London
from my
Windows

Books by Mary Carter

SHE'LL TAKE IT

ACCIDENTALLY ENGAGED

SUNNYSIDE BLUES

MY SISTER'S VOICE

THE PUB ACROSS THE POND

THE THINGS I DO FOR YOU

THREE MONTHS IN FLORENCE

MEET ME IN BARCELONA

LONDON FROM MY WINDOWS

Published by Kensington Publishing Corporation

London
from my
Windows

MARY CARTER

KENSINGTON BOOKS
www.kensingtonbooks.com

KENSINGTON BOOKS are published by

Kensington Publishing Corp.
119 West 40th Street
New York, NY 10018

All Kensington titles, imprints, and distributed lines are available at special quantity discounts for bulk purchases for sales promotion, premiums, fund-raising, educational, or institutional use.

Special book excerpts or customized printings can also be created to fit specific needs. For details, write or phone the office of the Kensington Sales Manager: Kensington Publishing Corp., 119 West 40th Street, New York, NY 10018. Attn. Sales Department. Phone: 1-800-221-2647.

Kensington and the K logo Reg. U.S. Pat. & TM Off.

eISBN-13: 978-1-61773-707-7
eISBN-10: 1-61773-707-0
First Kensington Electronic Edition: August 2015

ISBN-13: 978-1-61773-706-0
ISBN-10: 1-61773-706-2
First Kensington Trade Paperback Printing: August 2015

10 9 8 7 6 5 4 3 2 1

Printed in the United States of America

This book is dedicated to anyone who suffers from a hidden disability. You're not alone. May you find the strength to educate others as well as thrive.

ACKNOWLEDGMENTS

I'd like to thank my agent, Evan Marshall; my editor, John Scognamiglio; my publicist, Vida Engstrand; my production editor, Paula Reedy; and the rest of the staff at Kensington who work behind the scenes on all the aspects of bringing a book to life. Thanks as well to Hellen Candeland for sharing a few pictures of London from her windows with me.

Invisible threads are the strongest ties.

—Friedrich Nietzsche

CHAPTER 1

"May I have this dance, luv?" Ava's father asked her mother.

Oh yes. Please say yes. In the corner of her living room, Ava Wilder stood on tiptoe, clasped her hands, and held her breath, fearing if she exhaled, her mother would not dance. Ava's father held the record player's needle aloft, waiting for the yes to set it down and let his favorite song play. He had on his dancing shoes, the shiny black ones with the pointed toes, black pants, and the green sweater-vest Ava's mother had bought him for Christmas.

Such a good dancer, oh, he was so good. His glass of Scotch sat untouched on the shelf above the record player, two cubes of ice bobbed at the top, and the day's last beam of sun cut through it, striking it gold. While they waited, he turned his head, winked at Ava, and unleashed his drumroll of a smile. Ava's enthusiasm spilled out into silent applause. This way she could show her full support yet not shatter the moment with useless noise. Her mother loathed useless noise. Whenever she was tortured by useless noise, her face hardened. Then, the magic would be lost. *Oh, please soften; please soften.* Whenever she softened and they danced, the world glowed. Their living room pulsed with life, and Ava danced with joy. Joy, right here in their little town in Iowa.

Gretchen Wilder folded her arms across her chest and shook her head before glancing at Ava. The needle scratched down anyway and bossa nova music enveloped the room. "Tall and tan and young and lovely . . ." Her father lifted his arms up and moved his feet to the music. Yes. Oh, he was such a good dancer. Ava's right foot tapped along too. Someday she was going to be just like him. She would dance with her husband. She would never need to soften because she would never harden. His hips swayed as he sang along with Frank Sinatra. "Tall and tan and young and lovely." He was slightly off-key and it sounded funny with his British accent. Ava giggled. She wished she had a British accent, but hers was boring like her mother's.

"Come now. Dance with me."

Ava's mother shook her head again and stared at the tightly drawn curtains. "What will the neighbors think?" Could the neighbors see through the curtains? Ava would have to check next time she was in the yard. Ava's lips moved along with the song, although she didn't dare sing out loud.

"They'll think that we like to dance." Her father's voice was as upbeat as the music. He strode to the window and swooshed open the curtains. Faint stars were already starting to pop their heads into the sky. He turned to Ava. "Dance with me!" *Oh yes. Yes, yes, yes.* Ava glanced at the windows, then at her mother's pursed lips. Should she? Could she? Her father stood in front of her and planted his feet wide and firm. The tops of his black shoes were so shiny that Ava's nose, lips, and even the ceiling fan were reflected in them.

"Bertrand." Her mother's voice relaxed slightly. It was there, beneath her tongue, a slight hesitation. She was softening. He always made her soften.

Yes! The first shot of joy coursed through Ava. *Who cares, nosy neighbors. We're dancing.* Ava kicked off her shoes, grabbed on to her father's outstretched hands, and stepped onto his feet. They danced as the girl from Ipanema walked to the sea. Ava leaned back, stretched her arms as far as they would go, and forced her father to hold her weight. He sped up and the crown molding carouseled by. This was the best day ever. Her father was happy; her mother was softening. Dizzy, getting a little dizzy, but Ava didn't want to stop. Her shrieks filled the air. She straightened her head. The brown recliner, flowered sofa, and RCA television blurred into a mini-tornado of color.

Her mother headed for the kitchen. "She's going to barf on the living room rug."

"I won't barf!" Ava shouted. "Aaaaaaahhhhh." The scent of garlic and tomatoes filled the air. Wednesday. It was spaghetti night with the stretchy white cheese. Her mother baked it in the oven. Ava loved, loved, loved the stretchy white cheese. "Aaaaaaaahhh."

Ava's father gently brought her up, and he began to dance her to the front door. He held on to Ava with one hand and opened the door with the other.

"What are you doing?" Gretchen called from the kitchen.

"It's a beautiful night. Let's dance outside, Ava," her father said.

"What will the neighbors think?" Ava said. *Where did that come from?*

Her father just laughed and opened the screen door. "That we like to dance," they said in unison. And soon they were twirling on the front porch. Ava laughed and relished the cool breeze on her hot face. The aroma of marinara sauce mingled with the rosebushes below.

"Now, down the path." Her father danced her down the steps, one-two, one-two, one-two, and even though the music was distant now, deep inside Ava the beat continued to pulse. The sky was trying to hold on to the remaining streaks of blue, but orange streaks cut across it, deeper than any shade in her box of 64 Crayola crayons. "What do you say, little lady?" her father's voice rang out in the yard. "Shall we dance in the street?"

"We shall," Ava said, putting on her best British accent. They stepped just outside their brown picket fence. Fireflies blinked around them as they danced toward the curb. If only Ava had a jar. When they reached the strip of grass just beyond the sidewalk, Ava's father lost his footing, and stumbled. He dropped her hands and Ava's feet flew out, knocking her backwards. She smacked the ground, barely missing the concrete. Pain roared through the back of her head. "Dad?" Why wasn't he worried about her? Why didn't he cry out to her? Ava sat up. Her father was lying on the sidewalk a few feet away. Inside Ava's head, the music stopped and the needle scratched. And scratched, and scratched, and scratched.

She scrambled to her feet. "Dad?" Her voice came out as a whisper. Was he playing a game? He would never hurt her on purpose. He had never dropped her like that before. "Dad?" She said it louder this time, and her voice cracked. Once more, he did not answer. A strange thudding, like a heartbeat, pulsed through her ears as Ava inched over to her father. His eyes were open, unblinking. Was he having a laugh? Sometimes he liked to have a laugh. "Dad?" This was a scary game. She didn't like it. Did not like it at all. Dead. He looked dead. "Dad? Dad?" He would never do this to her, not when she sounded so terrified. Something was really wrong, terribly wrong. Ava screamed. The kind all the neighbors would hear. She tore up the walk and clamored up to the porch. She threw open the screen door. "MOM. MOM. MOM."

A clank sounded from the kitchen, followed by the sound of something crashing to the floor. "God damn it!" her mother yelled. "Ava! God damn it!" Ava knew the spaghetti with the stretchy white cheese smashing on the kitchen floor was the sound she heard, and saw it all in her mind's eye—noodles, red sauce, and the stretchy white cheese smeared all over the floor.

Her mother's heels clacked closer, and closer, and soon she appeared, fists clenched and eyes flashing. "Guess what you made me do?" she said. Who would make her soften now? No one. She would never soften again.

"Dad," Ava said. "Help." She whirled around and raced back to the curb, not even caring if her mother was following.

"What in the name of heaven?" her mother called after her, the first sign of worry creeping into her voice. Ava was standing over her father's body when her mother came down the walk, her face as pale as the stretchy white cheese that Ava would never eat again. "What did you do, Ava?" her mother wailed. "What did you do?"

What did she do? "Nothing." She didn't know. "Nothing." She really didn't know. "We were dancing."

"Dancing," her mother said. The word sounded different coming from her. It sounded evil.

"Dad," Ava said. "Daddy, wake up." Ava knelt down on the sidewalk. Pebbles cut into her knees, but she didn't move.

"I told you not to dance," her mother said. "I told you not to dance."

"Do something, Mom," Ava said. "Do something." She stared helplessly at her father. He was so still, so pale. "CPR," Ava said. It was a lifesaving skill. Her mother dropped to her knees next to Ava. Did she know CPR? She didn't pinch his nose or breathe into his mouth. She held his face between her palms.

"Bertie, Bertie, Bertie." Ava had never heard her mother call him Bertie. "Wake up; come on, wake up now." Ava wanted to tell her to blow into his mouth and press down on his chest. She wasn't quite sure how that would help. *Please, God, make him better. I will do anything you ask. Anything.* "Ava, go inside. Call nine-one-one. Then turn off the stove." Ava moved, somehow, up the path, the steps, and once again she burst through the screen door. She didn't stop until she reached the kitchen, where she darted in and slipped in a pool of marinara sauce. She hit the floor face-first this time. Noodles clung to her, and sauce covered her chest. She grabbed on to the counter and hauled herself up, then turned off the stove and snatched up the phone. Her fingers trembled as she hit the buttons, and she was smearing red sauce on everything she touched.

CPR. It's a lifesaving skill.

"Nine-one-one. What is your emergency?"

"My father," Ava said. "Help."

"What's your address, sweetie?" Ava recited it. There were so many questions, she wanted to get back outside. "Where is your father? Is he with you?"

"He's on the sidewalk. We were dancing. Outside." She leaked out each word like a confession, a plea for forgiveness. She wiped noodles from her, and as much sauce as she could. It looked like blood.

"How old are you? What is your name, sweetie?"

"Ten. Ava." Why was she asking her that? What did that matter?

"Are you alone?"

"My mother is outside. She's with him."

"Is he breathing?"

"I don't know, I don't know, I don't know. We were dancing outside. He's lying on the sidewalk. It's my fault! It's my fault!"

"It's not your fault."

"Help."

"The ambulance is on its way."

"Help."

"Can you bring the phone to your mommy, sweetie?" Ava never called her mommy. She was too old for that. Ava ran outside. Her mother was crouched over, sobbing, rocking.

"Mom. Nine-one-one wants you."

"You're too late," her mother said. "You're too late."

Too late. What did she mean? Too late. He was dead? Did she mean he was dead? That man on the sidewalk was not her father. Her father was alive. He could brighten a room just by walking into it. He was her dad. He was supposed to be there for her, watch her grow up. He was going to take her to London to see the Queen. He promised. He never broke his promises, so he couldn't be dead. They were going to visit her aunt Beverly. She was an actress in London and they were going to stay with her, and drink tea in rose-petal china cups with their pinkies sticking out, and eat something her father called trumpets. Ava's father laughed when she said it. "I wouldn't want to chomp on a trumpet." He winked. "Crumpet" was the word he said: It was more similar to an American pancake than a musical instrument. How could he be dead when she could still hear his laugh in her ear? Maybe she needed to beg.

No, please no, God. Please, God, please. Please. When that didn't work, Ava thought of everything she could have, should have, done that day instead. Ava should have run faster. No, she ran too fast; that's why she slipped. She should have been more careful around the sauce. She turned off the stove first. How could she be so stupid? She should have called 911 first. She was too late, too slow, too stupid. "I'm sorry. I slipped. I'm sorry. I'm sorry." She was too. Sorrier than she had ever been. Hot stabs of guilt assaulted her on an endless loop. *Make this stop. Please, make it stop.* Miracles existed, didn't they? Could she get a miracle, please? Just one. *Take me, God. Take me. I'm not even a good dancer.*

Her mother's wails echoed in the night. Up and down the block, neighbors flung open their doors and stepped onto the sidewalk, watching. Her mother was right. The neighbors watched. They saw. But for once, her mother didn't seem to care. "My husband. My love. My only love. He's gone, he's gone, he's gone. Why? Why? Why? Why?" Ava thought her mother was pleading with God. "Why, Ava, why?" She was wrong. Her mother wasn't pleading with God; she was pleading with her. This was Ava's fault. Her father was dead, and it was all her fault.

A fireman came into their class just last week to talk about CPR. He said it was never too early to learn because you could do CPR on animals too. That's why Ava really wanted to learn CPR. In case she had to save a dog one day. Maybe a poodle, or a beagle. She prayed she wouldn't have to put her mouth on something big and mean like a Rottweiler, or slobbery like an English bulldog. But she would. She would save any breed of dying dog. The fireman was going to teach it at the firehouse on Saturday. Ava had signed up. Her father was going to take her. But this was only Wednesday. It was never too early. But it was too late. *She* was too late.

CHAPTER 2

"You're ten years old. You know there's nothing you could have done to save him," the dork with framed degrees on his wall said. He also had fake plants. *Fake plants!* Ava wondered if he also pretended to water them.

"I could have done CPR!"

"Well, technically, yes, but that's like saying you could have flown him to the hospital, but you didn't because you didn't have a helicopter."

"Even if I had a helicopter, I don't know how to fly a helicopter."

"Exactly," he said. "You see?"

What a dork. On her way out he took a phone call and turned his back to her. She swiped one of the fake plants off the shelf near the door and threw it in the garbage bin outside. "Fake piece of shit," she said to the trash bin. Its plastic mouth just flapped back at her. She'd never said "shit" before, let alone stolen anything. Her father wouldn't like her saying that, wouldn't like it at all. Maybe if she said it God would send him back to straighten her out. Maybe he would see that she needed her father. She was going to turn into a cursing thief without him. Surely God wouldn't let that happen. Ava had never heard of anyone coming back to life, but miracles existed, didn't they?

If they didn't, she didn't care whether she was good or bad anymore. She knew she was supposed to feel bad, but she didn't. She'd spent ten years being a good girl and what did she get for it? The person she loved the most in the world was dead. She wasn't going to be good anymore. She wasn't even trying to be bad; she just didn't care.

Ava spent the first few days after her father's death doing every bad thing she could think of so that he would have to come back to life. She went through her mother's purse when she was in another room. She called five numbers in the phone book, said, "Help," when someone answered, then hung up. She drank milk out of the carton and stuck her fingers in every single dish well-wishers dropped by. She thought everyone was playing a joke on her, or trying to teach her a really giant lesson. The lesson was—learn CPR; it's a lifesaving skill. At her next therapy session she made the mistake of blurting this out to the dork. That repetitive thought, that her father was still alive and trying to teach her a valuable lesson, was a form of denial according to the dork psychiatrist. That made her really, really angry.

"Oh, so he's really dead then, is that what you're trying to say?" She thought he would get all embarrassed and feel bad, and apologize. She was wrong.

"Yes, Ava," he said. "Your father is really dead." She glanced at the shelf near the door where the fake plant used to sit. There was another one in its place. *Piece of shit*. He didn't even miss it. He just replaced it. He was trying to get her to do the same thing. Replace her father. *Piece of shit, piece of shit, piece of shit*. Why couldn't he be dead instead? She could bring fake flowers to his grave. Why did dorks get to live and wonderful people who could brighten rooms just by stepping into them have to die? Why? Why? Why? She wanted to smash something.

Maybe that's why everything in this dork's office was soft and plastic. Maybe everybody who saw him wanted to smash things. "Did you hear me, Ava?"

"Yes, I heard you. My father is dead. Why don't you open the windows and scream it for everyone to hear?"

"Are you worried about what other people think, Ava?"

She hated how he said her name all the time, as if she would forget what it was if he didn't constantly remind her. "I hate you," Ava said.

"I'm okay with that," the dork said. "I bet you also hate that your father is dead, don't you?"

Ava didn't think a man whose breath smelled like stale maple syrup should be allowed to say things like that to a child and get *paid* for it.

"Why do you look away every time I say that your father is dead?"

"Because he's not." *He's coming back. If I'm bad enough, he'll come back.* She wasn't going to say that to the dork. He wouldn't believe her. He would think she was crazy.

"He's not what, Ava?"

Miracles exist. They do. I believe.

"Ava, look at me." She looked at the dork. Long and hard. He swallowed, then adjusted his glasses. "Your father isn't coming back, Ava. You're grieving. It will get better. I promise. And it's not your fault."

"My mother said it was."

"We've talked about that. She was in shock. She didn't mean it."

"You don't know her."

"Maybe not. But I do know that it's not your fault."

"It is."

"What did you do?"

"You don't listen. It's what I *didn't* do. I didn't do CPR."

"Even if you knew CPR, a child can't do CPR on an adult man, Ava."

"Stop saying my name!"

"Very well." He sighed, leaned back in his chair. "You still wouldn't have saved him."

"I will next time."

"Next time?"

"I'll learn CPR and maybe somehow he'll come back, and it will happen again, and this time I'll be ready. This time he'll live." She hadn't meant to tell him, but he had to know that he couldn't keep telling her her father was dead and never coming back when miracles existed.

He leaned forward in his chair and looked at her. She scooted back. "Denial can be very dangerous. You need to accept that your father is dead."

Ava stood up. "Stop saying that! Stop saying that!"

"Denial over a long period of time can lead to psychosis. Do you understand what that means?"

"I hate you, I hate you, and your stupid maple-syrup breath, and your stupid fake plants." Ava swiped the plant off the shelf and hurled it at the far wall. *Oh no.* Why did she do that? Was she going to get in trouble? Was her father watching from heaven? She just wanted him to come back. The plant bounced off the window and landed on the floor. No dirt. Was that why the dork had fake plants?

A sad smile came across the dork's face. Ava did that. She made him sad. She was a horrible person. And she didn't know how to stop being one. She didn't know how to get rid of this pain that made her feel as if she were going to drown. She went to pick up the plant, then didn't touch it. She began to pace the room. She'd never felt like this before.

"I'm being punished for dancing outside."

"Ava."

"That's my name. Don't wear it out, don't wear it out, don't wear it out."

"Why don't we take some deep breaths? Will you stop for a minute and breathe in with me?"

"Why didn't we stay in the living room? Or on the porch. But not the path, not past the fence. Not outside. Why did we go outside?" She looked at the man behind the desk. Why wasn't he helping her? Why didn't he just tell her how to make it better? How to turn back time. She needed to find a way back to the living room. That's all she had to do, go back. Once, just once. If she and her father had stayed inside, this would have never happened. Inside, inside, inside, inside, inside.

"Would you please pick up Larry?" The dork pointed to the plant on the floor. He had named his fake plant Larry. If they were in court, she'd be resting her case. The judge would slam his gavel down; he'd be guilty and convicted of being a dork. He was alive and her father was dead. There was no justice in the world. "You don't want to carry this kind of pain longer than necessary. You don't want to make things worse than they already are. Do you?"

"You disgust me." Ava didn't know where that came from except it felt good to say. The guttural "uh" and the "gust." Maybe she'd grow up to be on the daytime soaps. An actress, like her aunt Beverly. Ava's mother said Aunt Beverly wasn't coming to the funeral. They'd waited so that she could. But she wasn't coming. Ava didn't talk to her. She wanted to call her and ask why. Her mother said not to bother. "That woman doesn't care about anyone but herself," she said.

The dork glanced at his wrist even though he didn't wear a watch. Ava wondered if the long dark hairs on his arm could tell time. You never knew with this variety of dork. "Our time is up. I'd like you to go home and think about everything I've said."

She did think about it. She thought about it a lot. *Outside.* Bad things happened to people outside. They should have stayed in the living room. It was her fault. She wasn't going to go outside anymore. She didn't even want to leave her bedroom. And every time she even *thought* about stepping outside of her bedroom, little colored dots danced in front of her eyes like psychedelic snowflakes. "Psychedelic" was a word they made up in the sixties. It meant someone was doing drugs and wearing brightly colored shirts, and tripping. Tripping was when you took a lot of drugs and it made you feel like you were either falling or taking a vacation. It also had something to do with bearded men, and guitars, and peace symbols, and women with long hair. They all had sex with each other too. It was called free love. Ava didn't quite understand it. Since when did love cost anything? There was a lot about the world she didn't understand, like why her father couldn't have had a heart attack on Sunday after Ava had learned CPR. Or even after they had eaten the spaghetti with stretchy cheese, because it used to be Ava's favorite and now she knew she could never eat it again. She would ask her father, but HER FATHER. WAS. DEAD.

She tried to leave the room a couple of times. She stood a foot from her door. She imagined a line in the carpet. She knew for sure that she was okay as long as she didn't cross it. If she even thought about crossing the line, her heart pounded so hard she felt as if she had a bongo drum in her chest and the back of her neck broke out in sweat. This was her punishment. This was what she deserved. Ava should have at least tried to do CPR. She knew she was supposed to blow into his mouth and push down on his chest and she didn't even try. She was a murderer. She'd murdered her own father. And she was so evil, she couldn't even bring herself to tell anyone what she'd done. But her father knew. Her father was in heaven and he could see and hear everything she did, and he knew Ava did nothing to save his life.

You would've saved me if I was a poodle, is that right? she imagined him saying.

She was stuck. Like a record.

Dance with me!

Blow breath into my mouth.

Pound on my chest.

Save me.

And she heard her mother's voice too. Over and over. *What did you do? What did you do? What did you do? You're too late. You're too late. You're too late. What did you do?*

Since she couldn't leave the room, or dance with her father, Ava was making a Victorian manor out of Popsicle sticks. When the stupid thing was finished it was going to have ten rooms and five bathrooms. An attic, a basement, ten fireplaces, an indoor pool, a gym, a chef's kitchen, a solarium, a gift-wrapping room, and a wraparound porch.

But she could already tell that it was nothing. A heap of sticks and glue. Not even a Popsicle shack. She should just stop. But she couldn't. Only when it was finished, only when the last piece had been glued on, and it was *perfect,* would she be free.

There was a knock on her bedroom door. Ava was dressed because she never changed into her pajamas the night before. She thought if she woke up and was already dressed it would be easy to open the bedroom door and step into the hall. She was wrong. She walked to the bedroom door and stared at it. The line in the carpet was still there. She could not cross it. There came a second knock, louder this time.

"Ava?" Her mother sounded concerned but also annoyed.

"I'm sick," Ava said. "Don't come in." *I'm a cold-blooded killer. Don't come anywhere near me.* The door opened. Her mother entered. A short man in a tan suit stood behind her. He looked wrinkled and forgiving. Big, round glasses gave him the appearance of an owl. Ava fully expected him to hoot. Instead, he stared at Ava, then smiled. She wondered if people made fun of him. He had a nice smile, but Ava did not smile back. He had the look of a man tiptoeing up to a tiger while holding a giant syringe.

"This is Doctor Gills," her mother said. A new doctor. Ava told her mother she'd rather drop dead than go back to the other one. The colored lights were back. Ava felt the ground beneath her feet sway. She suddenly didn't want them to see her Popsicle sticks. They were standing so close. They had tainted it. Her house. It would never be perfect. They'd ruined everything. And they were going to cross the line! She wanted them to move back behind the door.

"Stop moving," Ava said. It came out like a shriek. The doctor was going to think she was a terrible, terrible person. And he was right.

"Stop it," her mother said. She turned to the doctor. "See?"

See what? What do you see, Mom? Because I don't know who I am anymore. What do you see? Ava wished she knew how to get past her mother's unforgiving glare. How to soften her.

"It's all right," the doctor said. He put his arms up. "See? I'm not moving."

"This is ridiculous," her mother said. "I have had quite enough of this. Do you hear me? Enough?"

"Do you mind?" the doctor said. He turned to Ava's mother and smiled, moving his hand up and down as if to calm her mother down.

Good luck, Ava thought. Had her mother told the doctor it was all Ava's fault? She bet she did. "My father is dead," Ava said. They weren't going to leave. Ava marched over to the Popsicle-stick house and grabbed it with both hands. She brought it down on the table hard. Little bits smashed, and others caved in, and a few sticks flew into the air. Ava smashed it on the table again. And again, and again. *What have I done?* She didn't want to cry in front of her new doctor. She wanted her father. She was engulfed by a wave of grief. He was gone. She was never going to see him again. How was that even possible? Why her? She didn't want to cry. The tears came anyway. She didn't even feel like smashing her house anymore. She was going to have to start all over. She ruined everything she touched.

"I'm very sorry," the doctor said. "We can talk about that. We can talk about anything you like."

Ava stared at his ugly tan suit and green bow tie. She could see it now, her entire life laid out before her in a series of lousy fashion, wide eyes, fake plants, and stale, maple-syrup breath. *Ava, meet Dork Number Two.* Her life. Her life, her life, her life. Her life was going to be a never-ending revolving door of dorks.

"I want Aunt Beverly."

"She's not coming." Ava's mother kept looking at the doctor for reinforcement.

"Then I'll go see her," Ava said.

"She doesn't want to see *us.*" Ava's mother turned to the doctor. "That woman has never liked me."

"Do you mind if I talk to Ava alone?" the doctor said.

"I do mind," her mother said. "This isn't a session." She turned to her daughter. "You're grounded."

Ava laughed. "Good." She went over to her dresser, pulled out a pile of cards, and thrust them at the doctor. "Look at the stamps. She sent me things." They were all from Aunt Beverly. Funny cards, and letters, and postcards, and colored paper crowns for Christmas. Once her father told her that Aunt Beverly was sending "a few bob" so Ava could buy herself a gift. Ava actually thought that two guys named Bob were coming over to help her pick it out. When she finally admitted that to her father, he laughed so hard he had tears spilling out of his eyes. That was one of the best days of Ava's life. "Bevie's going to die when she hears that, luv." Then he actually started to cry. He was still crying when Ava's mother quietly pulled her out of the room. Otherwise, he didn't talk about his only sister much. But Ava knew her father loved Aunt Beverly. And that meant she loved Aunt Beverly too.

"Perhaps it would help if she could at least call her aunt Beverly," the doctor said.

"Yes, can I?" Ava said.

"No," her mother said. "And that's final." Ava looked at the doctor. He shrugged in defeat and lifted his arms in a Sorry-I-Can't-Help type of way. In the end, just another dork. He was dead to her. The little colored dots were back.

"Get out," Ava said.

"Don't you ever talk to me like that again," her mother said. Ava sucked in her lips and stared. The only way she could do that was if she never talked to her mother again.

Nineteen Years Later

CHAPTER 3

Queenie stood at Redlands Airfield Base, just sixty minutes outside of London, and rued the day he'd ever introduced the young barrister to his dear friend Beverly Wilder. Just because Jasper Keys had been dating and was now dumped by Queenie's niece—whom, it was quite obvious, Jasper was still pining over—didn't give the lad a right to insert himself into a forty-year friendship. Beverly was Queenie's best friend, Queenie should be the one helping her fulfill her last wishes. And skydiving certainly wouldn't be one of them.

The wind was chafing Queenie's face, horrendous for the skin (his face was his livelihood, among other bits), and the cuffs of his trousers were kissing the filthy ground. He'd wanted to wear them to the after-party after-party this evening, but even if they left now he wouldn't have time to dry-clean them. *Bloody hell.* He cast his eyes on the little plane waiting to whisk Beverly and Jasper into the sky. Bevie was planted in front of Queenie, waiting for him to read the skydiving agreement.

"You're stalling," she said.

"Of course I'm stalling. I'm hoping the rest of the little daredevils will get sick of waiting and take off without you."

Beverly huffed and her goggles slid down her nose. Between them and her skullcap, she looked like an elderly Amelia Earhart. "Hand it over."

"Poppycock." Queenie held the legally binding agreement away from her eager hand and scanned the skies for any signs of rain, or hail, or wind. *Blimey.* The sun was fat and bright overhead: the skies were blue.

Beverly thrust her hand up high and waved at Jasper, who was standing next to the little plane stretching his hamstrings. He waved back, then jogged over. *Bloody heartbroken barrister.* This was all his fault.

"Queenie won't give me the contract," Beverly said. Jasper turned to Queenie with an inquisitive look. Queenie would give anything to look that young again. And Jasper wasn't even young. Late thirties. Queenie never imagined there'd be a time when he longed to be in his late thirties. But here he was, old and fat, and getting the cuffs of his trousers filthy. All the pity went to aging actresses. What about aging drag queens? That was the bottom of the barrel. Gone, gone, gone with his youth. Spending his precious time left on earth trying to knock some sense into his stubborn best friend. And to what end? Beverly wasn't paying any attention to him; he might as well have been a gnat buzzing around the grass. "I have to read it first."

"Go on with you then," Beverly said.

"Do you need me to read it, mate?" Jasper asked. Queenie glared at Jasper. In that second, looking at his handsome, inquisitive face, Queenie could clearly see why his niece Hillary dumped him. Jasper was a nice guy. And nice guys finished last. Hillary, like most women, Queenie supposed, wanted the bad boy. Someone edgy and unpredictable. Tatted up and driving a motorcycle maybe. Just out of prison, why not? A beast in the bedroom. But this? Skydiving? Jasper was trying to be who he thought Hillary wanted, and he was dragging Beverly into it with him. *You've got the wrong end of the stick, lad.* Hillary wasn't ever taking Jasper back. She was a socialite; she craved attention and adventure. Jasper was steady-as-she-goes. He was trying to play the sexy adventurer and he was doing a piss-poor job of it. Queenie saw him standing by the plane, taking pictures, then furtively texting them to someone. Hillary. Pathetic. She'd dumped him and he was still pursuing her. *Loser. Loser, loser, loser.* Queenie took a deep breath and prayed for the strength to bite his tongue.

Look at the pair of them, dressed like fools in their suits and their goggles, waiting for Queenie to hurry up and read the agreement so they could jump out of a perfectly good aeroplane. Queenie had suggested they spend the day at Barrow's Market, buy up everything on the tables and have a grand do. Maybe even pop into the Tower, eavesdrop on the Yanks shouting, "Off with their heads!" every time someone snapped a photo. At least that would be good for a laugh. But no. Skydive. Beverly gets the devastating news that she's dying and what does she want to do? Skydive. Shouldn't she be grasping on to every last precious minute? This was utter madness. Jasper should be ashamed of himself. "What's on your bucket list, Bev, that we could do right now?" Jasper had said to her right after she'd told them the grim news.

Skydive. Beverly Wilder had always wanted to skydive. "There's something else—something important—and it won't come to me." She grasped her head while Queenie prayed she'd remember and it would have something to do with the holy trinity: eating, drinking, and shopping.

Skydiving. Bloody skydiving.

"Come on now, mate; the plane is going to take off without us," Jasper said.

Queenie cleared his throat. If they wanted to do this, he was going to use his stage voice so they would know exactly what they were getting themselves into. "The human body isn't meant to hurl toward the earth at twelve thousand feet." He peered at Beverly, whose face looked every bit of seventy-four, but her excited blue eyes could have been those of a ten-year-old. Especially with that silly cap, suit, and goggles. She was going to break his concentration. Queenie took a long, dramatic pause.

"Oh, do hand it over," Beverly said. She reached for it. He yanked it away.

"It says at best you could break an ankle, or end up paralyzed for life." He paused for dramatic effect. "At *best*, Beverly."

"If I do, it certainly won't be for very long and I won't ask you to wipe my arse," Beverly said. Weeks. The doctor said she had a matter of weeks. Queenie had a sneaking suspicion that Beverly had known something was wrong long before she finally went round to the doctor, and now it was too late. The cancer had spread. She would be dead in a matter of weeks. His sweet, precious Beverly. He didn't want to imagine his life without her. He was the funny sidekick; she was the star. He was supposed to kick it first.

"They're waving us over," Jasper said. "I've already signed my contract." He handed Beverly a pen, and turned on Queenie. "I can just get another one, mate," he said. *Cheeky lad.*

Beverly pointed at her skydiving instructor, who was indeed waving them over to his little plane. Then she turned her finger on Queenie. "I am going to get strapped to that ravishing young man over there, and I am going to jump out of that aeroplane, and I'm going to feel the wind on my face, and I'm going to *fly*. Then you can either pick my broken body up off the ground or take me out for a cocktail and stitch me up one side and down the other. But for now, you're going to give me that bloody contract, wish me British luck, and stay the hell out of my way."

"Oh, here." Queenie thrust the contract at her. "But you're buying the cocktails."

"To hell with the cocktails, I'll leave you my flat."

Beverly's beautiful flat. The words made a little pulse in Queenie's eye start to jump. She didn't have family other than some American niece she'd never seen or even spoken to as far as Queenie knew. There was a reason for it, something that was wrong with the girl, but Queenie couldn't remember the details. He was trying to remember when Beverly barked at Queenie to bend over.

"Don't I always?" he said as he assumed the position and she used his back as a table. When she was finished signing her life away, Queenie knew it was no use arguing any longer. He stood and waved at them as they made their way to the plane. *I'll leave you my flat.* Tears came to his eyes. It was like accepting an Academy Award.

Thank you, Beverly, thank you. Dear, sweet Beverly. The flat was in the West End of London. Beverly's family had owned it going back several generations. When her parents passed and her brother moved to America, it was all hers, although legally it was in both siblings' names. But then the brother passed. Beverly had been utterly heartbroken. Worse still, in her time of grief her brother's wife still couldn't let go of their petty grievances and wouldn't even let Beverly see or talk to her own niece. He used to rail against that woman every time he saw Beverly crying over a picture of the girl. Years passed with no contact. Beverly sent letters, cards, postcards, gifts. She didn't get a single thank-you in reply. "Gretchen isn't giving them to her," Beverly would say. "I just know it." The few times Gretchen returned Beverly's calls she hinted that Ava wasn't well. Ever since Bertrand's death, she'd—*how did Beverly put it? Recoiled from the world.* Queenie didn't know exactly what that meant except it sounded absolutely horrific. By the time Ava was grown up, Beverly was tired of trying, and too afraid to try to connect anymore. Surely the mother had poisoned Ava against her, and she didn't want to face that kind of rejection twice. Lucky for Queenie though, it meant the flat was his.

That was a terrible thought, but it's not like he said it out loud. If Queenie could perform magic he'd wave his wand and give Beverly a relationship with her niece. But he wasn't magic, and it certainly wasn't his fault. Queenie couldn't take on the weight of the world. He couldn't change his past, let alone anyone else's. And he had a right to be happy about his good fortune. Beverly wanted to give him the flat and he was going to humbly accept it.

Oh, wait until the lads heard about this. He'd be popular again, that's for sure. They'd probably want him to reprise his Streisand act. He'd finally be the one hosting the after-party after-party. *Oh yes, fabulous after-after parties.* The view of London from Beverly's flat was a showstopper. No more living with his brother in a tiny, smelly hovel. He would cherish it, he would! He wouldn't change a thing. He wouldn't even rearrange the collection of theater posters on her wall. Even though he thought it was absolutely hideous to hang *Pippin* next to *Cats*. It was all going to be his. But Beverly would be dead.

It was unfathomable. He would put it out of his mind straightaway.

Perhaps there were a few minor décor changes he would make. Nothing major. The lampshades with the pink tassels. Not even a drag queen could appreciate them. There was no other way around it. They would be the first to go.

Beverly stood at the opening of the plane. She was supposed to jump. Queenie was right. It was not normal to jump out of a perfectly good airplane and into the sky. They were so high. Nothing but clouds. She gripped the doorframe with both hands, and clung to life. Her instructor uncurled her fingers. "No turning back now, luv." He pushed them out.

Air screamed into Beverly's ears. Pain roared through her head. Her face flattened from the wind. She imagined she looked like one of those flying squirrels. But a few seconds later, the pain ceased, and the tunnel of air lessened. She remembered to arch her back and legs and throw out her arms like the instructor taught her. And then, she was flying.

Soaring, floating, cascading, gliding in the wind. She was like a bird. Everyone should feel this sensation once in his or her life. Everyone should feel this alive, this free. Her younger brother's face suddenly appeared before her. "Bertie!" Oh, how she missed him. She would be seeing him soon if heaven was for real. He wasn't smiling. But he loved adventures! Why wasn't he smiling? Because she'd failed. First she'd failed him, and then she'd failed Ava. Dear, sweet Ava. She should have tried harder. She should have been nicer to Gretchen, no matter how impossibly wrong that woman had been for her brother. She should have kept her opinions to herself. It drove a wedge between her and Bertie she'd never been able to repair. Ava had been a child stuck in the middle of stubborn adults fighting over petty bits and bobs. Beverly should have been the one to swallow the sword. Her pride had kept her from helping her niece. It was too late. Why hadn't she done anything? Oh, why hadn't she done anything? The clock was ticking. Was there anything she could do? Anything at all?

Help her! she could have sworn she heard Bertie yelling through the wind. *Help our Ava.*

They picked up speed; how could the ground be coming up already? She wanted to fly forever. She wanted to do it again. Faster and faster they approached. The instructor dipped back and she pulled her knees up for landing. Queenie was standing, grinning, and, good Lord, weeping. Their feet stuttered on the ground, and then Beverly, with her instructor on her back, fell face-first into the dirt. She heard Queenie gasp. But when they finally pulled her up, she was laughing. That was toptastic. Jasper landed right behind her. Smoothly, as only the young can land. She grasped his hands and together they smiled. Then, she remembered, and her smile evaporated.

"You look like you've seen a ghost," Jasper said.

"I have indeed," Beverly said.

"What's wrong?"

"Ava," Beverly said. She grasped Jasper's hands. "We have to do something about Ava."

CHAPTER 4

Ava was perched at her kitchen table, working on a cartoon strip about young lovers scaling Mount Kilimanjaro, when the doorbell rang. *Oh no. No, no, no.* Unexpected guests could poison her entire day. The doorbell rang again. She'd been just about to sketch the lovers reaching the peak, a triumphant feat to be celebrated, until it's discovered that one of them, probably the man, left the camera at base camp and it snowballs into their first big fight. That was the part she was looking forward to the most. Love didn't count until you'd survived that first big fight. The doorbell rang for the third time. *Leave me alone; I'm on a mountaintop.*

Ava picked up the remote and aimed it at the monitor hanging in the upper corner of the room. It flickered to life, illuminating the unwelcome guests as two uniformed police officers. Cliff, her boss in a way, and the one she was sleeping with, and most likely his partner, Joe. They looked funny together. Joe was a tall beanpole. Cliff was handsome all right, dark good looks and so muscular, but let's face it—he was short. Still, he was sexy. He had that gruff Napoléon thing going on, and he was good in bed. Not that Ava had anyone to compare it with. Unbeknownst to him, Cliff was her first. It was hard to play the field when you were afraid of the field itself. Cliff cupped his hand over his eyes and tried to peer into her windows. "Amateur," she said. Her windows were sealed with black sheets. He knew that.

Given the presence of his partner, Cliff wasn't here for a lunch-hour quickie. Too bad; sex with Cliff was always a nice distraction. Ava turned up the volume on the monitor. She could hear them conferring but couldn't make out the words. It was her day off. What did they want?

Ava stood and moved along the wall. Despite the black sheets, she didn't want to take the chance that Cliff could sense her movements. Why hadn't he called first? She'd wait them out. They'd leave eventually.

"Ava," Cliff said. "I know you're in there." His voice would carry down the block. To the neighbors. Of course he knew she was in here. She was always in here.

"It's my day off," Ava said. She was in her pajamas even though it was only two in the afternoon. There were very few perks to being an agoraphobic. Wearing your pajamas at two in the afternoon was one of them.

"It's a work emergency," Cliff said.

"Do you have a client with you?" She didn't want to sketch criminals today, only lovers.

"Open up," Cliff said. "You know I hate talking through the door."

"I'm not dressed," Ava said.

"I'm going to put the siren on."

That would draw the attention of the neighbors. Cliff knew just how to push her buttons. "Dammit." Ava opened the door. "Hurry," she said. Cliff and Joe stepped inside and Ava shut and locked the door behind them. Three locks. She checked them twice. Joe glanced at the locks, then at her horse pajamas, and then looked away. Cliff stared openmouthed at her pj's. "It's my day off," Ava said.

"We need you to do a sketch," Cliff said.

Ava sighed. "Why doesn't the department just switch to computer sketches like every other police department in the country?"

"Because we've got you."

Flattery wasn't going to work. The department was cheap, and old-fashioned. That was the real reason. Not that Ava was complaining. It paid the bills. "She or he?" Probably a she. It was normally a she.

"It's a girl."

"When?"

"Now."

"How can I sketch her now? I don't see her here." She smiled so that Joe wouldn't sense her hostility and figure out that she and Cliff were lovers. Ava watched Joe take in the black sheets hanging over her windows.

"Is this a bad time?" he asked politely.

"Yes," Ava said.

Joe put his hand over his heart. "I'm so sorry. Who died?" *Poor guy.* Ava bet his daughters ran right over him.

"My father," Ava said.

"Oh my God," Joe said. "We're so sorry to bother you. Our condolences." He tipped his hat and headed for the door.

"Nineteen years ago," Cliff said.

Joe stopped before his hand reached the doorknob. "Pardon?"

"Ava's father died nineteen years ago," Cliff said.

Joe frowned, then shook his finger at Ava as if he'd just figured out her secret. "Are you on a stakeout?"

"A stakeout?" Cliff said. He gestured to the black sheets. "She can't see out the windows. How could she be on a stakeout?"

"You're close, Jim," Ava said.

"It's Joe."

"Right, sorry. I forget that some people get to be called by their real names."

"Their real names?" Joe said.

"We don't have time for this," Cliff said.

"I had to change my name when I went into hiding," Ava said.

Cliff shook his head. "Cut it out."

Joe straightened up, hooked his thumbs into his pants. "You can trust me."

"I'm in witness protection."

"Holy shit. I knew it. I knew there was something . . . about you." He paused in the place where Ava was sure he wanted to say "odd."

"Seriously?" Cliff said.

"Please, don't blow my cover."

"Holy shit," Joe said. He took a step forward and lowered his chin. "Mob?"

"Would I be wearing horse pajamas if it *wasn't* the Mob, Joe?" Ava said deadpan. Joe squinted and considered her question. Ava should behave; she really should. But when you stayed in all the time, your pent-up energy had to go somewhere. It was too fun messing with people like Joe. And there was no real harm done.

"Get dressed!" Cliff said. "You're coming to the station." *The station?* Ava never went to the station. Never. "If I have to put you over my shoulder and carry you out covered in asses—"

"Asses?"

He glanced at her pajamas. "Mules, ponies, whatever."

"They're horses. Racehorses." It was her day off. She could wear whatever freaking pajamas she wanted to wear.

"It's the mayor's daughter," Cliff said.

"Emma?" Everyone knew the mayor's only daughter, Emma. Everyone loved Emma. A blond angel. A total sweetheart. She was just about to celebrate her sweet sixteen. A party for the ages. "Is she all right?"

"It was an attempted kidnapping. A man grabbed her just outside the mayoral home. She screamed and bit him. Bodyguards came running."

"Oh my God."

"You don't want him to get away, do you?"

Ava glanced at Joe, who became intensely interested in a porcelain cat on the windowsill. He reached out as if to pet it.

"Don't touch that," Ava said to Joe. "It's bugged." He jerked his hand away. God, Ava was an awful person. He was just too easy. Ava stepped closer to Cliff. "Bring her here," Ava said.

"High profile. Can't bend the rules on this one."

"I'm not prepared," Ava said. "You know I have to prepare."

"You don't have a choice. Not if you want to keep your job."

"Call Gary Vance." He wasn't as good as Ava, but then again, he also wasn't afraid of showing up to work.

"The mayor requested a female sketch artist. He requested you."

"By name?"

"Yes."

"The mayor knows my name?"

"Of course he knows your name. Your sketches have led to ten apprehensions in three years. Makes him look good. Like it or not, people know your name."

"But not your real name," Joe said. "Right?"

Cliff shot Joe a look. "What's it going to be? Either you come with me or you resign."

Shit. Ava couldn't lose her job. If she lost her job she'd lose her home. It was only a rental, but it was safe. But she wasn't prepared. She wasn't prepared. Did she have any Xanax in the medicine cabinet? "I'll get dressed." Ava hurried into her room. Getting dressed was easy. She didn't have very many outfits. She threw on black pants and a black top. She grabbed a blindfold from her top dresser drawer. She grabbed her cell phone and pushed the speed-dial button for her therapist, Diana. While it rang she hurried into the bathroom and opened the medicine cabinet. She rifled through the contents. No Xanax. She'd had no reason to refill the prescription. Cliff didn't mind hanging out at her place. He brought all her clients here. She could get everything she wanted delivered. Her mother stopped pushing her years ago. *Why did it have to be Emma? Poor, sweet Emma.*

Ava reached Diana's voice mail. Nobody was ever home. How easy it was for most people to go places, do things. Ava would kill to feel so free. She hung up and ran into the living room. "You're going to need to blindfold me," she told Cliff. "Carry me out to the car. You're also going to have to talk the entire time. I don't care what you talk about; just don't stop talking. And Xanax. You're going to have to find me some Xanax."

Ava and Emma sat in a back room of the police station. As requested, the windows were covered in Ava's black sheets. Ava was going to get through this, and she was going to help catch the man who tried to kidnap the mayor's daughter. Two bodyguards stood by the door, Cliff was in the left corner behind Ava, and the mayor's wife, Mrs. Rhodes, sat next to her daughter, holding her hand.

"Why the sheets?" Mrs. Rhodes asked.

Cliff stepped forward. "To protect Emma's identity." *Thank you, thank you, thank you,* Ava thought. He wasn't the best boyfriend in the world, but at that moment he really came through. She was going to owe him one.

"We just paraded through the entire precinct," Mrs. Rhodes said. "Take them off. They're morbid."

Cliff glanced at Ava, then nodded. He strode to the windows and took off the first sheet. Then the second, and the third. Ava could feel the open space behind them. Endless, open space. Eyeballs staring at them.

Ava slid down in her seat and hid behind her sketch pad as Emma described her attacker. "He was tall and strong. And his face was kind of puffy."

Pillsbury Doughboy meets the Hulk, Ava thought to herself. It helped her sketches if she related them to characters. Ava worked quickly and lightly, asking, as she sketched, the usual questions about the perpetrator's eyes, and forehead, and nose, and the shape of the chin. Why did Cliff have to take off the sheets? They were gone. Gone, gone, gone.

"He had a really big nose," Emma said. She sounded chipper. Ava expected her to cry, or sound afraid. She was very poised. Children of politicians were probably raised that way.

Ava nodded. "Lips?" She wished Cliff would just throw the

sheet over her head. If she sat under the table to sketch would anyone say anything?

"I don't know," Emma said. "It happened so fast."

"It's okay. Just say whatever you feel."

"Thin. I feel his lips were thin."

"Good." He should have made up another reason they had to keep the sheets up. Or Ava should have said they were hers. She was the artist; the room should be set up the way she needed. "Okay. When you're ready, open your eyes and I'll show you the picture. Remember, you're safe now." Emma nodded. Then, her eyes opened. Ava turned the sketch toward her.

Emma frowned. She cocked her head. Then, she shook it. Nobody had ever done this before. Normally they gasped in recognition. Was Emma in shock? "It's not him," Emma said.

She was in denial. Ava wasn't going to correct her. She more than anyone understood how powerful denial could be. "Okay, we'll work on it," Ava said. "Which part doesn't look like him?"

"Every part," Emma said.

Emma's mother glanced at Cliff. "This isn't working. We'll have to reschedule." With another sketch artist, she meant.

It was her fault for insisting they remove the sheets. Who did she think she was? Would she walk into Ava's home and insist she take the sheets off there as well? "Let's start over." Ava ripped the sketch out and set it on the table. She turned to a fresh sheet. "Start at the beginning—"

Mrs. Rhodes stood. "We're done here."

"Sometimes when a person is in shock—" Ava began.

"Does Emma look like she's in shock?" She had a point. Emma did not look like she was in shock. And Ava found that very troubling. Emma had almost been kidnapped.

"Emma, you have been very, very brave," Ava said. "But you don't have to pretend. Not with me."

"Pretend what?" Emma cocked her head.

"Yes, pretend what?" Mrs. Rhodes said.

Ava was upsetting them both. She was only trying to help. "Please, let's try this again."

Cliff put his arm on Ava's shoulder. "They have somewhere to be."

"What could be more important than this?"

"Somebody has a sixteenth birthday party," Mrs. Rhodes said. She shared a grin with Emma.

"You can't go on with the party." The words tumbled out of Ava's mouth before she could stop them.

"Ava?" Cliff said. Ava never interjected any personal conversation into her work. Cliff looked mortified. Mrs. Rhodes looked furious. Emma was simply watching Ava with open curiosity.

Ava shot out of her chair. "You have to cancel it."

"Why on earth would we—" Mrs. Rhodes started to say.

"At least postpone it."

"Do you want to come?" Emma asked. "You could sketch my friends."

Had the mayor's daughter really just invited her to her sweet sixteen? In theory, Ava would love sketching all those girls from wealthy families. Imagine, going to a party like that. It might just make up for all the parties she'd never been to. "I can't," she said. Her voice came out rushed, panicked. *Fire extinguisher, fire extinguisher, fire extinguisher.* "I'm already going somewhere." Ava slapped her hand across her mouth and thought about where she could be going, but her mind was a dark, swirling tunnel, taking out every thought in its path. Normal people went all sorts of places, didn't they? Movies and yoga, and book clubs, and bars, and birthday parties. Ava squeezed her hand around her charcoal pencil. It snapped in two. A splinter cut into her palm.

"Quite all right," Mrs. Rhodes said. Ava wasn't really invited. She was acting like a fool. This was why she didn't go out of the house. This was why! *It's never as bad as you think it's going to be.* The idiots who said that were right. It was worse. Much, much worse.

"I just want you to be safe," Ava said.

"Do you think he'll come again?" A thread of alarm came

into Emma's voice. Finally. She needed to be afraid. It was the only way she would be able to protect herself. Team Bozo by the door apparently weren't up to the job.

"No," her mother said. "He won't."

"You don't know that," Ava said. She turned to Emma. "I'm sure you have a lovely room." Emma nodded. "If you stay in your room for a while. Do you have Popsicle sticks? You can make a mini-mansion. I can show you—"

Cliff stepped forward. "Mrs. Rhodes, I apologize—"

"But it's labor-intensive," Ava said. "You have to wait for the walls to dry before you lay down the ceiling. That's the trick."

Mrs. Rhodes stood. She grabbed Emma by the arm and hauled her up. "Is this woman for real?"

"I'm deadly serious," Ava said. "Just lie low. Until they catch him. Wait. Or were you talking about waiting for the walls to dry? I was serious about that too."

Mrs. Rhodes snatched the sketch from the table and shoved it at Ava. "Catch him? Based on this?"

Ava tried to look at the picture, but little colored dots were parading in front of her, obscuring her vision. "If I don't have my party, he wins," Emma said. She laid her hand on Ava's forearm. Except for a few tumbles in bed with Cliff, and quick hugs, or pats from her mother or therapist, Ava wasn't used to being touched. Emma had a soothing touch, and Ava was surprised to discover she didn't mind it at all. But this was wrong. Ava was supposed to be soothing Emma, not the other way around. Emma looked deep into Ava's eyes. Ava wasn't used to that either, but she didn't dare break eye contact with such a brave young girl. "Don't you see?" Ava shook her head. She didn't see. "He might as well have snatched me and shoved me into a deep, dark hole."

"But—" Ava said.

"I'm going to be with my friends and I'm going to celebrate."

They were all getting up and moving to the door. Ava had failed. She'd failed. And that monster was still out there. The sketch remained on the table, untouched. Ava picked it up. "Shouldn't we get this to the media?"

Emma stopped. "I like your drawing," she said. "But it's not him." And then they were gone. Only Cliff remained, staring at her. Ava glanced down at the drawing. There was something so familiar about it. The shape of the face. The jutting chin. The big, warm eyes. She gasped. Ava had drawn her father.

"It's the sheets. And the Xanax," Ava said, following Cliff out the door. "It has to be."

"You didn't have Xanax," Cliff said.

"You gave it to me in the car."

"I gave you aspirin. You just thought it was Xanax."

"What? How could you?"

"Where was I supposed to get Xanax? The 7-Eleven?" Cliff was walking away too fast. The precinct was alive. Keyboards tapping, phones ringing, cops conversing. Where was her blindfold? Why was Cliff walking away? Had she embarrassed him? She wanted to go home. Home, home, home. She wanted to walk across the police precinct and pour herself a cup of scalding coffee, and maybe take a donut if there were any left in the box, which there probably weren't. But she'd never make it all the way across. She hated herself. Served her right that she wouldn't get to eat a chocolate, cream-filled donut. Served her right! Donuts were for those brave enough to walk across the room and claim them. Oh, the things outdoorsy types took for granted. It was nothing to them, nothing to walk across a room. And they had no idea how lucky they were.

A party! Emma was almost kidnapped and she was going to celebrate. Ava wished she had her life to live over. She wished she were the mayor's daughter. She couldn't breathe. The room was constricting and expanding like an accordion. She dived under the nearest empty desk, slipped a paper bag out of her pocket, and breathed into it. She needed to get her heart rate down. Adrenaline made all the systems in the body speed up, which was great if one was being chased across the Serengeti by a ravenous lion, but dangerous if you were simply trying to walk across a room. Over the long haul, getting this worked up too many times could damage her heart. And people said this was all in her head. *Breathe, Ava; don't worry about what other people think; just breathe.*

One. Two. Three. Four. Five. Six. Seven. Eight. Soon fatigue would set in and she would sleep. Somehow she was going to have to get out from underneath this desk and go home. Cliff would drive her. He might expect something from her when they got to her house. Sometimes she wondered if she was really into him or just really grateful. She didn't like to think about it. What did that make her if it was the latter?

She had to find Cliff's desk. She'd never even seen his desk. What kind of girlfriend was she? Was there a picture of her on his desk? Did he have a ball, a bowl of candy, or keys, a notepad with a list of suspects to interrogate? He'd never once complained that she had never come to his work, or his apartment. She would find his desk, find something about it to admire, compliment him, and get him to take her home. That monster was still on the street preying on young girls, his picture wasn't going to get distributed in time to warn the next victim, and that was all Ava's fault. This was why she never answered the door.

Ava crawled out from underneath the desk. Eyes all around were on her—she could feel them like lasers burning into her skull—but nobody said a single, solitary word. Which meant Cliff had told them all about her. She could only imagine the conversations.

She doesn't like to go outside.

What do you mean? She doesn't like the sun? What is she, a vampire?

I like the sun, you fuckers. I love feeling the sun on my face through the windows.

She has agoraphobia.

Is it catching? Hope you're wearing a glove.

Ha-ha. It's fear of the open marketplace.

A shopping disease? I wish my wife had a shopping disease.

Did they know she was sleeping with him too? Was she the laughingstock of the precinct? Ava kept her eyes glued to the floor so she couldn't confirm whether or not eyes were on her.

Perhaps they thought she'd lost something under the desk, a pencil perhaps, or an earring. She hoped they wouldn't notice she wasn't wearing any. She didn't even have any pieces of jewelry. She was not normal.

Eyes on the tile, which could use a good scrubbing, she kept walking. Past desks, and bookcases, and more desks, and there, she recognized his calves. Cliff was short, but he was strong. He was standing by his desk, talking on the phone. He had his back to her. Maybe he could get her a donut before he brought her home.

"I will reschedule with Gary Vance." Like she told him to do in the first place. Why didn't she trust her gut and stay home? "I'm sorry, sir. She's handicapped." Who was handicapped? Who was he talking about? "No, I'm not saying we have to use her—I'm just—"

Oh my God. He was talking about her. Her lover was calling her handicapped.

"Cliff?" She didn't mean to yell. He whirled around. Her eyes flew to his desk; she needed to ground herself. There were photos on his desk. How nice of him to keep photos of his handicapped girlfriend on his desk. If only she drove a car, she could get front-row parking. There were two photo frames. Which photos of her did he have? She lurched forward and grabbed the first one. She brushed a bowl on the desk and it toppled over the edge, shattering bits of glass and paper clips across the floor. She stared at the photo. Two little boys with dark hair and hazel eyes. Carbon cutouts of Cliff. They looked to be about six and eight. Sons. Cliff had two boys. Why didn't he tell her? Was he ashamed of her? Did he think she was unfit to be around his kids?

Cliff took the photo from her. She reached for the second. He tried to block her. "I'll scream," she said. The second was of a beautiful bride and groom. Cliff. And. His wife.

"You're married." It was a punch to the gut. Her voice came out strangled. She was stupid. So, so stupid.

"I'm sorry. I didn't want you to find out this way."

"Oh," she said. "Oh." This was why he didn't mind her

being—what was it he always called her? A homebody. *I like knowing where you are all the time.* Of course he did. She was the cheater's dream girl. He was right. She *was* handicapped. She was blind. A year. She'd been sleeping with a married man for an entire year.

He reached for the photo. She let him take it. He reached for her. "Don't you dare," she said.

"I'll drive you home."

"No. Get Jim."

"Who?"

"Joe." *Shit.* Now she couldn't remember anyone's name. She couldn't move. "Blindfold." She should make a scene. Why not? She'd never come here again, never work here again. What would a normal person do? Kick Cliff in the balls? Call his wife? At least knock everything off his desk and say something. *How dare you. How could you. I hate you.* Anything. Instead she stood, and she waited, as her body trembled, and her heart pattered, and sweat gathered on the back of her neck, and colored dots danced in front of her eyes. She was doing something, something very, very big. She was standing. She would not pass out; she would not make a scene; she would not give him that satisfaction.

"Joe is out to lunch," Cliff said in a low voice, near her ear. "Please, let me take you home."

He would never take her home again, never make love to her again. He was married. He was married and he was a liar. "No," Ava said. "I'll crash the car. If you drive me home, I'll make you crash the car and kill us both." Apparently her aunt Beverly wasn't the only one in the family with a touch for the dramatics.

"So what do you want to do? You look as if you're frozen in place."

"Blindfold me," Ava said. "And call my mother." What did he expect from a handicapped girl?

CHAPTER 5

Gretchen Wilder was no longer the woman Ava grew up with. The one who cared what the neighbors thought. The one who closed the blinds against the morning sun and left them that way all day, like an eye swollen shut. Bertrand's death had profoundly changed both of them, but instead of a left at the fork, Gretchen Wilder had taken a right. Gretchen walked into the police precinct dressed in cowboy boots, a short skirt with a tight white top, and with a red bandana around her neck. Line dancing. It was her latest thing. Everything in life could be cured by line dancing.

"Oh, Ava," Gretchen said. Cliff hadn't been able to find Ava's blindfold. Her own tears were doing part of the trick. Everyone, including her mother, was a tearstained blur. Unfortunately, not blurry enough. On display. Gretchen was on display.

"You look like you've had quite the day," Gretchen said.

"You look like you just auditioned for a remake of *Hee Haw*."

"I'm going to let that slide. Because of the day you're having."

"The worst day."

"I'm just going to pull off the Band-Aid. I'm sorry."

"What Band-Aid?"

"Your aunt Beverly is dead."

Ava hurried up the walk to her front door while her mother stopped to judge her mailbox. "It's spilling onto the ground!" Gretchen cried, bending to pick it up. Ava unlocked the door and stumbled in. Her mother was still complaining about the mail. Ava shut the door, leaving it just a little bit ajar so her mother could get in. She collapsed on the sofa. She had a good excuse about the mail, but she didn't want to defend herself anymore today. The regular mail guy used to bring the mail to the door. There was a new mailman now. Ava didn't know if the old one quit, got married, or jumped off a bridge. She wished he would've told her something. How hard could it be to send a postcard? She had so few people in her life. So now the new mailman was putting her mail in the mailbox. She should have moved it next to her front door, but she thought leaving it there would force her to get outside every day. So far, it hadn't exactly worked out. Her mother entered, plunked most of the mail on the kitchen counter, and presented the rest to her as evidence. "You have five letters from London."

"Aunt Beverly?" Ava grabbed for the mail. Had her aunt written her before she died? They were all from a barrister. *Jasper Keyes, Esquire.* "I was hoping one would be from her. That's it. I'll never have the chance to get to know her."

"Don't get me started," Gretchen said. She picked up one of the letters and ripped it open. "He wants you to call him right away."

"It's a federal offense to open someone else's mail."

"She must have included you in her will. I'm surprised."

"Mother, please. Can you please not speak ill of her?"

"She hated me. From the very start. Just because I was American and wasn't rich enough or posh enough for her."

Maybe she hated that you were hard. That you wouldn't dance. Ava kept her mouth shut. Her mother danced now. She had more on her mind than rehashing ancient history.

"Are you going to call him now?"

"What time is it in London?"

"It's probably around eight p.m."

"That's too late."

"He said to Skype him anytime."

"I think there's something wrong with the fact that you're dying to see what she left me. If anything. Maybe he simply wants to fill me in on the details of her passing."

"You won't know until you call."

"And you won't stop hounding me until I do. So have a seat, Mother; let's get this over with." Ava propped her laptop on the desk and she sat in front of it, while her mother perched on the sofa in the background. She didn't expect to reach him right away, so she was startled when she soon found herself looking at one Jasper Keyes, Esquire. He didn't look how Ava imagined a London lawyer—barrister—would look. She thought he'd be old, and gray, and admittedly wearing one of those white wigs the English still donned in court. She even imagined him dressed like Ben Franklin, except all in red. It was a far cry from the attractive man staring at her now. He didn't appear to be more than five years older than she was. Not that she was an expert at guessing ages, by any means. For all she knew, all that rain and fog in London kept Brits looking younger. Either way, there was something boyish and vulnerable about him. Maybe it was his wavy hair, the kind you wanted to run your hands through before handing him a brush. He looked tall, even though he was sitting down. He was wearing a navy T-shirt that made the blue of his eyes pop. People always complimented Ava on her blue eyes, but in her opinion his had hers beat. Especially with those eyelashes. Totally unfair. Perhaps his nose was a little big, and there was a hint of darkness underneath his blue eyes as if he could use a good, long nap, but there was no denying it, he was a very attractive man. He focused on Ava, but even though he smiled, he looked as if he'd just lost a dear friend.

Gretchen sat straight up, smiled at the camera, and adjusted her bandana at least ten times.

"First and foremost, I am so sorry for your loss," Jasper said after they introduced themselves. He looked at Gretchen.

"I love your accent," Gretchen said. "Very posh."

"My loss," Ava said. His eyes flicked to hers and stayed there. He was in pain. The thought hit her again. *Shit.* He was going to make her cry. Ava looked away. She wanted to reach out and grab him through the screen. She wanted him to bring Aunt Beverly back to life.

"I was very close to your aunt. We even went skydiving a few weeks back." Skydiving. Skydiving. Skydiving. With her aunt Beverly. A seventy-something-year-old woman. A million times the woman Ava would ever be. Apparently an adventurous spirit wasn't genetic. "I jumped right after her. Screaming my bloody head off. But Beverly. She was like a bird." He stared off into the distance. He loved her. That's why he looked so sad. A total stranger was grieving over her aunt. She wanted to comfort him, and pummel him at the same time. Her family. Her blood. Yet he was the one who got to love her. Ava wanted to ask Jasper a million questions about her aunt. She wanted to know, urgently, if Aunt Bev hated her. Was ashamed of her. Ever thought of her. She wanted to know if Aunt Bev thought she was handicapped.

"How did she die?" Ava had trouble spitting out the question. She didn't want to cry in front of Jasper; what right did she have to grieve for a woman she'd never met?

"She had terminal cancer. I think it started as breast cancer, but I'm not sure. It had spread quite rapidly. She didn't even go for treatment."

"Oh God," Ava said.

"But she didn't suffer long. She died in her sleep. Very, very peaceful."

"Unless she was having a bad dream," Ava said.

Jasper looked taken aback. "I don't think she was having a bad dream."

"How do you know?"

"She looked peaceful."

"Ava always thinks the worst," Gretchen said.

I don't! Ava wanted to shout. How could her mother embarrass her like that? Ava should have never let her in on the call. "Not always." It was the most she could sputter without tearing into her mother. Every time she even felt a tiny bit of anger it was engulfed by sadness. She hated that. She wanted to retain her anger. Diana agreed that would be healthy. But when it did come, Ava feared her rage would swallow everyone in her path.

"I'm sorry to cut right to business, but my schedule is jammed today—"

"Shed—jewel," Gretchen said, trying to imitate a British accent. "Oh, I could just eat you up."

"Mother."

"Perfectly all right," Jasper said. He held up his hand and grinned.

"I'm afraid I don't have long for this call either," Ava said. She wanted her mother gone so she could sit in the bathtub, and pull the curtain around her, and cry.

"Of course. In regards to Beverly's estate. She has technically left you her flat in the West End of London."

"What?" Ava said. It couldn't be true. Her flat? "Why?" A flat in London. She owned a flat in London?

"You don't sound happy," Jasper said.

"I'm shocked." She was. It just didn't seem possible. Was this a joke? A prank? Did Ava even want Beverly's flat? She wanted Aunt Beverly. But it had to mean something, didn't it? It meant her mother was wrong. Beverly did care. Maybe even loved her. Right?

"Oh my God," Gretchen said. She looked at Ava. "That was your father's flat once upon a time ago. Oh my God."

Ava gave her mother a look. She was practically bouncing on the sofa. Ava would also bet that her mother hadn't picked up on the fact that Jasper was grieving. She prayed her mother wasn't going to say anything unkind. It was about the third time replaying Jasper's words that something struck her. "Technically?" Ava said. "Did you say 'technically'?"

"And I must say, the West End of London is in high demand. It's the liveliest part of the city—"

"That will be lost on Ava." Ava stepped on her mother's foot underneath the desk. Gretchen kept smiling, but her eyelashes batted in acknowledgment.

"Technically?" Ava said.

Jasper looked as if he'd swallowed a snake. "I'm afraid there are some stipulations and conditions." His voice hitched at the end.

"What stipulations and conditions?" Ava asked.

He held up one finger. "First. You must live in the flat for one year." He stopped and waited.

"I see," Ava said. Aunt Beverly knew. She knew all about her.

"I'll do it," Gretchen said. "For Ava's sake."

"Alone," Ava said. "You are not allowed to live with me."

"He didn't say that," Gretchen said.

Ava pointed at Jasper. "He just said it. Sorry, my mum must be having trouble with your accent."

"I can understand you perfectly," Gretchen said. "You have beautiful diction."

"Please repeat what you said, Mr. Keyes."

"Jasper."

"Jasper." Ava lasered him with a look. He raised his eyebrows but did not speak. "Please repeat what you said about Aunt Beverly insisting I live there alone?"

Jasper made eye contact and held it again. A spark of electricity zapped through Ava. She never felt that with Cliff. Was this just grief? Was it because Jasper was close to Aunt Beverly? She looked away before he got the wrong idea.

He cleared his throat. "I'm afraid that is correct. The subject is to come alone. At least for the first year."

"Outrageous." Gretchen advanced on the computer like she was going to manhandle it. Ava tugged on her mother until she plopped into the chair next to her.

"We've lost the flat then," Gretchen said.

"Pardon?" Jasper said.

"Ava can't live there alone. Beverly knew that full well. This is a trick."

"Mother," Ava said. Oh, who was she kidding? Her mother

was right. Ava couldn't go alone. She planned on saying so when Emma's face rose before her. *Don't you see? If I don't have my party, he wins. He might as well have snatched me and shoved me into a deep, dark hole.* "I'll do it."

"Don't be ridiculous," Gretchen said. "You can't."

Jasper glanced at Ava. "I believe you may visit." Ava shrugged, then nodded. Jasper smiled. "But it's a limited number of days—" Ava nodded even more. "How many days?" Jasper posed it as a rhetorical question. Behind her mother's back, Ava held up three fingers. "Three days." His tone was emphatic.

"Three days?" Gretchen rose. "All the way to London?"

Ava was a terrible daughter. Her mother was misguided, no question, but she loved her just as fiercely. "How dare you disrespect my mother. Make it six days or no deal."

Jasper's mouth went through a few contortions. Was he trying not to laugh? "Six days." He rubbed his chin with his hand, then looked at Gretchen. "Perhaps we'll have to revisit the fine print."

"I'll fight for you, Mother," Ava said. Gretchen still didn't look happy. "Or we'll find you a nice hotel."

"Do they have country line dancing in London?" Gretchen asked. She hauled her leg up next to the computer and caressed her cowboy boot.

"No," Ava said. She shoved her mother's boot off the table.

"I believe they do," Jasper said.

"No," Ava said.

"I don't even know why we're having this conversation," Gretchen said. "Ava can't go to London alone. No matter what she says. She's agora—"

Ava lunged and shut off the monitor. "Mother! Stop!"

"What?"

"If I want him to know my business I'll tell him myself."

"But darling, you can't go."

"Why not, Mother? Because I'm handicapped?"

"You never leave the house. And you want to move to London?"

"I left the house today."

"You had a complete meltdown. You can't even walk out to your mailbox. You had to settle for a married man because who else would date a woman who won't go on any dates?"

The last comment was like a slap to the face. So that's what her mother really thought of her. *Wait.* She almost missed what her mother just said because of her hurt feelings. She advanced on her. "How did you know Cliff was married?"

"What?" Gretchen wasn't the actress in the family; she wasn't any good at it.

"You weren't there when I found out. And I certainly didn't tell you." Gretchen simply stared. "You knew. Oh my God. You knew Cliff was married and you didn't tell me? How? How did you know?"

"I ran into them once."

"Oh my God. How long ago?"

"It wasn't ideal but—"

"How long?"

"Shortly after you started dating."

"Oh my God. I can't believe you. How could you? He has two little boys. I could have wrecked their home."

"How? She wasn't going to find out about you."

"Oh my God. Who are you?" Ava hurried toward her bedroom. Pack. She was going to pack a suitcase. She stopped. She didn't have any suitcases. At least she had a passport. Because her father was British she had dual citizenship. She'd kept it updated over the years too. Not because she planned on going anywhere, but because she refused to lose that connection with her father. This would be the first time her passport would ever be stamped. London. The city she knew so well from books and movies. Buckingham Palace, and Kate and William, and her personal favorite, Prince Harry, because she had to love a rebel, and loads of tea, and Big Ben, and Notting Hill, and Downton Abbey, and clever little phrases like "Let's shag," and "Mind the Gap," and "I'm gobsmacked." Winston Churchill, and rain and fog, and the Tower of London—"Off with their heads!" Jack the Ripper and "London Is Burning" and "London Bridge is falling down," and rats, and pigeons, and Monty Python, and curried chips, the Thames, the Tube, and the plague. Ava's breath was starting to catch. Dots, she was seeing colored dots.

Oh, God. Her mother was right. She wouldn't be able to do it. *How do you know if you don't try?* Scrooge made a monumental change, didn't he? *Please, sir, a few pence for the crippled lad?* It was the city of her father. Maybe she'd feel close to him there. Get a little piece of him back. One thing was for sure. She couldn't stay here. Not anymore. She whirled around and headed for the kitchen. Her mother stayed on her heels.

"I'm sorry, I'm sorry. I told him not to hurt you—"

Ava opened the cabinet under the sink and fished out the box of extra-large garbage bags. Did the airport have any regulations about using Hefty garbage bags as a suitcase? Ava headed back to the bedroom, and once again her mother followed. Ava flung open the top dresser drawer and started throwing clothes into the bag.

"You can't pack your clothes in a garbage bag."

"Watch me." Ava grabbed a handful of panties and bras, and stuffed them in.

"I'll get you a suitcase."

"Now, can you get it now?"

"It's been a long day. You need to rest." Her mother approached, arms outstretched. Ava avoided them.

"I need to pack."

"You won't even make it to the airport."

Ava continued to throw clothes into the bag. She lifted it and a bra popped out. In a matter of seconds, the bag had a giant rip in the bottom. Hefty, her ass. "Piece of shit." Ava threw the bag to the floor. Her mother was right. This was stupid. She needed a proper suitcase.

"You don't have a plane ticket."

"I'll get one."

"This isn't the way to do this. You need a proper plan."

"I'll formulate one. Diana will help me. I'll get Xanax."

"Xanax? That's your solution?"

"It helps."

"You'll get addicted."

"You say that all the time. You're the reason I've been afraid to take Xanax. I can't listen to you anymore. I should have it on hand—I should have it now." *Maybe, just maybe, I could even handle you if I had kept up my prescription of Xanax.*

"Do you want to add being an addict to your troubles?"

Ava looked at her mother for a long time. She rarely ever confronted Gretchen. She realized a long time ago that it wouldn't change a single thing. Whoever Ava was, whoever her mother was, both completely imperfect, they were never going to change. Ava either accepted her mother for who she was now or wouldn't have a mother. But this was too much. Ava needed her to believe in her. Like the mayor's wife believed in her daughter. "You don't want me to get better, do you?"

"How can you say such a rotten thing? After all I've done for you? I hope you have kids of your own one day just so you know how it feels to have an ungrateful child."

"I can't help it. You're pushing me down like one of those crabs in a bucket, when you should be pulling me up."

"I don't get the seafood reference."

"Crabs in a bucket. You know. How one poor little crab tries to crawl out." Ava mimicked with her fingers. "But just when he gets to the top and you think the poor bastard is going to get free, the rest of the bastards yank him back down?" Ava yanked the imaginary crab back to the bottom of the bucket.

"I can't stand it when you use bad language. Certainly not the Queen's English, my dear."

"You're not listening. You missed the point entirely." God, nobody could push her buttons like her mother. Ava was so angry she was starting to shake.

"You're a crab; I heard you. If by that you mean crabby, I certainly agree. But I'm not the one yanking you down. Forgive me if I think you should start with your mailbox before tackling the UK."

"I'm doing this for Aunt Beverly."

"That woman never cared about us a day in her life!"

Ava shot off the bed. "She never cared about you. Not me. You."

Her mother's eyes welled with tears. *Oh, God.* It was a million times worse hurting her mother than it was getting hurt. This was why she never confronted anybody. "Do what you want," Gretchen said, picking up the bra on the floor and folding it. "You always do."

"I'm sorry I said that. Okay? I'm not going because I want to hurt you. I'm going for me. Because not going would be like hurling myself into a deep, dark hole and never, ever coming out."

"How is that any different than what you've been doing your entire life?"

Ava was wrong. That hurt worse. She bolted from the living room and fled to her bathroom. She slammed the door behind her. Her mother could let herself out. Ava sat in the bathtub, fully clothed, and pulled the curtain closed. *Breathe, Ava, breathe.* Aunt Beverly was dead. Her father was dead. Her mother resented her. Had her life been a deep, dark hole? It was hard to argue with. But she could change. People changed, didn't they? At the least, she could try. She was going to London. She was going to crawl out of the bucket if it killed her.

Gretchen picked up her purse near the computer. *That woman.* Of course she would find a way to stick it to Gretchen from the grave. She never liked her, never approved of her, did everything she could to convince Bertie not to marry her. Well, he married her anyway, and so Beverly threatened to never speak to him again. Then, after Bertie died, she had the gall to threaten to fight for custody. Saying that Gretchen couldn't adequately deal with Ava's condition. That a change of scenery might be good for her. She practically came out and said that Gretchen wasn't equipped to help her own daughter. The nerve of her! This coming from the woman who had never even met Ava. Gretchen didn't like to be crude, but that woman sure had a pair of balls. A hairy pair of balls. Oh, the fury she incited in Gretchen. It wasn't healthy then, and she could still feel the rage coursing through her veins now. Miss Famous Actress. Thinking her money could trump a mother's love.

Oh, the drama. It never ended. It still hadn't ended. Someone cleared his or her throat. Gretchen started. Who was that? Was someone in the living room? She whirled around, but saw no one. "Blimey," she heard a male voice say. It came out of the computer. She turned on the monitor. Jasper Keyes stared back at her.

"You're still there? How can you still be there?"

"She just shut off the picture. The call was still connected."

"And you kept listening? All this time?"

"I wasn't going to, I swear. I went to shut it off, and then I listened a bit more, and a bit more, and then the voices got too far away, and I got wrapped up in something else, here on my computer, and quite frankly I forgot we were still connected until I heard you come back into the room."

"I see."

"I'm sorry. I'm truly sorry." Jasper turned red.

Gretchen sank into the chair. "You knew about her already, didn't you?"

Once again, Jasper nodded. "Beverly said she had some challenges."

"She won't be able to do this," Gretchen said. "This is very cruel of that woman. Very, very cruel."

Jasper reached out as if he could touch her. "You've got the wrong end of the stick. Beverly's dying wish was to do something for Ava. Something to help her." He sounded sincere. Obviously Beverly had suckered him too.

How was it that such a dreadful woman could wrap so many people around her fingers? She had to control everyone and everything in her orbit. She was diabolical. "This isn't going to help. She can't even walk out to her mailbox."

"At least she's going to give it a go," Jasper said. "At least she's going to give it a go." He looked guilty of something. For a barrister he didn't have much of a poker face.

"What aren't you saying?"

"I didn't quite get to explain all the conditions," he said. "There's quite a bit more."

"That woman. Tell me everything."

"With all due respect. My instructions are to tell Ava."

"You'll tell me, and I'll tell her."

"I'm sorry—one moment—I'm getting a funny ripple on my screen—I'm afraid I'm losing you."

He was lying. There was nothing wrong with their connection. Gretchen gripped the screen with both hands as if she could shake it out of him. "What conditions?"

The screen went black. He was gone. "Bloody British," Gretchen said. She didn't know what Aunt Beverly was trying to pull now, but nobody was going to stop her from finding out. She wasn't allowed to come. The nerve of Beverly. Gretchen would see about that. All the guards at Buckingham Palace couldn't keep her away. Her little girl needed her whether she admitted it or not.

CHAPTER 6

Ava paid for two first-class tickets to London. It wiped out a substantial amount of her savings, but it was well worth it. Diana agreed to accompany her. Between her support and enough Xanax to choke a bull, Ava made it onto the plane. Ava was preparing her eye mask, headphones, and aromatherapy scents when Diana grabbed her purse from underneath the seat, unbuckled herself, and stood up. Then, she started to walk away.

Ava tried to get out of her seat, but the seat belt yanked her back down. "Where are you going?"

"The loo." Diana had been "speaking British" all the way through the airport. But Ava knew Diana wasn't going to the loo. She felt it.

"You just went before we got on the plane."

"What can I say? I may not feel my age, but my bladder does."

"You're lying. I always know when you're lying." It was true. Whenever Diana lied, all the Brooklyn drained out of her. Lying turned her weak, and polite, more like an awkward midwesterner.

Diana tugged on her turtleneck and shifted her eyes to the

left. "When a therapist doesn't tell the truth, it's a helpful prompt, not a lie."

"Bullshit."

"You used to be a lot easier to deal with."

"You've taught me how to stand up for myself."

"I'm so glad to hear you say that."

"Sit down; we're about to take off."

"I'm not going with you."

"You checked a suitcase."

"You keep it. But don't get your hopes up. Apparently it's illegal to fill it with Xanax."

"Please. Don't do this to me." Ava couldn't do this on her own. But she couldn't get off the plane either. There was no way she could face the airport again. Diana knew this. She was tricking her.

"Did I ever tell you how my father taught me to swim?"

"You can't do this to me."

"He pushed me in and walked away."

"That's horrible. That's child abuse."

Diana shrugged. "Perhaps. But I still swim every morning at the Y. Bon voyage."

"Don't." Ava unbuckled her seat belt and stood up.

In a flash Diana was back, gently pushing her back down. "Now you have both seats to yourself. The sleeping pills will kick in soon. If you make a scene they'll throw you off the plane. And your mother will win. She'll win."

Damn therapist. She knew just what buttons to push. Before Ava knew what was happening, Diana was gone, and she was alone. She had enough adrenaline coursing through her to keep her awake, but enough sleeping pills in her to make it all seem like a groggy dream.

Shortly after takeoff, Ava slept. She woke throughout the flight, but didn't want to see what was going on around her, didn't do much but make it to the loo, and that was only because the thought of pissing in her seat was way worse.

First class was wasted on her, that was for sure. She couldn't pay attention to television or movies, and when she tried to eat or drink she realized she had no sense of taste. All her senses were numb. Everything was just one loud hum. She kept her eye mask on, and her earplugs in. *This, too, shall pass.* And it did. Slowly, and torturously, but it did. Her legs were stiff. She couldn't wait to be off the plane. She also dreaded being off the plane. A rock and a hard place. That pretty much summed up her life. The plane began to descend; the pilot announced their arrival and welcomed them to London. Ava remained in her seat until every single other passenger had left the plane and the flight attendants were staring at her en masse. She wanted to ask for assistance, for a wheelchair.

She popped a Xanax and put herself on autopilot before she had to be dragged off the plane. She followed the throngs of people to the immigration line. She showed her British passport, for the first time. She made it. But now, she was in the middle of London Heathrow Airport, completely on her own, and wide awake.

Terminal 4. She felt terminal all right. *Huge. People. Fuck.* Purple signs hanging up high were telling her where to go. She wanted to tell them where to go. The infinite terminal was a minefield. She was just going to have to take step after step after step until she was blown to smithereens.

Who did she think she was? Loser, loser, loser. Handicapped. It was big; it was so big. She tried to remain calm, keep her heart rate down, but the space was absolutely massive. She had to get out of here; this was too wide, too open. This was not in her head. This was her brain perceiving a threat, then commanding her body to freak out. Lights, people, action. Was this Heathrow or Hollywood? She closed her eyes, but it didn't work. Sick, she was going to be sick. The line to the loo was stretched out the door and into the hall. *Oh, God.* Ava couldn't hide in the bathroom with that line.

There it was, next to the loo, a janitor's closet. It was open; a cleaning person must have just popped in to get a broom, or glass cleaner, or rat poison. Ava rushed over and squeezed into the small, dark space where she felt safe. Just imagine if she fell in love with someone who was claustrophobic. It would be a Greek tragedy. She wanted to sit, but she was jammed in next to mops, and brooms, and buckets. She would just stand. And breathe. She heard footsteps approaching. The cleaning lady was going to find her in here, she would startle her, the woman would have a heart attack, and Ava would finally get to use CPR.

Or she would startle her and the woman would jam a feather duster down Ava's throat, and she would die in a little closet in London Heathrow. Just as Ava was concocting a third scenario, the actual cleaning lady pulled the cart right up to the open door. She was texting. Texting! Or she could have been Tweeting. Facebooking. What was she saying? Something about the unspeakable filth of the flying public no doubt.

Ava looked at the cart. On top there was a pile of black garbage bags. Maybe Ava could put one over her head and just keep walking until she bumped into Baggage Claim. She waited until the lady stopped texting. "Can I use your phone?" Ava said in a calm, normal voice. The lady's head snapped up and she looked at Ava and she screamed as if Ava were standing there with a bloody cleaver and a severed head. "Stop," Ava said. "I'm not going to hurt you." *Great*. Now she did sound like a psychopath. Couldn't the woman see that she was suffering? "I need help," Ava said. Maybe she should have just let herself pass out instead. At least then she would have been picked up to a stretcher and maybe carried to her town car. For somewhere, at the other end of this terminal, if it ever did end, there was a driver picking up her bags and waiting for her with a sign. She hoped it didn't read: Total Nut Job.

"What are you doing? What on earth are you doing?"

"I just needed a quiet space."

"It's the cleaning cabinet."

"I am aware."

"Passengers are not allowed in the cleaning cabinet," the woman said. The tone of voice was as if she'd just caught Ava peeing in the supply closet. Ava was simply standing and breathing. People were so judgmental. The cleaning lady no longer sounded afraid, and she had stopped screaming, but she was hiding behind the cart. One false move and she would shove the cart at Ava as hard as she could. Ava could see it in her eyes.

"I just need your phone, your mobile, or I need a man with a cart—what is that in London Lingo? A trolley—you know. To drive me to Baggage Claim."

The woman thrust her arm out. "Baggage Claim is that way. You will not find Baggage Claim in here. Off with you then. Out, out, out."

She was being shooed away like she was a child or a rodent. Shouldn't they be a little nicer? Offer her a cold compress and a cup of tea? "Please. Just call for a trolley." Ava stepped forward and put a hand on her heart. "I've always counted on the kindness of strangers."

Apparently the cleaning lady wasn't a Tennessee Williams fan. Instead of helping her, the woman came from behind the cleaning cart, reached out as if to manhandle Ava. Ava grabbed a broom and held it across her chest. "Don't touch me," Ava said. "Just get a courtesy officer, or a trolley person, or a nice airline person who understands people with disabilities—and get them here right now."

"You have a disability?" The woman squinted at Ava. "Are you blind?"

"I'm not blind."

"And we've established you're not deaf, haven't we then?"

"So why are you still shouting?"

The woman's eyes flicked over Ava's perfectly good legs. "Can you walk?"

"Yes, I can walk."

"Then what on earth is wrong with you?"

"Not every disability is visible," Ava said. "Some are hidden." A strange, cold thought took root in Ava and began to grow. *Am I disabled?* She wanted to walk across the terminal by herself and she couldn't. She wasn't faking it, she wasn't seeking attention, and she certainly would have given anything to be like all of those normal people out there. Maybe she did have a disability. An invisible disability. Like Superman without any powers.

."You cannot stand in the cleaning cabinet. I've got work to do, I have." The woman reached for the broom and held it up like a sword.

Where did they recruit these workers? Prison? "I'm having a panic attack. Please stop talking to me." Ava snatched a black garbage bag from the cart.

"Oy," the cleaning lady said. "Rubbish bags are not for the public."

"So sue me." Ava fumbled opening it—those stupid plastic bags never wanted to open—but finally got it open and put it over her head. Darkness. That was better. She could still feel the woman staring at her.

"You're a right nutter!"

"Even if that's true," Ava said, "you shouldn't speak to customers like that."

"I'm getting airport security," the woman threatened.

"Finally," Ava said. "Do it."

The security officers treated her with the same respect she got from the cleaning lady. It wasn't until Ava dissolved into helpless tears that some sympathy crept into their eyes. She told it like it was. If she had to walk through this busy, humungous airport she would pass out. So they let her ride in the back of a trolley. And although she didn't keep the garbage bag over her head—oh, how she wanted to—she did keep it clutched in her left hand, head down, and her eyes covered with her right hand. "This, too, shall pass," she whispered to herself, over and over. "This, too, shall pass." So many echoes in the airport. Every sense bombarded. The smells of fast food and chemicals. Dings, and clicks, and footsteps, and beeps. The bounce of the trolley as they swerved to miss pedestrians. Ava wasn't crazy; everyone else was.

How did people do this day in and day out? Ava's senses weren't used to it. They'd atrophied. She wasn't equipped to deal with this. She was never, ever going to speak to Diana again no matter what she had packed in that suitcase for her. It was torture. It was that simple. It was torture for her and it was easy for everybody else. It made her feel enraged but impotent. As if she had a machine gun but no bullets.

The cart jerked to a stop. Ava flew forward; her chest hit the seat in front of her. *Ow. That really hurt.* For a moment she forgot about everything but the sharp pain in the top of her breasts. She wanted the driver to do it again and again. "Are we here?"

"I got you as close as we're going to get," the driver said. "If you need help the rest of the way we'll have to get a wheelchair and—"

Ava opened one eye. People swarming, shoving, moving. She shut the eye as quickly as possible. "Yes, please," she whispered. "Wheelchair." She didn't have to cry. She was shaking. And pale. Surely everyone would think she was British.

CHAPTER 7

Her driver looked like a member of ZZ Top. He had on a driver's cap, dark glasses, and was sporting a long beard. Ava had an urge to tug on it, see if it was real. He held up a sign: Ms. Ava Wilder.

Ava pointed to the sign and the driver from the trolley, who was now pushing her wheelchair, wheeled her up to him.

"'Allo," the driver said with a slight bow. He sounded like the chimney sweep in *Mary Poppins*. He took in the wheelchair and his eyes widened. "I didn't realize," he said.

"I can walk," Ava said. "I'm just a little weak right now."

"Of course," the driver said. He turned to the attendant. "I can take her from here."

"British luck to you," the attendant said to her driver with a parting glance at Ava. "Leave the chair at the curb."

"Jerk," Ava said under her breath. She clutched her suitcase on her lap as the driver wheeled her and Diana's suitcase out to the curb where a boxy white car was waiting. Ava felt every bump the wheelchair hit along the way, and every noise jangled her nerves. She squeezed her eyes shut.

They stopped. Her luggage was lifted off her lap and Ava listened as he put it in the trunk. *Boot, isn't that what they call it here?* Soon he was standing over her. "Do you need help? Shall I lift you?" Ava opened one eye. Just enough to see the car door open, black leather seats beckoning her inside. From what she could see, it was a cloudy day. It smelled like rain was coming.

"No, thank you." Ava stood, then crawled into the back seat, lay down, and since there weren't any covers, draped the plastic garbage bag over her face. Let the driver think she was a crazy American.

"Wait," she called just as he was about to shut the passenger door.

"Yes?" His voice sounded close. As if he'd popped his head into the backseat.

"Do you think I could keep the wheelchair?"

"Are you asking me to lift it?"

"Oh. Is it heavy? I thought you could fold it into the trunk."

"The boot?"

"What?"

"Are you asking me to lift it and toss it into the boot?"

"Well, I don't see how you would get it into the boot without lifting it." There was a pause, then laughter. He had a very nice laugh. He sounded younger than he looked.

"Do you expect me to steal a wheelchair from the airport like a common criminal?"

"Oh." "Lift," as in "steal." Lost in translation. She'd misinterpreted him on several levels. He was a goody-goody. The beard definitely didn't suit him. "Not when you put it that way." It was another few moments before she heard the passenger door shut and then he slammed down "the boot." She supposed that wasn't very cool of her, asking the taxi driver to steal airport property.

She waited until he was back in the car and they had pulled away from the curb. "I'm sorry."

"It's perfectly all right. I took a shopping trolley home once when I was ten."

"Ah."

"After my father found out my arse was so sore I couldn't sit for a week."

"Guess you'll have to go ahead and spank me." *Oh, God*. Did Ava just say that?

"What?" He swerved into the other lane, then jerked the wheel the opposite direction before he could get sideswiped. Horns blared and he blared his back. Red brake lights loomed inches ahead. "Bollocks." He slammed on the brakes. Ava was thrown off the seat and onto the floor. She'd bonked her head, but she didn't want to move. She liked it down on the floor better.

"So sorry, luv," the driver said. "Do you need some help up?"

"I've fallen and I can't get up," Ava said. Did they know that one in London?

"Should I pull over?"

"Without getting us killed? Unlikely." She crawled back onto the seat and made the mistake of looking up. Their eyes met in the rearview mirror, and she felt a tiny jolt as if she had just been Tasered. He had really beautiful blue eyes. "Your beard looks fake," she said.

"Maybe it is."

Ava put the garbage bag over her head. Cars honked again. There was at least a foot between him and the car in front of him and other drivers weren't having it. He moved the foot forward and stopped. Busy, busy planet.

"Only two suitcases," the driver said. "Must be a record." God, he sounded chipper.

"For a woman?"

"Pardon?"

"Must be a record for a woman?"

"No, no. No. Blokes too. Most blokes have more than two suitcases, especially if they're staying awhile."

"What makes you think I'm staying awhile?"

"You're going to a residential address, not a hotel," he said. She could hear him drumming his fingers on the steering wheel. Was she getting to him or was it the traffic?

She didn't bother telling him she had actually only brought one suitcase. That the other belonged to her traitor of a therapist. Was there some kind of ethics board she could report Diana to? That would serve her right. What could Diana have put in the other suitcase? Ava didn't need many outfits. Being a shut-in was certainly easy on the wallet. Really, all she needed was several pairs of pajamas. She would change into her horse pajamas the minute she got into the flat, cover the windows with sheets, maybe sit in the bathtub in the dark for a while. What were the chances there would be a bottle of wine at the flat? Not that she'd drink much. It wouldn't take much with all these pills.

"How is the temperature?"

It was freezing. "Great. Thank you."

"You're most welcome. Is this your first time in London?"

"I'm sorry. I have a migraine." That should be enough to get him to leave her alone. Europeans didn't need to be bashed over the head; they were schooled in subtlety.

"Dreadful. My ex-girlfriend is prone to migraines. Wait just a minute. Scratch that. Although technically she is my ex, I plan on getting her back. And in order to do that, I have to imagine— rather, create—my reality as if it's happening now." He pounded cheerfully on the steering wheel. "So she's not my ex; she's my current girlfriend—rather, she's my fiancée. My fiancée—my WIFE—my WIFE gets migraines too."

Ava suddenly perked up. He was mental. Just like her. How refreshing. There was a moment of silence and then he laughed at himself and shrugged. Self-deprecating taxi driver. Who knew. They were pulling out of the airport now; she could feel the turn and the acceleration of the car. Rain fell on the roof. "You don't mind if we chat, do you? Helps pass the time."

"I'm not really in a chatty mood."

"My iPod isn't charged, and there's no decent radio, so—"

"Why don't you call somebody?" *Who cares.*

"I think it's terribly rude to talk on the mobile while driving."

"I don't mind, really. As long as you're hands free."

"I hate when I'm in a taxicab and the driver is on his mobile—"

"You take cabs too?"

"Oh. Right. That must sound quite silly. Since I am, obviously, a driver myself. But I do take them as well. Once in a while, I do."

Ava slipped her hands into her purse—handbag or pocketbook, what did they say here? She rummaged around until she felt the round plastic vial. She edged around it with her thumb until she found the cap. She popped it and snuck her fingers inside. She scooted a pill up the side of the bottle and into her palm. It was a quick trip to her mouth. Xanax. Forget diamonds. That little miracle was a girl's best friend. She wasn't sure if it was actually time for one because the time change was messing with her. She just liked having something to do, and the floaty feeling was starting to wear off. Mission accomplished. All this, lying down, under the garbage bag. Ava would do pretty well as a blind person. The driver was still talking. Something about the architecture and the history of London. He had a pleasant voice. She didn't really care what he was saying; there was just something soothing about the noise of him. Everyone sounded a bit more pleasant with an English accent, even the cleaning lady who shrieked at her in Heathrow. It would be difficult to be on a jury here. The accused could be an axe murderer and still get off with that accent. *He probably did it all right, but he sounds like a lovely chap, doesn't he? Why don't we let him off? Be a good lad and don't sever any more heads, all right?*

Diana's warning barreled through her. *Don't abuse these pills. It's not a slippery slope; it's a slide straight to a life of hell.* It was too late, already in her mouth, down her throat, coursing through her veins.

"Jack the Ripper," the driver said.

"What?" Was she riding with a psycho? Was he going to chop her into little pieces? So much for trusting everyone with an English accent.

"I was saying you could take the tour. It's quite fun if you like a good fright now and then."

"I'm having a good fright right now."

"Does it help your migraine? Hiding under a rubbish bag like that?"

A rubbish bag. Not a garbage bag, a rubbish bag. "Not with you talking."

"If it doesn't help, you might want to look out the windows. Wouldn't want to miss your first glimpse of London now, would you?"

Maybe he was right. Didn't she come here to change? She could do this. Ava kept her eyes closed, but lifted the bag, then slowly sat up. She opened one eye. *Oh, God. Dizzy. Cars, so many freaking cars.* She cried out. He swerved, and then swore. Then apologized.

"You're on the wrong side of the road!"

"It's the side we drive on here, luv."

"Oh, right. Sorry, governor." She didn't mean to make fun of him, but he did just call her luv and "governor" kind of just slipped out. But instead of taking offense he laughed. At least he seemed to have a good sense of humor to go with those baby blues.

"Do you want to talk about *Downton Abbey*?" he asked suddenly.

Yes, I kind of do. "Why would I want to talk about *Downton Abbey*?"

"Americans are obsessed with it. Why do you think that is?"

"Maggie Smith," Ava said. "And the mansions, and beautiful clothing, and the servants versus the upper class. I've heard London is still very much about who's who. Money will only get you so far in the door—and I like that part—but you're only accepted into the inner circle if your name is such and such and you've been here since the dinosaurs roamed the earth. It's all nonsense if you ask me."

"Since the dinosaurs, did you say? Yes, I think we traced my family line back to the rex on my mum's side, brontosaurus on me dad's." Ava laughed. "You have a beautiful laugh," he said. "But I bet you hear that all the time." He stared openly at her through the rearview mirror. She wanted to thank him and tell him that she'd never heard that, ever. Cliff was more interested in a quickie than conversation or compliments. Of course now she knew why. At the time she simply thought he couldn't wait to have her. The driver was still watching her. Ava made eye contact with him and he smiled. "Welcome to London." His voice had lowered and for a second he sounded very attractive. Ava forced herself to look out a tiny section of the window. She didn't like beards, and even if she could get past it, she wasn't here to shag the driver.

Gray, rainy, blurry, busy. Why was everyone in such a hurry all the time? It had never made sense to her. Rushing to the grave. She, for one, planned on taking the slow boat.

"Do you like sports?"

"No." *Don't look at everything at once. Look at one thing at a time. One tree. One car. One building in the distance.* They were going too fast. How was she supposed to do this? She would look at the back of the driver's head. She would imagine sketching him. He had a nice neck. Underneath his cap his hair was light brown and wavy. She wanted to run her fingers through it. Maybe she was a nympho. *What do you call an agoraphobic who is also a nymphomaniac?*

"Football, cricket, rugby, darts?"

"No." *A slut who never leaves the house.*

"You like the theater then?"

In other words, Cliff's dream girl. "The theater?"

"Are you a loyal thespian?"

"My aunt Beverly is a stage actress. In the West End." *Was.* Why was she speaking of Aunt Beverly in the present tense? It didn't seem real. Even though Ava had never met her, she ached. She missed the fact that she'd never get to meet her. Talk to her about Ava's father. Ask what he was like as a little boy. Ask why she never made an effort to visit, why they never visited her. Why did Beverly leave her her flat? It must mean she had regrets. Did that count for anything? And what about Ava's regrets? Ava should have visited when she was alive. What did this look like? Coming only after she was gone just to inherit her flat?

"An actress, you say?"

"Was," Ava said.

"Pardon?"

"My aunt is no longer with us. She died."

"My apologies. I'm sorry for your loss." Ava was too. She was sorry about a lot of things. She simply nodded to the driver. "You've come to settle her affairs then?"

"I'm meeting with a lawyer. I guess you call him a barrister here."

"Ah. Barristers. They can be dodgy. Have you met him?"

"Just a video chat."

"What sort is he?"

"What do you mean?"

"I mean how did you find him?"

"He called me." This man was a little bit nosy.

The driver roared with laughter. "No, I meant how did you find him—as in what did you think about him? Dodgy?"

"No. I quite liked him." She laughed.

"What's funny? C'mon now. Give us a laugh too."

"Nothing. Just."

"Go on."

"Even my mother found him attractive. She was shamelessly flirting." *In her little cowgirl outfit.* Ava didn't mention that part. Oh, how her mother embarrassed her at times. Not that Ava was a saint. She had all but sealed her mother out of the London deal. It wasn't very kind of her. She'd have to have her mother for a visit soon. She just wanted to do this alone. Aunt Beverly was her family. Her last connection to her dad.

"Ah. Good-looking, was he?"

Ava raised her eyebrow. "Not in a traditional sense."

"A real uggo then?"

"No. If by that you mean . . . ugly."

"Ugly, yes. A real uggo."

"He wasn't. He was good-looking if you must know."

"But you said he wasn't. Not in the traditional sense."

"He had kind of a goofy air about him. But he had nice blue eyes. Like yours." *Oh shit.* The driver was smiling at her now. He thought she was hitting on him. "And I think he's tall," Ava added, wanting to distract the driver from the compliment.

"You think?"

"He was sitting down."

"So it was his personality that got you, was it?"

"He was friends with my aunt. They went skydiving together."

"He's an adventurer. A bloke you could really fall in love with, I suppose." He suddenly sounded twenty times more chipper.

Maybe the driver was gay. How could she tell? All British men seemed a little bit gay. "I wouldn't know about that."

"You wouldn't know about what? Falling in love?"

"Do you always get so personal with your passengers?"

"You're the first. So go on, answer the question. A pretty girl like you. Is there a special lad?"

Was he hitting on her? Did it matter? That was the beauty of taxi drivers, a built-in time limit; you could say anything you wanted to them because they eventually dropped you off. "There was. But he was married."

"That sounds complicated."

"I didn't know he was married."

"I'm sorry. Must have come as quite a shock."

"Shock is my middle name." Ava forced herself to look out the window. Maybe that's what was wrong with her. She was like an electric fence, ready to spark at any second. The cars looked boxier here. Like cute little milk trucks in the rain. She'd seen enough. She went back to looking at her hands. Her sketch pad was in her purse if things got too bad.

"Love is one of those things," the driver said.

"One of what things?"

"It's just hard. Even when it's going swimmingly."

"Let me guess. Your ex?"

"You've caught me."

"Complicated?"

"It is." He sighed. And waited.

"How so?" If he was going to talk the entire time, at least he could tell her the good stuff.

"Do you think you're supposed to know, I mean, really know when you're in love? Without a doubt?"

"Absolutely."

"Oh. Right then. That's me sorted." He gave a fake laugh.

"So she wasn't sure she was in love with you and that's why she broke it off?"

"You hit the nail on the head. 'I don't think we're really in love, do you?' " He shook his head, then met Ava's eyes in the mirror.

"I don't know," Ava said. Why was he putting her on the spot? "How would I know?"

"No, sorry. That's what *she* said."

"What?"

" 'I don't think we're really in love, do you?' That's what my girlfriend said to me."

"Oh." *Duh.* Chatting. Not really her wheelhouse.

"You see—it was a test, and I failed."

"What was your answer?"

"I said, 'You're not expecting the earth to move, are you, because that's a fairy tale. We're attracted to each other. We get on. What more do you want?' " The driver finished his speech and waited for Ava to respond.

Apparently she wasn't the only one out of touch. "Ouch."

"Bodged it, did I? Even if I was being honest?"

"When you're in love, the earth should move a little. At least that's what I believe." It *was* what she believed. Which meant she had never been in love either.

"Perfection," the driver said, almost to himself.

"No, God, no. Love is so far from perfect. It's hard. Sometimes it's searing pain. It's beautifully imperfect. But it just is. You never have to question it, because it's like air. You know that it's always there and you just breathe. I think love is about two very imperfect people falling in love with each other's flaws." Their eyes met again in the rearview mirror. There was kindness in his, that was part of it, but that wasn't all. He was looking at her as if he found her attractive; dare she say, he was looking at her as if he desired her.

"That was beautifully said, madame."

"Thank you."

He fell silent. Rain pelted against the rooftop and Ava found the vibration of the road soothing. Was he thinking about what she said? Would he go home and tell his ex that he thought she was beautifully imperfect? Maybe she should have kept her mouth shut. She didn't want to bear the weight of anyone else's burden. Her own was heavy enough. They were getting off the M4, turning into London. Even the names on the signs were startling. Chelsea, Battersea, Kingston. Buildings lined up on both sides of the street, clean and regal. Red double-decker buses, and fancy yellow license plates with black letters. London. She was in London. *Oh, God.*

She lay back down and placed the garbage bag over her head again. Much, much better. God, having a conversation was exhausting. She dozed off to an orchestra of sounds. Car horns, the thump and swish of the tires, the whistle of the wind. She didn't wake up until the car slowed down. They were pulling over. They had arrived. She could hear voices, and horns, and trucks backing up. London smelled like rain and baking bread.

But the pleasant feeling wore off quick as her brain began prepping her body for a five-alarm fire. *Danger. Outside. Danger.* Ava's heart immediately kicked into high gear. "It's a wonderful building," the driver said, looking up at it. "In the heart of it all."

"Goodie," Ava said. She was going to have to sit up. She was going to have to look at the building. She was going to have to ring the bell to the top floor and wait for Jasper Keyes to come down. He was supposed to meet her here. How long would it take him? How long would she be standing on the stoop? What would the driver think if she asked him to stand with her? He was probably busy. As soon as she paid him he would flee.

"I can help you out. I can get your luggage."

"Yes, thank you." She sat up, eyes closed, and waited.

He came around and opened the door. He was holding a large, black umbrella. The rain had stopped. But he was holding it open, waiting for her to seek refuge underneath. It was almost as if he understood. And it was still so gray that it wouldn't look odd at all. Her suitcases were perched on the sidewalk. She opened her wallet.

"The fare has been paid."

"What?"

"Your fare has already been taken care of."

"By who?" Was it "whom"? Brits probably cared about things like that.

"Perhaps it was the nontraditionally good-looking barrister."

"A tip then."

"Already paid."

Ava scooted over and the driver held his hand out. Ava felt a ripple of shock run through her as she took it and he helped her up. It so startled her, she snatched her hand away. "Thank you," she said quickly to make up for it.

"My pleasure."

Ava was actually touching the pavement. Now she would have to walk toward the building. One step at a time. She looked up at the black umbrella. Thank God he hadn't removed it yet even though it wasn't raining. He was astute, this driver. Maybe in his profession you learned to read people, just like a sketch artist. From behind them a car door slammed and suddenly a man was shuffling toward them. He approached Ava's driver.

"You're bloody late." The man snatched the hat right off her driver's head. What was going on? Were they sharing the taxi, switching shifts?

"Sorry," her driver said. "Traffic."

"Traffic me arse. This was the last time it was." The man put the hat on his own head and, sure enough, got into her driver's car and screeched away.

"Your taxi," Ava said. "Someone just stole your taxi."

"It wasn't mine," the driver said.

"You share the taxi? How are you going to get home?"

"I don't suppose you noticed that the car didn't look like a normal taxi?"

"How am I to know what a normal London taxi looks like?"

"You might if you—"

"Say it."

"My apologies. I didn't mean to carry this on as long as I have—"

"If I what?" Ava was feeling buoyed by the pills and the fear. She was right in front of the building; at least he'd done that much right. Her anger was actually helping her. "Didn't have a bag over my head? Is that what you were going to say?"

"Shall we go inside?"

"'We'? Who are you?"

He picked up her suitcases. Then put one down. Ava snatched it up. She didn't want it touching the ground. With his free hand he pulled off his cap. Then his ZZ Top beard. *Wait, those blue eyes. Wavy hair like sand. He's tall.*

"Oh my God," Ava said. "You jerk."

"I'm Jasper Keyes," he said. "It's nice to officially make your acquaintance." He smiled and stuck out his hand.

"You're Jasper Keyes." She sounded like an idiot, repeating what he just said, but she was so furious she couldn't formulate any other words.

"Madam." He bowed and tipped his missing hat.

"The barrister."

"If you must."

"You think this is funny?"

"I was trying to have a spot of fun. If you must know—"

"Must I?"

"I'm in training to become a stand-up comedian. My mate lent me his car, and I found this cap at a—"

"Unbelievable."

"I got us here safely, haven't I? Like I said, I'm in training to be a comedian—"

"You're not a comedian; you're a liar."

Jasper straightened as if slapped. Then his face flushed with color. "Oh, you've never lied, have you? What about—'Oh, and my mum isn't allowed to live with me'?"

"That is a lie that will save lives. Definitely mine and quite possibly hers."

"You assumed I was a driver."

"You were wearing a driver's cap and holding a sign with my name on it."

"I just explained all that. A spot of fun, research—"

"Fun at my expense. When I thought you were somebody else." Somebody she'd never see again.

"If this is about the rubbish bag, or the wheelchair, I won't say a word to anyone. I'll keep my gob shut and Bob's your uncle."

"Who's Bob?"

"Sorry. Lost in translation. I only meant—I won't say a word to anyone."

"I don't care about anyone. But if you never say another word to me it will suit me just fine," Ava said.

CHAPTER 8

It was a stately five-story redbrick apartment building adorned with black trim around the doors and windows. The massive front door had brass lion door knockers. It looked like a place Sherlock Holmes would live. The recent lashing of rain made everything smell fresh and tart. *Just like the new me,* Ava joked with herself. Because this was a new Ava. She actually had her feet on the ground in London, England. The thought almost lifted her like a balloon. *Steady. You might start to panic. Do not have a panic attack. Do not think about having a panic attack. Think about something else, anything else—*

This was Aunt Beverly's home. Ava would give anything if she were here to see that Ava had made it. The rest of the street was probably just as quaint, but Ava couldn't bear to look anywhere but straight ahead as if she were a horse with blinders on. Jasper had recovered from their row and was rattling on about a food market across the street. And the wine store and dry cleaner and some famous pub within walking distance. He had done his job, he had driven her safely to her location; shouldn't he just be off now?

There were people everywhere. Like roaches. Her stomach churned. She could be hungry, but she'd never be able to keep anything down if she ate. *Fire, fire, fire.* She was breathing too shallowly to add the word "extinguisher." "Top floor," Jasper said as he opened the door and waited for her to pass. He reached for her suitcase. "I'll get that."

"Are you the bellboy now?" Ava would carry her own suitcase. She didn't care what he did with Diana's. She didn't want to haul it up four flights, but she didn't want to owe him any favors.

With each flight, the thudding in Ava's heart eased slightly. By the time she reached the fifth floor she was breathing harder but sweating less. She reached for the door. *Keys. Right.* She didn't have them. What was taking Jasper so long? His voice rose up the stairwell. He was talking. Either on the phone or to a neighbor. So chatty. And loud. And peppy. She'd been hard on him back there. He was a friend of Aunt Beverly's. He was a barrister. He was the executor of Aunt Beverly's will. She would have to be nicer. She wanted to yell down the stairs, *Hurry up!* Laughter rang out. He was happy. He was standing somewhere between the first and fifth floor, just shooting the breeze, and laughing. It wasn't fair. Ava wanted to feel like that. She flung herself at the door. The doorknob jammed into her hip. She cried out.

"Hello?" Jasper yelled up the steps. He heard her. Soon his footsteps came pounding toward her. It wasn't logical, but she just couldn't stand there, so she flung herself at the door again. "Are you trying to break into your own flat?" Jasper sounded incredulous.

"I have to use the restroom," Ava said. "Loo," she added.

"Perhaps we should try these." Keys dangled from his fingertips. She wanted to tell him to go away, but her tongue felt swollen to three times its usual size. She felt like Alice in Wonderland, shrinking by the second. A huge tongue and a shrinking body. "Are you okay?" She gestured to the door. She waited, holding her breath until he inserted the key in the lock. The door sprung open and Ava stumbled in. She dumped the suitcase by the door, turned, and faced the living room. She could breathe again. It was gorgeous. A generous space with light wood floors, cozy furnishings, and three large dome-shaped windows that overlooked London. *Best not gaze out quite yet. Look at the décor instead.*

The walls were covered in theater posters. Cluttered, most might say, but these were Aunt Bev's things and Ava loved it. The sofa and a matching set of chairs looked Victorian. They were red with gold trim. Beverly lived out loud, that was for sure. An Oriental rug covered the floor, there was a piano against the near wall covered in pictures, and books, and plants, and a coffee table was overflowing with various magazines, books, and other objects. Each one would require careful scrutinizing; each one was a little clue, a connection to Ava's aunt.

But Ava could take her time with that later. When she was alone. And calmer. What she really wanted was the bedroom. She was exhausted. The Xanax was supposed to last twelve hours, but for her it was more like twelve seconds. A door just beyond the living room was ajar. She headed for it. Sure enough, there was a queen-sized bed. A thick white quilt was draped over it hiding the frame. Ava dropped to her knees and lifted the quilt. *Thank God.* She could fit. The bathtub was another option, but she was already here. A normal person would wait until Jasper Keyes was gone, but she'd reached her limit. She told him not to come up with her. She crawled underneath the bed. It was dusty. Aunt Beverly had never swept or mopped under the bed. Ava was going to start sneezing. But she couldn't move. Darkness. Refuge. She practically hugged the floor and marveled as her heart and breath began to slow. She could fall asleep right here. Jasper's footsteps headed her way. "Ava?"

He startled her and she inhaled. Dust went up her nose. She sneezed. *Shit.* Was he still here? Maybe if she was really quiet, he would just go away. If only she had shut the door. Then she could pretend she was taking a nap on top of the bed. But she'd left it wide-open. From the gap between the quilt and the floor she could see his black shoes standing in the doorway. They weren't polished like she thought a barrister's shoes would be polished. They were scuffed. He wore them a lot. Or perhaps he only wore them when he was impersonating cabbies. She sneezed again. *Darn it.* She'd always been a repetitive sneezer.

"Are you all right?" He sounded alarmed.

"I'm just looking for my earring," Ava said.

"Would you like some help?"

"No, no, I'm fine."

"Would you like me to leave?"

"Yes, please."

He was silent for a moment, then shifted his feet. "I wanted to show you a few odd quirks about the flat." She was now the oddest quirk in the flat. She wondered if he was thinking the same thing. Not much of a comedian if he wasn't. Or he was too polite. Comedians had to be brutal. She'd have to tell him not to quit his job as a barrister. "Ava?"

"Another time. Please." He had to go. She wanted to be alone. Take a bath. Sketch. Fall asleep. None of those things were possible with him lurking about the place. Her black sheets were in her luggage, along with a miniature hammer and nails. So many windows in the living room. She might have to pull some sheets from the bed.

"I'm going to leave you some information on the kitchen table. A map of the London Underground, a map of the area, and a note with some basics—food market, pubs, deliveries, that sort of thing." *Deliveries.* The word rang in her ears like bells in heaven. Deliveries. She was in a big city. She could have everything delivered. Everything and anything. She sneezed. "Gesundheit."

"Thank you for everything. I think I tore my stocking. I'm too embarrassed to come out with you here. You can see yourself out, can't you?" Ava wondered if he was going to point out that she was wearing pants.

"Of course, of course."

"Thank you for the ride."

"I'm leaving my business card as well. As soon as you're up to it, you'll need to come to my office so we can discuss the stipulations of your year here."

Stipulations? What stipulations? "No problem." Oh, it was going to be a problem all right. He was going to have to come here.

"It's in the financial district; all you have to do is walk two blocks to the Tube—"

"Get out. Now. Please."

"Right then," Jasper said. "Cheerio."

She listened to his footsteps, the opening of the bedroom door, the closing of the bedroom door, footsteps, then finally the opening and closing of the door to her flat. She was alone. She could breathe. She sneezed. Five times. Apparently Aunt Beverly had never felt the need to seek refuge under her bed or there wouldn't have been so much dust. Ava crawled out, stood, and then ran to the bathroom. There was no bathtub, just a shower. Ava wouldn't be able to hide out in a bathtub anymore with the shower curtain pulled around her. She was going to have to start cleaning underneath the bed.

CHAPTER 9

Approximately twenty minutes after Jasper left, Ava stuck one foot out into the hall, and braced herself in the doorway as if she were in danger of an invisible force shoving her out of the flat. She wouldn't be able to relax until she knew she was alone. Even if he did have really nice blue eyes, and was tall. She'd learned a lesson from Cliff. No more short men with tall egos. Jasper also had the kind of laugh that made you happy just listening to it. Was he telling the truth about all that stand-up comedian stuff? It still didn't make things right, but she could hardly fault him for practicing his craft, and trying to have a laugh at the same time. The girl who told a police officer she was in witness protection really shouldn't judge.

The suitcases sat by the door. Ava kicked Diana's, then knelt down and opened it. Folded in neat little piles on top were black turtlenecks. "Unbelievable." So Diana had meant to come. What happened? Was Diana afraid of flying? *The hypocrite.* Ava didn't want to dig around anymore. It wasn't her suitcase. She zipped it back up and went to pick hers up instead. The second she grabbed the handle, someone called her name. "Ava." Ava jumped and let out a little shriek.

"So sorry," Jasper called out from behind the door. "I didn't mean to startle you."

"Why are you lurking outside my door?" Ava asked.

"I'm not lurking. I had made it halfway down the block when I turned around."

One minute Ava was daydreaming about his eyes and height, and the next she was being rude. It wasn't her fault. She needed space to process this. She wasn't used to talking to strangers for long periods of time. She wasn't used to talking to anyone for long periods of time. What was it going to take to get him to leave? "You shouldn't have turned around." He didn't answer. She could hear him breathing. Did he run back up the stairs? Did he forget something? "Why did you turn around?"

"There are some things you need to know."

There were probably a lot of things she needed to know. Like how to get rid of strangers at the door. What did she need to know? She'd been through an ordeal. She needed a bathroom, a bedroom, and water, so she could take her Xanax. She was sorted. She didn't want anything else today. "You can tell me another time."

"I can't."

"Why not?"

"Because if he comes home before I have the chance to tell you about him, you're liable to stab him in the neck with a fork."

He? He who? What home? "Stab who in the neck with a fork?"

"Your flatmate." His voice took a forced upbeat tone.

"My flatmate? I don't have a flatmate." If he was trying to scare her, it was working. Why was he trying to scare her?

"Right. I'll start with that, so. You have a flatmate." By "flatmate" was he trying to tell her that she had a mouse? Or a cat? She didn't quite get the British sense of humor. She looked right, toward the living room. Across from it was the kitchen.

Was there any evidence anywhere that somebody else lived here? Ava hurried into the kitchen. "Ava?" Jasper called. "Did you hear what I said?"

"I heard!" Ava yelled. "I just don't understand."

It was not a modern kitchen by any means, but it was neat. The cabinets were white, and the floor was made of dark blue tiles. The appliances were older, also white, but as long as they were functioning, Ava could live with them. She even had a combo washer and dryer in the kitchen. That was a bit odd, but hey, maybe she could throw cups and saucers in with her panties and save loads of time. At the far end of the kitchen was a small set of table and chairs situated by more dome-shaped windows. She scanned the floor for cat food or mice droppings. Nada. She opened the fridge. It was packed. The day before Thanksgiving packed. In fact, a large turkey covered in cellophane took up the middle rack. Either someone had stocked the fridge for her arrival or she indeed had a flatmate.

A flatmate. No. No, no, no, no, no. The kind who walked on two legs? She couldn't do it. She wouldn't do it. This was her flat. Hers. She walked over to the front door and pressed her ear against it.

"Still there?" Ava asked.

"Still here."

"Say that again."

"Still here."

Jasper laughed. Ava bit her lip. He wasn't going to make her laugh. Not until he explained himself. "I meant the bit about having a flatmate."

"Why don't you let me in?"

"I can hear you just fine through the door."

"It is absurd to conduct business through a closed door."

"How could I have a flatmate?"

"Let me in and I'll explain everything."

"This is the second time you've lied to me. Why should I believe anything you say now?"

Jasper sighed. "I didn't mean to lie. Haven't you ever gotten carried away?" Ava thought of herself hiding underneath the desk at the police station, hiding in a closet in Heathrow, and, of course, her stunt a few minutes ago involving a nonexistent earring and the dusty underside of Aunt Beverly's bed.

"Fine." Ava unlocked the door. Jasper looked guilty. Tortured, actually. *Good. He should be.* "Explain."

Jasper stepped in. He filled the room. She never knew a person could give off energy that you could actually feel. Ava *felt* him. He was way too familiar. Why? Was she just grasping on to anyone who knew and loved Aunt Beverly? Was she delusional? This man was a total stranger. Cliff definitely had a presence, an animal attractiveness. But Jasper's effect on her wasn't just sexual. Standing this close to him, she had visions of throwing herself in his arms, and trusting him to take care of her the rest of her life. *Whoa. Where did that come from?* Ava had never wanted anybody to take care of her. Not even herself. This was a new feeling and she didn't like it. She certainly didn't know how to handle it.

"Living room or kitchen?" Jasper asked.

"For what?" She didn't care what he said. She was not going to tolerate a flatmate.

Jasper met her eyes. *Anything. Name it.* "For our talk."

"Right. I refuse to have a flatmate. How's that for a talk?" Ava headed for the kitchen. "I'm starving."

"Why don't we get some takeaway? There are menus in the drawer."

"But there's a fridge full of food."

"It belongs to Queenie."

"Who?"

"Queenie. Your flatmate."

"I don't have a flatmate. If someone's been living here, she'll have to leave."

"He."

He? Oh, no. No, no, no. This isn't happening. "I don't care."

"His name is Queenie. He's an actor. And a drag queen. He was Beverly's best friend."

"I see your mouth moving, but you're not making sense. You said Beverly left the flat to me." Jasper looked sheepish. "Hello?"

Instead of confessing this was all just another joke, Jasper headed into the kitchen and opened a drawer. He lifted out a stack of menus and tossed them on the counter. "Takeaway menus," he said. "Anything you'd like. I would have cooked for you, but this isn't my flat and—"

"It's a one-bedroom apartment. How can I share a one-bedroom apartment?" *Don't get worked up. Don't fall for another joke. Of course you don't have a flatmate. Don't take the bait.* Her nerves were tingling. If he said the word "flatmate" one more time the colored dots were going to appear.

"Queenie will take the sofa."

"No. He won't. There is no Queenie. You're just messing with me."

"Let's start over," Jasper said.

"Too late," Ava said.

"Welcome to London." Jasper bowed. He straightened up. "I promise, everything will get sorted. You mustn't worry."

"I mustn't worry," Ava repeated. The words sounded so funny, so foreign, even though they were both technically speaking English. This was so absurd. He was putting her on. And she was eating it up. She was jet-lagged. And starving. She started to laugh.

"What's so funny?" Jasper was keen to delve into anything that made her laugh. Perhaps he *was* studying to be a comedian.

"I've never used the word 'mustn't' in my life," Ava mused.

"Oh, you should try it. It feels good. Mustn't." Jasper walked toward her. She was still leaning against the kitchen counter. Before she knew it, he was right in front of her. "Mustn't," he repeated, lifting up his chin.

"You're insane."

"Say it."

"Mustn't."

"Mustn't." He imitated an American accent. "I mustn't go to Mickey D's." She laughed. He *was* a bit funny and his eyes lit up when she laughed. "I mustn't, like, hang ten." He tried to sound like an American surfer.

"You're an idiot," she said, still laughing. "Is that what you think of us? We eat hamburgers and we surf? Is that all?"

"I mustn't watch *So You Think You Can Dance*." He broke out in a frenetic imitation of a dance.

Ava laughed harder than she had in a long time. It felt good. And strangely, it hurt too. "Mustn't," she said.

"Just tilt your chin up a bit." He reached over and touched her chin to tilt it up. Ava felt a shock run through her. Here she was a stranger in a strange kitchen with a strange man, touching her. And it didn't feel strange at all. *Strange.*

"There you are. Now say it. 'Mustn't.' "

"Mustn't."

"Brilliant."

"I mustn't drink tea, eat biscuits with jam, and watch telly." What was she doing? Flirting? Was this an unwelcome side effect of the Xanax?

"By George, I think you've got it." He was still touching her chin. She didn't realize it until right that moment. And then he realized that she realized it, and their eyes locked as electricity passed between them. His touch seemed to reach all the way inside her. She knew it sounded completely insane, but it was as if he was looking into her soul, and she into his. He dropped his hand.

Mustn't, she said to herself. *Mustn't believe him when he says I have a flatmate. Mustn't, mustn't, mustn't.* Ava walked over to the counter, picked up a takeaway menu, and pretended to read.

"See anything you like?" Jasper said.

Ava couldn't focus on the words. Did she need glasses? Was it in a foreign language? "Not yet," she said.

"It might help if you turned it right side up."

Ava glanced up at him. He was smiling and there was literally a twinkle in his eye. She glanced at the menu. Oh, God. He was right. It was upside down. Xanax hangover. She was definitely having a Xanax hangover. Maybe she needed more. She also needed to be alone. She was getting flustered and it was all his fault. "I knew it was you. In the taxi." She was going to start an argument. Anything to avoid these feelings she was having for a total stranger. She'd obviously been locked inside too long. What other explanation was there for the fact that she was wondering what would happen if she walked up to Jasper, grabbed him by the tie, and led him into the bedroom? She'd never desired a total stranger before; she'd never had a one-night stand; her lifestyle hadn't permitted any of this. Her first day in London and here she was very, very close to propositioning a man she had just met for sex. She didn't want Cliff to be the last man she'd had sex with. But Jasper wasn't just any man. Not some taxi driver she'd never have to see again. He was her aunt's friend. He was a barrister. Ava was seriously losing it.

"Come on now. You didn't know."

"I knew your beard was fake."

"I'll give you that. I thought you were going to tug on it and the jig would be up." He smiled at her, and once again a jolt of electricity surged through her. They didn't call it chemistry for nothing. But Ava wasn't casual sex material. She wasn't exactly girlfriend material either. *Oh, God.* What material was she? Was there part of her that had suspected Cliff was involved with somebody else but didn't want to face it? *No. No.* She had no idea. None. But she also didn't question the limitations of their relationship. Because she had wanted him there. It was too much to think about right now.

"So, you're all right?" Jasper asked.

No, I'm not all right. I want to invite you into my dead aunt's bed. Does that sound all right to you? "Of course I'm all right. Why wouldn't I be all right?" Was she flushed? Could he tell she was turned on? Why was he asking her that?

"I'm sure it's quite a shock to find out you have a flatmate."

"Cut it out. You're not getting me again."

"Pardon?"

"I know I don't have a flatmate. The jig is up." Right? He had to be putting her on. Right? Why wasn't he just admitting it?

"I swear, this isn't a joke," Jasper said.

Oh, God. He sounded very, very serious. Ava lost her appetite. "I can't possibly share a one-bedroom flat with a stranger." Who was she kidding? She couldn't share it with a stranger if it were a mansion.

"He won't be a stranger for long." Jasper was trying to sound upbeat, but his voice cracked at the end. "Trust me. He's a decent bloke."

"I don't care if he's the actual Queen. It's not going to happen."

"I'm afraid you don't have any control over that."

Ava put her hands on her hips. They needed to do something other than wrap around Jasper's neck and strangle him. "Where is this flatmate?"

"He agreed to give you a few days to settle in."

Ava looked around. "Am I missing something? Is there another wing to this flat?"

Jasper threw open his arms. "Thai? Italian? Chinese?"

"Am I to guess my flatmate's ethnicity now?"

Jasper laughed. "Maybe you're the one who should do stand-up comedy. No. I was referring to the takeaway."

"Well, take away this. I refuse to have a flatmate."

Jasper strode into the living room. Ava followed. "Do you like to watch telly?" He pointed to the television as if she might not quite know what one looked like.

"Are you really a barrister?"

"Of course. Why?"

"You avoid conflict like the plague."

"That explains why I settle out of court a lot." He waited for her to laugh. She didn't. He gazed out the windows, his face rapturous. "Isn't this a stunning view?"

"Yes," Ava said. She'd have to take his word for it. She couldn't look. She would hang her black sheets as soon as he left.

Jasper scanned the walls of pictures and theater posters. He lifted a small framed photograph off the wall. It was a picture of Beverly, Jasper, and another man standing in a field. A small airplane was in the background. Jasper pointed to the man. "This is Queenie. They were best friends."

Ava studied the portly bald man with gray sideburns. He was grinning for the camera and had his arm around Beverly. He looked like a nice best friend. But a terrible flatmate. "And he lived here with Aunt Beverly?"

"No. But he's going to live here with you."

"Wait. He didn't live here with Aunt Beverly?"

"No."

"Then why in the world would he move in with me?"

"Because." Jasper stopped. Ava could actually see beads of sweat form on his forehead. He removed a handkerchief from his pocket and dabbed at them.

"Jasper?"

"The flat isn't quite officially yours yet."

Why not? He just meant she had to sign some papers first, right? Then why was he sweating? "What do you mean?"

Jasper swallowed. He looked at the view again as he spoke. "You and Queenie are competing for the apartment."

"Come again?" Ava suddenly understood the urge to shoot the messenger.

"There is a list." Jasper removed a piece of paper from the breast pocket of his suit and held it up. "Right here."

"A list?" Ava said.

"Stipulations."

"You had better start speaking the Queen's English."

"Right. So. I explained to you on the video chat that one of the stipulations of ownership was that you must live in this flat for an entire year."

Ava opened her hands. "And here I am."

"What I didn't get a chance to tell you was that in addition . . . there is this list." Once again Jasper held up the piece of paper. "You have ninety days from now to complete the items on the list. If you do not, then I'm afraid that Queenie will inherit the flat."

"Oh my God." For a second Ava was tempted to snatch the list out of his hands. She changed her mind. Whatever the stipulations were, this was not good. This was bait and switch. This was some kind of a game. What stipulations? Was her mother right? Was Beverly a master manipulator? This certainly didn't seem right. Or kind. What was on that list? Jasper wasn't saying, and there was no way Ava was going to validate it by asking. She ran to her suitcase and pulled out her black sheets. This was what she could count on in this world. Her black satin sheets. She didn't even care that he was watching as she held them up to her nose and inhaled. They smelled like Febreze dryer sheets. List. List, list, list. Ninety days or Queenie inherits the flat. What kind of cosmic joke was this?

Heart hammering, she strode toward the dome-shaped windows. All she had to do was raise her head and there was the heart of London sprawled out before her, in all its glory. She quickly draped the sheets over the windows. She would need to get out her hammer and nails to cover them completely, but this was a start. When she had used up all three sheets she turned back to Jasper. Just being that close to the windows had elevated her heart rate and made her perspire. She knew she looked like she had just jogged a few miles. She couldn't worry about that right now. She waited until Jasper made eye contact with her. One by one the sheets fell to the floor in a heap. She wouldn't look. She would have to nail them in the minute she got the chance. She didn't want to do it with him here. What kind of person packs a hammer and nails in her luggage? "What exactly is on the list?" He held it out to her. She shook her head. "No. I want you to tell me."

"Wouldn't you like to order your dinner?"

"I've lost my appetite." This was her flat. Wasn't it? She hadn't given up her entire life in America, risked death to fly here, just to end up living with some flatmate she never agreed to, competing for the flat. Stipulations? Why hadn't Jasper mentioned any of these things before she'd upended her life? Thank God she found this out now. Her stupid lust, her stupid crush. *God, Ava, you are so naïve.* She stormed back into the kitchen, yanked open the fridge, and removed the platter of turkey. Jasper entered the kitchen and stared at her. His eyes dropped to the platter of turkey. He looked terrified. She would have laughed except she was too angry with him. She left the fridge door wide-open, almost daring Jasper to reprimand her. This was her flat. Aunt Beverly's flat. Aunt Beverly wanted Ava to have it. She didn't care who these friends were. They weren't her family. Queenie's turkey was taking up her fridge. Well, not anymore. She ripped away the cellophane, grabbed a turkey leg, and pulled until it came off. Globs of fat dripped to the floor. Jasper looked positively rooted to the spot. She smiled. She was going to stand at this counter and eat whatever she wanted out of her fridge, flatmate be damned. She wasn't even hungry. But she would not be bullied. She would lick every single thing in this fridge, providing it didn't look like it had been licked already.

"That's really not the best way—"

Ava stuck out her tongue and slowly licked the turkey leg from top to bottom. She couldn't tell if Jasper was turned on, or horrified. Either way, he couldn't take his eyes off her. She stuck the turkey leg in her mouth and sucked on it. *Take that, Queenie.* She popped it out of her mouth long enough to speak. "Delish." She held it out to Jasper. "Want some?"

Jasper shook his head. "Quite all right."

"I want to be alone now," Ava said.

"We've come this far. If you wish, I'll read you the list."

"Oh, goodie," Ava said. "I'll just suck on turkey while you talk." Jasper sighed, made his way to the little kitchen table, and plopped down on one of the chairs. Ava needed a sheet for that window too. She'd take care of it the second he was gone. "Beverly left the flat to Queenie first," Jasper said.

"Oh," Ava said. Aunt Beverly didn't really want Ava to have the flat. And why should she? Ava wasn't really family, was she? Not in the way that Ava wanted a family. Not in the way they would have been a family if her father had lived. She didn't just lose her father that day; she lost everyone. Even her mother to an extent. Gretchen had been a happier person with Ava's father. "I see." She didn't see. She didn't want to cry in front of Jasper.

"Please, Ava," Jasper said. "Will you sit down?" He pulled out the other chair. Ava brought the turkey to the table and sat. "After Beverly jumped from the aeroplane she had an epiphany."

"Me," Ava said.

"You," Jasper said.

Ava threw down the turkey leg, wiped her hands on her jeans, and folded her arms across her chest. "Go on."

Jasper set the list on the table and kept his hands over it, as if protecting it. Then he began swirling the piece of paper around the tabletop. "It's quite simple, really. If you wanted you could probably get them done in a week." His voice cracked at the end. Ava wondered what his ex-girlfriend was like. She probably didn't like nice guys. Jasper was definitely "a nice guy." This time Ava was starting to see how annoying nice guys could be. Ava bet his ex had walked all over him. She had an urge to draw a cartoon of a woman doing just that—literally walking on Jasper Keyes.

Ava snatched the piece of paper from underneath his hands. She was going to get turkey grease all over it and she didn't care. She looked at the list.

See Big Ben
Walk along the Thames
Visit Buckingham Palace
Tour the Tower of London
Go to an English pub
Sit on a bench in Hyde Park
Go to a show in the West End
Go to a club in the West End
Navigate the London Underground (Tube/subway)
Ride the London Eye

CHAPTER 10

It was a list of normal, touristy things to see and do in London. Things most people would want to do. And Ava wouldn't be able to do a single one of them. It wasn't a fun list; it was a death march. "I have to do all these things if I want to keep the flat?"

"Yes. Once you've completed this list—"

As if.

"—ninety days from now—then you simply must continue living in this flat for one year. After that, it's yours to do with as you wish."

Tears instantly filled her eyes. *Dammit.* She did not want to cry in front of Jasper. Or anyone. A flatmate. A list. This was an ambush. Aunt Beverly knew that Ava was a freak, and she had done this just to prove it. Ease her conscience that she hadn't lifted a finger for Ava ever since her father died. Maybe Beverly had been cruel to her father too. She remembered him crying over her that one day. She remembered knowing there was some reason Beverly wasn't visiting, but not knowing exactly what it was. Frankly, Ava always thought it was because Aunt

Beverly didn't approve of her mother. Didn't approve of Americans. Ava hated this. She hated being angry at her father's only sibling, but really. How could she? Ava never would have imagined that Beverly could have been so cruel.

Ava couldn't do a single thing on this list in ninety days let alone all of them. It was impossible. The flight home felt equally impossible. She never wanted to see the inside of that airport again. Maybe they could knock her out entirely. Or Ava would have to simply lock herself in the flat, refuse to let Queenie inside, and force them to drag her out kicking and screaming. Ava wanted to pick up the turkey leg and throw it at Jasper's head. It was probably the kind of behavior they expected out of an American nutter anyway.

"You can go now," she said. "I'm going to fight this."

"Fight this?"

"Yes. Through the courts."

"I see." Jasper ran his hands through his hair again. "That is always an option. But it would take a lot of time, a lot of money."

"Are you threatening me?"

"No, of course not. I'm giving you the facts. It's really quite simple—"

"For you maybe. And definitely Queenie. Does he have a list?" One look at Jasper and Ava knew he didn't. "I see. Get out." Ava stood up. "I'm asking you to leave now." Jasper nodded and rose from his chair. He looked like he wanted to say a million things to her, but Ava didn't want to hear them. She headed for the door. Jasper exited once more, but this time he lingered in the hall, and this time Ava waited.

"About Queenie." Ava waited some more. "He can be a bit overly dramatic."

Join the club. "So can I." She might have been an agoraphobic, but Ava was no pushover. She was highly functional. Just in a very small area.

"Look. I know you're upset. And I'm sorry. But your aunt Beverly wanted to help you."

"Help me?"

"Of course. She wanted you to experience the world. Or at

least this little corner of it." Beverly had no clue what life was really like for Ava. Neither did Jasper. "And as far as Queenie is concerned, having a flatmate could actually be a good thing."

Now he knew what was best for her? "How so?"

"London is expensive. There are building fees that I don't think you can afford unless you find a job." He let the rest linger. He didn't add the obvious. It would be nearly impossible to get a job if she never left the flat.

"How much are the building fees?"

"I don't have the exact figure. But I believe all considered it's close to a thousand pounds per month."

"That's insane!"

"That's London."

"I can't face the airport. I can't." Ava reached out. She didn't mean to, but the thought of the airport ignited a panic in her, and she reached out her hand to Jasper. He took it and held it. He looked her in the eye. She was back to liking the nice guys. He looked at her with compassion. Not pity, but genuine concern. How could this man she just met care about her so much?

"Ava, listen to me. You're not going anywhere."

"But the list—"

"Forget about the list. I'm sorry. I'm a wanker. I should have let you settle in."

"You should have told me before I left America."

"Maybe. But God, I'm glad I didn't." They held eye contact. He let go of her hand. Ava stepped back. "I mean, here you are, right? This isn't so bad."

"Sure. Maybe they'll be the best ninety days of my life."

"Forget about the ninety days. One thing at a time." He glanced behind him as if he was worried someone might overhear. "It's to your advantage to get along with Queenie. Maybe he'll let you have the flat even if you don't complete everything on the list."

"Or anything?"

Jasper looked away, then back at Ava. "Let's just take one step at a time," he said again.

"Why? Why is she doing this to me?"

"Please believe me. Her heart was in the right place."

"How? By luring me here under false pretenses? Then humiliating me with this impossible list?"

"Not to mention forcing you to live with an actor?" Jasper smiled. Ava did not. "Right," he said. "It *is* all in the timing."

"I think Beverly had you fooled," Ava said.

"How do you mean?"

"I can tell you're convinced that she meant well. But maybe you just don't understand women." *Maybe that's why you got dumped.*

"You're right about that. I don't understand women. But I think I understand you."

"Good for you." Ava slammed the door shut. She rested her forehead against it. She had the urge to bang her forehead against the door but not while Jasper was still there. And he was still there. She waited to hear his footsteps.

"Any questions before I leave?" Jasper said. Ava couldn't believe it. He just wouldn't go away. Why did that thrill her so?

"How will you know if I've really done any of the things on the list?"

"I'm to accompany you."

Ava opened the door again. He looked at her with something akin to hope in his eyes. What did he want from her? "You're a nice guy, Jasper."

"Thank you."

"It's not a compliment. Women like bad boys, and comedians who are too nice just aren't funny."

He took a step back. Ava hated herself. He was only trying to help. But he shouldn't be here, looking at her like that, making her light up inside. "I see. Thank you for the character assessment." She was seeing him angry for the first time. He was sexy when he was angry. Ava left the door open, and walked away just to see what he would do.

Along the wall separating the living room from the kitchen was a little bar. It was stocked with liquor but not wine. Ava went over and picked up a bottle. "I wouldn't drink his Scotch if I were you," Jasper called out.

"Aren't you lucky that you're not?" She put the bottle up to her mouth and drank. By the time she had swallowed, and wiped her lips, Jasper Keyes was gone. That flat was surprisingly empty without him. Ava retrieved the hammer and nails from her suitcase, picked the first sheet up off the floor, and went to work.

Three stiff Scotches later, Ava staggered over to the windows and stared at her silk sheets. Maybe she should take them off. She'd come this far. If she only had ninety days in London, she should at least look at it, shouldn't she? Could she do it? In Iowa she definitely needed sheets. She was on the ground level. Anyone could sneak up and look in. The outside was right there, pushing to get in. But here, she was up high. Removed. Maybe if she took the curtains off, she could get used to the idea of London. If she was only going to be here for ninety days she couldn't just hide. Slowly, she advanced, grabbed a corner of the first sheet, and tugged. Before she could change her mind, she whipped off the last two sheets. And then, she looked.

All of London stood at attention before her, slightly muted behind a pearl gray sky. The river Thames to the far left. The Houses of Parliament stretched out, regal and proud. A cathedral stretched into the air. The London Eye rotated in the distance. And just below, a busy street lined with shops, and trees, and pedestrians. Ava didn't need to go out to experience London; London had come to her.

She'd been reading up on London ever since she was a little girl. First, when her father was alive, so she could tell him all the places she wanted them to go, and then, especially after he died. It made her feel closer to him, knowing where he was from. So she read everything, imagined herself everywhere— and here all those magnificent places were at her fingertips, just outside her window. She was so close. Separated only by panes of glass.

Every single place she'd read about, searching between the pages for her father. Had he wandered the halls of St. Paul's Cathedral? Had he sat underneath a tree in Hyde Park? Had he watched the Changing of the Guard at Buckingham Palace?

Chased fat pigeons at Trafalgar Square? Had he stood by the Thames and wondered about his future wife, his daughter? Why couldn't he be here? She missed him just as much today as she did when she was ten. Her father. What would he think of her now? Surely he'd be so disappointed. Not his Ava. He would never have imagined his little girl was a freak. *Dance with me!*

Now here she was. Nineteen years later. So many wasted years. The Ava her father knew was a vibrant little girl who had friends, and went to school, and took piano lessons every Tuesday. She raced her yellow bike up and down the street every evening before dinner, got scrapes on her knees from playing in the dirt, and the rain, and the snow. Even Ava couldn't believe it had all come to a crashing halt. At first everyone was so kind, so patient. Her two best friends, Andrea and Susan, visited her like clockwork. They didn't even make fun of her for staying in her room. "Take your time," her teacher said, sending homework each week, checking in. And Ava did take her time. Boy, did she. She took the rest of the school year. After that came the heated meetings between the school and her mother, the yelling (her mother at Ava), the threats, the tears, the paperwork from the psychiatrists advocating homeschooling. For the time being, everyone said. For the time being.

But Ava got used to Greta, the in-home tutor, and so did her mother. Ava did her homework, got good grades. She fought with her mother less. Eventually everyone got used to it, and nobody pushed Ava anymore. After the first year Andrea and Susan visited less and less. Instead they talked on the phone. And then gradually the calls stopped too. Ava couldn't blame them, but it hurt. Greta was Ava's only friend, unless you counted the psychiatrists, which Ava certainly didn't, or the young girl across the street, a pretty woman named Heather who popped her head into Ava's room on holidays to say hello, or the series of goldfish that swam in and out of her life. Other than that there was the odd visitor now and then, a few family members on her mom's side, but no one substantial. Ava wanted to be saved, yet when anyone tried to do just that, to get her to go out, she fought tooth and nail. Secretly there were times she wanted to be outside so bad she physically ached. But the minute she touched the doorknob, her entire being revolted. She'd been at war with herself. She wanted to want to feel the sun on her face, the wind through her hair, taste the rain on her lips, or scoop snow into her hands. She kept waiting for a miracle. Her father to show up at her door and forgive her. Eventually she covered the windows with construction paper so she would forget. The few times a year she was forced outside she was so medicated it was like a queasy dream. So much waste. So much time to make up for. Could it even be done?

Ava inched closer to the window until she was looking down. She felt like a tightrope walker, on the night of her very first show. She was doing it. It was terrifying, but she was doing it. There were so many people on the streets. Living their lives. Walking, without a care, down the block. They were not afraid. Their palms were not sweaty, their hearts were not tripping, and little colored dots were not dancing in front of their eyes. They were just out and about, and had never known life any other way. Ava placed her hands on the window. She was leaving her prints. Was it enough? Compared to everyone out there, she really wasn't here. "I'm dead," she said. She might as well have been.

The view, miraculous to anyone else's eyes, was a gun to the head. St. Paul's Cathedral, right outside her window. Built in the shape of a cross with a dome crown intersecting the arms. Filled with the Golden Gallery, the Stone Gallery, and the Whispering Gallery. All places Ava would never see, but she could close her eyes and imagine them. One of the largest domes in the world. Weighing in at sixty-five thousand tons. And it was right outside Ava's windows. The highest point in the city. A fourteen-hundred-year history.

The London Eye. She'd never ride a Ferris wheel, never, let alone one that was four hundred and some feet tall. Even if she did everything else on Aunt Bev's list, that one would be the one to take her down. There it was, her nemesis, rotating on the south bank of the Thames. *Look away!* Her eyes darted to Canary Wharf, one of London's two financial districts. What a beautiful skyline the buildings made. Finally she gazed back upon the Houses of Parliament—the Palace of Westminster. Now that looked British. Royal and elegant, its ancient stone façade and spikey bits running along the top like points in a crown. *Big Ben, you old clock tower, you. I feel as if we're old friends. I know you from children's books and movies, and photographs. I see you. Do you see me?*

So much could be glimpsed from these windows. Rows of redbrick flats just like hers. She had lost too much already; she couldn't lose this. This was the closest she had come to living in the past nineteen years. She would find a way to fight for this flat.

Panic began to bubble within her. The little colored dots appeared. If she let this go too far, soon she wouldn't even be able to look out the windows. She had to ground herself, wipe her mind of emotions, replace them with facts. She snatched up her sketch pad and pencil and hurried back to the living room. From here, she had the best view of the streets.

The people and cars below weren't so tiny they looked like toys, but they weren't quite real either. It made it easier to look. Men and women in suits, with briefcases and bulging handbags, strode purposefully down the footpath, heads down, mobiles in hand. Some elderly folks pushed carts, or brooms, or shuffled along. People came in and out of the grocery store directly across the street. So close, yet so far away. Ava's eyes lit on the sign. Sainsbury's. Mothers pushed prams and tried to balance the older kids who clung on to their legs. Bicycles weaved in and out of traffic that moved in fits and starts. Cars lurched; then the drivers slammed on their brakes, and laid on their horns. Double-decker buses lumbered by. She loved their shiny red color, eye-popping even through the gray. Ava wondered if they would let her hop on but never hop off. She began to sketch them all, her hand skating across the page as she tried to take it all in. The next thing she knew, her page was full, and she had to start a new one. She was astonished to discover she could draw the outside with no adverse reactions. There it was, in front of her on the page, and she was okay!

God, this was like being outside without being outside. For a second she wondered if she was cured. Ava had seen a program once where a deaf child had been given a cochlear implant. She watched the moment when the child heard raindrops on the roof for the first time. Saw the astonishment on the child's face. Ava felt like that child. Not hearing for the first time, but being for the first time. Seeing, hearing, almost touching. Existing out and among others. From a safe distance. The best of both worlds. Who needed the telly? She could watch people all day long, and sketch them. After twenty solid minutes staring down at them, it hit her. It might be a cliché, but it was true—people never looked up. She was a shepherd looking down on her flock.

Maybe Beverly was right. Maybe coming here was all she needed. Imagine if in a few days, or a week, she was cured? A whole new person. *Okay, breathe. Don't get too far ahead too fast. Take a break from the windows.* London would be there.

She turned to the walls. So many cool theater posters. Had Beverly been in all these productions? *Les Mis, Cats, Pippin, Mary Poppins, Monty Python*—there were photographs too. Aunt Beverly onstage in all different costumes. She looked like a genuine star. Ava studied the woman in each picture. Beverly was beautiful. Not only in her younger years, where Ava was shocked to see she resembled her, but she'd aged beautifully too.

There was one remarkable difference between Ava and Beverly. Her bright smile. The kind that could light up a room like Ava's father. She looked alive.

And the outfits, oh, the outfits. Each picture sported a new dress. White and tight with sparkles. Red silk. And a variety of little black dresses. Plenty of accessories too. A green felt beret, a chunky blue necklace, a cigarette holder. She didn't just look glamorous; she was glamour. It was as if she had stamped *I AM HERE* in every single picture. Ava had yet to go through Beverly's closets; did any of these outfits still exist? She'd save the discovery until later, relish the anticipation.

Ava would never get to see Aunt Beverly onstage. But Ava

knew stage presence when she saw it, and Beverly Wilder had been the real deal. Ava tore herself away from the photos, imagining herself in one of Beverly's outfits, imagined how she would walk, talk, and think, if she were Beverly. She tried to smile. It wasn't natural.

She entered the kitchen and approached the window at the far end. Whereas the living room looked out toward Highgate, this one looked out to the Thames. In front of the window sat the little two-seater table. Sitting in the center were the maps Jasper mentioned. The top one leapt out at her. The London Underground. She hadn't even touched it and she could feel a panic attack coming on. She didn't even want to look at it. People. Underground. Moving about like a colony of ants. She liked a good, dark hiding space as well as the next person, but not when others were down there with her. Dark spaces were supposed to be small enough to hide in, not expansive and unending. Rushing, shoving, breathing the same stale air as everyone else. No thank you. It would ruin her love of small, dark places forever. Who would she be without a sanctuary? She would have nowhere left to run and hide. Never, ever, ever. She wouldn't even open the map. She didn't even want it in the house. Burn it. She would burn it. She picked it up by the edges like it was a dead rat she was being forced to touch.

She found matches in a kitchen drawer. Did Beverly smoke? There were no signs of cigarettes but plenty of melted candles. For all Ava knew, Beverly had weekly séances. She went to the sink and held the tip of the flame to the map. As the fire licked the edges she had to rotate the map to keep from burning herself. *London's burning.* When she was finished she stared at the ashes in the sink. Then she turned the water on high. They didn't so much go down the drain as plaster themselves to the edges of the sink. She washed her hands twelve times and then wiped up the remnants of the map with a paper towel and discarded them in the bin next to the refrigerator.

How many hours had it been since Jasper left? Two? How could she miss him? A man she'd only just met. How was it possible that his absence had already left a void? Ava wasn't used to liking people, let alone missing them. It wasn't a pleasant feeling; it was more like a low-grade ache. How ridiculous to miss a stranger. She must be homesick and she was transferring that onto Jasper.

Ava walked over to the little bar again. It was stocked with glasses and liquor bottles and a bin waiting to be filled with ice. It even had tongs. Beverly liked to entertain. *I wouldn't drink his Scotch.* What did Jasper know? Besides, how was Ava to know if it was Queenie's Scotch or Aunt Beverly's? *Finders, keepers.* Ava poured herself another. She held it up to the windows. The liquid glowed in the setting sun. "Here's to us," Ava said. Aunt Beverly. Her father. Her mother. And her. "Here's to us." She drank it in one go. It hit her chest like a gunshot. She choked and sputtered. It was a good kind of pain. Warmth coursed through her. She set the glass down with a plunk. That was enough for one day.

Ava entered Beverly's bedroom and opened the double closet on the far wall. Outfits stretched for miles. Shelves were lined with boxes and accessories. The beautiful bits from the photos, they were all here. Shoes lined the bottom of the closet, in every color and heel. She even had actual nightgowns hanging. Silky ones. Ava touched a pink one, then brought it to her nose and inhaled. It smelled as if it had been dry-cleaned, then never worn again. Ava took her clothes off and left them on the floor of the bedroom. She slipped the nightgown over her head. She wasn't Ava; she was a young actress, a beautiful woman in a negligee and—Ava reached and opened another box. And a green beret. She placed the beret on her head and laughed at her reflection in the mirror. One more. She opened the third box to find a long cigarette holder. She was a beautiful young actress in a rose negligee and green beret, holding an elegant cigarette holder between two fingers, smiling into the eyes of strangers, and declaring to the world: *I am here.*

CHAPTER 11

The next morning Ava was eager to sit by the windows again and sketch. The wonder of observing the city from above trumped the worries that she only had eighty-nine more days to enjoy it. Last night she had come to a decision. She wasn't even going to try to tackle the list. Beverly couldn't manipulate her if she refused to participate. Maybe she would fight it in court, but she didn't even want to think about that. She just wanted to enjoy the eighty-nine days.

Ava made a cup of tea and brought it into the living room. An emerald velvet stool sat in the center of the room. Ava scooted it to the center window. This would be her office. She sat, feet *en pointe,* as if she were a ballerina, her elbows propped on her knees so that she could lean forward, and imagine she was one with the windowpane. Maybe if she gazed out long enough, she would soon feel as if she was an integral part of the scenery, an inanimate object, no blood, no bones, no beats, no breath, no pulse. She was no more or no less than a latch on the window, one that would take considerable force to pry open.

Ava had lost track of what day it was. She was pretty sure it was Tuesday. People were going to work, starting their day. She could almost feel them as they hurried below. The windows opened like shutters. Before she could talk herself out of it Ava unlatched the set in front of her and pushed them open. The air was much warmer than Ava had imagined. Today, the skies were blue and the sun glinted off windows up and down the street. Beneath Ava's window was a tiny ledge. It was only about a foot wide and three feet long. She could sit on the ledge and rest her feet on it. If she dared. Parts of her would actually be outside. In London.

Don't, don't, don't, don't, don't—
I can pull them right back in.
You're going to die, you're going to die, you're going to die—
I'm already dead.

She stuck a foot out on the window ledge. The grates were cold and smooth on her bare foot. She stuck the other out. Her heart rate soared. She wanted to bring them back in; it felt as if she were holding them over hot coals. *Keep them there. Your seventy-something-year-old aunt jumped out of a plane after being told she was terminally ill.* Ava could manage to keep her feet out on the little balcony. Or whatever it was. Plant holder most likely. Would she be able to squeeze her entire body out there? Ava was petite, and flexible. She bet she could. She pushed herself out. There was barely room to sit, but she was technically outside. Totally safe, completely removed but still part of everything and everyone below. Her feet joined those on the pavement, as she grasped a shopping bag, hurrying to an exciting destination, answering her mobile, and juggling a dozen things before she had to rush across town to meet her lover for espresso. God, she wished she had an espresso right now. Any one of those Londoners below could right now, if they so desired, get an espresso. They had no idea how lucky they were.

Ava closed her eyes and just sat, feeling the air on her cheeks. Gratitude enveloped her. This was a surprise gift. Ava never imagined her life could have changed so dramatically. She wondered if her father was up there watching her, if he had arranged for this little miracle. No matter what, she was thankful. She sent a little prayer upward, thanking him, and saying hello and thank you to Aunt Beverly. Even if she had concocted that horrendous list.

When her face felt as if it was starting to burn, Ava crawled back inside and spent the rest of the day sketching. She read a few chapters of a murder mystery off Beverly's shelf of books. She noticed how some words were spelled differently over here. "Colour." "Harbour." "Rumour." It appeared as if the Colonists had dropped the *u* along with British taxes. *Take that, England; we don't need* u. She laughed, then looked around as if Jasper were right there to laugh with her.

She made herself a turkey sandwich. And then another one. *Thanks, Queenie.* She would give her mysterious flatmate this: He was an excellent cook. When would he be here? Jasper said a few days. She didn't want a flatmate. This place was way too small. Maybe if she told him he could have the flat in eighty-nine days he would find somewhere else to stay. Seemed like a small price to pay for stealing the flat from her. Why didn't Beverly give him a list too? Not one like Ava's, of course, but a list of things *he* would be terrified to do. Wasn't everyone afraid of something? And even if he was only terrified of one thing then he should be forced to do that thing ten times. Fair was fair. She wouldn't worry about it anymore today. Every second she worried was a second wasted. Ava napped. She showered. She tried on outfits, and shoes, and accessories from Beverly's closet, modeling in front of the bathroom mirror each time, her own private catwalk. She made sure to put everything back where it was. The closet was so pristine she didn't dare leave it any other way. Twice she had an official tea break. She liked the ceremony of it. Picking out a teacup, placing the little bag in the cup, waiting for the kettle to shriek. It gave one something to do. The day passed quickly. That wasn't so bad. She could get used to this life. When night fell, she eagerly resumed her post at the window.

People led such fascinating lives at night.

I see London. Not France. Not anyone's underpants. Although she saw a few women in short dresses and skirts, so perhaps she could see a few knickers if she cared to. Lights sparkled. Cars blared their horns. High heels clacked on the sidewalk. Voices rose and fell. Ava was almost giddy. A pair of binoculars sat on the shelf in the living room. Would it make her some kind of pervert if she watched people through them? No, she was simply an artist, an observer of life. She picked up the binoculars and set them on her emerald stool. More tools of the trade. She was hungry. She didn't want to eat any more of Queenie's leftovers. She wanted her own food.

She opened the drawer with the takeaway menus. Places that delivered. And everyone delivered. Indian, Chinese, pizza, Greek, sushi even. *Imagine!* Ava had never tried sushi in her life. She'd also never been to high school, or college. Homeschooled, and an online degree from Iowa State University. At least she did have some live discussions with classmates and professors over the computer. She'd also made some friends on Internet chat groups about art and, ironically, travel. *Friends.* Listen to her. She'd never met any of them face-to-face or even video chatted with them. And she never told them she was an agoraphobic. Although once she met Diana she'd made real progress. Diana was eventually successful in getting Ava out of the house. Once a month at least, down the street, and back at first with Diana by her side.

Then once every two weeks, trips to the market, and around the block, and eventually Ava made it to Diana's office every week for her appointments. And finally after a year of this, and a portion of the nest egg from her father's life insurance, Ava was able to move out of the house—God, the Xanax and support that had required. Then came the day she saw an ad online for the police department. A freelance sketch artist. It was like a gift from heaven. Thank God the local police department was still accepting sketches the old-fashioned way. Ava really felt like her father had a hand in that one. Ava glanced back at the menu in her hand. Funny, all the memories that Indian food could stir up in her. What choices. What an incredible city in which to be agoraphobic. She never wanted to leave.

Indian food was one of her father's favorites. She actually made a mean curry if she did say so herself. Money. She needed money to order food. She only had American dollars. Should she call and ask Jasper for help? Where was he now? Having dinner with his ex? At a pub? About to do his stand-up routine? She wondered if he was any good. She hadn't been very nice to him. It wasn't smart to alienate anyone here. Maybe she should call him just to apologize. But first, she had to figure out how to get food.

Maybe Aunt Beverly had some cash somewhere. It was odd, going through her dead aunt's flat looking for pounds. But surely Aunt Beverly would want her to eat? And where were all of Aunt Beverly's family photos? Ava wanted to see baby pictures of her dad. Hell, she wanted to see any pictures of her dad. Either Beverly didn't have any family photos or Ava hadn't discovered her hiding spot.

Maybe she should just have another Scotch instead and worry about eating in the morning. She poured herself a Scotch and went back to her velvet stool. She took the shot, and picked up the binoculars. She maneuvered them over the streets, finally zeroing in on a couple walking arm in arm. The woman was wearing a red dress and heels. The man, a smart gray suit. They were probably going to the theater.

Ava sketched the couple. She guessed that they had been together for a long time. Definitely not a first date. First dates didn't normally link arms, did they? Really, how was Ava to know? But she could imagine. *Come to my house, my sofa, my bed.* She thought of Jasper, imagined him walking toward her as she walked backwards. He would walk her right up against the wall—any London wall would do—and kiss her until she was dizzy. He'd pick her up, carry her around. He'd carry her to every single place on the list. At a bench in Hyde Park he'd lay her down and crush his body on top of hers. She'd say, *I never knew it could be like that.* He'd take her in the Tower of London surrounded by ghosts of past prisoners. His mouth, and hands, and words would distract her on the London Eye so that she wouldn't have to think about the ride; he'd ravish her in the London

Underground; they'd ride bareback at Buckingham Palace. They would be dirty at every single tourist spot on the list. By the end of the eighty-nine days he'd march into court with his white wig and burning desire and declare the will unjust. He'd fight for her, do anything to keep her. Queenie wouldn't stand a chance.

Enough! Thank God nobody could read her perverted mind. *No more fantasizing.* Ava picked up the binoculars and tried to find the couple out on their date. They were gone. She'd missed them. They were on their way to their very real life, while she sat up here, wasting hers on stupid fantasies about men she didn't even know.

After the theater, or the dinner, or the drinks, or the movies, would the couple stroll along the Thames? They were probably meeting other friends. And of course they would go out for drinks. Talk about their jobs, their kids, the play. Not one of them would realize how lucky they were to be out and about. Not one of them would imagine someone like Ava, afraid to go out, worse than a vampire, for she was equally allergic to the moon. Maybe all that Scotch hadn't been such a great idea. Ava was still hungry. She slipped on another nightgown of Bev's and went to bed.

Ava had a difficult time falling asleep. Could she still claim jet lag? She glanced at the clock by the bed. Nine p.m.? It was only nine p.m.? She would've sworn it was after midnight. No wonder she couldn't sleep. Had all her dirty thoughts about Jasper screwed up her biorhythms? Funny that she wasn't thinking about Cliff. Her attachment to him had been more of a necessity than a real connection. Jasper had ignited something in her she didn't even know existed. She'd never considered herself oversexed. Suddenly she was consumed by it, bombarded by lust for this total stranger. Seemingly overnight she had transformed into a pervert.

So what? London screamed sex. And sex was a pleasant distraction. Too bad it required another person.

Did it though? Did it really?

Fantasies didn't require another person. Porn didn't require another person. She wasn't going to watch porn. She couldn't. Could she? No, she could not. Why not? Because it was degrading to women. Maybe not to all women. Maybe some porn stars really enjoyed their job. Ava didn't have to be a prude about it. Maybe a little adult entertainment distraction would help her sleep. It was a biological fact that an orgasm was relaxing. She was in London. Nobody would know. She certainly wasn't going to tell anyone, would never send a postcard home: **WATCHING A BRITISH PORNO, WISH YOU WERE HERE.** She could at least see if she could get any porn on Beverly's television. Just for a laugh.

Oh, God, that wasn't cool. Using her dead aunt's cable to watch porn? What kind of a person was she? But Aunt Beverly was outrageous, too, as far as Ava could tell. Aunt Beverly would have probably put it on the list if she had thought of it. *Watch a British porno.* It was research. It was either that or lie here all evening fantasizing about Jasper.

Ava wouldn't watch very much of it; she would just see what she could find on the telly.

Aunt Beverly's television was new. It was HD. There weren't as many channels as Ava had in America, but there were enough. And there it was. *British After Dark* or *BAD.* That was funny. Ava would just have a look. She glanced around. Maybe, even though they were up high, she should put the sheets back on the window. Ava set about the task, hammering as quietly as she could, just in case any nosy downstairs neighbor would wonder why she was hammering again. It was probably impossible that anyone would put hammering together with porn—no pun intended—but they might wonder why she couldn't make up her mind as to where to hang her pictures. Once the sheets were back in place, she turned back to the screen. She pushed the MUTE button just in case her neighbors liked to listen. They could get their own porn.

Just for a laugh, she'd watch a bit. There were so many titles. *A Royal Pain*—how tacky. She wasn't going to watch whatever that was. *London's Coming. Piccadilly's Sex Circus. Bucking the Ham at the Palace, The Tower of London.* Guess that one worked as is. *Going Down on Abby. Banging Big Ben.* Maybe if she watched that one she could cross Big Ben off the list. Besides, she was only watching the free previews. That didn't really count. *Banging Big Ben,* it was.

She glanced around before settling onto the sofa. This was insane. But kind of fun. Nobody would ever know. She pushed PLAY. The screen filled with two naked women and one man. The male actor indeed lived up to his name. His Member of Parliament was impressive, and it was definitely in working order. *A working stiff. Ha!* Maybe Ava should do stand-up comedy. Ava wondered if they had British accents, but she didn't dare turn the volume up. Soon the women were kissing as Ben played with his impressive erection. Ava couldn't believe she was watching this. Just a few more seconds.

It wasn't long before the women stopped kissing and started servicing Big Ben. It reminded Ava of the job she did on the turkey leg. And then, she imagined Jasper standing in front of her. She imagined unbuckling his belt, unsnapping the button, unzipping his pants. She didn't expect Big Ben, but she had the feeling Jasper would be nicely staffed as well. She laughed. Since when did she become a walking romance novel? *Penis.* There, she could say it. It just sounded a bit odd. *Cock.* That wasn't much better. Lady parts weren't great either. "Vagina" or "pussy." The British sometimes said "quim," didn't they? That was a strange one too. Maybe she'd stick with "Member of Parliament" for him—and what? "Victory Gardens" for her? She was insane. She shouldn't have skipped dinner.

Jasper could be dinner. It would be nice to make him feel good. She never fantasized about giving Cliff blow jobs. She did it, of course; they all expected it. But with Cliff, she did her best to make sure it would be over quickly. He wasn't that big, so it wasn't like she was ever gagging on it, although it turned him on if she pretended like she was. God, men were such strange creatures. Luckily, it never took him long to climax. But that was hardly a glowing endorsement. Ava thought she just hated doing it, that all women probably hated doing it. But here she was fantasizing about going down on Jasper. What would it be like to put her mouth on him, make him moan? What was wrong with her? Maybe it was London itself. She was so sexed up on this side of the pond.

Stop it. Do not fantasize about Jasper. He's in love. He told you so himself. Watch Big Ben, instead. He was a beautiful man, really well developed all over. *Bet he comes right on time too.* No wonder he was such a tourist attraction. When you thought about it, most porn was either boring, or downright funny. This was no exception. The women were both on their hands and knees now, and Big Ben looked like he was trying to decide whom he was going to introduce his member to first. She was surprised the trailer was this long. She hadn't accidentally bought the darn thing, had she? What if she had? Or was British porn free like health care or certain museums?

What if it got charged to the cable bill? What if her new flat-mate got the cable bill?

Somewhere a door slammed and suddenly the volume was on full blast. Definitely British accents, sounded more like two male voices and a female—but Ava hadn't touched a single button. Suddenly the voices came to a dead halt. She pushed the MUTE button, still confused. Immediately moaning filled the air as Big Ben mounted the girl on the left—funny, Ava thought for sure he'd start with the one on the right—

And then someone cleared his or her throat. The door slamming, the voices. It hadn't come from the television. Ava froze. She tried to shut off the television. Instead she froze the three-some in place, whirled around, and saw three people standing in her living room.

She recognized Queenie right away. The round body, the bald head, and despite the pudgy face he somehow still had high cheekbones that suggested he could definitely pull off dressing as a woman. The only difference was his facial expression. Always smiling in the pictures, now he stood with his mouth open like a living rendition of *The Scream.* Next to him stood a beautiful woman about Ava's age. She was tall, with long black hair. Her face was pretty, although truth be told she looked a bit pinched.

She, too, had her mouth hanging open. And behind them stood Jasper. Ava found the POWER button on the remote and shut the porno off. She stood, heart hammering in her chest, face absolutely hot with shame. This could not be happening. How could she make this not be happening? Nobody spoke. They were waiting for her to speak.

"I—I—"

"We knocked," Jasper said. "Several hard raps on the door."

"That's what she said," Queenie said. Before she even processed his comment, Ava held out her hand for a shake. Queenie just looked at it and smirked. "Sorry, doll. We don't know where that hand has been, or do we?"

"What?" Ava looked at her hand. *Oh, God.* "No. I was just—it was a laugh. Your list. It said 'See Big Ben' and I was flipping through channels and that one was called *Big Ben.*" She left "Banging" off the title, hoping every little bit of decency would help. From the looks on their faces, she was wrong. "I just turned it on for a laugh." Thank God she didn't pick *Going Down on Abby,* thank God.

"Quite understandable," Jasper said. His shaky voice and absolutely crimson face once again said otherwise.

"I was flipping channels and just ran into it. I can show you—" Ava picked up the remote.

"NO," all three said at the same time. Even worse! Surely they'd all watched a porno at least once in their lives, right? Of course they had. And look at them staring at her as if they were asexual amoebas and she was the freakiest of freaks.

Jasper cleared his throat. "Ava, this is Queenie, your flatmate." Ava went to shake hands again, and then remembered. *Screw him.* Instead she curtsied as dramatically as she could.

"Is that Beverly's nightgown?" he said. Ava just stared. She'd forgotten she was wearing a nightgown. It was probably see-through. What was the protocol? Stand here as if her bits weren't on display or run to her room and slam the door? Queenie produced a slow smile as Ava debated her options. He folded his hands over his large stomach. "And here I thought you were going to be a bore," he said. "But I can see Beverly in you, all right." *He could?* Ava liked the sound of that. "Looks like I won't be needing a strand of your locks for that DNA test after all." His voice carried the theatrics of a stage actor.

Locks? DNA test?

"This is my *friend,* Hillary," Jasper said. He gave the beautiful woman a slight push and she stumbled forward, then turned and glared at him. *Unbelievable.* He was hanging around with his ex, trying to be her friend. He really didn't get women.

Hillary turned to Ava. "How do you do," she said. She was as prim and proper as the Duchess of Cambridge herself. Tall and slim with perfectly coiffed brunette hair. She was wearing a gray suit. It was quite possible she'd never watched a porno in her life. And unlike with Queenie, there was no grin. She didn't step forward, or hold her hand out to shake. Jasper was in love with an Ice Queen. Figured. Nice guys liked to be tortured. And they thought Ava was the pervert. She resorted to the only thing the Brits might do if they were in her situation.

"Cup of tea?" she said.

They blew on the steam. They slurped. They looked everywhere but at her. She had changed back into jeans and a T-shirt, but still nobody would look at her. They didn't comment on the sheets on the window either, but they glanced at them often. Ava wanted to tell them she'd taken the sheets down and enjoyed the view, but then she'd have to tell them that she only put the sheets back up to watch porn. This was awful. Maybe she could face Heathrow Airport again, because right now all she wanted was to be anywhere but here.

"I never would have come if I had known I was to have a flatmate," Ava said.

Queenie put his hand on his heart. "Darling, believe me. I don't want to live with a Septic either." Hillary laughed. It was the first time she'd vocalized anything.

"Queenie," Jasper said. His tone was a warning: *Be nice.*

"A what?" Ava said.

"Queenie," Jasper said.

"She said she read some kind of an online slang dictionary. I'm just testing her retention."

"A Septic," Ava said. "I didn't come across that one."

" 'Septic tank,' which rhymes with 'Yank,' " Queenie said. "What?"

"It's not personal," Jasper said. He was talking quickly as if to outrun trouble. "It's what we call all Americans."

"Septics?" Ava said. "You call us Septics?"

" 'Septic tank' rhymes with 'Yank,' " Queenie sang out.

"Gee thanks," Ava said. "Much easier to swallow." *Shoot.* That made her think of the porno again. Why did this have to be happening? Ava lurched to her feet. She jostled the table. Teacups rattled. "I have to go to bed."

"I take it you've already claimed the bedroom?" Queenie said. "I thought maybe we'd draw crowns."

"Draw crowns?" Ava said.

"It's a British tradition. Whoever draws the pointiest crown wins." He patted down his pockets. "I seem to have misplaced mine. Did you bring yours, Jasper?"

"Enough," Jasper said. He turned to Ava. "He's having a laugh."

"At my expense," Ava said.

"I can't help it; I'm hungry," Queenie said. He got up. "I've been dreaming of this turkey all day." It wasn't until Queenie reached the refrigerator that Ava remembered the turkey. What was left of it.

"Wait." She turned to Queenie, but it was too late. He opened the fridge and gasped as if he'd just seen his own corpse. He reached in, grabbed something, and turned around. He held the turkey carcass up by the thread of a bone.

"My turkey," he said. "It's been massacred."

"First I just tore off a little piece, but it was so good—you're an excellent cook—"

"You filthy, filthy girl."

"Queenie, enough." Jasper stood.

"I don't care if you watch porn all day and all night, but this!

This makes you a filthy, filthy girl." Queenie shook the turkey carcass. "I basted him for hours. I'm on a protein diet. This was breakfast, lunch, and dinner for a week!"

"I'm sorry. I'll get you another one."

"Will you?"

"Yes, of course."

Queenie made a beeline to the kitchen window and ripped off the sheet. Then he pointed out the window. "The market is right across the street. Why don't you just walk over there *right now* and replace my turkey?"

"I have to change my American dollars into pounds."

"Oh, is that all?" Queenie said. His voice went from high to low. "They take plastic."

"I can call them. Have it delivered."

"Not this late you can't."

"You can order takeaway tonight," Jasper said to Queenie.

Queenie whirled on Jasper. "I basted for days!"

"You're just upset about your audition," Jasper said. "Why don't you pour yourself a Scotch?"

Scotch. Shit. What's left of it. Hot pinpricks of shame invaded the back of Ava's neck. *I wouldn't drink his Scotch. Shit.* Would he notice? A scream rang out. A wail, really. Like that of a mourner throwing himself on a grave. Dramatic? He was a walking telenovela. Queenie stormed toward her with the near-empty bottle.

"I thought it was Aunt Beverly's!" Ava said.

"Sean Connery gave me this bottle of Scotch," Queenie said.

"Oh my God." Ava's hands flew to her mouth. Queenie smirked. "Did he really?"

"He could have," Queenie said. He shook his fist in the air. "He could have!"

"But did he?"

"It's my Scotch. It's almost gone." Queenie hugged the bottle to his chest, then kissed the top. Jasper approached. Hillary kept her distance, watching them like a snooty hawk, high up on her perch.

Jasper placed his hand on Queenie's arm. "Ava is your guest."

Queenie shook Jasper off. "Some guest. Lock up the silver-ware."

"She's Beverly's niece," Jasper said.

Queenie stopped talking. He put his hand over his mouth. Then looked mournfully at the bottle. "This Scotch is worth over two hundred pounds."

"I'm sorry," Ava said.

"You, my dear, are an alcoholic."

"Enough, enough," Jasper said.

"I am not," Ava said. "I was stressed."

"Alcoholics are stressed."

"I am not an alcoholic."

"What are you then?"

Agoraphobic. Trapped. Dead.

"Perhaps you're a sex addict?" Hillary offered.

"Didn't used to be," Ava said. She glanced at Jasper. Their eyes locked. Flames roared up the side of her face. *Shit.* She looked away. He continued to stare at her until she could feel her face heat up. "Call me a Septic," Ava said. "I don't care." She ran out of the kitchen, into the bedroom, and dived under the bed. She lay on the floor listening to her heartbeat against the boards. She could hear voices in the kitchen, talking. Talking about her. Jasper was probably telling Queenie to be nicer. *You won't have to put up with her long; she'll be out of here in eighty-nine days.* That man was Beverly's best friend? That woman was Jasper's *friend?* British pornos were free? The more Ava got to know the outside world, the less she understood it.

CHAPTER 12

Ava was up early. She crept out into the living room. Queenie was a snoring lump on the sofa. Surely a grown man would prefer his own room and bed. She would keep quiet, not because she wanted him to have his sleep, but because she wanted her peace and quiet. She tiptoed to the kitchen, opened the cabinet, and stared at the boxes of tea. *Ugh.* She'd kill for a nice cup of coffee. Did anyone in London drink coffee or was it tea, tea, tea? There probably wasn't a coffeemaker either. She headed for the kitchen table. Every single sheet had been stripped off the windows. They were folded neatly on the kitchen table. Next to them were a hammer and a box of nails.

In case you want to put them back up.

It had to be Jasper. Even his handwriting was a turn-on. Sharp, strong lines. Why did he have to be in love with that snobby ice twig? She looked like she'd be no fun at all. High maintenance. Then again, Ava could only imagine what Hillary had said about her. Why did she have to turn on a porno? She never watched them. It was for a laugh. But of course, she'd been caught. It was too late to fix it; first impressions were everything, and in Queenie's and Hillary's minds she was probably a pervert. A sex addict. *You know that girl who never leaves the house? It's because she's addicted to porn.* Thank God she'd already met Jasper. Although her first impression of him was that he was a bearded taxi driver, she'd gotten past that, so maybe she could redeem herself. Not that she was ever going to fit in anyway. She was the Septic. The outsider. How ironic. There was a first time for everything. For someone who never left the flat, Ava sure had managed to cause a lot of trouble. She went back into the living room.

The lump was still snoring. So much for the stereotype that all Americans were fat. She was thin, and the British invader on the sofa was not. Just one crack about America and fat and she would nail him. He slept cocooned up in a blanket. Maybe they did have a few things in common. One minute she was staring at the lump; the next minute his arms shot out and he yelled, "What's my line?" Ava laughed loudly, then slapped her hand over her mouth. Queenie's hands remained extended; then one slowly pulled the sheet from his face. "Where am I?"

Ava took a step forward. "You're in my flat," she said.

"You," he said.

"Me," Ava said.

"Why are you hovering over me? Am I keeping you from a porno?"

"Now that's not funny."

Queenie stared at her for a moment, very somber. Then he started to laugh. "You're quite wrong about that. It's my favorite story in a long time." His cheeks jiggled as he laughed. Ava started to laugh with him, until the full meaning of what he said smacked her in the face.

"Story? As in you're going to tell people?" She'd be the laughingstock of London. "Please, don't," Ava said. "I was watching it for a laugh." She took another step. "You don't gossip about your flatmates. Only the lowest of the low would gossip about their flatmates."

Queenie slowly sat up and rubbed his eyes. He was like an over-grown child. "So we're flatmates now, are we? I thought you were kicking me out." He rubbed his eyes again, then glanced at a clock on the bookshelf behind him. He let out a cry. "Four-thirty? In the morning?"

"I take it you're not a morning person."

"Luv, the only time I'm up at four-thirty in the morning is if I hadn't gone to bed yet."

"How often is that?"

"All the time. I don't suppose you like parties, do you?"

Ava didn't answer. Aside from when she was a child, she had never really gone to a party, so how was she supposed to know? "Don't any of you people drink coffee?"

"Us people?" Queenie said. "You mean the gays?"

"No. British people."

"I can't speak for the rest of the Queen's subjects, but I love coffee."

"There's no coffeemaker here." Queenie closed his eyes and turned his head toward the sofa cushion. *Oh my God.* He was so easy to read. There was coffee here somewhere. "Where is it?" Ava asked.

"You've already desecrated my turkey and invaded my Scotch. Why should I share my espresso?"

Ava gasped. "Espresso? I'd love, love, love an espresso."

Queenie groaned. "I don't suppose you'd go back to sleep if I promise to make you one in, say, four hours?"

"Four hours?"

"You're right. Make it six."

"I'll just turn the flat upside down until I find the espresso and then I'll make it myself." Ava turned for the kitchen. She heard a loud thump. She turned. Queenie was lying on the floor next to the sofa. His hands shot up again.

"I'll get it, I'll get it. Do not touch my espresso maker." He hauled himself up. His boxers sagged and his shirt rose above his belly. "Don't stare at my fat," he said. "It's not polite."

Ava turned around. "You look fine."

"Darling, you may be Beverly's flesh and blood, but you're

no actress. The doctor said I had to lose weight. I would be thinner by now if you hadn't eaten all my protein."

"I'll make it up to you."

"You can look now." Ava turned around. He was wearing a blue kimono. "You could have made it up to me already," he said, wagging his finger at her. "All you had to do was give Sainsbury's a bell."

"A bell?"

"On your mobile."

"A bell on my mobile." She had no clue what he was talking about.

"A fucking phone call?"

"Oh. Give them a bell. I get it. Cute." She paused. "Give who a bell?"

"Sainsbury's! They could have delivered twelve turkeys by now."

"I need pounds," Ava said. "I only have American dollars."

"They take plastic."

"I don't have plastic."

Queenie gasped and put his hand over his heart. "No cards?"

"No."

"No credit?"

"No again."

"How do you shop?"

"I pay cash."

He turned his head and stared at her out of one eye as if she were the sun and he was about to go blind. "And you won't go to the bank?"

"It's not a matter of won't; it's a matter of can't." Why should she explain herself to him? She was always explaining herself. And it never did any good. Unless he could experience it for himself, Queenie would never understand that being outside was pure terror.

He pointed to her stool. "Sit there." Ava flashed him a smile and obeyed. My God, the things she was willing to do for an espresso.

"Single or double?" he asked her.

"I love you," she said.

He handed her the perfect espresso with a dollop of whipped cream in the daintiest cup. "Thank you." He pulled up a chair and propped his own espresso in his lap.

"Bev got me this robe," he said, running his hand along the silk. Ava must have been too obvious about looking at it. She wasn't used to other people being around.

"She had style," Ava said. It was probably best not to mention that she'd been trying on everything in Beverly's closet.

"Oh, luv, that she did."

"What was she like?"

"Bev?"

"I always—" Ava stopped. She'd always thought she'd have the chance to get to know her. But she wasn't going to pour her guts out to Queenie. Just because he got up at four-thirty in the morning to make her an espresso didn't mean they were suddenly best friends. Then again, she did want to learn everything she could about Beverly before her ninety days were up.

"You always?" Queenie said.

"I always thought I'd have time," Ava said. "To get to know her."

"She thought the same about you," Queenie said.

"Do you mean that?"

"Of course I mean it. You sound surprised."

"Beverly didn't even come to my father's funeral." How could she not come to her own brother's funeral? It was unforgivable. Ava took a sip of her espresso. Scalding hot. The back of her throat burned. Her eyes watered. It was bliss. She hoped they served espresso in heaven.

"And how would you know that?" Queenie said.

"Excuse me?"

"That she didn't come to your father's funeral?" He knew. He knew her most shameful secret. Ava hadn't gone to the funeral either. She'd stayed in her room under her bed. It was unimaginable that they were going to put her father in a box and put him under the ground. So she got under her bed. To see if she could figure out what it would be like. And she didn't want him to be afraid. So she told herself it wasn't that bad. And it wasn't. And she didn't come out all day. Ava slammed the espresso down.

"She didn't come, she didn't come."

Queenie sighed, put his espresso on the windowsill, and got up with a groan. He walked over to the bookshelf and came back with a photo. Beverly had hid it behind a book. It was a picture of Ava's father's headstone with a huge bouquet of red roses lying on top. Ava gasped. She held on to the picture, examining it, trying to find out how it had been done. Had someone else sent Beverly this picture? Who?

"She went," Queenie said.

"But, but, but." *She didn't see me.* "My mother said—"

"Your mother wouldn't let her see you. She said you were traumatized. Beverly stayed for six days trying to see you. Six days. She even missed a matinée. And darling, Beverly Lee Wilder never missed a show. Never. That woman could have been shot in the chest at intermission and she would stumble onstage holding a bloody handkerchief over the wound. Only one show in a fifty-year career. Trying to see you."

Trying to see me. Me. Was he telling the truth? What did this mean? She never knew. "Why? Why wouldn't my mother let her see me?"

"Darling, it was a long, long time ago. There's no good in getting all mussed up about it now."

It didn't feel like a long time ago to Ava. It felt like yesterday. A "yesterday" that changed everything. "Do you know why?"

"You'll soon find that I know very little about anything. You should talk to your mother."

The liar who raised her? "Aunt Beverly didn't approve of my mother," Ava said. "That's why she and my dad barely spoke. I guess Beverly hated us Septics."

"Do you always do that?"

"Do what?"

"Come to your own conclusions without any factual evidence to back them up?"

"What are you? A barrister in your part time?"

"Because I use fancy words like 'evidence'?"

"Beverly and my father didn't speak. I know they used to speak before he married an American woman. Is that enough evidence for you?"

"Are you sure caffeine is a good mix with your disposition?"

"I'm sure, Mary Poppins." Ava picked up her espresso and downed the rest of it. She had whipped cream on her lip. She left it there, as if daring Queenie to say something. He didn't. She finally wiped it away. "So what did Beverly tell you about my father?"

"Uh, uh, uh. Weren't you just lecturing *moi* about how flatmates don't spread gossip?"

"About each other. We can certainly gossip about other people. Otherwise, what would be the point of having a flatmate?"

"From your end, I'd say, turkey, Scotch, espresso, porn, and all your living expenses taken care of. From my end, that certainly is an excellent question." He thought she was a weakling. He thought she had nothing to offer. He was confident she would fail and the flat would be his. Ava turned to the window. A few people were out now. A man in a suit smoking a cigarette on the corner. Another young man sweeping the sidewalk in front of the market. Anger coursed through her. She was a grown woman. Not a child, a woman. She should be able to make it across the street to the market.

She would force herself to do it. Maybe even today. "Is it your father's death that did it?" Queenie asked.

Ava whirled on him. "Did what?"

He waved his hands around as if trying to make more words materialize. "Your condition."

"My condition?" If he was going to be rude, she was going to make him say it.

"Beverly said you weren't like this when he was alive."

"Like what?"

Queenie sighed. "I'm not the enemy, you know."

"I'm not either."

"So let's call a truce."

"I didn't know we were at war."

"So let me help you."

"Help me?"

"Yes. We can go out together. Take a walk around the block. There's a great little pub at the end of the street. I'll buy you a pint."

"That sounds lovely."

Queenie's face brightened. "Well, that was easy. We'll go late this afternoon. Before the tourists show up."

"Not today. I have to wait for my prescription of Xanax to arrive." Ava had almost a full bottle of Xanax left, but he didn't need to know that. Xanax or no, she wasn't going to be rushed outside. There was no hurry whatsoever.

"Arrive?"

"Not in the mail. My psychiatrist will contact a doctor here that can prescribe it and I'll pick it up."

"I see."

"Unless you have any?"

"I'm fresh out."

"That's it then. I can't go today."

"You can't go out without it?"

"Trust me. You don't want to see me try." Ava smiled. Her cheeks hurt. How did people do it, pretend all the time?

"You may not believe this, Ava, darling. But we all want to see you try."

What was this? He seemed as if he genuinely cared about her. For a second she wanted to throw herself at him, hug him. Beverly's dear friend. He could be like an uncle. He was a good cook, and he was probably a lot of fun at parties. But he was also an actor. This sudden kindness could be nothing more than a ploy to steal her flat. She wasn't going to fall for it. But she couldn't alienate him either. He had very practical uses. *Survival of the fittest. Forget that. Survival of the smartest.* "Can I trade you my American dollars for pounds?" Ava asked. "Or are those septic too?"

"Not at all," Queenie said. "American dollars are welcome. As long as you give me twenty percent above the exchange rate."

"That's hardly fair."

"Then go out and go to a bank."

"Ten percent," Ava said.

"Fifteen."

"Fine." Ava went to her purse and handed him three hundred dollars.

He reached for his wallet, which was propped on the coffee table next to the sofa. He dug in and came out with twenty pounds. "I'll get the rest to you later."

"I'll take the dollars back until you do."

"I need to take the dollars to my bank and exchange them for you. Unless you want to go to a bank today?"

Go to a bank, go to a bank, go to a bank. He was getting on her nerves. He might as well be asking her to rob a bank. "Will you do it soon?"

"Darling, the banks here don't open at five in the morning. And from now on, neither do I."

"I'm just not used to the time change."

"I'm going to back to sleep," he said. "I wouldn't wake me twice if I were you."

Ava went back to the bedroom to get dressed even though she still had close to three hours before the market would open. She would do it; she would go. For once in her life, she would just do it. That's what everyone said. *Just do it. It's not as bad as you're making it out to be. It's all in your head. What's the worst that can happen?*

Do you hear that, Ava? It won't be that bad. It was the market. A jolly place where pleasant Londoners went to buy food. Surely she could manage that. It was right across the street.

Fire extinguisher, fire extinguisher, fire extinguisher. Little colored dots appeared at the mere thought of crossing the street. This was so ridiculous. Why did she have to go through this? She wanted to smash everything in sight. This wasn't fair. Why couldn't she trade places with someone else, see how easy it was to walk outside? She'd give anything. Anything.

And what did it mean that Beverly was at her father's funeral and her mother wouldn't let her see Ava? Cruel, it was just cruel. Ava was going to have to confront her mother. All that money on psychiatrists, yet she wouldn't even let Aunt Beverly help Ava. Was her mother at all to blame? The homeschooling, keeping family away, the ridiculous doctors?

Not entirely to blame. Ava wouldn't have gone to school. Her mother would have had to have her committed. Maybe she should have. Neither of them could change the past. But one of them was certainly going to have to explain it. And this time, Ava wouldn't settle for anything but the truth.

She would call her mother, lie in bed until Sainsbury's opened, and then be the first in line. Aunt Beverly had a red rotary phone. Ava enjoyed rolling her fingers through the numbers. It was after eleven p.m. in Iowa. It was technically the day before there, right? What a strange thing, as if she were calling back in time. She got her mother's voice mail. She was probably line dancing.

"I know," Ava said. Then hung up. *There*. Let her mother think about that one. Ava got dressed for the market. That was step one, wasn't it? Fake it until you make it. She lay on top of the bed. She drifted in and out; she replayed her life so that she went to her father's funeral, where she was embraced by Aunt Beverly, who instantly adored Ava. She took Ava and her mother to London to live. Ava never had agoraphobia again. They went to all the touristy spots together. Ava accompanied Beverly to the theater and played in Beverly's dressing room when she was onstage. Soaked in all the applause from the wings, attended all the parties. Ava went to a private school. What did she become? A famous dancer? An actress? It wouldn't have mattered. She would have been a girl who lived her life outside. Parks, and parties, and parades. Ava drifted off, watching the fantasy her do everything a girl should do, and then some. She even went skydiving with Aunt Beverly. She grew up to be the kind of girl Jasper Keyes could fall in love with. Fall in love with and enjoy the rest of his life with. An active life. Full of hiking, and faraway trips, and mini-adventures. Ava slept. And then, she woke up and glanced at the clock beside her bed. It was time. The market opened in twenty minutes. Perhaps it wouldn't be so bad if she was the first in. The streets wouldn't be too crowded. She would get in and out. It would be easy. *Lies, lies, lies, lies.* How did she know? Maybe if she just pretended to be normal, she'd make it across. Maybe if she stopped making such a big freaking deal out of it, she could do it. Didn't they say the most complicated problems often had simple solutions? *Don't think.*

She picked up her keys. She had twenty pounds. She looked over at the market. There were only a few people going in and out. She went to the front door of the apartment. She opened it. She closed it. She went into her bedroom and shut the door. She crawled on top of the bed. She could feel the market glowing, calling to her like an alien ship. What was she thinking? Leave the flat? She couldn't even make it out the front door. She got under the bed. She sneezed. *Bloody hell.* This was no way to live. She sneezed again. *Bollocks.* Cursing in British didn't help either. London hadn't changed her. She was still her. *Wherever you go, there you are.* Ava hated that saying. Ava was handicapped. What did people trapped in wheelchairs do? People who wanted to get up and walk, but couldn't? Did anybody blame them? Did they stand over them, shouting at them to get up and walk? People were constantly standing over her, telling her to get over it, to go outside. They were yelling at a cripple. And they made her feel worse. She wanted it way more than they did. Shame on top of rage. Too many years of it. Cliff was right. Ava was handicapped. Doomed to sneeze underneath dusty beds from London to Timbuktu. Ashes to ashes, dust to dust. What would Jasper think if he could see her now? She would stop flirting with him. He deserved better than this. He deserved better than her.

CHAPTER 13

It was Ava's ten-day anniversary. She was going to mark the occasion with a special series of sketches. A young man who lived in a building across the street had captured Ava's attention. The brick dwelling was a one-story rectangular structure at street level. It was next to Sainsbury's. She'd yet to make it there, but that was Queenie's fault. He'd actually bought her groceries, a "Welcome to London" do-over. It even included a bottle of Scotch. But the food was almost gone. She would have to go to the market soon.

In the meantime, she was fascinated with the young man across the way, and his nondescript building. Given the location and foot traffic, it was obvious that the building was prime commercial real estate, yet it had no sign, and the windows were always covered with dark curtains. Was he a fellow agoraphobic who had worked up to sweeping the sidewalk? There were support groups online for agoraphobics, but Ava had never taken any comfort in them. "You're isolating again," Diana would say. "Give them a chance."

"They're strangers," Ava would say. "I don't feel any kinship with them."

"You haven't given it enough time."

She didn't want to give it time. She didn't want to give them a chance. She didn't want to be in some kind of insiders' club. She didn't want to listen to others describe their panic attacks in every gory detail. What she hoped would be a group focused on overcoming their fears turned out to be people going to a place just to kvetch. Even worse were the videos online of people who actually had filmed themselves having panic attacks. Who in the world wanted to see that? It was embarrassing. Some of them seemed totally unhinged. It made Ava want to slap them across the face and yell, *Snap out of it!* "I'm not that bad," Ava would say to herself after viewing yet another spectacle. "I'm not that bad." Was she? Was that why she couldn't stand to watch? *They're holding up a mirror to you, Ava, and you can't stand looking at your own reflection.*

But she did like sketching the man across the street. He always came out to sweep at three p.m. He looked to be in his twenties, with brown skin and dark hair, Middle Eastern or Indian descent. He had such a calm demeanor that Ava liked watching him. He would sweep first, then lean against his building and smoke a cigarette. He held it like a joint, pinching it between his thumb and index finger, and then, just as it neared his lips, he'd squint and thrust his head back, as if it were being forced on him. That was the part Ava found fascinating. Like he was eating a wriggling cockroach on a dare, every day at three p.m. He only smoked one, and he always behaved as if every second was torture. Was he facing his fear of smoking? The thought made Ava laugh. Maybe she could sketch a series of people trying to overcome outrageous "fears." People tightrope walking, running out into traffic, running *into* burning buildings, trying to adjust to being waterboarded. It made her feel better to laugh even if there was no one around to share it.

Sometimes, when there was a breeze, Ava could smell the cigarette smoke wafting into her flat. At those times she felt as if she was truly mingling with the world. How could she not be if she could actually smell it? See the wisps of smoke floating through the air? Did he know how funny he looked? None of us did, Ava realized. None of us realized how completely ridiculous we really were.

Life's short. Go outside. That would be Ava's motto if she ever conquered this. She wouldn't let people complain, or explain, or excuse. *Life's short. Go outside,* she would say, her arm outstretched in a commanding gesture. Someone could build glass boxes for agoraphobics. Set them on street corners and force agoraphobics to stand in them like they were David Blaine conducting a spectacular magic trick.

What are they doing? outsiders would muse, circling the box.

Maybe it's really hot in there, another would say. *Look how they're sweating.*

How long before the participants were throwing themselves against the glass, smashing their noses and lips against the scorching pane, begging for someone to throw a sheet over them? Would they eventually get used to it, enjoy the great outdoors, or simply die in their little glass boxes, alone in the crowd and misunderstood? Maybe they could set the boxes in the woods. Ava often wondered if she would like the woods in the fall with giant red, yellow, and orange leaves cascading on top of her. She could imagine them twirling down, no two alike, gently sticking to the glass box until they completely covered her. Buried her, even. She could trace them with her finger, the spikes, the dips, the stem. She would want to be there the night of a full moon, bathe in its radiant light. Maybe even on Halloween, with the smell of a campfire in the air, and a hay wagon circling the perimeter. Maybe after a while she would be brave enough to get out of the box. She wanted to hug a tree, feel the strong trunk against her body and the rough bark underneath her fingertips. Or the beach. No, not the beach; there was no end in sight, sand and sand and sand and sky. Water without walls. Endless open space. Ava would rather die.

Stop it. Stop, stop, stop.

Ava refocused her binoculars on the man across the street.

He flicked the cigarette nub to the ground, smashed it into the pavement with his foot, and then swept it up into his dustbin. Maybe someone inside didn't know he smoked and he was sneaking out every day to indulge in his vice. But why look so miserable doing it? Ava couldn't make out the brand. Not that she needed that kind of detail for her sketch. It was his expression she captured on the page. The agony. The odd fear. To be fair she sketched other sides of him too. Sweeping the street. Leaning against the building. Who else was inside? What was inside? Was he in college? Was this the family business? Why bother to sweep when five minutes later someone would drop a piece of trash at your doorstep? Was it simply the ritual of doing it that he liked? Was it meditative to sweep a city footpath? Did it make him feel like he was doing his part to clean up society? Should she do that? Could she do that? Find a broom and simply stand on the stoop of her building sweeping? She'd have to think about trying it. So far all she'd managed to do was find a broom. Sometimes she stood in front of the window with it, imagining she was outside. Sometimes she imagined she was sweeping grime off the London skyline.

Sometimes she would see a few men dressed in business suits enter the young man's building. Always men, always brown skin. Maybe they were accountants. Or private detectives. Or an Internet company. It seemed to defy the odds, that he wouldn't look up even once. *Outsiders* thought they saw the world. But they didn't. They had blinders on, too; they just didn't know it.

Oh, the things she'd been learning. Ava could spend hours people-watching out her London windows, and sketching. It was the best job in the world. She wished Beverly were here to see it. Maybe she would see it wasn't such a bad way to live. Maybe she would take back the stipulations. Forced sightseeing, it wasn't right. This was the real London, at least her little slice of it, right outside her window. Had Beverly also spent hours looking out? *Happy Anniversary, to me.*

Ten days. Ava couldn't believe she'd been in London for ten days. She hadn't seen much of Queenie lately; he mostly communicated through Post-its on the fridge, bathroom mirror, and the bar in the living room: *Paws off my meat, Please hang your towels on YOUR rack, Are you drinking my Scotch again??!!*

But he wasn't all bad. Queenie had come through with a few more pounds. She was almost out again; she'd have to confront him about the rest. Either way, Ava wasn't going to starve. But just in case that day came, every day she visualized herself going to the market. In the meantime, and in addition to Queenie's food offerings, she was getting takeaway. The takeaway in London was such heaven. That alone was a reason to stay forever. She started ordering three lunches because they were always the least expensive. Then she had something to heat up in the microwave for the next two meals. And, oh, did she love the takeaway in London. The Indian food was divine. She could also get burritos, Chinese, pizza, and Greek. But mostly she ordered Indian. And sometimes Queenie took pity on her and brought her home a few requests from the market. Namely peanut butter and jelly—or jam, as they said here, and bread. That and coffee and she was a happy girl. Could she make Queenie like her enough that he would own the apartment but want to keep her on as his flatmate the rest of his life? Highly doubtful.

She'd seen very little of Jasper since the embarrassing porno fiasco. It was probably for the best. It was normal to think of him for hours a day. Who else did she know?

Three p.m. That meant it was espresso time. Her taste buds were primed for the rich treat. Ava headed to the kitchen to make one. She opened the freezer, where Queenie kept the espresso. A barren frozen tundra stared back at her. Gone were the bags of veggies, the mint chocolate-chip ice cream, the microwavable meals, and the espresso. All that remained was a single tray of pathetic ice cubes. She slammed the freezer door shut. It bounced open again. She shut it less violently the second time although what she really wanted to do was rip off the door and hurl it out the window. She took a step back and stared at the fridge.

Please. Let there at least be crumbs. She opened it. White, white, white, empty, sad, bleak. Not a single bottle of salad dressing or stick of butter to be seen. It was so white she had to shield her eyes. How could he? One by one she threw open the cabinets. Dishes, cups, martini glasses, and alcohol shakers, and salt and pepper, and tea, boxes and boxes of tea, but nothing edible to be found anywhere. It was as if the entire cast of *The Walking Dead* had come through and cleaned out every edible morsel.

Queenie. That diabolical bastard. And just when she was starting to like him. This was beyond cruel, especially since he had taken her three hundred American dollars and so far had only given her what amounted to sixty pounds in return. He was probably keeping the rest to make up for the Scotch, and the espresso, and all his groceries. Perhaps that was justified. But leaving her to starve? It was sadistic. She'd spent so much on takeaway lately she doubted she had more than ten pounds left. She headed for the little table by the windows. Sitting in the middle was a note.

> *Gone for a few days!*
> *Enjoy the market!*
> *Queenie*

CHAPTER 14

Why, that big weasel. Queenie said he'd be gone for days. He was trying to force her out of the flat. What was next, tear gas? She grabbed the phone and called Jasper. It went to voice mail.

"Can you stop by and exchange some American dollars for pounds? Queenie took all the food out of the fridge and I'll need to order takeaway." She hung up. That felt awful. She was a grown woman. Everyone was right. She ought to be able to go to the market across the street. In the bedroom, she opened the wardrobe. In addition to her nightgowns, Ava had started wearing Aunt Beverly's clothes. It made her feel close to her. Forget shoes, you could really get to know people by slipping into their outfits. Aunt Beverly had flair. She was flirty and daring and that's just how Ava felt when she wore her aunt's dresses. She pulled out a short red dress. The phone rang. Jasper. She lunged for the bedroom phone.

"Hello?" She tried to slow her breaths so she wouldn't sound desperate.

"Thank God, you're there." Queenie's voice boomed through the phone.

Where else would I be? Was he calling to apologize? The nerve. She'd make him work for it. "Who is this?"

"It's Queenie."

"Queenie who?"

"Queenie who owns your flat."

"Not yet you don't."

"You sound grumpy."

"No food in the house will do that to a girl."

"You haven't gone to the market yet?"

What a cruel man. She wouldn't give him the satisfaction. "I am about to go. What can I do for you?"

"I need my lucky charm."

"I told you there's no food."

"I—What?"

"Are you talking about breakfast cereal?"

"No, I'm not talking about breakfast cereal; I'm talking about an actual lucky charm."

"Oh."

"I have an audition and I have to wear it."

If there was one thing Ava believed in, it was superstitions. She couldn't even hate Queenie enough to deprive him of his lucky charm. "What is it?"

"It's a gold coin around a chain—can you look in the sofa cushions?" Ava nodded even though he couldn't see her, took the cordless phone, and headed to the living room.

"You were supposed to give me pounds for the rest of my dollars," she said on the way.

"Sorry. I was in a rush."

"Did you leave any pounds?"

"Luv, if I could afford to leave pounds just willy-nilly we wouldn't be fighting over Beverly's flat."

"Well, I won't be able to mail your lucky charm even if I find it." Ava dug into the first sofa cushion. Change. But not a gold coin on a chain. And it didn't look like enough change to buy food. Well, maybe an apple. Was it worth risking an attack just to walk across the street and buy an apple? Was it a real gold coin? The second sofa cushion held a pen, crumbs, the cap of a pen, and a piece of paper. Ava unfolded the paper. It had one word on it. "BREATHE."

"I'll send a friend to get it—and he can bring you a basket of food or give you pounds."

A basket of food? What was she, Little Red Riding Hood? "I found a note that says: 'BREATHE,'" Ava said.

"Beverly always wrote herself notes before shows," Queenie said.

"She did? Why?"

"Stage fright."

This was news. "Beverly had stage fright?"

"She would get a touch of the nerves now and then. The notes helped her." A touch of the nerves. Just like Ava. Only Aunt Beverly still functioned. "What about my charm?"

Ava lifted the third sofa cushion, and sure enough there it was—a large gold coin with Shakespeare's big face smiling at her. Ava pulled it out. It was way too golden to be real. The chain, however, looked real. "Is it the Bard?" Ava said.

"Oh, thank God. Thank God, thank God, thank God."

"Call me Ava."

"My friend's name is—"

"Why don't you just ask Jasper to pick it up? And I'll take pounds over a basket of food."

"Why do you want Jasper?" Queenie's voice rose an octave, and if Ava didn't know better she would say that she just made a teeny tiny mistake. "Does somebody have a little crush?" She took it back. She'd made a monumental mistake.

"I know him. I do not know your friends."

"Somebody has a little crush."

"Stop saying that."

"You'd better not let Hillary find out. You think I'm bad? My niece is a hellcat." Hillary was Queenie's niece. Had anyone ever mentioned this before? Ava was back to not liking Queenie.

"They're broken up."

Queenie laughed. "That doesn't mean she's going to let anyone else have him."

"He's not a trinket; he's a person. Besides, I don't have a crush on him. We're just friends."

"She's also high society. London high society."

"I don't care." Ava didn't even know what that meant. Designer clothes, and polo matches? Royal invitations? Old money? Who cared.

"You *should* care. She's a Hell Hath No Fury kind of broad."

"How many times do I have to say it? I don't have a crush on Jasper. I have a boyfriend back in the States."

"You do?" He didn't even try to hide his surprise. "Don't you miss him? Don't you want to go back home?"

"He's going to visit me here instead." *Imagine Cliff here.* She couldn't. Not just because she hated him; he just wouldn't fit. His Pabst Blue Ribbon beer drinking, blue-collar ways. *Oh, God.* Was it happening to her already? Was she becoming a snobby Brit?

"He's not allowed to live in the flat, not until the year is over. That is, if you complete the list first." Queenie sounded truly alarmed. Now Ava wished Cliff really was coming just so he could invade Queenie's privacy. "Is he a hermit too?"

"I'm not a hermit! Hermits don't like people. I like people. *Most* people." Ava gravitated to the window. The London Eye was turning in the distance. Cars, and lorries, and people, and dogs, and bicyclists were all out en masse. Busy, busy people.

"If you're not a hermit, then what do you call yourself?"

"Ava."

"If I wanted to refer to your condition."

"Why would you be referring to my condition? To whom?"

"I'm a drag queen. You don't need to lecture me on labels. We're all gay, and bitchy."

"But you *are* gay and bitchy."

"That doesn't mean I have to wear the label. A small percentage of the time I can also be masculine and mushy."

"Just how I like my manly men. Mushy."

"I'm just saying I'm an aging, gay, bitchy drag queen and I'm not ashamed of it."

"Fine. I'm agoraphobic. Is that what you want to hear?"

"I think 'bitchy' applies to you as well, luv."

"Stick it."

"Have you ever thought about getting together with others who are like you?"

"So the Mother Ship can call me home? Oh, gee, I've thought about it. Only problem is none of us are willing to meet because we all insist on being the host." God, Ava could kill him. Why was he being so nosy?

"Maybe you could meet online—"

"I have to go."

"Where?"

"Just because I'm an agoraphobic doesn't mean that my time isn't valuable, that I don't have things to do."

"You're right. I've been schooled. I'll give Jasper a bell and tell him to pick up my charm. Unless you want to call him."

"Nope."

"And until he gets there . . ." Queenie paused.

"Yes?"

"There's twenty pounds in the tin of Earl Grey in the kitchen." He hung up. Ava went to put the lucky charm down on the mini-bar, then put it on instead. The heavy coin felt comforting against her chest. She could see why Queenie liked it. She went to the kitchen and found the tin. Sure enough, there was twenty pounds. She took it out and put it in her bra. Where else was he hiding pounds? Ava checked in a few other tins. Nothing. She opened drawers and dug into tea boxes. Nada. At least she had twenty. Would Jasper be able to make time to see her again? He'd been busy the last ten days. Not that she'd expected any kind of regular visitation. But she sure wished for it. She thought he liked her too. Maybe that's just how people behaved with each other. How was Ava to know? She had so little to compare it to. Queenie was right about one thing; she did have a little crush on Jasper.

Hillary is definitely the Hell Hath No Fury type.

Well, she didn't have anything to worry about when it came

to Ava, now did she? Jasper would never choose Ava over Hillary anyway. Would he?

What time was it in the States? She could use a chat with Diana, despite her betrayal on the airplane. Ava would eventually need more Xanax. Could Diana find a way for her to get a prescription in London? Or would Ava have to find a psychiatrist in the UK? Were there any who would make house calls? Ava's stomach gurgled. Her immediate concern was food.

Maybe if she opened the window and yelled down at some-one on the street they would take pity on her and toss up some-thing to eat. Would they simply think she was a lazy cow? Once again, she wished people could just understand. One of the pit-falls of having an invisible disability. Maybe she should get a T-shirt made up. *THE INSIDE GIRL.* Or she could start a blog. *The In-sider's Guide to London.* High society. Like Hillary was famous or something.

Ava brought her laptop over to the window. She wanted to show Diana the view. She looked down at her hand. She was still holding the piece of paper from the sofa. *BREATHE.* She tried to pay attention to her breaths as she put through the video call.

Ava watched herself in the camera as she listened to the com-puter trying to chirp through.

"Hello?" She heard the voice too. It sounded garbled. Under-water. Seconds later the picture came on. Diana's hair was a mass of frizz. She had huge dark circles under her eyes. "Who is this?" she demanded. *Uh-oh.* From the looks of Diana it was three o'clock in the morning.

"Traitor," Ava said. "What kind of doctor are you?" She hadn't meant to start with that, but her mouth usurped her brain.

Diana rubbed her eyes. "Who is this?" Good God, apparently Diana wasn't a morning person.

"It's Ava. From London. Remember me? The one you aban-doned?"

"Ava." Soon Diana's face was on the screen. She kept moving her face closer and closer to her own computer's camera, giving Ava a full view of all her wrinkles and pores. A view Ava could have done without.

"It's good to see you. Even though I'm really pissed at you." Ava meant it. It was really good to see Diana.

"What time is it?"

"I don't know. I haven't figured it out."

"From now on, figure it out. You can't just call me in the middle of the night."

"And you can't just leave a person like that without an apology."

Diana sighed. "I'm sorry. But you're there, aren't you? Well done."

"Gee, thanks. I feel so much better. I'll let you get back to your beauty sleep now."

"Oh, don't. You've already gotten me out of bed and you look like you haven't slept in days." Ava looked at herself on camera. She was a fright too. Dark circles. In need of a haircut. But how in the world could she go to a hairdresser when chances were very good that midway through her shampoo or, worse, little foil packets of highlights Ava would be seized by a panic attack and have to flee? She wished Diana would just cure her already. If a scrappy Brooklyn Jewish woman stuck in Iowa couldn't help her, then who could? "Talk to me." Diana's truckdriver voice cut through the air. She pulled her glasses to the bridge of her nose and leaned forward until her entire face filled the computer screen.

"It's good to see you." Ava was repeating herself, but it was true. She had no idea how much she missed Diana until she was there before her. What about Cliff? How would she feel if she saw Cliff right now?

Diana smiled and threw open her arms as if to hug Ava. "You made it."

"I made it." Ava threw her own arms open. Tears filled her eyes. "No thanks to you."

Diana didn't comment. "Tell me everything, starting with the flight."

Ava wiped her tears and bit her lip. She didn't want to spend her time with Diana crying. She wasn't even sad. It was just such a relief to talk to someone who knew her. Who understood her. Once upon a time she had Diana, her mother, and Cliff. Now she just had Diana. She couldn't imagine losing her too. "I don't remember a thing about the flight. I was drugged like a Clydesdale horse." First class. She missed the hot towels, the champagne, the chocolates, the nuts. She'd slept straight through.

"What about when you landed? Did you make your way to Luggage okay?"

Ava felt a flash of heat rise up her neck and flare from her cheeks. "Easy breezy." No use going into the bits about the janitor's closet, the rubbish bag, and the wheelchair. Ava grabbed the laptop and stood. "Would you like a tour of the flat?" She was proud of it. She wanted to show it off as if it were her own.

"No, it will make me dizzy."

Ava started to walk around anyway. She really wanted Diana to see the flat. "It's lovely. Very spacious. Beautiful light wood floors, and an open floor plan—"

"Ava, put that computer down or I'm going to hurl."

"Sorry." Ava set the laptop down but remained standing. "It's four flights—sixty-two steps—up to the flat, but the view from the windows is so worth it. You can see all of London—"

"Ava, oy. Please sit down." Diana slapped her hand over her forehead. Ava took a deep breath and plunked down on the seat. She looked out the window but could feel Diana staring at her. "What's going on, Ava?"

Ava turned to the screen, her damn eyes still overflowing with tears. She was tired. Seeing a friendly face, even if it was grouchy, was overwhelming. "How could you not come with me? And what about all those turtlenecks? You don't need them?"

"I have more. But I'd appreciate it if you'd like to mail the suitcase back to me; I would appreciate that."

"No."

"You don't have to do it right away. Spend a few days imagining yourself going to the post office. Baby steps, visualization. Just like we talked about."

"Maybe you should have spent a few days visualizing yourself staying on the plane with me. Are you afraid to fly?"

"I'm too tired for this. What's really going on? You look like you're about to cry."

"I'm going to lose the flat."

"Lose it how?"

"Aunt Beverly knew about my condition. I only get to keep the flat if I go out and do certain things within the first ninety days." *Eighty days now.*

"What sort of things?"

"Touristy things. See Big Ben. Not the porno, the real thing." Diana arched an eyebrow. Ava plowed on. "Tour the Tower of London. Ride the Tube. Ride the London Eye. Sit on a bench in Hyde Park. Go to an English pub. All lovely, lovely, impossible things to do. Can you believe her?"

"How does it feel?"

"How does what feel?"

"To meet yet another person who doesn't understand your condition?"

"I think she was trying to help."

"That's not what I asked."

"It sucks, okay? The whole world thinks I'm a joke!"

"I don't think you're a joke."

"You're paid too well."

"Ava."

"I'm kidding. Maybe they're right. Maybe I should just get over myself."

"We've been through this. It's not in your head."

"I know." Ava knew what Diana was waiting for her to say. They'd talked about this ad nauseam. "My body reacts to everyday errands like anyone else's would in times of crisis."

"Fight-or-flight response," Diana added.

"I'm just going to the market, but my body thinks I'm being chased by a wild boar." Ava laughed. You had to laugh. Otherwise it would just kill you. It sounded funny. It just didn't feel funny at the time.

"Your panic attacks are not in your head."

"I know. I step outside and I truly feel like I'm about to die."

"What your aunt Beverly is asking you to do is unreasonable for someone with your condition."

"So I'm going to lose this flat."

"Maybe you should speak to an attorney."

"The executor of the estate is an attorney." Jasper's smiling face appeared before Ava. "He's rather good-looking."

"Is he now?"

"And funny. He's actually pretty funny." Ava didn't want to tell her about the taxi ride. She wanted to keep this memory for herself. It had been so long since Ava had actual stories of her own to tell. She was afraid if she told it she'd lose it. She wanted to hold it close a little longer. Secrets were delicious. Keeping it almost made her feel high. Or was it just thinking of Jasper that made her feel that way?

"Is he your age?"

"Yes."

"Married?"

"No. But he's pining over his ex-girlfriend." Hillary. High-society wench. Jasper seemed too down to earth to fall for that.

"Well, you know what they say."

"I never know what they say. I don't even know who they are."

"The best way to get over an old love is to get under a new one."

"Brilliant advice. I'll just straddle him and that will be that."

"But you may need to get another attorney."

"I don't have the money to fight this. Queenie is going to get the flat."

"Who is Queenie?"

"One of Aunt Beverly's best friends. He's an actor too. We're sharing the flat."

"You have a roommate?"

"Yes. Doesn't that suck?"

"I rather like the fact that you won't be alone."

"Oh yes, he'll be the first to discover my body."

"Your sarcasm is a little heavier than normal. I'm fine with it. As long as you recognize you're doing it."

"I recognize."

"Could he be your safe person?"

"Not a chance. He's my archenemy."

"He's your archenemy?"

"If I don't complete the list in eighty days now, then the flat is his."

"I'm beginning to think your aunt was quite the manipulator."

"Jasper says she had already promised the flat to Queenie when she felt bad about me."

"Is that why you think she wanted you in London? Because she felt bad?"

"I don't know. I'm trying to learn about her. Through her things. Through Queenie. And Jasper."

"You're mentioning this Jasper a lot."

"Am I?"

"Maybe he could be your safe person."

No. She couldn't get too close to Jasper. What kind of a girl-friend would Ava be? Jasper was an adventurer. A bloke who liked jumping out of airplanes. She wasn't going to hold any-one back. "You were right the first time. Definite conflict of in-terest."

"You haven't left the apartment since you arrived?" Ava shook her head. "You've made progress. Just going to London is huge."

"I hid out in a janitor's closet in Heathrow Airport." *Damn.* Ava never could keep a secret.

"You made it from your house in Iowa all the way to London, England. I don't care if you spent the night in the janitor's closet. That's huge."

"I was on a lot of Xanax."

"You are refusing to recognize your accomplishments."

"I don't think throwing a fit, hiding in a closet, and wearing a rubbish bag over my head is much of an accomplishment."

"That's a lot to throw at me at this hour. Do you need to dis-cuss any of those incidents?"

"No."

"Does the list require you to enjoy doing these things?"

"No."

"Then I'll help you. If you can make the trip from America to England, you can tackle this list one by one."

"Have you ever looked at the map of the London Underground? Lines going every which way? I still can't get the image out of my mind." Choking her, that's how it felt, like the lines were choking her.

"Let's start small. Is there anything near your flat of interest to you?"

"There's a grocery store right across the street. If I held up the laptop to the window you could see it."

"That's a fabulous start."

Ava reached for the laptop.

Diana threw her hands up like she was protecting herself from a blow. "Not literally!"

"Sorry." Ava's knee started to bounce. She had energy now. God, Diana was a good therapist.

"Are you taking your medication?"

"Yes. But I'm going to run out soon." The bottle was half-gone. Ava was going through them too fast. She kept this to herself.

"I'll see if I can get any referrals in London. In the meantime why don't you start with the market? Use the technique we used to get you to work. One step at a time. You can turn back at any given moment. Are you sure your roommate can't be your safe person?"

"I'm sure. He's my pain-in-the-ass person. He hates me."

"I wish you had someone there."

"Like Cliff?" Did he feel at all guilty for what he'd done? Did her mother?

"He did serve a purpose."

Or two. "Jasper wants to be a stand-up comedian. But he's not funny. Should I laugh at his jokes anyway?"

"And now we're back to Jasper."

"I'm not interested in Jasper."

"You seem sexually aroused."

"I hate it when you say things like that."

"Your pupils are enlarged and you're smiling more than usual."

"He's cute, that's all. And funny. And aggravating. And his ex-girlfriend who he's still pining for is high society, and according to Queenie she'd unleash the seven circles of Hades on me if she knew I liked Jasper, and they all caught me watching British porn. Are you happy? Is that what you wanted to hear?"

"Our time is up. Go to the market."

"What am I, a Little Piggy?"

"Yes. But we've had enough of the one who stays home." Diana wiggled her fingers and then bowed her head. She was hunting for the correct button to end the session. Seconds later the screen went black. *Great.* Now Ava would wonder until their next appointment if Diana thought she was a pervert.

CHAPTER 15

Ava stood in front of the full-length mirror in the bedroom while she put on a pink dress Beverly had hanging in her wardrobe. It looked as if it was from the fifties. Ava slipped it on and looked in the mirror. She grabbed a hat from its hook. A little white number with some netting hanging down. Ava was somebody else. An actress herself perhaps. If not a member of high society, then perhaps at least somewhere in the middle. She slipped on a pair of Aunt Beverly's flats. Ava and her aunt had worn the exact same size. Ava would literally get to walk in Beverly's shoes. Not a mile, that would be pushing it. But across the street, to Sainsbury's. *It's never as bad as you think it's going to be.*

Ava spent thirty minutes visualizing herself successfully going to the market. She sat on the emerald stool and imagined herself gliding down the stairs, floating almost, then easily, happily, normally crossing the street, entering the market, and buying a few bits and bobs. *Piece of cake.* Maybe she'd get that too. Cake or death? Wasn't that what Eddie Izzard always said? *Would you like cake or death? Cake, please.*

Here's hoping. It was time. It was now or never. Today the market, tomorrow something from the list maybe. She could do this!

Just before she reached the door she stopped to remove Queenie's lucky charm. Then again, maybe it would work for her too. She left it on. *That's it.* With Beverly's dress and Queenie's lucky charm, she could do this.

One step at a time. Ava opened the main door to the flat. *Oh, God.* The floor beneath her began to sway. This wasn't fair. This wasn't what other people had to deal with. She gripped the keys in her hand along with her purse. Should she write some kind of a good-bye note, just in case? She slammed the door behind her. That felt good. If only she had something to slam all the way there. Just go down the first three steps. That was all she had to do. One step. Two step. Three steps.

But I don't want to go to the food mart. There's tea in the flat, isn't there? All I want is a nice cup of tea.

One more step.

Four steps. *Creak.*

I told you I didn't want to go. Don't do this to yourself. You're the same girl in London you were in Iowa.

Ava tripped on the next step and then she was tumbling. *Oh God. Protect your head!* She grabbed for the rail, but she was going too fast skidding down the stairs on her bum—that's how the Brits would put it—and it really hurt. She came to a stop at the landing of the first set of steps. She grabbed a rail and hugged it for dear life. Her heart was thudding in her chest. If she opened the buttons on her dress her heart would probably leap out. That would show them. All of them. She'd love to see their reaction if her heart was out of her chest, flopping on the floor like a fish. *Take that, assholes.* Now she was stuck. It was either back up the stairs or down three more flights. This really sucked. So far this was way worse than she'd imagined it.

She heard the main door to the building open. Was it Queenie? Jasper? A neighbor? If it was Queenie or Jasper, how would she explain the fact that she was sitting on the stairs, shaking? Her flat was the only one on the fifth floor, but there were two on the fourth, where she was sitting. She heard a door open and close. It was a neighbor on a lower floor. *Just get to the main door of the apartment building, Ava. If you want to turn around from there, you'll turn around.* She closed her eyes, held the rail, and continued down the stairs. There were only three flights left.

Run, Ava, run! The building is on fire, the building is on fire, the building is on fire. She ran down the stairs, flames licking at her heels. *Go, go, go.* What a racket she made, *clunk, clunk, clunk* in Beverly's flats. *Fire, fire, fire, fire.* By the time she reached the main door to the building she had to stop, bend over, and gasp for air. She did it. She made it down four flights of stairs. How was that for a little cardio? She wished there were a water fountain nearby. Why hadn't she thought of bringing bottled water? Because she was going across the street, not to the Sahara Desert.

She pushed open the main door as if it were a perfectly normal thing for her to do. She pushed through a roar that was sounding in her head. Outside; she was outside. The ground swayed again. She grabbed on to the rail. Five steps here. Then she'd be on the sidewalk. Five steps. She was outside. She brought out Aunt Beverly's note, the one she found in the sofa cushion. *BREATHE.* She did. She focused on the word as she inhaled. Then exhaled. She was sweating. How did people remain pretty while outside? She realized her eyes were closed. She forced them open, but stared at her feet. *One thing at a time.*

There was no official crosswalk in front of her building; it was just a little side street. She would have to walk almost half a block farther to cross at a light. *Don't think; just move.* She darted across the street. Cars, it was jammed with cars. *Shit.* She wasn't thinking about the cars at all. She watched in horror as a black sedan barreled toward her. She squeezed her eyes shut. She heard tires squeal, and horns blare. She opened one eye. The black sedan had stopped barely an inch from her. Other cars were jammed up next to it. The drivers were all laying on their horns. Ava's heart beat so loudly she was sure everyone could hear it. She couldn't believe what she'd done. To her, the outside was so terrifying that truly dangerous things—like running out into traffic—hardly seemed frightening at all. That's what was going to get her killed. *Move, Ava; you have to get out of the street. Move.* But she couldn't. It was as if she were paralyzed.

"Bloody hell. Are you trying to get fucking killed?" *No. I'm*

just no longer in control of my body. I'm trapped. Maybe my body is try-
ing to get me killed. What in the world did one do about that?

"Get out of the fucking way!" Horns kept blaring and the
threats kept coming. She still couldn't move. People were stopped
on either side of the street, staring, and trying to figure out why
someone would stand in the middle of traffic. The man she
sketched, the Middle Eastern or Indian one, was leaning against
his building, smoking his cigarette. He moved toward her as
angry horns continued to beep. Ava watched as he walked out
into the street and held up his hands to the cars. He came right
up to Ava, took her by the elbow, and began to pull her across
the street. She let him. When they reached the curb, he helped
her up, and then walked away. She froze again. She wanted to
call after him. Thank him. She couldn't speak. A mute, standing on the sidewalk in London. But she had made it down four
flights of steps and across the street to the grocery store. She
was pathetic. Because the thought of crossing the street again
was swallowing her whole. The man she sketched was watching
her. He came toward her again while others brushed past. One
man hit her with his briefcase. They looked much nicer when
she was sketching them from above.

"Are you all right?" He had an Indian accent, so she was
wrong about him being Middle Eastern. His accent was light,
mixed with a bit of a British accent. Maybe he had lived here
most of his life. Ava pointed to the market like the Grim
Reaper, hoping he'd understand. She couldn't speak. "Sainsbury's?" he said. "You want to go to market?" She nodded. He
held out his arm and she took it. Together they walked the few
steps to the market. The moment they were inside Ava felt a
rush of cool air. There. She was here.

It was huge. So big. Open and wide. Not too busy, but it didn't
look this big on the outside. This was a huge mistake. The young
man looked at her. Was he waiting for a tip? She should give him
one, but she only had twenty pounds.

"Thank you." It came out like a whisper.

"Right then," he said. He was gone. She missed him. The lights
were so bright. So painful. She put her hands over her eyes and

bent over. Two Xanax hadn't been enough; she should have brought the bottle with her. All the things ignorant people always said to her bombarded her:

If you just force yourself to do it, you'll be fine.
What's the worst that can happen? It's not going to kill you.
It's all in your head.
Everybody has to force themselves to go out once in a while.
You just want attention.
You must be exaggerating.
It can't be that bad, can it?
Yes. It freaking can. Screw them. Screw all of them. This wasn't for attention. Ava wanted to die.

"Hallo?"

Ava removed her hands, stood up, and opened her eyes. A few feet away a girl with short spikey blond hair was openly watching her. She had on a Sainsbury's apron. She had tattoos up and down her arm and a nose ring. She was stocking shelves. Ava wondered if they let her behind the counter looking like that. Not that there was anything wrong with the way she looked, but Ava figured most places in England would be a bit . . . proper about their staff. She glanced at the people behind the registers. It was hard to tell what they looked like because the colored dots had arrived.

"You all right, luv?" The girl was in front of Ava holding a can of Heinz beans. "You look like you're going to do a header."

"I have twenty pounds," Ava said. "You can have half of it if you just get me something to eat, anything, and then"—Ava pointed behind her—"help me back into that building across the street."

"You're the girl who just stopped traffic," she said. "Almost got yourself killed, did you?"

"I didn't mean to."

"What's wrong with you? Are you mental?"

"I'm dizzy. I might, as you say, do a header."

"What do you want to eat?"

"Bread. Butter." *Like prison.* "Lunch meat. Fruit?" Ava didn't know if she had enough for all that. "Espresso," Ava said to the girl's back.

The girl picked up a basket as Ava stood still. Her pink dress was getting soaked in sweat. She hated herself. This wasn't worth it. She'd rather starve inside her flat. So much for walking in Beverly's shoes. She was still Ava. She closed her eyes.

"Miss?" Someone touched her on the elbow. She jumped. "Why don't you just come over here." She let the person move her. She didn't open her eyes. Soon she was leaning against a counter. "Victoria will come get you when she rings out. Did you bring bags?"

Ava opened one eye. "Bags?"

"Most people care for the environment. So they bring bags. They care about the seals and the birds, they do."

"I didn't bring bags."

"Right then."

"But I do care. I care about the birds, and other sea creatures, all of them. I care about all of them and I don't want them getting caught in my plastic."

"Right, so," the clerk said. "You didn't care this morning though, did you?"

This was even more humiliating than she'd ever imagined. Why didn't she just order in? "Do you have delivery? Can I order online?" He just stared at her. "You could come get bags from me first, and then you could deliver."

"You want us to come get bags from you, then bring them back here, just so we can deliver them to you all over again?"

"Pretty much. But. You know. Filled with food the second time."

"That's outrageous."

"Not if you care about the environment."

"You're a cheeky one, aren't you?"

"Do you deliver?"

"We deliver after two from Monday to Thursday. Do you live far?"

"Across the street."

"Across the street." He pointed. She nodded. "And you want

us to deliver?" He said it like he was disgusted with her. Like he thought she was rich and lazy. Like she didn't give a shit about poor sea creatures. Why didn't she bring bags?

"I have a disability."

"What is it?"

He wasn't going to believe her. She could see it in his eyes. He would think she was a nutter. She leaned in and lowered her voice. "Actually, I'm conducting an experiment."

The clerk looked around. "Am I on a hidden camera show? A practical joke, like?"

"I'm an actress," Ava said. "Researching a role."

"What sort of role?"

"I play a lazy, septic American woman who loves plastic bags despite the fact that they clog up the oceans and kill innocent sea creatures. It's a terrible role, about a terrible woman, living an awful life. But it's union work. Pays pretty good."

The clerk nodded. "Would I have seen you in anything?"

"Do you watch American television?"

"I watch loads of it."

"I'm only on Canadian television," Ava said.

"Oh, right, so."

This was torture. Where was Victoria? Finally Ava saw her spikey blond hair.

"Vic," the man talking to Ava said. "She's an actress. Canadian television."

"Right," Vic said. "No wonder I don't recognize her."

"Why don't you help our actress home with her plastic bags?"

"You didn't bring bags?" Vic said.

"Sue me," Ava said.

"Right," Vic said. She turned to the male clerk. "Then a smoke break?"

"I thought you were going to quit that filthy habit."

"I thought you were going to lose two stone."

"Be back at half past." The man bowed to Ava, glared at Vic, and then strode off.

"Do you mind?" Ava said.

"Don't be daft. Off we go then."

CHAPTER 16

Vic walked fast. Too fast. She wasn't frightened of the outdoors at all. But since she had Ava's groceries, Ava didn't yell at her to stop or slow down. Maybe sprinting was the way to go. Maybe if Ava sprinted everywhere she went she would be cured. Bag boys could stand on the curb in front of Sainsbury's and Ava would just zoom by and grab them.

"Ava!" Vic yelled at her. *What?* Ava had just taken a few steps into the street. A car whipped toward her from the opposite direction. It was going the wrong way. This was it. She was going to die. Everyone was wrong. It was just as bad as Ava had imagined it. Powerful arms grabbed her from behind and yanked her to the sidewalk just as the car screeched to a halt. Horns everywhere blared, and the driver of the car and those of every other car on the street were honking at Ava like the European version of *Groundhog Day*. She still didn't even know who saved her, or whether or not she was glad the person did; she was doubled over, dealing with the *thump, thump, thump* in her head. Twice in one day? Who runs into traffic twice in one day? Outside was no place for her. It was no place! Here came the colored dots. The nausea. Maybe this time she really was going to die. Would Jasper think about her from time to time?

"What's happening? Were you hit?" A male voice with an accent. A dark head appeared on the sidewalk. The man was lying on the ground in order to make eye contact with Ava. It was the Indian man once again.

"Twice in one day," Ava said. Her tongue was thick. Maybe it was swelling inside her mouth and soon she wouldn't be able to breathe.

"You owe me two lifetimes," the man said with a smile.

"What's that?" It was Vic. She was out of breath, standing next to the Indian man. She was pointing to something on the sidewalk.

"It's mine," he said. "I dropped it to help her. She just ran right out into the middle of the street. Again!"

"She's American," Vic said. "But for some reason she's on Canadian telly."

"No wonder I didn't recognize her," he said.

"Is that fertilizer?" Vic asked.

Ava moved her head slightly. Sure enough, splattered on the sidewalk was a trail of fertilizer, next to a large, torn bag discarded on the sidewalk.

"I dropped it to save her," the man said.

"Why do you need fertilizer?" Vic asked.

"I have a garden," the man said. "Do you have a problem with that?"

"The coppers might," Vic said. "That's a big bag."

"Very paranoid of you, and very racist."

"If you see something, say something," Vic said.

"Oh yes? And what is it that you see? I am from Bombay."

"Bomb," Vic said. She curled up her nose.

"You're a nasty girl. And here I just saved your mate's life."

"She's not my mate," Vic and Ava said at the same time. Ava couldn't hold herself up anymore; she landed on her knees on the sidewalk.

"You have a garden in the West End?" Vic just wasn't going to quit. Ava had assumed because of her tattoos and piercings that she was more of an open-minded sort. She was wrong about everything and everyone.

"I built a garden in the alley," the man said. "I'd show it to you, but I don't like you." He knelt down near Ava. "Be more careful crossing the street."

"I'm sorry," Ava said.

"He could be making a bomb," Vic said.

"You'd need a lot more fertilizer than my one bag," the man said. "A hundred bags. Maybe more."

"Oh, is that so, is it? How would you know?"

Ava had to get home. She didn't care about groceries. She'd have to arrange to be completely knocked out when it was time to go back to America. Maybe they could drug her and put her on a ship. But go home to where? They'd probably rented out her house. And she didn't have a job anymore. She didn't belong anywhere. She might as well just rot and die here, and get added to the fertilizer.

"Is there something wrong with her?" the man asked Vic.

"She's a shut-in," Vic said.

"I never told you that," Ava said.

"I know panic attacks," Vic said. She looked at the man. "What's your name?"

"Deven."

"Deven?" Vic said.

"It means 'one who pleases others.' " Deven stared Vic down. Vic's pale face immediately flushed as she stared back at him. Then she stuck her chest out and began playing with her hair.

"I'm Ava," Ava said with a little wave of her hand.

"Nice to meet you!" Deven leaned down and yelled it in her ear.

"Not deaf," Ava said.

"Is she ever going to get up?" Deven said.

"I'll help you get your fertilizer inside if you help me carry her across the street," Vic said.

Ava wanted to argue, but she knew if she tried to stand on her own her legs wouldn't work. They would buckle. She would fall again. She wanted Jasper.

"You're supposed to look right before you cross," Vic said. "It even says so on the street. There's an arrow and everything."

"Thanks," Ava said. Was sarcasm universal? She needed a mobile. If she had one she could call Jasper. What was he doing right now? Sitting in his office with a cup of tea? Did he ever go to court? Did he think Ava was a total nutter?

Vic dropped Ava's groceries next to her. People going by looked at the three of them, but nobody stopped. Deven and Vic were soon holding the broken bag of fertilizer between them and scooting it toward the nondescript building next to the grocery store. Ava remained on the sidewalk. She was trembling. Her stupid body. *Just try it. Try picking up your groceries and crossing the street again.* Ava grabbed the bags. She took a deep breath. She stood. Blood rushed to her head. Vertigo hit hard and fast and it was no joke. She wasn't experiencing a bit of dizziness; the entire sidewalk was flipping over her head. Everything but her, around her, in front of her, above her, was moving.

"Oh, God, help me." Ava squeezed her eyes shut. She took a tiny step. The world tilted. This wasn't fair. She had tried to go to the grocery store. Was that so wrong? Why was this happening to her? Why couldn't she just go to the fucking grocery store?

"Ava?"

"Jasper?" She let out a sob at the sound of his voice. Where did he come from? Before she could censor herself, she threw herself into his arms. He was stiff at first, then wrapped his arms around her.

"It's all right," he said. "I've got you."

"Everything's spinning," Ava said. "Like a ride at a carnival. Make it stop."

"I've got you," he said again. Before Ava knew what was going on, Jasper had scooped Ava and her groceries into his arms and was crossing the street. Ava didn't mention Vic or Deven—they chose a bag of fertilizer and their lustful hormones over her; screw them.

Jasper jogged across the street. Ava was petite, but she still felt bad; she couldn't be easy to carry while jogging. But she didn't say a word. She wanted to get inside more than she wanted anything else in the entire world. And soon he was opening the front door and the cool, dark hallway greeted her. Ava let out her breath, which came out as a sob. Jasper set her down and Ava stumbled, then grasped the railing to the stairs. She held onto it like a life raft. The relief was immediate. But her legs were still shaking.

"What are you doing here?" she asked Jasper.

"Queenie called me about his lucky charm," he said. "Was just popping by when I saw you on the sidewalk."

"Looking pathetic."

"Looking as if you needed a hand."

"Thank you."

"It really is difficult for you, isn't it?"

"Torture. It's torture."

"I'm so sorry." Jasper pointed to one of the bags in Ava's hands. "But looks like you made it."

"With a little help from strangers." *Who abandoned me for a bag of shit.*

"It still counts."

"It's not on the list though, is it?"

"I don't think your aunt Beverly quite understood the nature of your difficulties."

"She's not the only one. I don't understand it myself."

"Let's just get up and have a cup of tea, shall we?"

"Is that the British answer for everything? A cup of tea?"

"I'll pour you a Scotch too. Just don't tell Queenie."

"Now you're talking, mate," Ava said.

Ava sat on her emerald stool while Jasper moved about the kitchen. She liked him being here. Hell, she just liked him. He hummed as he put the kettle on and set teacups on the kitchen table. It was a ceremony, a ritual. Even if Ava wasn't as nuts about tea, she could see the pleasure in having a ritual. Across the way Vic and Deven were standing on the sidewalk looking at the spot Ava had previously occupied. Ava had to laugh. She felt sort of bad, but then again, they did abandon her. If they were to look up they might see Ava through the window and Ava could wave. *Oh, shoot.* They were crossing the street. Soon the buzzer shrieked through the flat. Ava jumped. How did they know which flat she was in? They must be buzzing every single unit to see which one she would answer. If they kept this up, all her neighbors would hate her. Good Lord, Beverly must have had a hearing loss. She was going to have to do something about that monstrous noise before she had a hearing loss too. In the kitchen, a teacup rattled against a plate and Jasper yelped. He popped his head into the living room. "That about took my eardrum off."

"Right?" Ava was relieved it wasn't just her. For a moment she had wondered if staying inside all the time had increased all of her senses.

"Are you expecting company?"

"It's the girl from Sainsbury's," Ava said. "Probably checking on me."

"I can go."

"No. Please. Unless . . . you have to go."

"I made time in my schedule for the visit."

"Great. I'll just get rid of her." The intercom buzzed again. Ava pushed TALK. "Hello?"

"Ava?"

"Hi, Vic," Ava said. "What do you want?"

"Crikey. You vanished."

"Sorry."

"What happened?"

"Made it home."

"Are you being held against your will?" Ava felt someone staring at her. She lifted her head and made eye contact with Jasper. Very long eye contact.

"Oh, do say yes," Jasper said. Ava laughed.

"I'm fine, thank you." Ava started to walk away.

"Deven has a garden in the alley. It's brilliant." Apparently Vic thought the intercom was a telephone. Ava went back and pushed TALK.

"That's great."

"I have a green thumb, not a trigger finger," Deven piped in. Vic laughed. Loudly. Ava didn't need to see her to know that she was probably playing with her hair and pushing her chest out again.

"See you later," Ava said.

"Order your groceries online next time," Vic said.

"Got it," Ava said. She turned to Jasper with a smile and a shake of her head.

" 'A green thumb, not a trigger finger'?" Jasper said.

"Apparently he's a gardener and not a terrorist."

"That's London for you," Jasper said. "A story on every corner." He was putting away her groceries. Ava should help, but she loved that he was doing it for her, so she watched instead. She brought her hand up to her hair, and then touched her neck where a little pulse had started to beat. Her neck felt strange. Why did it feel strange? Naked. Queenie's lucky charm! It was gone. *Oh, no.* Had it fallen off in the grocery store, or in the street, or on the sidewalk?

"Are you all right?"

"Fine, fine." She should tell Jasper she had lost Queenie's lucky charm. He could go out right now and look for it. But she didn't want him to leave. Even more to the point, she didn't want him to think she was the kind of flatmate who wore other people's things. She had just been trying to keep it close so she'd remember to give it to Jasper. So far Jasper hadn't mentioned it. Which meant he was truly here to see her and he'd forgotten all about it. Ava didn't have time to analyze that; there would be hours, maybe days, to indulge in that later. Tell him or don't tell him? *Shoot.* Maybe Vic or Deven had found the charm. She'd call Vic at the market later and ask. Otherwise there was no way Ava would be able to trace her steps, and there was also no way she could admit to Queenie that she'd worn it and lost it. No way. She wanted to grab her binoculars and see if she could spot the charm, but she didn't know how she'd explain it to Jasper.

They sat, and Jasper drank tea, and Ava drank Scotch out of

a teacup. So civilized. After the third sip, a sly smile stole across Jasper's face.

"What?" Ava said.

"Anything good on telly lately?" He was talking about the porn. Ava froze. Then he laughed. It was funny. He was funny. Finally, Ava laughed too.

"I was so mortified."

"Ah, it's perfectly natural, I suppose."

"You suppose. Like you never watch porn."

"As a teenaged boy, sure. I could have been Wanker of the Year. But never when I thought someone could walk in on me."

"I certainly didn't expect you to barge in either!"

"That was quite obvious."

"What did they say about me?"

"They?"

"Hillary. Queenie. Do they think I'm a pervert?"

"Oh, yes. They do."

"Damn it."

"What do you care?"

"Do you think I'm a pervert?"

"In a good way." Ava laughed again and looked at Jasper. He stared back. He was so close. He shot up and moved to the counter. He leaned against it and folded his arms across his chest. He was muscular beneath that gray suit. Ava had an urge to press her body against his, to feel his stomach plastered to her stomach. And she definitely wanted to kiss him. Instead she took a sip of Scotch from a cup meant for tea. Maybe the Brits weren't as civilized as they appeared. Maybe they drank all that tea to cover up all the perverted thoughts they had. Maybe she would start drinking a boatload of tea.

"Why did you move over there?" Ava asked.

"Because I wanted to kiss you."

CHAPTER 17

Ava put her teacup down and stood. "I would have kissed you back." There it was. In the open. An admission. They were here. Admitting their attraction. Queenie was gone. The bedroom was so very close.

"Would you have?" It was a challenge. He was flirting with her.

"Don't believe me?"

"The proof is in the pudding." Ava headed for him as he came toward her. They stopped when there was barely an inch between them. Jasper's hand trailed down her body, and she shivered. He leaned in to kiss her.

"I'd make a horrible girlfriend," Ava said.

"You're not too good at the sweet talk either."

Ava laughed, then quickly stopped. "You deserve better. You deserve someone adventurous."

"I see. Such as someone who packs up and moves to another country?"

"It's the only thing I've ever done."

"You don't give yourself enough credit." He looked at her lips. "I want you."

"I want you too." He pulled her into him. Before she could ruin it again, his mouth was on hers and he was kissing her like she'd never been kissed in her entire life. So much for nice guys being boring. The kiss was electric. When he released her he left her wanting more.

"I might be gone in eighty days."

Jasper put his hand on his head. "God. I'm around you for any length of time and every ounce of intelligence drains right out of me. You make me incredibly stupid."

"Great speech, Romeo. Was 'You complete me' getting old?"

"What?"

"Not a fan of American movies, I take it."

"I'm quite fond of American movies. And television—" Jasper tried to keep a straight face, but ended up laughing. "Just like you might be a fan of *Downton Abbey* or, uh, *British After Dark*."

"All right, all right."

"Their acronym is 'BAD.' Pretty good, right?" He pulled her in and nuzzled her.

"You were saying how stupid you were?"

He laughed. "I am. Because I forgot to tell you the good news. The most amazing news."

"What?"

"Now, it's not for sure, but it's a good sign. A very good sign indeed."

"How long are you going to drag this out?"

"Sorry. I must admit I like to tease."

"It's not a bad skill to have." They locked eyes, and she could tell they were both thinking of making love.

"Indeed."

"Sorry. The good news."

"The almost good news."

"The almost good news."

"Queenie has an audition for television in a fortnight."

"Oh. Good for him." She tried not to sound disappointed. She had thought the news had something to do with her.

Jasper laughed. "Not just good for him. He told me himself. If he gets on telly, he'll be making plenty of money."

"Again. Good for him."

"Enough money to get his own place."

"His own place. You mean?"

"He said he'd sign over the flat to you. You won't have to do a thing on that list. No more worry, no more stress, no more ticking clocks. This will be home, Ava. Your home. That is, if you want it to be."

"More than I've ever wanted anything in my life."

"And it's my fondest wish that you'll be open to this." He pulled her in and kissed her again.

"Queenie would really do that for me?"

"He's grown quite fond of you too. I told you it paid to be on his good side."

"I can't believe it. That's amazing news. Do you think he'll get it?"

"The part calls for an aging drag queen."

"Oh my God. That's exactly how he refers to himself."

"It's fate."

"It's a miracle."

"He's even booked himself a rehearsal room for the next month. Going to give it all he has. I just need to pick up his lucky charm, and I'll be off."

"Oh," Ava said. *Oh, God.*

"Don't worry," Jasper said, misreading the look on her face. "I'll be back." He put his hand on her chin and tilted her face up. "And maybe we can pick up with some teasing?"

Ava's hand fluttered to her neck. "Does he ever audition without his lucky charm?"

Jasper laughed. "The queen go without his crowning jewel? Never. He's the most superstitious bloke I know."

"Oh, God."

"You look pale. What's wrong?"

"It's gone," she said. "I lost it."

"You're joking, right? Tell me you're joking."

"I wore it to the market. For good luck." Ava pointed at the windows. "When I came back, it was gone. Not very lucky after all, is it?"

Jasper ran his hands through his hair. "I'd better go look for it. You went across the street at the light—"

"No. I crossed right where you come out the door."

"But that's right in the middle of traffic."

"I'm aware."

"You ran out into the middle of traffic?"

"Not on purpose. I was so focused on making it across, I just didn't look."

"Didn't you see all the cars?"

"I did when they almost hit me."

"My God."

"He's never going to forgive me, is he?"

"I'll find it. So the middle of the street, the footpath, then I suppose I have to search the entire market."

"Where did he get the charm? I can buy him a new one."

"I'm afraid you can't. It was given to him by someone very special."

"Would he know it wasn't the same one?"

"It was from a special celebration at the Globe Theatre. They don't make them anymore." Jasper headed for the door.

"I'm so, so sorry," Ava said.

Jasper hurried back to her, grabbed her, and kissed her. "I'm going to find it. But if I don't . . ."

"Yes?"

"You have to let me tell Queenie that I lost it."

Ava shook her head. "I won't let you do that."

"You have to. He's going to go nuclear. You wouldn't have a chance of staying in the flat then."

Unless she completed everything on the list. But Jasper didn't have to say that. Because he'd seen her today. He knew she wasn't faking it. He knew she couldn't do it. "But he's your friend. He'll be mad at you."

"Mad? No. He'll never speak to me again."

"I can't let that happen."

"And I can't lose you. I've never met anyone quite like you."

"Thank you. I think."

He tilted her head up, and kissed her. Slowly. Purposefully. Then, he let go. "Wish me British luck."

"The Best of the British to you."

He winked. "I'm going to find it." And then he was gone.

For a full minute she stood, tracing her lips with her finger, trying to memorize everything about his kiss. She prayed he found the charm, but if he didn't she couldn't let him take the blame. She ran to the windows and grabbed the binoculars. Jasper stood on the footpath trying to stare out into the middle of the street. There were too many cars. Besides, if it was there, it would be destroyed. He must have come to the same conclusion, for he headed to the stoplight, where all the sane people crossed. Should she tell Queenie and just get it over with? Should she just pack it up and go home? How much was a lucky charm worth these days? If Ava found one that cured her agoraphobia, it would be priceless. Why did she have to put it on, and take it outside? What in the world was wrong with her? How could one well-meaning person cause so much trouble in so little time?

CHAPTER 18

Ten days. Jasper had managed to stall Queenie for ten days. Some poppycock about how the lucky charm would work best if he didn't wear it until the audition. But now that was four days away and Queenie was foaming at the mouth. In the next hour, over a friendly lunch, Jasper would have to break it to Queenie that his lifeline was gone. Jasper could think of a million things he'd rather do, including what he was doing now, strolling down Oxford Street, with Hillary at his side. Just like he'd done a million different ways on a million different days. Except it felt different this time. Because he was different. They were different. But he wanted Hillary at the lunch so that she could offer Queenie a bit of comfort when Jasper cut his heart with the news. There was no time to lose; Ava was on the verge of a breakdown, and several times had almost confessed to Queenie that she lost the charm. Jasper couldn't let that happen. She had enough stress in her life without living with an enemy. And if Queenie knew she was the one who lost the charm, there was no doubt about it: his wrath would rival every wicked Queen in fairy-tale land. The only shred of hope now was if Queenie realized how silly it was to be so attached to an inanimate object, to infuse it with so much power. *Buck up. You can win this audition on your own, mate.* It made Jasper shudder to even think about saying it.

Ava Wilder. He'd been saying her name to himself for the past couple of days, as if it would help him piece together the puzzle of her. He'd told her the truth. He'd certainly never met anyone like her. His feelings had taken him completely by surprise, and he was normally so prepared for everything. Hillary was chatting away on her mobile, which normally drove Jasper mental. Today, he was relieved that she was otherwise occupied. Jasper wanted to think about Ava. No. He had no control over it whatsoever. He couldn't stop thinking about Ava.

"No, no, no," Hillary said. "I know the match will be lovely this year; I'm so looking forward to it." The person on the other end of the mobile must have said something hilarious, for Hillary threw her head back and laughed. It was one of the less than perfect things about Hillary Swanson. Her laugh sounded like an animal being butchered. Hard to believe he'd actually contemplated living with that for the rest of his life. Not that he'd ever say a thing like that to her.

Jasper wasn't good at hurting anything. People, animals, including insects. He was a scooper. See a fly in the flat and he'd grab the nearest newspaper, spend way too much time trying to scoop the fly up and let it go. Not that Hillary was a fly. If she were any insect she'd be more of the stinging type.

Oxford Street was alive. There were the usual tourists window shopping, vagrants begging, kids whizzing by on skateboards, traffic jams, the typical buzz of London on a Saturday morning. "Cheerio." Hillary dropped her phone into her handbag. They stood in front of Marks & Spencer. Jasper took one look at the swarms of people coming in and out and stopped.

"Care to step in for a bit?" Hillary said. It wasn't so much a question as a command.

"Actually, I don't care to step in at all." God, he'd always wanted to say that. It felt just as good as he'd always imagined.

"We'll just pop in and pop out."

"The last time you said that we went in on a summer's day and came out to three inches of snow." Hillary laughed and clobbered him with her handbag.

Did Ava like to shop? She wouldn't like getting to the shop, but would she like it once she was inside? He wished he could build her a series of tunnels to the world. He didn't understand much about her affliction. Fear of the marketplace. That certainly ruled out Oxford Street, or all of London, he supposed. It was one giant shopping extravaganza. Jasper used to be a bit afraid of the marketplace himself. Especially when it came to Hillary and her charge card. Another thing he didn't have to worry about anymore. Faults aside, Hillary was a beautiful, decent girl. But recently it had occurred to Jasper that he didn't want a decent girl. He wanted someone imperfect and indecent. Someone like Ava.

"What?" Hillary said. "You've been acting the fool all day."

"I'm sorry," Jasper said. "I can't do this."

One of Hillary's perfectly arched eyebrows shot up. "Oh for God's sake. I'll meet up with you at the pub then."

"Righto." Hillary squinted and gave him a look. He'd better watch himself. Hillary had a keen eye for a lie. *Rubbish.* On top of it all, Jasper was going to have to try to eat with a subzero appetite.

"Cheerio." Hillary kissed Jasper on the cheek. First the left, then the right.

"Cheerio," Jasper said. Hillary started off. "Wait." She stopped. Maybe he shouldn't be doing this, testing her, but he just had to confirm something. He reached into his pocket and handed her the brochure. The one he'd been keeping in his breast pocket all week. It was a flyer for his upcoming stand-up debut. If they were going to be friends, he ought to be able to share his hopes and dreams. Hillary glanced at the flyer.

"You're too polite." She swooshed it away like it was an insect.

"Pardon?"

"Either don't take it, or take it and drop it like everyone

else." This time Hillary yanked it out of his hand and dropped it on the ground. "See?" she said. She churned it into the ground with her heel. Jasper stared at it. It never crossed her mind for a second that he was trying to share something with her about his life. Ava had learned more about him in one taxi ride than Hillary had in years.

"Half-one?" She looked at him.

"Half-one," Jasper said. Hillary nodded, then disappeared into the swarm. Jasper bent down and picked up his flyer. *THE LAUGHING DEN. Open Mic Night.* He looked at the date. Thursday week. Not long now. A jolly good endeavor even if he wouldn't have any friends in the audience. He knew he'd be imagining Ava in the front row cheering him on, warming him with her American laugh. Screw Hillary. What had he ever seen in that woman? He smoothed it out the best he could and put it back in his breast pocket.

It felt wrong. To be sitting at a cheerful pub, just a five-minute walk from Ava's flat, yet they all knew there was zero chance she would walk through the door. Would she like it? This old English pub with the dark interior, animal heads on the wall, and over a hundred beers on tap? This was one of the happier pubs in London, for it drew in a lot of tourists. Tourists thought London was jolly. Pubs with smiling bartenders. Original copies of Dickens's novels lining the shelves. Royalty. Architecture. Shopping. Curried chips. Hop-on, hop-off buses. Trafalgar Square, and Buckingham Palace, and Big Ben, and Westminster Abbey, and the Thames, and the London Eye. Perhaps even the pigeons seemed exotic. Cheerio!

They didn't stay long enough for the weather, garbage, expense, or even loneliness to get into their veins. Maybe Ava was better off only seeing London from her windows. Maybe it would remain a jolly place. Still, that wasn't really living, was it? Jasper couldn't imagine being afraid of the outdoors. He would do anything to help her, anything.

In the meantime, Jasper was regretting that he hadn't tried to talk Beverly out of the list. One thing was for sure. She wouldn't have concocted it if she knew how deep Ava's disorder really was. It wasn't just a matter of "forcing her out of her comfort zone." Beverly meant well, but it wasn't going to help anyone. As long as she wanted it, the flat was intended for Ava. Jasper knew it for a fact. The problem was, he wasn't sure Queenie saw it that way.

Jasper waited while Queenie got comfortable. Eating, for Queenie, was pure pleasure, an art form. First Queenie moved his pint glass to his left. Then he took his silverware out of his napkin and arranged it on the table, next he placed his napkin on his lap, and finally he gazed at the plate of curried chips in front of him with undisguised lust. Jasper let him enjoy a few bites before he began.

"When I saw Ava less than a fortnight ago, she was outside, coming back from Sainsbury's."

Queenie let his fork clatter to his plate. He looked outraged. "She didn't bring home a turkey."

"I think she was too busy trying to *breathe.*"

"I basted him for days." Queenie met Jasper's look. "The turkey," he added.

"This affliction isn't just in her head. She almost got hit by a car. She looked like someone having a heart attack."

"It does run in the family."

"Don't say that."

"Sorry." Queenie took another bite of his curried chips while Jasper drank his beer. "I've been warned to watch my cholesterol meself." He paused midair, another chip heading toward his mouth. He stared at it as if contemplating his next move, then shrugged. "I'll start tomorrow." He devoured the chip.

"You do know that Beverly fully intended the flat to go to Ava no matter what."

Queenie was slow to respond. That wasn't a good sign. He took his time setting down his fork, then dabbed his lip, put his napkin in his lap and looked at Jasper. "So?"

"So. It was meant as encouragement. Motivation. You know how Beverly felt about motivation."

Queenie lifted his head and became very serious. "Motivation is everything."

"Exactly. Beverly wanted Ava to have an adventure. The list was a 'Welcome to London' gesture, not a forced death march."

Queenie squinted at Jasper, then poked his fork at him. "That's exactly what Ava said about the list. Forced death march."

"Did she now? She put it just like that?"

"Don't play me. You two are conspiring against me!"

"I swear to you. I never heard her put it like that. How do you like that?" Jasper grinned. "Great minds think alike."

Queenie jabbed at his chips. "How does this concern *moi?*"

"You got me thinking when you generously offered to let Ava have the flat if you get on telly—"

"Hold your horses." Queenie put his hand up. "I didn't say it for a fact. I said I would consider it. But only if I took the lead and the show was going to be picked up. It was a bit of daydreaming." He set his pint down and stared at Jasper. "You didn't say anything to her, did you?" Jasper shook his head. "Vocalize it."

"Mate, listen. We have to tell her the flat is hers no matter what."

"But it's not."

"Yes, it is."

"It's in writing. If Ava doesn't complete the list in seventy days—tick, tock, tick, tock—then I get the flat."

"Beverly just didn't want the flat abandoned. She didn't want Ava to sell it or, worse, she didn't want Gretchen Wilder to profit from it. She wanted Ava to live here. In a strange way it was her last attempt to feel close to Ava."

"What's your point, barrister boy?"

"If Beverly were alive and saw the extent of Ava's agoraphobia, she would drop the stipulations immediately. And you know it." Jasper wasn't normally so direct. But he could see Queenie's wheels churning. Jasper was there when Beverly broke the news of the flat to Queenie. He understood it was to go to Ava no matter what.

"You're saying I should just hand over the flat, even if she doesn't complete the list?"

"Yes. As long as Ava lives here for one year, the flat is hers no matter what."

Queenie sighed. "I've already compromised by saying I'd think about giving her the flat if I get the part on telly. I don't want to discuss it anymore. Now where's my lucky charm?" Queenie held his hand out.

"Beverly would be ashamed of you."

Queenie gasped and jabbed his fork at Jasper. "Take that back."

Jasper should have saved that one for later. After he admitted he lost the lucky charm. Now Queenie would be even more riled up. Jasper had seen Queenie throw fits before. He certainly didn't want to be on the receiving end of one.

"Can't you even try to put yourself in her place? Imagine if you lost your lucky charm. How well would you do without it?" *What are you doing? Easy, mate. You're walking the plank, lad.*

"I certainly wouldn't lock myself in the flat and never come out."

"Very well, you're not getting it back." *Brilliant. Or stupid. Definitely stupid. You wanker.*

Queenie stuck his hand out. "Give it."

"No." Bloody hell, what was he doing? It just fell out of his mouth.

"I'll sue."

"Funny, that's what Ava is threatening too."

Queenie gasped again. Jasper wished he'd quit doing that. Forget cholesterol, all that gasping couldn't be good for Queenie's heart either. "You would honestly keep my lucky charm. The one given to me by my dead lover?"

"You intend on keeping the flat. The one not really given to you by your dead friend."

"Should I be contacting another barrister?"

"Why? Because I'm trying to talk some sense into you?"

"Because you have a conflict of interest." Queenie made the proclamation as loud and dramatic as he could, complete with an outstretched arm and a finger pointed at Jasper. Given the width of the table, Queenie's finger was now less than an inch from Jasper's nose. For a moment he considered snapping at it.

"You've got the wrong end of the stick. I'm trying to uphold Beverly's intentions."

"That's not what I was referring to."

"Out with it."

"You have romantic feelings for Ava. How do you think Beverly would feel about that?" Queenie leaned in and lowered his voice. "Not to mention Hillary." A cheer rang out from the group of rugby players. Jasper looked around just in case Hillary or anyone who remotely knew her was in the vicinity.

"I don't know what you're talking about."

"Oh, please. The two of you have been struck with the stupid stick. Do you know what's more annoying than a flatmate who never leaves? A flatmate that never stops smiling." *She feels the same way. She feels the same way. Smiling.* Like Jasper was doing right now. Queenie wagged his fork in Jasper's face. "See? What a load of bollocks. A month ago you were pining over Hillary like a man about to kill Cupid."

"Speaking of Hillary," Jasper said.

"We won't. At least I certainly won't." Queenie retreated as far as he could into his side of the booth. He was frightened of his own niece. It was like watching a vicious tiger turn into a mewling house cat.

"She's been very attentive lately. Do you think she's still in love with me?"

"She's a bloodhound. She doesn't want you back, Jasper. She just doesn't want to see you with a Septic."

"Well, that's none of her business now, is it?"

Queenie gasped. "Don't play with fire."

"You're saying I'm not supposed to date Ava because my ex-girlfriend wouldn't like it?"

"Wouldn't like it? She'd burn down the flat."

"Fuck."

"You wouldn't be able. Not after she was done with your balls."

"Queenie."

"Better I say it now than let you suffer later."

"You need to help me."

"Help you chop off your own head? It would be my pleasure. How can I help?" Queenie held up his index finger. "And before you ask, I'm all out of rusty axes."

"Why don't you feel Hillary out for me? See if it would bother her if I was to start seeing Ava." It was ridiculous to be worrying about this. Hillary was the one who dumped him. He shouldn't give a fop about her feelings. But Hillary was lethal when it came to jealousy. It was her worst quality. And Jasper didn't care how she treated him, but he certainly didn't want her plotting against Ava. *God, women.* When it came down to Hillary and Ava, Hillary was truly the crazy one. Why had that been so appealing to him before? Thank God. Thank God he was no longer under her spell. Or rather, thank Ava.

"Stay away from Ava."

"What if I can't? What if I'm in—"

"NO." Queenie banged his spoon against his pint glass as if he were about to give a big speech. "Do not say that. You're mental. This is lust, nothing more."

"It's not just lust."

"It's mostly lust. It'll pass."

"I can't stop thinking about her. I. Can't. Stop."

"Can you truly live with a woman who never leaves the flat?"

"She'll get there. As long as we don't push her."

"See! You're rooting for her to get the flat."

"Of course I'm rooting for her to get the flat; that's what my client Beverly Wilder intended."

Queenie threw down his napkin like a dueler throwing down his glove. "Even if she makes progress, I don't think she's ever going to be completely happy running about."

"Probably not."

"Is that the kind of life you want, Mr. Jumping from Aeroplanes and Taking Off for Holiday Wherever the Wind Blows?"

"I want to cure her."

"You can't."

"She deserves it."

"Don't tell me you've shagged her."

"No. We just kissed. Twice. Maybe three times. It depends how you count."

Queenie gasped. *What a dreadfully annoying habit. How did Ava put up with it?*

Annoying habits. What did Jasper do that drove Hillary mental? He'd have to think on it, then start doing more of it. A lot more. "What can I do that would turn Hillary off?"

"Tell her about wanting to quit your job as a barrister to become a stand-up comedian. That should start things off."

"I tried. I handed her a brochure for my Open Mic Night. She thought it was rubbish someone handed me on the street. She dropped it to the ground without another glance."

"When is it?"

"Thursday week."

"I'll get her there."

"What?"

"I'll bring Hillary. She'll see you make a fool of yourself onstage. You'll tell her it's your dream and you're going to do it no matter what. You'll quit your job. She'll freak out. And before you know it, you're dumped. Again. She'll be so disgusted by you, she'll walk you down the aisle when you marry Ava."

"Do you really think so?"

Queenie slammed his fist down near his plate. "Have you gone completely mad? Beverly wanted you to help her disabled niece, not drag yourself into her pitiful life."

"Don't talk about her like that. Don't you like her? Has all this turned you heartless?"

Queenie had the decency to look a little sheepish. "There's something a bit appealing about the girl, I'll admit."

"See?"

"In an 'oh, look at the poor pup romping around on three legs' kind of way. She's handicapped, Jasper."

"Who doesn't have their share of problems? You can't audition for anything without your lucky charm." *Bollocks. Why did I bring that up again?*

Queenie's hands flew to his neck. "Give it back!"

"Sorry, mate. I left it at the office."

"Well, go get it. That was the whole point of having lunch. I only have four more days until the audition. Can you imagine seeing me on the telly?" Queenie grasped his hands like he was praying. "Then, *perhaps,* I can buy my own flat and your little head case can have hers."

"Right, so. That would be brilliant. But even if you don't get the part—"

"Do not jinx me, do not jinx me."

"Right. Where did Alfred get that charm, by the way?"

"I've told you a hundred times."

"Then one more won't hurt, lad."

"A commemorative event for the Globe Theatre. It coincided with our anniversary."

"Brilliant. Truly one of a kind." *Shite.*

"Truly. Should we go to your office right now?"

"We're waiting on Hillary."

"Until we get this whole mess sorted I think you should stay away from Ava," Queenie said.

"But."

"No buts. You keep your hands, lips, and schnozzel away."

"Schnozzel. Really?"

"Away."

"I'm supposed to accompany her when she does anything from the list."

"If she does anything on the list."

"When."

"Conflict of interest. We'll assign someone else." Queenie reached onto the seat and hauled up a pile of notebooks, swatches, and magazines, and dumped them on the table.

"What's that?"

"My redecorating plans. In case I don't get the part. I'll console myself by redecorating my new flat."

"I can't believe you."

"A girl can dream, can't she?" Queenie's head immediately

snapped to the left. Jasper followed suit. Hillary was making her way toward the table, her arms filled with Marks & Spencer bags.

"Hello, lads," she said. She plunked down next to Queenie. Her eyes landed on his pile of decorating ideas. She clapped her hands. "I can't wait to get my hands on that flat," she said.

"You?" Jasper said.

Hillary put her hand on Queenie's arm. "Us," she corrected.

"We were just discussing this. I was reminding Queenie that Beverly intended the flat to go to Ava. Whether or not she completes the list."

Hillary looked at Jasper. He would hate to be on her witness stand. Any virile male would walk off cupping his balls.

"Then she shouldn't have put it in writing," Hillary said. "Because it will stand up in court."

"Not if Queenie doesn't fight it."

"He won't have to fight it. When the ninety days are over and she's done nothing from the list, the little Septic will crawl home, and the flat will be ours."

"Ours?" Queenie said, arching his eyebrow.

"We're family, are we not?" Hillary said. Queenie shrugged, and Hillary punched him on the shoulder with a laugh.

"That's not nice." Jasper threw twenty pounds on the table and stood. "Beverly would be ashamed of both of you."

"What's gotten into you?" Hillary said. Queenie made a slashing motion across his throat while Hillary wasn't looking.

"I'm trying to honor Beverly's intentions. So much for letting her have the flat if you get on telly, isn't that right, mate?" Queenie looked up, startled. He had just pressed a piece of pink fabric to his cheek.

"Telly or no telly, we're not giving up the flat," Hillary said.

Queenie buried his head in the decorating binder.

Jasper stood. "I have to get back to the office."

"Thank God," Queenie said. "When can you get me my lucky charm?"

This was it. Queenie wasn't ever going to let Ava have the

flat. Even if he did get on telly. There was no use pretending now. "I'm sorry, mate. I lost it. It's gone."

Queenie's hands flew to his neck. "No. No! You're lying."

"I'm sorry, but it's the truth. I tried to retrace my steps, but no luck. I'm sorry. It's gone."

"I want to die. Oh, God, I want to die."

"Now you know how Ava feels. Every single time she steps outside."

"You're doing this to bully me into giving her the flat."

"Look at me. You know what kind of liar I am."

"A terrible liar," Hillary said.

"I'm sorry. The lucky charm is gone."

"You've ruined my career. My entire career. It's over. I'll never be the star. I'll never be on telly. But you can be sure as Christmas I'm getting that flat. I don't care if you love her or not."

"What?" Hillary said. "Love whom?"

Jasper looked at Hillary. "I'm going to become a stand-up comedian," he said. It was the only thing he could think of to throw her off.

Hillary threw her head back and laughed. Somewhere, pigs were getting slaughtered. "As if being an actor weren't hideous enough," she said, patting Queenie on the shoulder. She turned back to Jasper and grinned with all her teeth. "That's the funniest thing I've heard all day. Why doesn't one just give up on life altogether and become a clown?"

Jasper took the binder, turned it upside down, and shook it out over the table. Pieces of fabric and design patterns rained down. Queenie grasped for all the bits, gasping and sputtering, while Jasper walked out.

"Soon to be sixty-nine more days!" Queenie yelled after Jasper, shaking his fist. "I'll be the proud owner of a West End flat in sixty-nine more days."

CHAPTER 19

Ava perched on her stool and opened her laptop. London was only half-gray today. Strips of blue cut through the remainder of the sky, offering a little bit of hope. It made Ava hungry. After Queenie's apoplectic reaction to her not having plastic, Ava had applied online for a credit card. It was in her pile of mail this morning. She never knew it would be that easy. Then again, she didn't have any debt and she had a decent savings. And this was without mentioning that she might soon be the proud owner of a European flat. She'd put in her mother's address in Iowa, and when the card arrived her mother had graciously mailed it. They weren't talking a lot these days, but at least they were somewhat communicating. The mail here was delivered to a little room on the first floor, but Queenie always brought hers up. There was just one note from her mother with the credit card: *You need this for?* Her limit was only $1,000, presumably because she had very little credit to begin with. But a thousand dollars was plenty. She put on some music, and a black silk robe that she had taken to calling her dressing gown.

She danced around the flat with her credit card before settling onto her stool with her laptop.

Food! Mangia! *Yum!* Most girls would take their plastic to Marks & Spencer, Harrods, or Selfridges, but Ava had her eye on Sainsbury's.

She would order groceries online, then request that Vic deliver them. Or she could just invite her over like a normal friend might do, have her in for tea and crumpets, but what if Vic didn't think of her as a friend? Or normal? She did kind of disappear on Vic and her mysterious gardener friend, Deven, although that was after they disappeared on her. Were Vic and Deven in love? Had they already shagged? Ava loved all the British terms. *Shagged.* Made her think of doing it on carpets from the seventies. Whether or not they'd had sex, Ava couldn't believe how fast Vic had bonded with this guy. Ava had been drawing him for days and didn't feel the need for anything more.

Then again, her feelings for Jasper had taken off like a rocket, hadn't they? She'd felt a spark with him from the moment she saw his handsome, grief-stricken face on the video, and she'd even been attracted to him when he was posing as a bearded, lovesick taxi driver. When the chemistry was there, it was undeniable. She would have sworn it wasn't possible to feel so connected so fast. Maybe it was because Beverly loved him, and he her; maybe it bridged some kind of gap. All she knew was that he triggered her like no one else had ever done. And she liked it. That was the wild part. She actually liked feeling this way. It was like a drug. Thoughts, feelings, fantasies. How did people deal with all these things happening to them? It made it hard to get on with the business of life. Always waiting, wondering, hoping he'll walk through that door. When was he going to walk through her door again? How fast were these things supposed to go? Could she confide in Vic? Tell her she and Jasper had kissed? Tell her about the list? That's what friends were supposed to do, confide in each other.

Ava had never felt such a deep need for a friend before.

Then again, Ava had never had so many things bubbling inside her, dying to get out. Hunger first. Ava pulled up the Web site for Sainsbury's. This would be fun. A virtual-shopping experience in London while looking out the window was very close to the actual experience, wasn't it? Especially if Ava imagined herself in the aisle, pushing a cart and picking up items as she clicked. It was nobody's business but hers how she enjoyed her life. Who said people were better off with fresh air? If she wanted some fresh air, she'd open the windows. But not today. It probably smelled like exhaust and pigeons anyway. So many cars, and lorries, and fat gray birds. She'd get her fresh air from a fan. Her eyes flicked to the computer screen.

Welcome to Sainsbury's online groceries
Free delivery after 2pm Monday to Thursday

How lucky she was that this was the age of the Internet. Ava couldn't imagine being agoraphobic at other times in history. How isolated she would have been. Nothing to read but perhaps a classic by the fireplace. Then again, that didn't sound so bad either. A rocking chair, a blanket, and a tin cup of whiskey. Maybe she would leave the curtains open a peek so that she could catch a glimpse of snow falling outside the cabin. But what would she do when the cupboards were bare? Who would bring in the firewood? She would have to have a husband who didn't mind a wife who never left the house. Or the cabin in the woods. Or the turret in the castle. Such husbands would be up to no good the minute they were out of sight. But there would be nothing she could do about it if she was using them for her very survival. What a world. It sucked to be dependent on someone, but it sucked more to be alone. Jasper was someone she could trust outside the house. But Jasper was also someone who deserved a woman on his arm, accompanying him on his adventures.

Focus. With a click of a built-in mouse, she could order in anything she liked. She even heard of a person—she couldn't remember if it was a woman or a man—who purposefully stayed inside for an entire year, ordering everything they needed and wanted online. Was it too late to tell Jasper she was a blogger doing a social experiment? *My agoraphobia is just a cover. I'm doing a study on technology and social media and how it has isolated all of us in these little cocoons. To prove it I'm going to stay in my flat for a solid year, order everything online, and have all my social interactions through a screen. It's horrid, yes; that's the point. I'm sacrificing my freedom for the good of the people. The British People. Starting with ordering some tasty lunch.*

She couldn't believe all the items she could purchase from the comfort of her own home:

Cadbury Dairy Milk Swirl Ice Cream

Yes. She would take two boxes. They were on sale this week for only two pounds! She could get two bottles of selected wines for ten pounds. A tab at the top read: *Favourites.* She scanned the list.

Loyd Grossman Pasta Sauce

She didn't know who Loyd Grossman was. Should she? Oh, what the heck. If he was important enough to have a sauce named after him, why, she was going to try it. If they named one after her would it be Septic Sauce?

Round Pound Deals

Who didn't want a good round pound deal? Ava certainly did.

Colour Persil. Small and Mighty.

Ava hadn't given a single thought to laundry. Mainly because she'd been raiding Beverly's closet. Looked like she'd be washing all her clothes in the sink for the near future. Might as well get a bottle or three of Colour Persil.

Heinz Ketchup and Beans

No thanks. The last thing a shut-in needed to do was eat a load of beans. If she did, she'd definitely have to open the windows.

Brioche Pasquier Croissants

Hell yes! Eating foods she'd never heard of was educational. She was being a tourist. She could eat a Brioche Pasquier Croissant while looking out her window at all of London, sipping on Earl Grey tea. Watch the London Eye rotate. Take in the crowds in the West End. Ava didn't care what anyone else thought. She was in a new and foreign place. She was observing life. Memorizing the points of interest, the shape of the buildings. She watched the world at sunrise when the first glint of morning light bounced off windows, and at sunset when the night sky leaked behind the skyline seconds before it started to glow. It was riveting. Sparkling. Exciting. New. Ava felt alive. A true show, morning and night, and Ava had a front-row seat. It changed day to day, never the same shades, or shapes, or pace. Life was ever constant, and there was something profoundly comforting about that.

"If you knew how much I appreciated this, you'd let me stay," Ava said aloud. She paused, in case Aunt Beverly wanted to rattle a teacup or the windows. "For an actress you're awful quiet." Ava suddenly had an urge to sketch Beverly. She'd find every picture she could of her aunt and sketch her. That's how she got to know people. But she'd have to do that later; right now she needed to finish her food shopping.

Emma's Plain Creamed Fairies

Now that sounded a bit homophobic. She ordered them anyway.

Emma's Rock Buns

Personally Ava would have called them Emma's Rock-Hard Buns. She ordered them.

Flora Original Spread
Copella Orange Juice with Juicy Bits

They all sounded like porn. She was going to order everything that sounded foreign and dirty.

Good 4 U Alfalfa & Radish Shoots

Well, maybe not everything.

Ginsters Cornish Pasty

Now she was thinking of strippers and tiny chickens. Seriously. These people were sexed out.

Gu Zillionaires Puds

WTF? Where did she begin?

Quorn Meat-Free Mince

Minced what? Not meat, but still a mystery. No thanks. She'd stick with the beef.

Sainsbury's British Beef Roasting Joint. Taste the Difference.

Ava would taste the difference all right; she would taste London. She could see London out her window and taste it. That was an adventure. That was progress. And British Boneless Pork Crackling Leg Joint. Large. Less than five pounds a kg. How much was a kg? Damn her lack of metric system upbringing. She'd just get it. Queenie could eat some; didn't he say he was on a protein diet? Maybe she could order him an entire pig, roast it on a spit in the flat. *I'd like to make amends. Have a sow.*

Here we go. Sainsbury's British Whole Chicken with Pork, Sage & Onion Stuffing. *Ooooh*, Sainsbury's Beef Sandwich Steak. They had everything. They were just begging her not to leave the flat.

Mr. Brain's Faggots

What in the wide world of London were those? Mr. Brain's Faggots. It sounded gross, and once again homophobic, and somewhat Jekyll and Hyde–ish, and there was no way she could resist buying them. She wished her father were here to laugh with her. Ava froze. She hadn't thought so fleetingly of her father before. Not in an upbeat way like that. *Strange.* Maybe it was being here in Aunt Beverly's home. Her mother was probably worried too. Ava should call her. She had been waiting until she'd actually successfully gone out and done something. She didn't want to hear: *I told you so.* Mr. Brain's Faggots. She definitely wasn't in Kansas anymore.

Ice Lollies

Then again, maybe she was.

Weight Watchers Beef Hotpot

Now that was the way to lose weight.

Duck and Game
Bacon and Gammon

What the hell was gammon? Ava was starting to get dizzy. Whatever it was, you could get it smoked, unsmoked, with pineapple and cheese, sticky honey glaze, or rosemary and thyme. Heck, maybe Simon and Garfunkel would come over and sing while you cooked. British this, British that. They were very patriotic about their food. Saute British Gems with Rustic Salsa Verde. FruitBroo Elderflower & Lime Iced Tea. British Gems Potatoes.

The words on the site were starting to blur. Somewhere she remembered reading: From Field to Fork in 48 Hours. *How about from field to flat in two hours, Sainsbury's?*

Sainsbury's Kiwi Fruit, Ripe & Ready. British Sweet Chili Chicken Wings—She was ordering too much, but she couldn't stop clicking. She checked her cart. Over four hundred pounds. Four hundred pounds! Nearly half her credit limit. *Wait.* She'd order some of their canvas bags, too, for surely her order could choke a flock of seagulls. She didn't know how many bags it would require, so she ordered twenty. *Yowza.* She'd just stop looking at the credit card total. It was for later anyway. Wasn't that the whole point of it? Buy now, worry later? *Oh, God. Over six hundred pounds now. Those damn gulls better appreciate it.* Oh, she missed the red velvet cake with buttercream icing. She'd always wanted to try red velvet cake. It sounded so royal.

Gobshite. Now *this* was British porn. She shouldn't have ordered two of everything that sounded dirty. Or so much meat. Would they talk about her? *That mysterious woman who orders boatloads every single time. We hear she never leaves the flat. Maybe she has a broken leg like Jimmy Stewart in* Rear Window. If only Jasper would have lifted that wheelchair like she asked him to. She'd have to look into getting another one. She could probably do it online. Craigslist. As part of the experiment she could compare how people treated the Ava they thought was normal to the Ava in a wheelchair. It would be an eye-opening exposé. They would never glare at her, or shove past her, or whisper about her, or judge her, or ignore her, or scream at her if she were in a wheelchair. She alone would dare to throw open the velvet curtain and show the world the true Wizard.

More aptly, she would sit on her stool eating red velvet cake. Sure beat "curds and whey." Not an agoraphobic, but a social experimenter. *Thank you, Ava, for doing what we could not. I hear she's vowed to stay inside her flat for three hundred sixty-five days in a row, ordering everything off the Internet. Can you believe that? Poor girl, how ever will she manage? I would go stark raving mad. She's so brave. So brave. I wish I had her fortitude.*

CHAPTER 20

Vic showed up at the door, her face obscured behind a mountain of groceries. Behind her stood Deven, equally burdened.

"You came," Ava said. Deven glared at her, then dropped his bags and headed back down the stairs. Ava picked up the bags and stared after him. That was odd. "Is he mad at me?" She looked around Vic and yelled down the stairs, "I saved a lot of seagulls today!"

"He said you could feed his entire village with your order," Vic said. "The trolley's overflowing. We couldn't get it up the stairs."

Vic shoved her way in and dumped groceries on the kitchen counter. She put her hands on her hips. "Are you having a party?"

"A party for one," Ava said.

"You're a pig," Vic said.

Ava took a step back. Vic just said whatever came to her mind. Not a clue that it might hurt her feelings, or was it . . . not a care? Ava wasn't a pig. Was she? "I'm conducting a social experiment."

Vic reached into her Sainsbury's apron and pulled out a pack of cigarettes. She went to the window and threw it open. "Mind if I smoke, luv?" Ava did mind. But she didn't want Vic to leave.

"Make sure you blow it out the window," Ava said.

Vic lit her cigarette and sat on the windowsill without any hesitation. She turned to Ava and studied her.

"What kind of social experiment?"

"The kind where you stay inside your flat for an entire year and order everything online."

"Christ. That's idiotic."

"And brave."

Vic shook her head, then blew smoke out her nose. "Where'd you disappear to the last time? One second you're kissing the ground, and the next, poof. Vanished."

"I ran into Jasper."

"Jasper?" Vic's voice rose an octave.

Ava wanted Vic to leave. Where was Deven with the rest of her groceries? She headed for the kitchen to start putting them away. "My barrister."

"Ooo la, la. I didn't realize you had your own barrister." Vic pushed herself to a standing position and began walking about the kitchen as Ava put away groceries. Vic touched everything, with nail-bitten hands, infecting every surface with snaky trails of smoke. What had Ava been thinking? She didn't know this girl from Adam. She wasn't very nice. Not nice at all. Where was Deven? "Whose flat is this?" Vic held up a carving knife and ran her finger along the blade. Ava wanted to yell at her to put it down.

"Sort of mine," Ava said. Vic's head snapped to attention. *Uh-oh.* Had Ava said something she shouldn't have? *Don't talk to strangers, don't talk to strangers, don't talk to strangers.*

"Sort of? It's either yours or it's not, isn't it?"

"Can you please put down the knife and smoke the rest of that out the window?"

Vic put the knife up to her own throat as if she were holding herself captive. "If you tell me how you sort of own this flat."

The Mob was alive and well in London. "My aunt Beverly owned this flat. She's bequeathed it to me—but there are conditions."

Vic tossed the knife in the sink. Even though Ava had seen it happening, the clatter still made her jump. Vic stepped toward the window, never taking her eyes off Ava. She sat on the sill, inhaled, and blew the smoke out her nose. Ava wondered if the smoke would eventually rust her nose-piercing. "What conditions?"

Deven entered, arms outstretched like Frankenstein, four bags hanging on each limb. He stared at Ava as he let his arms drop and the bags slid to the floor.

Ava put on a bright smile. "Thank you."

Deven did not smile back. "This would feed my village for a month."

"It's for science," Ava said.

"You said it would feed your village for a week!" Vic yelled from the windowsill.

Deven shook his fist. "Possibly one year."

"Doesn't quite have the hang of bartering, does he?" Vic winked at Ava.

"Would you like some water?" Ava asked Deven. He nodded, then went to the kitchen sink, turned on the faucet, and drank directly out of it.

"I have glasses," Ava said.

He held up his hand and waved her away.

"What conditions?" Vic said.

Ava kept staring at Deven. She wanted him to stop that. She got out a glass and tapped him on the shoulder. He turned, swallowed, and then started to cough.

"You've choked 'im," Vic said. "For every seagull you save you lose one poor Indian boy from across the street."

Ava pounded him on the back. "Sorry. Sorry." Deven wiped his mouth with his sleeve and walked over to Vic. The water was still running. Who were these people? She shut it off and put the glass away. The entire floor was covered with groceries. She ordered all this? Deven was right. There was enough here to feed a village for a month. What kind of person was she? She couldn't eat all this.

"Bloody hell. If you don't tell me what conditions I'm going to jump out the bloody window," Vic said.

"Me too," Deven said.

Oh, please do. Ava didn't want to tell them now. But she didn't see a way out. "This is going to sound silly."

"Oh, believe me, it already does, luv."

"If I want to keep this flat I have to live here for one year—"

Vic slapped her thighs and jumped off the window. Deven stared at her ass. "Is that all? I could live in a bathtub full of urine in the middle of Sussex for a year if it meant I owned a flat like this."

"I as well," Deven said. "I would even supply the urine."

Ava wrinkled up her nose. "There's also a list."

"A list?"

The more Ava tried to make things sound like no big deal, the more Vic zeroed in on them. "A list of things I must do within ninety days—well, sixty-six days now, or is it sixty-five? Or Queenie will inherit the flat instead."

"Who the hell is Queenie?"

Ava had spent the past few weeks wondering the same thing, but it sounded kind of mean when Vic said it and she felt bad. "He's my flatmate."

"You're competing for this flat with your flatmate?"

"Yes."

"Is this going to be on telly? Like *Big Brother?*"

"God, no."

"Pity. Show me the list." Ava hesitated. She didn't like how intense Vic was getting. "Go on."

Ava held up her finger. She went to the bathroom where the list was taped to the mirror above the sink. She hoped reading it every time she was in there would somehow reinforce it, help her visualize doing it, seep into her skin and erase all her fears. God, this was a mistake. Vic was going to chew her up and spit her out. Then again, maybe that's what Ava needed. A little tough love. A kick in the butt. Ava grabbed the list, took it to the kitchen, and handed it to Vic.

One by one Vic read the list items out loud. Deven nodded along, smiling in approval. Vic finished the list, then crumpled it up and tossed it across the room.

"Hey," Ava said. She ran to retrieve it.

"You're joking me, aren't you?" Vic said. She stubbed out her cigarette on the windowsill and left it there. Ava wanted to swat it off. If she happened to push Vic out the window at the same time it would be purely by accident. "What kind of a competition is this? You could knock these out in one day."

"No. I couldn't." She just had to ask them to leave. That was it. She never had a problem asking Cliff to leave, so why was she finding it so hard with Vic? She was afraid of her, that's why. Vic was scrappy. She'd probably gotten in a million physical fights in her life. She could bust Ava's lip open.

"Two days at the most then," Vic said.

Ava eyed the pack of cigarettes. "Can I bum one?"

"Ah course," Vic said. Ava didn't normally smoke, but what a brilliant idea. Smoke out Queenie. Payback for emptying out the fridge and cupboards. Ava lit a cigarette, inhaled, and choked. The coughing went on forever.

"Crikey," Vic said. "You're a virgin."

"I just want to smoke out my flatmate," Ava said. The instant she said it, she realized that it wasn't true. A few minutes in Vic's presence and she missed Queenie. Fond of him even. She rushed to the kitchen and ran her cigarette under water. "I forgot. He's allergic."

"The guy competing for your flat?"

"Yes."

"What do you care then? Even more reason to smoke, isn't it?"

"It's probably better to get along while we're living under the same roof."

"This is because of your problems, isn't it? Your panic attacks?"

"Yes," Ava said. Vic had known this all along. She was trying to force Ava to say it out loud. She suddenly remembered Queenie's lucky charm. "Did you find a gold coin on a chain?"

"A gold coin on a chain?" Vic repeated.

"The day I came into the store."

"Sounds important," Vic said. "Valuable?"

"No," Ava said. "It's just a lucky charm."

"It's not real gold?" Vic said.

"No," Ava said. "It's not." Did that mean Vic had it? "There's a reward." Ava studied Vic, but the girl didn't move a muscle. Not so much as a blink or a twitch. "Have you seen it?"

"The coppers might have it," Deven said.

"Have what?" Ava said.

"Your lucky charm." He glanced at Vic. "They almost took my fertilizer."

Vic smiled. "That's shit. Get it?"

"I don't understand," Ava said.

"Fertilizer is shit," Vic said. "Horse shit, cow shit, pig shit—"

"Not that. I don't understand why the coppers would have my lucky charm." Ava looked at Deven. He tried to stare back but ended up blinking ferociously.

"Vic called them and told them I could be a terrorist," he blurted.

"You did what?" Ava said.

Vic grinned. "I wanted to see if they'd come."

"They did," Deven said, nodding. "Quick and in force."

"I ran away," Vic said.

"What happened?" Ava asked Deven.

"I had to show them the garden. They let me keep the fertilizer."

"Do you feel any safer?" Vic said, throwing up her arms in a what-has-the-world-come-to kind of way. "I certainly don't."

"What does this have to do with my lucky charm?"

"Maybe you dropped it on the footpath in front of Deven's and one of the coppers fingered it on his way in."

It was such a ludicrous scenario, which meant only one thing. Vic was lying. She had the lucky charm. "Please give it back. I'll pay you."

"Did I say I have it?"

"You haven't denied it either."

"That's London for you. Sometimes it takes things from you and you never get them back."

Deven stood near the window, peering down at Ava's pile of sketches on the floor. The top several were of Deven, in various poses in front of his building. "What in the bloody hell?" It was comical to hear him swear. But this wasn't the time to laugh. He shook the picture at Ava. "Who are you? Are you stalking me?"

Ava laughed; she couldn't help it. "I'd be the world's most pathetic stalker."

"Are you a spy?" Vic said. "Is he a terrorist after all?"

"I'm just a girl. I like to sketch."

"I'm not a terrorist," Deven said.

Vic walked over and grabbed the sketch out of Deven's hand. "Looks like a Wanted poster to me. She really captured your scowl."

"I don't have a scowl," Deven said, his expression matching the one on the sketch to a T.

Ava grabbed her other sketches. "I'm just passing the time. See?" She held up the sketch of the couple on their first date. Vic squinted.

"They look like cartoons," Vic said.

"People like cartoons," Ava said. She put the pictures away. They felt soiled now. "I need to rest. I'll see you to the door."

"What's it like then? Your agoraphobia?" Vic's voice was loud. She didn't care who heard her.

"It's like you're going to die," Ava said.

"A right in-valid," Vic said.

"Don't pronounce it like that. 'In-valid.' Like I have no value."

"You have value," Vic said loudly.

"Thank you."

"Your life doesn't though, does it?"

Ava clenched and unclenched her fists. "Good-bye."

"We just got here," Vic said. "You haven't even offered us tea."

"I have to unpack the groceries. Maybe next time."

Vic and Deven ambled to the door. Deven exited, but Vic stopped before she reached it. "I have to go to the loo," she said.

Damn it. Couldn't she wait? Ava pointed to the bedroom. *Through there.* Vic disappeared into the bedroom, shutting the door behind her. Why did she do that? The bathroom had a door of its own; she didn't need to shut the bedroom door too.

"Do you think she'd steal anything?" Ava said.

"Most definitely, yes," Deven said.

Shoot. Should she go in there? She turned back to Deven. "Do you like her bossing you around?"

"No," Deven said.

"Then why put up with it?"

Deven looked up, as if someone he admired were floating on a cloud just above him. "She has the personality of the butchiest lesbian, and the body of a straight girl. She's every woman who has ever rejected me all rolled up into one. Colored ponies couldn't drag me away."

"Wow," Ava said. "I didn't realize you had reached the colored ponies stage so fast." Deven nodded very seriously.

When Vic emerged from the bathroom Ava eyed her pockets for bulges. It was hard to tell, what with the apron and all. Should she frisk her?

"Crikey, that's some wardrobe you've got in there," Vic said.

"Everything belongs to Aunt Beverly. You shouldn't be going through her things."

"Chillax," Vic said. "Isn't that what you Yankee Doodle Dandies say?"

"I'm hardly a fitting representative for the rest of the Yankee Doodle Dandies."

"Riding on a pony!" Deven said. He bobbed his head and smiled. "I'll bet it was a colored pony too."

"What if Deven and I help win the competition?" Vic asked. "What would you give us?"

"There's nothing you can do," Ava said. *Go now. Just go.*

"Oh, there's always something that can be done," Vic said. "And I'm usually the girl they ask to done it." She laughed at her own mispronunciation. "I'm sure we can think of something."

"That's not necessary," Ava said.

"What's his name? Queenie?"

She was relentless. Ava had made a huge mistake inviting her here. *Hello, box. Meet Pandora.* "Thank you again for the groceries."

"Does he have a last name?" Vic asked.

"Please," Ava said. "I can handle this."

"How would Queenie feel if he knew a terrorist was living right across the street?" Vic smiled and put her arm around Deven.

"That wouldn't work," Ava said. "But thanks."

"I'll think of something," Vic said. "Maybe we could rotate use of the flat. A time-share."

"No," Ava said. "I don't want your help. Sorry. Good-bye." She tried to shut the door. Vic lodged her foot in it.

"I'm telling you. I can make this happen."

"If they even think I'm cheating, Queenie gets the flat."

"He doesn't have to know."

"Do I have to know?" Deven said. "I don't think I want to know."

"Go home, little terrorist," Vic said.

"Will I see you later?" Deven said.

Vic shrugged.

"Both of you need to go," Ava said.

"Not until you say you want my help," Vic said.

"I don't."

"I've decided. I'm going to help. I'll start by digging up dirt on your flatmate."

"No. I said no. All right? Now get your foot out of the door and go home."

Vic winked at Ava. "Right, right," she said loudly, as if they were secretly being recorded and had just discovered it.

"I mean it," Ava said. "Don't do anything."

"What if you and Deven got married? He could do the things on the list." Deven looked like he'd swallowed his own tongue.

"No," Ava said.

"Marry me, then," Vic said.

"Please don't," Deven said.

"I won't," Ava said.

"We'll talk terms later," Vic said. "After I've proven my worth."

"If you wanted to prove your worth you'd give me the lucky charm back." Ava tried to nudge Vic's foot out of the doorway.

"What's it worth to you?"

"I'm not trading you the flat for it if that's what you're asking."

"What about your flatmate? Would he be willing to trade me his share of the flat for the charm?"

"If you have that charm you'd better give it to me. Stealing is a crime."

"I'm just saying I'll keep me eye out for it, I will. Especially if there's a reward."

"I'll pay you a reward. A hundred pounds. Deal?"

"I'll give you a ring if I come across it," Vic said. She turned and started down the stairs.

"It has no value to anyone else. It's just sentimental. Two hundred pounds?" Ava called after her.

"Cheerio!" Vic called back.

Ava slammed the door. Did Vic actually have it or was she just messing with her? So much for friends. So much for friends, so much for charms, and so much for colored ponies. Ava headed for the kitchen, where she had every intention of stuffing herself into the next life.

CHAPTER 21

Don't think; just run. Ava stood at the bottom of the steps of her building, facing the main door. If she didn't start warming up, going out in little increments, she'd never build up to anything on the list. Vic's visit had really shaken her. Vic saw her as vulnerable and was more than ready to swoop in for the kill. Did she actually think Ava would just hand over a portion of her flat to a total stranger? *Just go outside the damn door. Open the door and stand on the stoop. That's all.* There was only a small window in the door and it was so old and dirty that all Ava could see was a blur of colors and shapes. She was wearing one of Diana's black turtlenecks and jeans. At the time Ava thought it might assist her with channeling her inner therapist, but now she was sweating bullets, and it felt like someone was slowly strangling her. Why did Diana love these things so much? *Do it. Just do it.* Ava closed her eyes, pushed open the door, and stumbled out onto the stoop. The air was cool against her flushed cheeks. The noises, the smells, the vibrations. Horns, and voices, and cars, and sirens. She smelled coffee, and bacon, and dirt. *Get this over with.*

Ava opened her eyes and sprinted down the stoop. Muggy air accosted her. It felt wet even though there was a break from the rain. She was right. It also smelled like exhaust. She tripped on the third step. She grabbed the rail, but it was too late. She fell down the other three steps, landed on her hands and knees on the sidewalk.

"Ava?" Vic called. Ava peeled her stinging palms off the ground and stood. She lifted her left leg, then the right. She didn't think anything was broken. "Ava? You're outside. You're outside, luv." Ava tried to keep her head straight ahead but slid her eyes across the street. Vic was standing with Deven in front of his building, smoking. Great, he'd changed his one smoke break to coincide with hers. And this time he looked like he was enjoying it. Which meant he'd picked up two bad habits, Vic being the worst of them. Ava just held up her hand in an approximation of a wave. *Keep going. Don't think.*

Ava took a step, and then another. *Put one foot in front of the other. And soon you'll be walking out the door. . . . Great.* Now she was going to have that bloody Christmas carol in her head all day long. Maybe death wasn't the worst thing after all. At least if she died she wouldn't have to feel like this anymore. That was something, wasn't it?

"You off, luv? Going to do something on the list?"

Bugger off.

"Want us to come with ye in case you do another header?"

Run, Ava, run. Run away from her. Ava ran. She pumped her legs and her arms as fast as she could. She was doing it. Running down the street past a wine shop, dry cleaner, and apartment buildings. Emergency sirens pulsed and shrieked in the distance. She could relate. A man with a briefcase blocked her path; she darted to her right and plowed into a young woman lost in her headphones.

"Ow," the girl said. "You gobshite!"

"Sorry," Ava said. She wanted to push the girl to the ground and stomp on her face. She didn't do it on purpose.

"Watch where you're bloody going!"

"Sod off," Ava said quietly to the girl's back, watching her blond ponytail bounce away.

The colored dots swarmed Ava's vision. That was enough for today. She turned around and made it step-by-step back to the building by fastening her eyes on the pavement. London was chewed gum, cigarette butts, and abandoned advertisements.

"Back so soon?" Vic called when she'd climbed the first few steps. "Or forget your lucky charm?"

Ava whirled around. "Do you have it?" she shouted. Her voice cracked. She wasn't accustomed to shouting. Or talking, for that matter. Her vocal cords had atrophied.

Vic laughed. "Why don't you come see?"

Ava shook her head. One of them was a terrorist all right. Ava jogged the rest of the way up the steps and threw herself at the door. It didn't open. She didn't, did she? *Keys.* Oh, God, how could she be so stupid? So careless? She'd forgotten to bring her keys.

Typical. Normal people always remembered their keys. What did Ava bring instead? A turtleneck. Perfect for suffocating and strangling her on this hot summer day. *Nicely done, nicely done.* The colored dots began to disco. Ava collapsed on the top step and buried her head between her knees. She wanted to rip the turtleneck off. Was it illegal to sit around in a bra on your stoop in London? There were just some things the guidebooks didn't cover. *Think, Ava, think. What can you do?* The one little window in the main door was made of thick glass. Even if she did find something to throw at it she was pretty sure it wouldn't break, and even if it did break, it was so high up it would be impossible to stick her hand in and open the lock.

She would have to start buzzing neighbors. Hers was the only flat at the top, but the other four floors had two flats each; at least eight other people lived in this building. Someone had to be home.

Ava lifted her head. A wave of dizziness crashed over her and she put it back down. She lifted her head again and looked across the street. Deven and Vic were gone. She put her head back down. That was probably for the best; she didn't want to owe Vic any favors. But surely Vic had seen that Ava was locked out? Had she taken off on purpose? Ava didn't know a lot about friendship, but she definitely couldn't trust Vic and thought she'd be lucky if she never had to deal with her again.

Keeping her eyes closed, Ava scooted around on the step until she was pretty sure she was facing the front door. She pawed her way, hands and knees, to the door; then, using the knob, she hauled herself to a standing position. Were Londoners paying any attention to her? Was a crowd gathered behind her photographing her ass for Facebook? From the times she'd observed them from her windows, Ava was pretty confident that nobody was paying any attention to her. In Iowa the Fire Department would have arrived by now and neighbors would be camped out on her lawn with binoculars and a bag of chips.

Ava gripped the knob and took deep breaths. She still wasn't ready to open her eyes again, so she began to feel along the door heading for the right side, guessing that's where the buzzers were located. She felt hot, scratchy brick. Her fingers played up and down it searching for a panel. To an outsider it probably appeared as if she were a lunatic scratching at the walls. The rough edges of the brick cut into her palms the harder she pressed. She liked it. The pain felt good. The more she concentrated on the scrapes in her palms and fingers, the less she noticed the colored dots. She stopped, took a deep breath, and then opened one eye. She traversed the wall in front of her bottom to top. No panel. *Darn it.* She slid her eyes to the left. There it was, a rectangular bronze panel with buzzers. *Great. Nothing going on here, folks. I just like wearing turtlenecks at the hottest point of the day and scratching at the walls until my palms bleed. Surely you do too. Cheerio!*

Ava sidled to the left and examined the panel. There were nine buzzers. *Please, somebody be home.* If they all had typical day jobs she would be out of luck. The buzzers didn't have names, just flat numbers. Ava started at the bottom with 1a. She laid her finger on it for several seconds, then released and waited.

She listened for the buzz but wasn't able to hear proof that the buzzer worked. She pressed the next one up, again holding it for several seconds. Once again there was silence. She continued to press, up, and up, and up, this time using both fingers, and then finally using all fingers and the sides of her hands to press as many buttons as she could at one go. Pound, pound, pound, that felt good. She began to punch each buzzer with her fist. Then both fists. She was having a boxing match with the buzzers. The pain felt good. When she finally pressed her own buzzer, just for the hell of it, she heard it shriek. *Good God.* She was right about that deafening level; she could hear hers from all the way out here. So why couldn't she hear a single peep from the others? Either nobody else's was working or hers was the only one set to DEFCON 1.

Damn it. Who were these working-class neighbors with good hearing? Did they know she had moved into the building? Had they been friends with Aunt Beverly? Was Queenie friends with anyone in the building? Big cities were so cold. So many people packed into so little spaces, hardly any privacy anywhere you went, crammed into tubes, and lifts, and bars, and restaurants, and shops—yet nobody would answer a distressed buzz. Maybe the only way outsiders survived was to deny anyone was next to them at all. And people called Ava weird.

What now? She was absolutely baking, and if the dots continued for much longer she was going to pass out. *Step right up, folks. Watch the agoraphobic go down.* Would Londoners step right over her? Assume she was a drunk? *Public loo.* She needed to find one and lock herself in a stall. Who cared what happened after that? Salvation was a cool, dark space where she could rip off this turtleneck.

Don't think; move. She ran back down the steps, then took a right on the footpath and it was déjà vu time. Past the wine shop—probably no public restroom in there, although a bottle of wine might help, past the dry cleaner, where there was a long line and, again, probably no public restroom, then past apartment buildings. Didn't Queenie or Jasper mention there was a pub up here somewhere? She kept going and, sure enough, she saw a sign hanging overhead, a crest of some kind, flanked by regal lions holding giant mugs of ale. She didn't even register the name of the pub because her vision was blurry; it was all she could do to remain upright, fighting both dots and dizziness. Her breath become more and more labored, perspiration soaking her entire body.

She picked up speed and flung open the door of the pub. It was dim and smelled of stale beer, and curry. There were patrons in the pub, and waiters, and bartenders, all furry blobs to her; she could only see patches of them, like a living, European quilt. She lurched ahead, praying the restrooms were in the back. Halfway there she slammed into a curved piece of metal; it jammed into her, just below the breastbone. She registered what it was just as the serving tray crashed to the floor.

"Bloody hell!" the waiter who had been holding it screamed. "Look what you did." The floor was smeared with burgers, and chips, drowning in ale.

"Loo," she said. "Loo, loo, loo." She hooted it like an owl, then ran straight ahead and burst through a pair of swinging doors. Fluorescent lights, a grill, steel counters, ham sizzling, coffee gurgling, and curry, curry, curry, curry.

"Oy. You're not allowed in the kitchen, mate!" a chef yelled.

"Loo, loo, loo, loo," Ava hooted.

"Out the doors, to the left, across the restaurant, down the stairs, around the supply room, down the little hall, and to the right," a man wielding a large butcher knife said.

Ava opened her mouth to scream and instead squeaked like a little mouse. *Too far, too far, too bloody far.* "Bollocks," she said. A short boy elbow deep in dirty dishes stopped what he was doing and approached.

"I show you?" he said.

"Loo." Ava nodded. "Loo, loo."

He started ahead of her when Ava grabbed his soapy hand. He looked startled for one moment, and then met her eyes, gave her a nod, and led her out of the kitchen. Ava shut her eyes as much as she could as the boy led her past the mess on the floor. The surly waiter was hunched over it, staring, as if he could make the mess clean itself up if he glared hard enough. They passed the men's restroom on the main floor and Ava cursed under her breath. By the time they got to the stairs on the other side of the room, Ava knew she was seconds from passing out. "Wait." She grabbed the rail and stood at the top of the stairs. "Got it. Thank you."

"Do you need to go to hospital?" the boy said.

"No, thank you," Ava said. *Possibly. Probably.*

"It's down the stairs, then follow the hall as it curves around to the other side. You should run into the loo." She nodded, and he bolted.

Ava sank to the step. She was going to claw her eyes out if she had to wear this turtleneck for much longer. Diana was bat-shit crazy to wear these things. Ava began to slide down the steps on her bottom. At least if she fell, she probably wouldn't hurt herself.

The cement floor and cellar walls were painted red. Seriously. Why couldn't the men's room be down here? *Wankers.* She should have asked the dishwasher to bring her a pint. Or would that have been weird? She began to walk the hall. "Tall and tan and young and lovely." She hugged the wall. Tears came to her eyes. She'd avoided that song whenever she could. There was no one down here. *Thank God.* She grabbed the turtleneck and pulled it over her head. It stuck. Ava left it there but kept inching forward. "Short, and pale, and frightened, and lonely, the girl from America goes walking, and when she walks she panics, and says, 'Loooooooooooo.'"

Her voice was muffled by the turtleneck. She struggled but managed to pull it off the rest of the way. Her hair levitated like a science experiment. Static. She continued to sing and then twirled the turtleneck above her head like a lasso. She took the turn and came face-to-face with a long line of women trailing out from the door marked: Ladies. A mass of denim, colorful pumps, and hair, blocking mecca. They turned, some together, some wondering what the others were looking at, and, just a hair slower, stared. Ava could only imagine what she looked like. Bra exposed, crazy eyes, science-experiment hair, twirling a turtleneck, and singing, "Loooooo." *That's right. She's here. The Septic has arrived.*

CHAPTER 22

Ava sat in the stall, on the floor. The lid to the commode was closed, and the turtleneck rested on top as a pillow. Ava had wiped down the floor first with soap and paper towels, once all the wenches had left. She waited them out. Thank God she didn't have a weapon or she would have brandished it. Not a single one asked her if she was all right even though she had been sitting on the floor in the hallway. At least she was here now. There were two stalls; she'd taken over one, so the rest of London was just going to have to share the other. She didn't have a plan from here. There were no more options. This was it, her final resting place. She'd spend the rest of her life hugging a commode in the cellar of an English pub. She probably wasn't the first. Women filtered in and out, and some noticed her, and knocked on the stall door. "Are you all right in there? Too many pints?" *She's blotto? At this time of the day?* Was she sacked? Jilted? Snorting coke? Did she have any to share?

Approximately thirty minutes into her stay, a male voice boomed through the space. "Sorry, sorry, coming in, ladies, all right? All right, then, all decent, all right? I'm coming in." She heard footsteps; then large brown shoes appeared underneath the stall door. He knocked. "Are you all right in there, luv? Should we call an ambulance?"

"I'm fine," Ava said. "Thank you."

"You're sitting on the floor, " the manager said.

"I'm aware."

"That's not all right then, is it?"

"That's relative."

"Are you snookered?"

"If that means drunk, then, no. I wish." This was so embarrassing, this was the worst day of her life. Maybe crawling under desks at the police station and discovering Cliff was married in front of the entire precinct was a tad bit worse. But strangely, she cared more about what they thought of her here. London felt like home.

"Right, then. Who can I call, luv?"

"Ghostbusters." She couldn't resist.

"I'm calling an ambulance." He moved to the door.

"Wait." He came to a halt. "I'm having a panic attack. I just need to sit here for a bit. If I can borrow your mobile I can try to find Jasper's number. He works at a law firm in Canary Wharf. Or Queenie. He's a drag queen somewhere in the West End; I don't know how many clubs there are—"

"Queenie? From down the street? Used to come in with Beverly?"

"Yes, yes. Oh thank God. Yes." This was probably his local. *Thank you, thank you, thank you.*

"That bitchy queen hasn't shown his face in here since his bar tab shot up to over a thousand pounds."

"Oh." *Shit. Shit, shit, shit.* "I'll pay his bar tab if you call him to come pick me up." With what? The rest of her credit card wouldn't cover it all. But it would have to do for a start. Otherwise he was going to have to take a sweaty turtleneck as payment.

"You'll pay his full tab?"

"Nearly half. Or Bob's my uncle."

"Who?"

Apparently she hadn't used it correctly. "As soon as I get back to my flat and get my credit card, I'll call you with the number."

"Right."

"Otherwise, leave me here all day, or call an ambulance. I give up."

"Why were you having a panic attack?"

"Because I was outside." *Screw them. Let them figure it out for themselves.* Ava was sick of having to be the ambassador of ago-raphobia.

"You were having a panic attack because you were outside?"

"That's right."

"You don't like to be outside?"

"That's right."

"Oh." *Bugger off.* "Why not?"

"I'm agoraphobic. It's a severe phobia. It's not in my head; I'm not a nutter. When I'm outside my body reacts as if I were in severe danger. I go into fight-or-flight mode. I panic. Okay? Either I pass out or I find cover. Today, I found cover. I'm sorry to say that it's at your establishment. I'm an arsehole, all right? I'll never be a lion enjoying a frosty mug of ale."

"Darling, this is a British pub. All of our patrons are total arse-holes."

Ava laughed. "Thank you. Thank you for being kind."

"How do you know Queenie?"

"He's my flatmate."

"The one he inherited?" *Oh, great.* How many people had Queenie told?

"Yep."

"Can you believe that? Guy inherits a flat in the West End, worth a load of money, and he still comes in here saying he doesn't have the cash yet. Whining about the money he's spend-ing per month on the flat."

Oh. Queenie was the one paying all the fees, whatever they were. Ava didn't know it was that hard on him. Then again, the flat was going to be his, so she was not going to feel sorry for him.

"I'll pay nearly half his tab, I swear," Ava said. "I'll call my credit card in as soon as I get home."

"I'll see if I have a number for him. I know a few of the clubs where he works; I'll put in some calls."

"Thank you."

"Would you like some water?"

"No," Ava said. "But I'd really love a pint."

She was halfway through her pint of Boddingtons when the door opened and she smelled lilac perfume. Thick heels clacked toward her.

"Ava?"

She was so happy to hear his voice. "Queenie."

The other stall door opened. He sat on the toilet. His heels were black and at least three inches. He was wearing red fishnet stockings. She was dying to see the rest of his outfit. "Sorry to bother you during work," she said.

"It sucked, as you Americans would say. My Downtown Diva act was incorrigible. I was booed offstage. Booed. For the first time in my life."

"That's awful. I'm sorry."

"Jasper is the one who should be sorry."

"What? Why?"

"That heathen lost my lucky charm. With the most important audition of my life coming up. I stalled them once believing a miracle was going to happen. But I can't stall them again and I'm ruined. I'm completely ruined. I wish I was dead." He gasped, then began to sob.

Oh, God. Ava knocked her head on the lid of the commode several times. "Don't cry. I'll fix it. I'll fix it. I swear to you." *Oh, God.* She broke him. She broke a British drag queen. Did Vic have it? She had to get it back.

Queenie sniffed loudly, then blew his nose. "Enough about my disaster of a life. How can I get you home, luv? I can't carry you in these heels."

"Could you bring my Xanax, a shirt, and a blindfold from my top dresser drawer?"

"Sound like my Friday nights," Queenie said. Ava laughed. He was being so kind. She didn't deserve it. Tears welled in her eyes. She didn't want to cry in front of Queenie, but there was no stopping it now.

"Shhh," he said. "It's all right, luv. You did it." A hand snuck under the stall. She took it. His felt as clammy as hers. *What a pair.*

"Did what?"

"Why, you went to an English pub. One item off the list, now, isn't it?"

Ava was so stunned she stopped crying. "Does it count?"

"I'm told you have a pint of beer," Queenie said.

"Boddingtons. It's good."

"It certainly counts. In fact, ending up locked in the loo is going above and beyond. Now you're just showing off."

"Not exactly what Beverly had in mind," Ava said. "She would be so disappointed in me."

"Now you listen to me, Ava Wilder. Beverly would be over the moon that you're here. Over the moon. She loved Bertie more than anything in the world, and she loved you. It was her dying wish to bring you here, so I don't ever want to hear you say something like that again."

Ava came out of the stall. She went to the sink and splashed water on her face. She looked in the mirror. For a few seconds she didn't even recognize herself. Who was she? She turned around and looked at the closed stall. Queenie's feet were turned in. "I want to know her. I want to know everything about her and I know nothing."

Queenie sighed. He crossed his legs. "I don't know how to fill you in on seventy-four years of her life."

"Just tell me something. Anything."

Queenie planted both feet on the floor again. "She was smart. You wouldn't know it unless you hung around her long after the curtain went down and the applause ended. Her public face was more flirty than intellectual. Oh, she craved the spotlight. But once home, out of her costume and makeup, she was usually curled up with a book. Mysteries, biographies, history. She liked facts, and sometimes flung them at you like weapons. Always on me to read more. But unlike her, I'm pretty shallow. What else? She spent a great deal of time thinking about Bertie, trying to rewrite the past. She spent a great deal of time trying to figure out how to connect with you. She liked crossword puzzles too. And she was damn good at them. She had a shopping addiction. Clothes, as you can see from her closet. Hardly wore anything more than once. She liked a good party. Any kind of celebration, really. Any occasion where she could dress up, pop open the champagne, and pretend to be someone else for a while."

"Someone else?"

"I don't think Beverly ever quite felt comfortable in her own skin."

"But she was an actress. So confident."

"Onstage, yes. Offstage? Well. She was rarely offstage. It can be lonely, always wearing a mask."

"But she didn't wear it around you?"

"Oh, she did. Most of the time. Once in a while, she'd relax."

"I'm glad you were her friend."

"Don't you worry about that. Beverly always had an entourage. Although I don't think she had a single female friend. Beverly was more comfortable around men. I don't know if it was out of jealousy, or the fact that she could be crude, like a man, but again, also wanted that spotlight. She drank as much whiskey as she did tea, and when she was younger she slept with a lot of men but only fell in love with a few."

"Why didn't she ever marry? Have kids?"

"Oh, she would tell you it was because she never found the one."

"And what would you tell me?"

"Beverly hated the very idea of commitment. It was stifling to her. She loved the theater. She loved romance. She loved a good party. Real life was always a glaring disappointment. So she fell in love with unattainable men. Married, the bad boys, the ones who rejected her. Oh, I could write a book on Beverly. She was complicated. But when it came to those she loved—

like Bertie, like you—that was very, very simple. You say you don't know her, but I see so much of her in you. She's there, luv. Inside you. She's there."

The words speared Ava. Was it true? Was Beverly a part of her? "I wish I could live my life all over again. I'd be different. I would. I'd have come to visit. Told her I loved her. I'd have been braver. I swear. I'd have been so much braver."

Queenie sighed. "Oh, luv. We all have our ways. Beverly was afraid to fly, did you know that?"

"She jumped out of a plane."

"That's my Beverly. Death took the fear right out of her."

So that was the trick. Ava would get over this right before she died. Typical. Ava went back into her stall and sat on the commode. She was suddenly so tired. "Is that why she didn't want my dad to marry my mom?"

"Oh, I'm sure it was a huge part of it. She didn't want your father to go to America in the first place. Oh, she threw such a fit, begging him not to go."

"She flew there for the funeral."

"She was just like you. She needed pills, and cold presses, and hot presses, and every other bloody thing just to get on the plane. Oh, she was terrified. Absolutely terrified. The trip to Bertie's funeral was the last plane ride she ever took. That is, until she went skydiving."

"Did my mother know Beverly was afraid to fly?"

"Well, Bertie certainly knew, so I would have to assume so."

"She still thought Beverly hated her. She thought it was all her fault."

"Beverly was the coolest person in the world if she liked you. She had such an orbit, and people loved being sucked into it. But I will admit she had a cold side to her too. She was so heartbroken about Bertie. Their parents died when they were young, so Bertie was really not just a brother; Beverly in some ways thought of herself as his mother. Either way, she couldn't bear to see him go, and each year that passed without him visiting her made her more and more bitter. I don't think your poor mother really ever stood a chance."

"Did Beverly ever tell you any stories about her and my dad growing up?"

"Oh, she loved telling stories."

"I can't get enough. I want to hear more. I want to know all her stories."

Queenie slapped his thighs. "I'll tell you what. Let's get you home, get you all set up on your stool, maybe a little espresso, or Scotch if you're really good, and we can talk about Beverly until we can't keep our eyes open. Do we have a deal?"

"Deal."

"Okay, luv. You wait here just a little longer. I'll get your accessories and be right back." He stood.

"Queenie?"

"Yes?"

It's me. I lost your lucky charm. I'm the one. "Thank you."

"You're welcome, luv. It's certainly not the first time I had to drag a gal out of the loo."

A while later, Ava was back in her flat on her emerald stool, wrapped in one of Queenie's dressing gowns and gazing out the windows, while Queenie ferried back and forth, handing her an espresso, then biscuits, and finally a Scotch as he settled in next to her.

"What's with the refrigerator?" he said. "Are you having a party?"

A party? Oh, the food. She'd forgotten all about it. "Maybe," she said, testing out the thought like a swimmer dipping a toe in the water.

Queenie's spine straightened up. "Who told you? Jasper?" He sounded thrilled.

"Could be," Ava said. What on earth was he talking about?

"Nobody this ancient needs to celebrate his birthday," Queenie said.

Ah, his birthday. "I won't force you if you don't want—"

Queenie rose, put his hand on his heart. "But if you were to insist."

"Which clearly I am," Ava said deadpan.

"It's a little early, but I see the logic. Weekend parties trump Monday parties, don't they?"

"That's what I was thinking."

"Friday or Saturday? Wait. Surprise me."

"Okay."

"Friday. No. Saturday. Saturday definitely."

"Of course."

"And you know some of those queens can't show up until late, late, late. Then again, if you happen to say something like *this party is hush-hush, exclusive,* then they'll be calling their understudies faster than Prince Harry drops his pants."

"That's devastatingly clear."

"Ooooooh. A surprise party. I love it." Queenie ran over to the minibar and held up his little address book. "I tend to just leave it lying here," he said, tapping it. "Only contact those with a star next to their names."

"A star. Right."

"Not an X."

"X does not mark the spot."

"Unless."

Oh boy.

"I would invite the Xs if . . ." He let it hanging as if he wanted Ava to finish the sentence for him.

"You were playing tic-tac-toe?"

"No, silly. Do you think you could pretend, just for that night, that the flat is mine?"

"Yes. I can do that."

Queenie clapped his hands and jumped up and down. He was surprisingly graceful for a big man. She'd have to catch his act one of these days. "Then invite the Xs too. Oh, this is going to be my night. And maybe. Oh. Never mind." He fluttered his eyelashes and looked at her.

"Go on."

"Maybe you can let it slip that I'm going to be on telly."

"You read my mind."

"And cake. You know who makes the best cake?"

Death. Give me death. "Why don't you leave me a list?"

"As in who's naughty and who's nice? Smashing idea. I've got to start working on my surprise face. There's an art to it, you know." He gave a sample of a surprised face.

"Keep working on it," Ava said.

"You are going to hide, and then jump out, and yell, 'Surprise!,' aren't you?"

"We are now." At least she liked the hiding part.

"That's good. I have the sudden urge for cake. You know who makes the best cake?"

"Just leave me a list, Queenie. I'll follow it."

"Good girl."

Ava laughed as he trounced off to the bathroom. *Oh, God. A party.* She had no choice now. She'd start planning the party and double-check everything with Jasper. *Jasper.* God, she couldn't wait to see him. Look in his eyes, touch him, smell him, take in his blazer, or blue jeans, or whatever the hell he'd use to cover his tall, muscular frame. A party. Like she was a normal person. He could be her date. Ava had never even been to a party and now she was going to throw one. She thought of Emma, the mayor's daughter. How had her party turned out? Had they ever caught the potential kidnapper? Ava's mother would know.

She picked up the phone and dialed her mom. Voice mail picked up. "Mom? It's Ava. Call me back." Ava hung up, feeling hurt. Her mother was punishing her. Or she was just so relieved that Ava was gone, out of her hair, that she was constantly out having a good time. Could her mother have a boyfriend? Ava hoped so. She hadn't been with a single man since Ava's father. Bertrand had been the love of her life. God, Ava wanted peace with her mom. She'd lost just as much as Ava had, maybe even more. When her father was alive, her mother laughed a lot. She always softened. She was crazy in love with Ava's father; even Ava could see it. And although she hadn't done it on purpose, Ava certainly had put her mother through the wringer over the years. She felt bad about that. Ava wanted her mother to be happy again. She wanted it for both of them. Maybe they could even have a real mother-daughter relationship. Learn to truly enjoy each other's company. Go places together. Imagine that. But first her mother was going to have to answer the phone, and in the meantime Ava still didn't have an answer to her question.

Ava opened her laptop and Googled "Emma Rhodes." Immediately a picture of a man sprung up. *Sketch Artist Helps Identify Kidnapper.* He'd been caught. *Thank God.* He'd been working with one of the landscaping crews. *Evil bastard.* Ava pulled up the sketch done by Gary Vance. It was a remarkable likeness, one of his best. She wasn't jealous, just relieved. In fact, she didn't miss being a sketch artist at all. She much preferred cartoons, and caricatures and happy things. She'd definitely have her sketch pad on hand for the party. It would calm her if the crowd got to be too much. Ava set the sketch pad down, then went to the minibar and picked up Queenie's little black book. She opened it and a little fabric square fell out. It was a dark red. Was this a fabric sample for a new outfit? She'd never seen him dressed as a woman except for his heels and stockings when he came into the pub. By the time he returned to the pub with her Xanax and blindfold, he was once again in men's clothes. She wondered how he would dress for his party. She should make an effort to go to one of his shows, just like she should go to Jasper's comedy sets. Why did all her new friends have to be so darn talented and outgoing?

Queenie came back into the room, robe on, towel thrown over his shoulder. Ava held the swatch up. "What's this?"

Queenie gasped, then snatched it out of her hand.

"Nothing," he said.

"It fell out of your address book."

"It's nothing."

"A new outfit?"

"Yes. Mrs. Claus. Ho, ho, ho."

Liar. Why was a little piece of fabric such a big secret? "Why haven't I ever seen you in drag?"

"Because I have a dressing room at the theater. Believe me, if I brought home all my outfits you'd have nowhere left to sit." He whipped the fabric sample out of her hand and headed for the kitchen. "Espresso?"

CHAPTER 23

Dance club music pumped through the flat. Ava had never been to a dance club, but she was pretty sure this was the type of loud, rhythmic music they would play. Beverly's speakers might have been old, but they were mighty. Voices rose over the music. The place was packed. The invite was just as Queenie directed:

Isn't it a DRAG?
Time stops for no Queen
Exclusive invite
Celebrate the bash at his brand-new flat
(And he might just be on telly soon!)

And so they came. And kept coming. Ava had never met this many people, let alone called them friends and—in some cases—mortal enemies.

It turned out Queenie's friends had been dying to get a look at her, as well as the flat. They arrived with booze, and food, and chocolates, and flowers, and boas, and buzzers. They fussed over Ava so much she almost forgot it was Queenie's birthday and not hers. From the looks of it, she wouldn't even have to use up much of her stash of food. Trays of appetizers rotated around the flat. Cheese and crackers, dips, crab cakes, stuffed mushrooms, it just kept coming. These people were amazing. Ava loved them. Queenie couldn't be so bad if he had this many cool friends. They were Aunt Beverly's friends, too; she recognized some from the plethora of photos on the wall. They came straight and they came gay. They came dressed in drag and dressed to die for. There were no awkward silences because nobody was awkward and nobody was silent. They talked as if they'd known Ava all her life. Ava didn't have to say much about herself because they filled in the gaps, as if Mind the Gap applied just as much to parties as it did to the Tube. Everybody had an opinion about everything. Ava could have sat all day just listening to snippets of conversations or words that stuck out at her as being "British."

Bangers and mash . . .
Primrose Hill . . .
Bubble and squeak . . .
Toad in the hole . . .
Apple crumble and custard . . .
There is one dungeon in North London I'll always remember fondly.
It's closed now. It's probably an Abercrombie and Fitch.
I got absolutely bollocksed at the office party and shagged an intern. . . .

Several of the conversations just added to Ava's fears.

The Tube? It's horrific. Swarms of dirty people pushing and shoving. Last week a bloke fell off an escalator and cracked his head. You're smart to stay away from that death trap.

London's dirty. Not round here with all the shops, but my end, the South End of London, people leave trails of rubbish as if they're trying to lure you somewhere like Hansel and fucking Gretel.

I'm sick of the rain. It seeps into your pores, you know. I'm thinking of moving to Spain. Have you been to Spain? Oh, you have to go. The Spanish are so laid-back. I could have shagged the entire island of Ibiza. Not like Londoners. They'll bite your head off, they will. Although I will miss the buzz. Always something to do in London, it's electric.

The culture, that's why I stay. The museums, the opera—

When was the last time you were at a museum or opera that didn't involve dildos?

Shut your mouth, Franco. The ballet—the theater. You must know what I mean, being Beverly's niece and all, luv. Wasn't she just a marvelous actress?

It's an international city. I don't know anybody who's actually from London. At any given day on the Tube you hear a hundred languages spoken. German, French, Japanese, Arabic—

Peals of laughter, snippets of British accents, and footsteps rang out.

"Love the dress, luv," a man sporting a fedora said. Ava was wearing a green silk kimono with yellow stitching. God, she loved Aunt Beverly's wardrobe. She'd also liberally applied her makeup. She almost looked like someone else, like an actress playing a role. She might have entirely forgotten who she was, if it weren't for a few rotten apples who had had the nerve to come right out and ask her if she was agoraphobic. "Shh," she said, putting her finger to her lips. "I'm an artist conducting a social experiment."

"How's that, luv?"

"I'm spending an entire year inside the flat, just to see if in today's wireless age it can be done." They leaned in, wanting to know more. "You know. Can I order in absolutely everything I need?"

In London, of course you could, they said.

"Can I maintain friendships?"

"We're here, aren't we?"

"Maybe even romance?" Ava blushed on this, and immediately scanned the room as if Jasper would materialize.

"Luv, this is London. You can even order in a mate," one of the drag queens screeched. The small crowd whooped at that. Ava kept up with the charade and begged them not to tell anyone.

"Is it a blog?" someone asked. "Can we follow it?"

"I'm saving it all for a book," Ava said. "*The Insider's Guide to London.*" They liked this too. They laughed. Ava felt warm inside. No wonder Jasper wanted to be a stand-up comedian. It was like a high, making people laugh. "Please, just don't tell anyone. Can't compromise the experiment," Ava said again. Heads nodded; people promised. She assumed the British gossip vine worked the same way it did everywhere else. It wouldn't be long before the rumor spread. She wasn't agoraphobic, a shut-in, an invalid! She was an artist, conducting a social experiment. *She's writing a book, don't you know?* The Insider's Guide to London. *Brilliant!*

As the festivities raged on, Ava found that she much preferred watching to participating. Perhaps it was too much too soon. She grabbed her sketch pad from the bookshelves in the living room and made her way over to her emerald stool. She began to sketch the nearest person to catch her eye. He was a short man, but thin, and he held himself very straight. An important man, maybe a director? He had on a gray suit with a pink tie. He was wearing green eyeliner. He was very animated, moving his hands almost like an orchestra conductor as he spoke. She began to sketch him. The bow tie was the piece that interested Ava the most, along with his dramatic hand gestures. He was like a cruise ship host. So soon she found herself sketching a cruise ship, with the bow-tie man at the helm, waving his arms, telling embarking passengers where to go. She made his grin the exact same size as his bow tie. She gave him a bubble and a caption: *The "Luv" Boat.*

From behind her came the peal of laughter. She looked up. An extremely tall black man was the source of the mirth. He was dressed in a blue-rhinestone skirt and a black wifebeater shirt. Long black boots and a wig with wavy black hair down to his ass. He was stunning. Light caramel skin with features both strong and delicate. Fake eyelashes and purple eyeliner ringed green eyes. Ava knew her mouth was hanging open.

"You're beautiful," she said.

"And you must be drunk," he said, then laughed some more.

"Completely sober," Ava said.

"Well, we'll have to do something about that, darling, won't we?" He held out his hand, and when she offered hers he kissed the back of it.

"I'm Ava," she said.

"Everyone knows who you are, luv. Welcome to London, Ava. I'm Francis."

"Hi, Francis."

"My friends call me Franco. That means you now. Your aunt Beverly was one of my dearest friends."

"I'm sorry for your loss," Ava said. An ache rose in her. She should be the one experiencing the loss; Bev was her family. Ava was in her flat, wearing her dress, talking to her friends. She could only grieve for missed opportunities.

"What do you think of your little flat in this end of the world?"

"I love it."

"Who wouldn't."

"Queenie!" Franco yelled. "You have to see how she captured George."

All heads turned to her, including George, her bow-tie man. George gazed at his picture; then he, too, roared with laughter, along with Franco. The crowd parted and there stood Queenie. He was wearing a long black gown with sequins. He was in full makeup, complete with a shaggy blond wig. Ava couldn't believe the size of his purple-tinted eyelashes. He was the ugliest yet somehow the most arresting woman she had ever seen.

"There's the birthday girl again," Ava said. Queenie fluttered his lashes. It was the second outfit he'd worn since they yelled, "Surprise!" He'd shouted so loud she wasn't surprised her eardrums were still vibrating. She had to give it to him; even she thought he was truly surprised for a minute there. He wrapped his arms around her and smashed her to his bosom. He smelled of Scotch and baby powder.

"Beverly would be so happy," he said.

"Don't squash the artist," someone called out. "Not until she does me."

"Why not?" somebody yelled out. "Everyone else has." Laughter rolled in, one wave after another.

"Oh, me first, darling," Franco said.

Queenie released Ava. "I wondered what you did in that thing all day," he said, looking over her shoulder at her sketchbook. "Remarkable." Ava picked up her sketch pad, ripped out the portrait of George, and handed it to him. He grinned ear to ear. This was much better than sketching criminals. These people were happy to recognize themselves.

"Will you sign it?" George asked.

"Of course." She had never been asked to sign one of her sketches. The police certainly never wanted her name. She autographed it, and then paused over a new sheet while a crowd hovered around her. So many people. Little colored dots began to swim in front of her face. *Oh, no. Not inside too, please not inside too.*

Fire extinguisher, fire extinguisher, fire extinguisher. Ava put her hands over her eyes. She could just announce a game of hide-and-seek. She'd hide under the bed.

"Give her some space," Queenie said. "Come on, come on." He began to physically pull people away. "Ava does better if you just act natural," he said. "Right, luv?"

Ava swallowed hard and nodded. "Not easy with this bunch," Queenie said in a stage whisper before whipping his dress to the side and flouncing off into the crowd. Ava sat on her emerald stool and gripped her sketch pad.

"I want to be a rock star," Franco called from across the room.

"Perfect," Ava said, focusing on the sketch pad. "I can see you in the spotlight."

"Can you, luv?"

"With those looks? You have to be under the lights." Men in the crowd laughed and a few slapped Franco on the back.

"Give me leather pants," Franco said.

"Draw them half off!" someone else yelled out.

"That's not until the finale," Franco said.

"Mince pie, hot from the oven!" Queenie yelled.

"Why didn't you tell us she was so talented?" George said.

"I didn't realize," Queenie said. "I thought she had no talents whatsoever."

As Ava sketched Franco, she heard someone walk up, saw a glimpse of long brunette hair. She looked up to find Hillary gazing at her.

"That's quite good," Hillary said. She sounded surprised. Hillary didn't think much of her to begin with, would never imagine Jasper having a crush on her.

Did Jasper have a crush on her? Or was she projecting? Her heart began to thump. If Hillary was here, did that mean Jasper was here too? Was he watching her? Did he think she was good? Where was he? She finished the sketch of rock-star Franco. She gave him a bubble: **Don't hate me because I'm beautiful.** Franco snatched it out of her hands and howled. He immediately started passing it around.

"Don't hate me because I'm beautiful, Queenie." She could tell he'd never heard the saying before. She could totally claim it as original.

"I don't hate you because you're beautiful," Queenie said. "I hate you because you're young."

"Ish," Georgie called out. "He's young-ish."

"How would you draw me?" Hillary said.

The socialite from hell? "You could have a shotgun wedding," Ava replied. It just popped out of her mouth.

"What's a shotgun wedding?"

"Yes, tell us." Even Queenie looked on eagerly.

"You've never heard of a shotgun wedding?"

Heads shook back and forth.

"Well. The origin goes back to the Wild West. When a young

lady was dating and became pregnant her father, shotgun in hand, would force her and the man who got her that way to marry. So today, when a pregnant woman marries her lover it's often referred to as a shotgun wedding."

Laughter rolled around. "Shotgun wedding," Georgie said.

"Shotgun wedding," Franco repeated. He mimed holding up a shotgun. Georgie mimed having a pregnant belly, then slapped his hands on either cheek, mouth opened. Ava laughed. Hillary simply stared. In fact, she seemed to be vibrating a little.

Franco placed his hand on Ava's shoulder. "Would you like a cocktail, darling?"

"Please," Ava said.

Hillary hovered over Ava, hands on her hips. "Are you implying that I might be with child?" Her eyes were flashing. "Or are you saying I'm fat?"

"Fat? Of course not. You're a twig."

"I'm a two-bit whore then, is that what you're saying?"

"Of course not. No more than I'm implying that Francis is a rock star—"

"Darling, I *am* a rock star."

"Or Georgie is a cruise ship director."

"All aboard," Georgie called out.

"Not helping!" Ava shouted out.

Hillary's eyes were literally flashing.

"So why did that just pop out of your head?" Hillary said.

"I don't know. I'm just trying to be funny."

"You are funny. Throwing a party for Queenie on one hand and threatening to go to court on the other." *Going to court*? Had she heard that from Jasper? How could Hillary say that in front of all these people?

"Go to court?" Queenie said, popping up like he had bionic hearing. "Why would you be going to court?"

"It's nothing," Ava said. "I didn't mean it." Where was Jasper? Hillary was still standing there. Ava turned over a new sheet in the sketch pad. "I can make you a judge, or a police officer, or a high-society girl—or the Wicked Witch of the West End." *Oh, no.* Why did these things keep shooting out of her mouth? Because she loathed Hillary and she couldn't hide it. What did Jasper ever see in her?

"The Wicked Witch of the West End!" Franco yelled into the crowd.

"Did you have a shotgun wedding?" Hillary demanded. God, she'd really upset her.

"No. I—"

"Of course not. Because your man was already married with children, wasn't he?" *Oh my God.* She was referring to Cliff. How did she know about Cliff? Jasper must have told her. How could he? But she'd never told Jasper about Cliff, had she? This just didn't make any sense. "Not to mention what a cruel thing it would be for you to have children in your condition."

"Excuse me?" Ava gripped the pencil so hard it broke in her palm.

"Would you lock them up too? Never let them see the sun?"

"Hillary!" Jasper's voice rang out. He was here. He heard. Soon he was standing beside Hillary, looking at Ava.

"You told her," Ava said.

"Ava," Jasper said. He reached for her.

Ava shot off the stool. "Did you happen to mention I didn't know he was married or does that not matter at all?"

"You're fighting the will?" Queenie asked, stepping forward. "On what grounds?"

"I have to go," Ava said. She wanted to shut herself in the bedroom. Under the bed, she needed to get under the bed. But she couldn't move.

"What's wrong?" Franco said.

"She's not very functional," Queenie said in another stage whisper. Those were just as annoying as his gasps.

"I'm highly functional," Ava said. "Just in a very small area."

"How could you even afford to fight the will?" Queenie said.

"She could sell sketches at parties," Franco said.

"She could make a fortune," Georgie said.

"Except the parties would always have to come to you, wouldn't they?" Queenie said.

"Ah, right," Georgie said. "The social experiment."

"The social experiment?" Queenie said.

"Ava is undercover," Franco whispered. "She's writing a book. *The Insider's Guide to London.*"

"Are you now?" Queenie said.

"And she's on Canadian television!" someone yelled out.

Queenie gasped. "Queenie is going to be on telly," Ava said. "Very soon."

"Ava," Jasper said. "Let's go somewhere." He took her hand. Ava started to rise from the stool. Queenie pushed her back down.

"It's my party," Queenie said. "No serious talk." He pulled Jasper away.

Hillary was still standing over Ava.

"What do you want?" Ava said.

Hillary put her hands on her knees and bent down so she was in Ava's face. "Jasper is not your friend. You won't need to ring him, see him, or talk to him."

Ava stood up. "You don't get to tell me who my friends are."

"He pities you. You know that, don't you? You're not mistaking that for some kind of affection, are you?"

"Hillary. Enough." Jasper was back. He took Ava's hand, threaded through the partygoers, and walked her out the door.

CHAPTER 24

"Please. Just give me a chance to explain." Jasper sat on the top step and patted the spot next to him. Ava passed him by a few steps, then turned around, but remained standing.

Jasper looked at her. She hated how turned on she could get by his gaze alone. It wasn't fair. "Are you browned off? You look browned off."

"How could you?" she said. "How did you even know about Cliff—that's number one. But tell Hillary? She hates me. You not only gave the enemy a gun; you also threw in the ammunition and loaded it for her."

"Would you by chance be speaking of a shotgun?" Jasper kept a straight face, but Ava could tell he was trying not to laugh. She bit her lip. That woman had no sense of humor. "Sorry. It's not what you think, Ava."

"I think you've had quite enough laughs at my expense." Jasper reached for Ava's hand, but she pulled it away and leaned against the wall. "I've never slammed my head against a wall," she said. "But I understand the desire."

"I would never purposefully hurt you. Tell me you know that."

"Don't manipulate me. We're not in court. You're not wearing your wig."

"Manipulate you?"

"You're being lawyerly trying to get me to answer a certain way."

Jasper stood up. "It hurts me that you think I would say nasty things about you behind your back. I would never do that. Never."

"But you did."

"No, Ava. I didn't. The day I first called you on video chat, remember?" Ava nodded. She would never forget. The spark had been there from the moment they first locked eyes. "Hillary was there."

"Why would you make a business call with her in the room?"

"She wasn't in the room when I placed the call. She still had keys. Let herself in. Maybe I should have interrupted the call to deal with her—but I thought it was almost over. I didn't know what was going to happen next."

Ava thought back to the video call. She certainly didn't mention Cliff. "Why in the world would I have said anything to you about Cliff? I'd only just found out I'd been sleeping with a married man a half an hour before we spoke."

"You had a fight with your mother about it."

"That was after I shut off the video."

"You turned off the monitor. The call was still connected. I heard everything."

"Oh, God."

"I didn't mean to listen, but your voice carries." Ava stared at him. "All right. Maybe I meant to listen a little. But only because I was concerned about you. No, that's not right either. I was fascinated by you. All right? So I listened." Ava sank to the step. Jasper sat next to her and put his arm around her. "I'm sorry that happened to you. You didn't deserve that."

"Neither did his wife."

"Neither did his wife," Jasper agreed.

"Why does Hillary hate me so much?"

Jasper clasped Ava's hands and brought them into his lap. "Because she knows how I feel about you."

Ava swallowed. "And how do you feel?" Was she really going to do this?

"Smitten?" Jasper held her gaze, and there it was again, that little jolt. That left her tingling. Smitten. Yes, smitten.

"Me too," Ava said. Definitely smitten. "Queenie accused me of having a crush on you weeks ago."

Jasper raised his eyebrows. "Is that right?" He sounded thrilled.

"Apparently I was mentioning you a lot."

"Never underestimate that man." He leaned into Ava as if he was about to divulge a secret. "He caught me smiling."

"Smiling?"

"Apparently, ever since I met you, I've been smiling like an idiot."

They looked at each other, smiling. Jasper leaned in and kissed her. When he pulled away they went right back to smiling. *What a pair.*

What was she doing? She couldn't maintain a relationship with a man like Jasper. Hillary was right. She could never be a proper girlfriend, let alone a proper mother. It would be cruel to lead Jasper on. She pulled her hands away.

"Don't do that," Jasper said. "Don't run away."

"I'm not good enough for you."

Jasper reached in his pocket and pulled out a postcard. He handed it to Ava.

Open Mic Night

"You're going to do it?" Jasper nodded. "That's great. That's so great." Ava was proud of him. Even if he bombed, at least he was trying, following his dream. She hoped he didn't bomb though. But if he did bomb, she really hoped he didn't blame her for encouraging him.

"Do you really mean that?" Jasper asked.

"Of course. Why wouldn't I?"

"When I tried to tell Hillary, she didn't take it seriously for one second. She threw the flyer on the ground. Now that's someone who's not good for me. You?" He put his hand on her face, caressed her jawline with his thumb. "You are nothing but good for me. And you haven't even heard the best part." Jasper grinned. Whatever he had to tell her, he was excited about it.

"What?"

"I'm going to quit my job to pursue comedy full-time."

"What?"

"Because of you."

"You're going to quit your job—as a barrister—because of me?"

"You sound alarmed."

Ava stood. "You're just going to quit? Before you start making a living from it?"

"Yes. Yes. That's exactly what I'm saying."

"Because of *me?*" *Oh, please, God.* She could not have that burden on her. Should she tell him? Tell him he wasn't any good?

Jasper stood. "I'm sick of playing it safe. You have to take what you want in this life. Take it by the reins, or the horn, or the saddle knob."

"Saddle knob?"

"I was running out of rodeo metaphors. What's the thing on the saddle that you hold on to? What do they call that?"

"The horn."

"Oh. Right. So. So—when they say, 'Take life by the horns'— I mean the horns of a bull—you know, just reach right up there and grab those horns. But I can't say 'horn' twice, now can I?"

"Can we move past the grabbing? Don't most artists have a day job? You know, just until they're sure that they can make a living at their . . . hobby?"

"Maybe the ones who don't believe in themselves. Who doubt. But I met you, and I don't have any doubts. Not anymore. You've inspired me to be as brave as you are."

"Are you making fun of me?"

"Of course not. You've come a long way already. Can't you see it?" He gestured. "We're standing in the stairwell. You didn't even hesitate."

"I'm not afraid of stairwells."

"But we're closer to the outside."

"Keep talking, Romeo."

"Sorry." He took her hands. "I think you're doing remarkably. You're throwing a party. And they all love you."

"It's my first party. Ever."

"You're changing. I can see it." Jasper leaned in. He was going to kiss her. Ava put her hands on his face and gently pushed it back.

"Do you pity me? Are you making fun of me?"

"Of course not." He took her hands and held them. "Why would you say such a thing?"

"I don't want to be the reason you quit a perfectly respectable job."

"To pursue my dream."

"Isn't that . . . just a little bit reckless?"

Jasper turned away from her, headed up to the landing. "I don't believe this. You don't believe in me either."

"That's not fair. How can I believe in you? I've never even seen you perform."

Jasper grabbed her and pulled her into him. "You're right. You're right. Will you come? Do you think you could do it?" He was pleading with her. She could see it in his eyes. This was what their relationship would be like. He would be supportive up until a point and then he would expect her to be normal already. To go out and do things. To live. Perfectly normal requests. Ones she'd never be able to satisfy.

"I can't do it. I can't come."

"I see. Okay. Okay. I didn't mean to push."

"This is why we can't see each other. Smitten or not." Ava faced the door to her flat. Her heart literally ached for Jasper's touch.

"Wait. Just because I asked I didn't expect you to say yes." Jasper stayed on the landing. Ava looked down at him. She wished he could save her. But he couldn't. This wasn't just in her head. She had a biological condition. One that could turn him into a prisoner too.

"I hate this. I hate me."

"Don't say that. Don't ever say that."

"I'm a shut-in, Jasper. You're not. This is where our story ends."

"You're making remarkable progress. Why can't you see that?"

"I've only done one thing on the list. And even that was an accident."

Jasper came up behind her. "I've been thinking about what you said. About fighting the will in court. And I think you're right."

"I can't afford to fight it."

"I'll represent you."

"And lose all your friendships?"

"Beverly was my friend too. And I believe with all my heart that she had no idea what she was setting in motion. It was her intention that you get the flat." Jasper reached her and put his hands on her waist. "I hate to see you sad."

"It means a lot that you would fight for me. But I won't do that to you. Or Queenie. The only way I'd ever consider being with you is if I tackled that list."

"I don't care about the list," Jasper said.

"I do."

"You do?"

"At the very least, I want to make the effort. That's what counts, isn't it? The effort?"

"Yes. Yes, that is exactly what counts, Ava." His hands moved up her back and he pulled her into him. "The effort is everything," he whispered into her ear. "It's everything."

Ava rubbed his back. He smelled good, he felt good, and he was right here, wanting her. She wanted to be with him. But only if she could make real progress. Only if she could be who Jasper needed her to be. At least part of the time. She had to earn it. She had to earn him. Ava pulled away, placed her hand on Jasper's face, and ran it along his jawline.

Jasper reached up and trailed his finger along her cheek. "I've felt a connection with you from the moment I laid eyes on you. I can't stop thinking about you. I can't stop smiling. I can't stop saying your name over and over again in my head. But I'm a coward too."

"You? A coward?"

"When you asked me how I felt about you, I said 'smitten.' That was a lie. I'm not just smitten. I'm falling in—"

Ava put her fingers over his lips.

"Don't," she said. "If I lose the flat, I won't be staying in London."

"You could stay with me."

"How? Where?"

"With me."

"We can't rush this. I don't just come with baggage; I'm lugging the whole damn carousel."

"Has anyone ever told you you talk too much?" Jasper whispered. Jasper began to walk Ava over to the wall. When she was pressed flat against it, he put a hand on either side of the wall, and kissed her. Soon Ava relaxed into the kiss, and then she began kissing him back. Jasper's hands went around her waist. Ava broke away.

"God, I wish I didn't have a party going on. I want to take you to my bedroom. Right now."

"We could go to my place," Jasper said. Ava froze. He caught the look on her face. "Sorry. I wasn't thinking." Ava broke away. "It's okay."

"It's not. That's a perfectly normal thing to say to a woman who wants to sleep with you. Only I'm not normal. I'm never going to be normal."

"I don't want you to be normal. What is it you said about love? It's imperfect. You're positively imperfect."

The door flew open and Hillary stepped into the hallway. She glared at Ava, then Jasper. "You're going to regret this," she said to Ava.

"Good," Ava said. "If you don't have regrets, it means you're not really living."

Ava walked into the flat and headed for the bedroom. The party was still going strong. They were so loud and animated they didn't notice Ava come in at all. Thank God there was no one in there, no one making love on the bed, no one in the bathroom. Of course she couldn't close herself in, because they would have to come through the bedroom to use the loo. She dived underneath the bed. At least she'd cleaned it. There was also a sheet and a little pillow. She touched her lips. Just seconds ago she was kissing Jasper. *Maybe I'm falling in . . .* Her lips still burned. Oh, how she wanted him. If she were someone else she would have been on her way to his flat by now. He probably had a lovely flat. It would be tidy, and organized. She'd see to it that they made it a little dirty. Why did she have to stop him? It would have been the first time a man had ever told her he loved her. She could have checked things off of a real list then—a life list. She was never going to change. She was never going to be normal. She couldn't do that to him. She certainly wanted to, and she probably could, but she wouldn't. She just wouldn't.

CHAPTER 25

The next morning Ava was barely awake when the buzzer screamed through the flat. Given the pitch of the bloody thing, every dog in London was probably barking in her direction. When was she ever going to remember to ask someone to fix that? Could she figure it out herself? Grab a knife and cut a couple of wires? Who the hell was buzzing her anyway? For a few groggy seconds she forgot all about the party. She slid off the bed and padded to the door. The smell of stale alcohol brought back the first reminder. The evidence was stacked up. Literally. Empty bottles standing proudly on tables. Water rings. Food wrappers. Overflowing ashtrays. Every surface screamed, *We partied last night!* Huh. She would have thought Brits and drag queens would have been a bit more tidy. She glanced at the sofa expecting to see the lump that was Queenie. It was empty. Did he get lucky last night? At least he had the decency not to stay here. This flat wasn't built for privacy. The buzzer rang again. "Who is it?"

"Candygram!" a loud voice rang out. It wasn't coming from downstairs; someone was at the door to the flat.

"Candygram?" Ava was trying to stall so she could recognize his voice.

"I've always wanted to say that." Peals of laughter rang out.

She hadn't been sure about the voices, but she sure recognized the laughter. "Franco?" Ava said.

"And Georgie."

Ava opened the door. They stood, looking fresh, as if they had gone to bed at a decent hour after a nice cup of herbal tea. Gone were the lavish outfits, hairpieces, and makeup of the night before. Instead, each was wearing a tracksuit and runners. Georgie's was purple; Franco's was bright orange. Franco was just as beautiful as a bald man. His smile was infectious. Ava glanced down at her horse pajamas. "Did you forget something?" They were each holding bags, and plastic bins, and held them up in unison. Tinfoil sat on the top of Georgie's box.

"Let us in," Franco said, pushing his way in. "We brought product."

"Product?" Ava said.

"I used to do hair," Georgie said. "And today I'm going to do yours." They immediately commandeered the kitchen, setting down their stuff, and arranging things to their liking. Franco pulled a chair over to the sink while Georgie whipped out a black apron and put it on.

"Ta-da," he said.

"You want to do my hair. Here?"

"Luv. We felt so sorry for you last night." He put his hand on his heart.

"You did?" Why did he say it like it was a good thing?

"We talked about you all night long," Franco said. "Everyone did."

"Wonderful news," Ava said. "Thanks for that."

"Don't be a poor sport," Franco said. "Everyone loved you. Your sketches were the hit of the party." Ava. The hit of a party. Words she never imagined hearing. But she couldn't help feeling she was more of a freak-show attraction than anything else.

Georgie began to run his fingers through Ava's hair. "I can't imagine not being able to get my hair done. Running out of the salon mid panic attack with your foils still on."

"It was the most frightening thing we've ever heard," Franco said.

"Really?" Ava said. "Not all the stories of how death is waiting at every London corner?"

"It was your hair gave us nightmares," Georgie said. He placed his hands on Ava's shoulders and guided her to the chair. "You just sit your 'before' self down."

"Who says I want an 'after' self?" Ava said.

"Man up," Franco said. He handed Georgie a very large, very sharp pair of scissors. "We're going to cut."

"And highlight," Georgie said.

"Highlights? I don't want highlights," Ava said.

"What about streaks of dark red?" Franco said to Georgie.

"Brilliant," Georgie said. "Like mahogany."

"Mahogany?" Ava said. She didn't like the sound of that. "Like a piano?"

Franco towered over her, holding a makeup brush. "Georgie is going to do your hair; I'm going to do your face."

"Please don't ever say that again," Ava said.

Franco threw his head back and laughed. *God, what would it feel like to be him?* So confident and carefree. Surely he'd taken his share of prejudice and abuse, but he was totally comfortable in his own skin. Not just that. He flaunted it. "We're going to bring out your inner slut."

"And then we'll try to coax out your outer slut," Georgie added.

Ava shot out of the chair. She hadn't prepared for this. She liked to prepare for things. "I love this idea," she said. She held her hands up and slowly started to back up. "But I'm just not ready to confront either of my sluts."

"We're your sluts now, luv," Franco said. His long arms shot out. He pulled her in and pushed her down in the chair again, whipped out an apron, and threw it over her.

Ava tried to pull it off, but he was already tying it tightly in the back. "What about next week?" she said. "I'll check my calendar."

"You don't have a calendar," Franco said.

"Next week is too late," Georgie said.

"Too late?" Ava said. "Am I dying?"

Franco laughed and punched her in the shoulder. "After all those cocktails last night, I certainly am." He pinched his cheeks as if they weren't already glowing.

Ava gripped the arms of the chair and squeezed her eyes shut as if she were about to rocket into space. "I need time to think about this. Look at pictures in a magazine maybe."

Georgie was setting up little plastic bottles. A chemical stench soon overpowered the tiny kitchen. Georgie shook one of the bottles, and beamed. He definitely had cruise director teeth. "We have just landed an ongoing Friday gig at the hottest club, just two little old blocks away, and you are going to be our guest of honor." He said it so matter-of-factly. *Just two little old blocks away. Is that all?* All Ava had to do was reach up and grab the scissors. Then plunge them into his heart.

"I see what's going on here. You think you can cure me with a new hairdo." Ava stood. "I'm your new pet, am I?"

"You need a drink," Franco said.

"Get the agoraphobic girl outside. Maybe all she's been missing all these years is a few piano streaks in her hair." Ava stood her ground, and made direct eye contact without smiling, but Georgie and Franco didn't look away.

"What if it *was* all you were missing, luv?" Franco said.

"All Cinderella needed was a few rags, and a pumpkin," Georgie said.

"You're grossly underestimating my condition," Ava said.

"We saw you in Beverly's dress last night," Georgie said.

"You know all her outfits?" Ava said. Heat rose to her cheeks. What did they think of her? Wearing a dead diva's dress.

"Do you know why Beverly was such a great actress?" Franco asked.

"Scotch?" Ava guessed.

"She's got you there," Georgie said.

"She was never herself," Franco said. "Beverly Wilder was always playing a role."

"Don't you think that's kind of sad?" Ava said.

"Sad? She was the most alive person I've ever met," Franco said.

"And talented," Georgie said, running his finger lovingly up and down the blade of the scissors.

Ava inched back toward the chair. "Did she ever talk about me?"

"All the time," Franco said. "She loved you to pieces. That's why we're here."

"Exactly," Georgie said. "So shut your gob and let us work our magic."

Franco pushed her down in the chair for a third time. He leaned down and spoke directly in her ear. "If you get up one more time, I'm using chloroform."

"Very funny."

"Try me," he said.

Ava folded her arms. Georgie began pinning little chunks of her hair to the top of her head. Franco was beautiful and Georgie was meticulous. If they couldn't help her, who could? "Bring it," Ava said. The pair cheered. Georgie began to apply color to various strands, wrapping them in tinfoil. The smell was hideous and he had a bit of a rough touch. Still, she dared not cry out or complain. She couldn't believe that they had actually come over here to do her hair. She wasn't going to complain.

Franco put on music, and pulled an enormous bottle of wine out of his bag. "Juice time," he sang. He poured everyone a generous glass. Georgie was deep in concentration, but Ava happily took hers.

"It must make it hard to date," Georgie said about fourteen foils into it. "Never going out on the prowl."

"He wants to know if you're a virgin," Franco said.

"I do not," Georgie said. "It just occurred to me that your beaus would have to make house calls."

"True," Ava said. "That's why I only shag delivery boys and old-school veterinarians." Georgie and Franco gasped in unison. God, drag queens were fun to be around. "Kidding," Ava said. "I've never shagged a veterinarian. But the Domino's boy? Now he comes in thirty minutes or less or it's free." Ava laughed. Franco and Georgie just stared at her. "Lost in translation."

"Pity," Franco said.

"But I did have a boyfriend. He was a police officer." Good old Cliff. Was he still married? Had he found a new mistress? One he would be forced to take to movies and motel rooms?

"We heard," they said in unison. *Shit. Hillary and her big mouth.*

"I love a man in uniform," Franco said. "And out of it," he added with a wink.

"Were you in love?" Georgie asked.

"No," Ava said. "Just lust." Jasper flitted across her mind. She felt heat rise into her cheeks. *Maybe I'm falling in—*

"We're going to let this sit," Georgie said. He took off his gloves and picked up his wine.

"So. What about the London men?" Franco said. "Anyone catch your fancy?" His voice was suddenly an octave higher. Ava's alarm bells went off.

"I've barely left the apartment," Ava said.

"Notice how she avoided the question," Georgie said.

"Oh, I noticed," Franco said.

"You seemed pretty chummy with Jasper last night," Georgie said. He topped off Ava's wine. Ava glanced at their wine-glasses. They looked as if they hadn't been touched. In fact, Franco was sipping out of a bottle of vitamin water. What were they doing to her? Why wasn't she drinking vitamins?

"He's a friend," Ava said.

"Handsome fellow, wouldn't you say?" Franco said.

"I'd say," Georgie said. "What do you say, Ava?"

"It's hard to believe Jasper and Hillary were ever a couple," Ava said. She tried to sound casual.

"You say that as if they're over," Franco said.

"They are over," Ava said. Franco and Georgie exchanged a look. "Aren't they?" Of course they were. Jasper was falling; she was falling. A net. Were they falling without a net?

"Is anything ever really over?" Franco said.

"Yes," Ava said. "When things are over, they're over." What was going on here? She'd better be careful or she was going to give her feelings away. What was it about getting her hair done that made a woman want to divulge every secret underneath the sun?

"Somebody has a little crush," Franco said, clapping his hands together.

"On Hillary?" Georgie said. "You're gay?"

Franco swatted Georgie. "Not Hillary." They turned to her at the same time.

"Jasper," they said in stereo.

"Shit," Ava said.

Franco jumped up and down. "We got it! We got it!"

"Oh, he's going to love you when we finish with you," Franco said.

"Let's not get her hopes up too high," Georgie said. Franco and Georgie exchanged a look.

"What?" Ava said. "What was that?"

"Nothing. It's just . . . You don't really want a British man, do you?" Franco said.

"Why not? What's wrong with British men?"

"Where do we start?" Georgie said.

"Wait. Are you talking about straight British men or gay British men?"

"Honey, we're talking about Brits of both sexes. You don't want us. We're not *Downton Abbey*."

"We don't always have straight teeth."

"Or big dicks."

"We're pompous."

"Boring."

"Workaholics."

"Snobby."

"Very dry sense of humor."

"Show her."

"How many barristers does it take to screw in a lightbulb?"

"Why would we screw in a lightbulb when we have a perfectly good bed?"

Ava's head was starting to hurt, and truth be told, her scalp was starting to burn. "Should we rinse this off now?"

"Not yet," Georgie said. "I've got you on a timer, darling; don't worry about a thing."

"What about a Latin man?" Franco said. He began to sway his hips, à la tango-for-one.

Ava drank more wine. It almost seemed as if they were on a mission to turn her against Jasper. It was as if . . .

Hillary sent them. *Oh, God.* The hair. Had he done something hideous to her hair? Georgie wouldn't do that, would he?

Hell hath no fury like Hillary Swanson. Was she going to be bald? Ava knew she didn't have the kind of head that could pull off bald; she just knew it. Was this what she deserved? Who cared what she looked like when nobody was going to see her anyway?

"Take them off," she said, reaching for her foils. "Take them off."

"What's the matter?" Georgie asked. "Are you having a panic attack?"

"More wine?" Franco said.

Ava snatched Franco's vitamin water out of his hands and drank the rest of it down.

"That was rude," Franco said. "I'm only half-hydrated."

"Rude is pretending to be my friend. Rude is making me go bald."

"Bald?" Georgie said.

"What are you doing to me?" Ava said. Georgie and Franco put their hands up, as if surrendering. "I thought you two liked me."

"Of course we like you," Franco said. "Why else would we be here?"

"Hillary," Ava said. "And don't you even think of lying about it."

Georgie sighed. "You don't want to cross her."

"So she did send you," Ava said.

"We have minds of our own. Your hair is going to be fabulous. But yes. She suggested we do a little reconnaissance."

"And she helped us get the gig at the club. The club that's only two little blocks away."

"Why is she doing this? She's the one who dumped him," Ava said.

"Jealousy makes the heart grow fonder," Georgie said.

"What is the deal with you and Jasper?" Franco asked.

Ava didn't have to speak. Her face did it for her.

"Oh my God," Georgie said. "You're in love." Franco clapped. Georgie swatted his hands away.

"We won't tell her," Franco said. "We're on Team Ava."

Team Ava. She'd never had a team before.

"We'll tell her you have a mad crush on Jasper, but he flat out rejected you," Georgie said.

"We'll tell her Jasper is still madly in love with her. That will turn her off."

"Tell her Jasper is going to quit his job as a barrister to become a stand-up comedian," Ava said.

"No," Franco said. "It has to be believable. Can you imagine?"

"Is there any possibility that you're a lesbian?" Georgie said. "We could go with that one too."

"Especially if we butch up her hair," Franco said.

"You are not butching up my hair," Ava said. Georgie began removing foils. "Right?" Ava said. "Right?"

"How about this? We won't butch up your hair if you promise to at least try and make it to the club on Friday. You can take a taxi if you wish."

"Of course," Ava said. Georgie and Franco cheered. *Idiots.* There wasn't a chance in hell she was going to their club. Georgie continued with her hair, Ava drank the rest of the wine, and Franco pulled out a flyer for their club and stuck it on the fridge with a magnet that read: Upstage Me at Your Own Risk.

CHAPTER 26

Ava stared in the mirror long after Team Ava had left. She stood, naked and alone. Her hair was cut in long layers, angled in toward her face. Streaks of dark red made her eyes look darker, almost green. She still recognized herself, but it was like staring at an alter ego. Bad Ava. Sexy Ava. Daring Ava. "The possibilities," she whispered. She tried on a black silk night-gown of Beverly's. There was no doubt it had been dry-cleaned and never worn again; the tag was still on and plastic was still over it. The woman certainly did dress young. She only kept it on for a few seconds before slipping on sweatpants and a T-shirt. She picked up her sketch pad and headed for her emerald stool. She sat and stared out the window. It was foggy again today. She hadn't seen Deven outside his place in a while. She hoped he was okay. Vic was going to eat him alive. Yet he wanted her to, didn't he? Would a peaceful world ever exist? Where you didn't have to worry about crime, or prejudice, or lovers who just wanted to bulldoze you? Probably not. It was too bad the good people couldn't win out. She had met plenty of good people in London. Some strange ones too. Like every-where, she supposed. But how was she to know? Ava had been so few places. She concentrated on sketching the scenery. It was too foggy to see the details of any particular person. She started with the London Eye. God, she couldn't imagine why on earth people would want to ride that thing. Then again, was it much different from looking out these windows? Ava imag-ined what it would feel like if her flat were rotating. *Oh, God.* Yes, it was much different. Nauseating. She'd might as well call it: The-London-Eye-Will-Never-Ride-You.

"You were quite a hit with my friends," Queenie said. Ava jumped, then turned around. Queenie stood dressed in his black ball gown from the party but wig gone, makeup smeared underneath his eyes, yet he was the one who gasped. "Georgie." His hands did cartwheels. "Georgie did your hair."

"What do you think?"

"You look like a different person."

"I know."

"You look incredible."

"Thank you." She wasn't going to mention that she had Hillary to thank. And that she couldn't wait for Jasper to see her.

"You should go clothes shopping. Or at least order some-thing online."

"Maybe." Ava smiled and went back to sketching. Queenie dropped to the floor and began looking under every piece of furniture in the vicinity.

"What are you looking for?" Ava said.

"My lucky charm."

Ava froze. She'd forgotten all about it. She had also forgot-ten to tell him. Tell him it was her. The new Ava told the truth. "I thought you said Jasper lost it?"

"But you gave it to him here, correct?"

"Yes."

"And from the looks of you two, he probably didn't leave right away, so maybe he never actually made it out of the flat with it; maybe it's still here somewhere." He looked toward the bedroom, then back at her with a grimace. He jerked his head in the direction of the bedroom. "Did you check? You know. Everywhere?"

"Can't you just buy another? Maybe on eBay?"

Queenie hauled himself up. He was sweating. He looked like her before one of her panic attacks. "I told you. You don't buy lucky charms. They have to be given to you."

"Oh."

"I can't stall the audition anymore. It's in two days. I won't get the part if I don't have my lucky charm."

"Do you think someone from the party took it?" Ava said. She was a bad person. But they were getting along so well. The last thing she needed was Queenie blaming her for not getting a part on the telly.

"Georgie," Queenie said. He gasped and put his hand over his heart.

"Why Georgie?"

"Because he's going to the same audition. He wants me to fail. Everyone knows I need my lucky charm."

"Who gave it to you?"

"The only man I've ever loved."

Even though drama was his middle name, there was a ring of truth to this statement. *Shit.* "You broke up?" Just Ava's luck. If Queenie still had the love of his life he probably wouldn't be staking claim to her flat.

"He passed away. Five years ago."

"Oh." Why did she take it outside in the first place? Didn't bring her much luck. Should she tell him it was totally useless? "I'm sorry."

"It's not your fault."

"I'm still sorry."

Queenie nodded, then picked up his robe and headed to the bathroom. Ava filled the espresso maker and put it on the stove. By the time Queenie returned she had a cup waiting for him. His eyes widened and he placed his hand on his heart. They took their espressos to the living room and sat looking out at London.

"I don't have anything of my father's," Ava said. " Just. A song."

"A song is good."

" 'The Girl from Ipanema.' "

"Nice choice."

"Except I've never listened to it since."

"It's too painful?"

"He was playing it when he died. We were dancing to it."

"I can think of worse ways to go."

"I never thought of it like that."

"He was listening to his favorite song; he was dancing; he was with his beautiful daughter."

Ava hadn't meant to bring it up. "He was too young. I was only ten. It ruined the rest of my life."

"I'm sorry. Beverly was torn to pieces too."

"Was she?"

"Yes. She loved Bertrand."

"You talk about him as if you knew him."

"I felt as if I did." Just like Ava felt she knew Jasper, and Queenie. Love had tentacles. It reached.

"What did she have against my mother?"

Queenie looked away, then headed for the kitchen. Ava followed. She watched him put the kettle on and remove a teacup from the cupboard along with a bag of tea. The Brits were probably the only people in the world who could drink a cup of tea after a shot of espresso. "Well?"

"I don't want to troll through ancient history."

"I do."

"No."

"It really hurt my father that Aunt Beverly didn't like my mother. And it really hurt me that she didn't try harder to be in my life."

"What about her? She lost her only brother."

"Lost him? To us? His family? To America?"

"Are you close to your mother?"

"I knew it. Aunt Beverly hated her because she's American." That reminded Ava. Her mother had never returned her phone call. Didn't she want to know what Ava meant by *I know?* Maybe she was glad she was gone. Ava had been too much to handle. Ava's agoraphobia had ruined her mother's life too. She'd never thought of it like that. She'd been too selfish. She should insist her mother come for a visit while she still had the flat.

Queenie took his tea to the table and sat down. Ava followed him. "I think Beverly was most upset by the change in Bertrand after he married your mother."

"Everybody changes when they get married."

"Does she still worry about every little thing?"

"No. She was saved by country line dancing."

"Beverly tried. You have no idea how much she tried."

"Missing a few matinées? Is that it?"

Queenie slammed down his teaspoon. He jumped up and flew into the living room, where he opened a small cabinet next to the sofa. Ava had never paid any attention to it. He lifted out a box and shoved it at her. "I don't want to answer any more questions." He took his tea, went back to the table, and turned his back on her. Ava sat on the sofa with the box.

She opened it. A pile of envelopes wrapped in a lavender ribbon greeted her. Cards. All marked: Return to Sender. Ava would have recognized the loopy script anywhere. Her mother was the one who had sent them back. Ava began to finger through them. The first ten were addressed to her, the next several her mother. Ava slammed the lid shut. What were these? Birthday cards, Christmas, valentines? Why would her mother do that to her? How dare she? What had Aunt Beverly done that had made her mother hate her so much? Ava didn't want to open them now. They were festering sores; they were glaring accusations. She knew it anyhow, deep down; she knew there had to have been letters, and cards, and postcards. She definitely wasn't going to read them in front of Queenie. Someday, she would read them. But only when she could savor them, read them without rage in her heart. Her mother was still alive. If she hated her, who would she have left? She put the box back in the cabinet and poured herself a Scotch. She'd buy more for Queenie later.

And she'd get his lucky charm back one way or the other. Tricky Vic. How could she get her to give it back?

Ava heard Queenie answer the phone in the other room. His voice went from friendly to Swiss yodeling. "Now? The audition is now?" He flew out of the room, his face glistening with sweat. "They had a cancellation," he said. "They want me to audition now."

"Okay, okay. You can do this."

"Not without my lucky charm."

Ava went to the kitchen. There was a drawer that held string, and tape, and scissors. She gathered them up and turned to Queenie. He was right behind her with an inquisitive look. "Do you have anything else that belongs to your lover?"

"Not with me. Everything I own is in storage."

"Okay. Okay. Tell me about him. What did he like?"

"Forget it. I'm not going to get the part."

"Don't be so dramatic."

"Don't be so agoraphobic."

"I'm trying to help you."

"You're saying I'm crazy for knowing what I know."

"I'm telling you, you can get roles without your lucky charm."

"You are hardly the person to be throwing stones. You aren't even in a glass house. You're in a glass palace."

"That almost sounded like a compliment."

"It wasn't."

Ava dug around the bookshelves. She opened the drawer of the end table next to the sofa. On her third attempt, she found an American fifty-cent piece. Her father must have sent this to Beverly once upon a time. It was approximately the same shape and size as Queenie's lucky charm; it would probably even have the same weight against his skin. Ava taped it around the string. "Close your eyes." Ava slipped it around his neck. Queenie gasped and his hand went for it.

"No touching, no looking. It's your lucky charm."

Queenie opened one eye and looked at her. "Is it?"

"Repeat after me. 'It's my lucky charm.' "

"If it works so well, why don't you just make yourself one?"

"Because I'm not at the lucky charm level."

"I have to get dressed." Queenie flung open the closet and pulled out a suit. He held it against him.

"Dapper," Ava said. She never saw anyone change so fast. When he was ready, he stood in front of her. The new lucky charm was hidden underneath his white shirt and bow tie. He touched it. "It's your lucky charm," Ava said. "It is." Queenie nodded and headed for the door. "Queenie?" He turned around. "What if?"

"What if?"

"Your lucky charm didn't bring you luck, but you brought the luck to it."

"How so?"

"It sat against your skin, soaked up your unstoppable energy, and carried all that love you had for . . ."

"Alfred."

"Alfred. You brought the luck. Maybe you lost it because it was time you passed it on to someone else. You know. Like blowing a kiss."

Queenie cocked his head and considered it. Then he considered her. "I guess I'm off to test your theory."

"Good luck."

Queenie squeaked. His hands flapped. Ava didn't know if this was some sort of ritual or he was literally trying to fly. "You never, ever say that to an actor."

"Sorry. Break a leg."

He exhaled. "Better." He pulled himself together, flung open the door, and slammed it on his way out. Ava ached a little after he was gone. Could this be it? Would he get the part, become a television star, and give up the fight for this flat? He'd still be friends with her, wouldn't he? Come for a visit? She put the kettle on for tea. She went to the window, and it hit her. She put the kettle on as a reflex to comfort herself. She smiled. Maybe she was becoming a little bit British. She sat on her emerald stool and watched Queenie walk up the street with a bounce in his step. And then, he stopped. He turned. And he looked up at Ava and he waved. She waved back. When he walked away again, she felt like she had just won the lottery. He was going to his audition without his crutch. And he looked up, and he waved. She made that possible.

She liked him. She liked him underfoot. She liked his blue silk kimono, and red scarf strung over a chair, or a door, or a sofa. It was like the middle-aged gay man's version of *Where's Waldo?*, UK-style. She liked the shuffling sound his slippers made in the morning; she liked how he flapped his hands when he got excited; she liked when he had a pep in his step. She liked his vocalizations. Screams. Gasps. Squeals. He was walking drama. Lucky charm her arse. She hoped her tips helped. The fate of the flat aside, she really wanted Queenie to get the role. She could see why Aunt Beverly loved him. Once you got past the bite, he was all bark. He was an excellent chef too. If only this flat were larger. Maybe they could have split it indefinitely. Then again, maybe there was nothing he loved about her. It would probably be an unimaginable drag for anyone, let alone a queen, to have a roomie who never left the room.

CHAPTER 27

Here it was, another Monday morning in London. Ava was surprised she could keep track of the days. After the bustle of the party and Franco and Georgie's visit, and the excitement around Queenie's audition (he still hadn't returned; Ava was dying to know how it went), the flat felt unnaturally still. Was it always so quiet? The place seemed more suited to laughter, and the clink of glasses, or even a gasp or two from Queenie. But it was just her, and the dome-shaped windows, and her new mahogany-striped hair, and her emerald stool. Lonely. That's how she felt. It was a new feeling for her; she normally relished being alone. London was spread out before her, offering some comfort. In a city you were never truly alone, now were you? And she had her mother, whom she hadn't spoken with in quite some time.

Ava picked up the phone and called her mother. It went to voice mail. Same as it had most of the other times she'd called. "Hi, Mom. It's Ava. I miss you. I'm sorry that Aunt Beverly wasn't nice to you. I'm sorry we fought. I hope you come visit. Call me." She hung up. *God. So quiet.* Everyone was probably out *doing* something. Day after day. Was it ever challenging for them to find something new to occupy their time? Didn't anybody just sit around anymore?

Maybe it was time to at least think about tackling something on the list. She'd start with Intermittent Exposure Therapy. It was a commonly used method for phobias. If you were, say, terrified of spiders, the therapist would start acclimating you to your phobia by showing you pictures of spiders. Once you could look at the pictures without clawing your eyes out, they might move on to, say, showing you a live spider in a glass jar. And so on down the line. Ava didn't want to think about it anymore or she was going to develop a fear of spiders. Instead, she'd start with something a little more pleasant. *Sit on a bench in Hyde Park.*

Ava shoved the sofa against the bookcase. She set the emerald stool in the middle of the flat. Aunt Beverly had three plants, all ferns. They were situated on the top shelf of the bookcase along the wall. Ava removed the plants and placed them around the emerald stool. She set a chair in front of the stool, and propped up the laptop. She went to YouTube and typed in: "Hyde Park."

There were multiple videos to watch. They panned over the beautiful yet so very large park. A cheery flute accompanied the video. Hyde Park, a chipper male voice with a London accent told her, was where Londoners went to ride bikes, jog, stroll, take a boat ride, or play with their dogs. The videos showed pictures of Londoners doing just that. It was one of the eight royal parks in London. Ava had to admit that adding the word "Royal" to anything suddenly made it seem a lot more important than your average park.

Three hundred and fifty acres. Wow. Her heart didn't like hearing that. Soon Ava felt as if she had already jogged or biked or boated through the entire place, all along the Serpentine lake.

A Metropolitan police station was located in the park. Ava wondered if she would feel safer if she sat on a bench near the station. Speakers' Corner was a fascinating discovery. Every Sunday people could come to this corner and speak on any subject. From the videos Ava clicked on, it appeared they mostly argued with one another over religion.

Nearby was the Marble Arch. It used to be at Buckingham

Palace until Queen Victoria had it moved when she was renovating. *Imagine. Moving an entire arch. A bit more of a procedure than getting a new gazebo, but apparently she had the pull.* Benches lined the area in addition to a giant horse head sculpture called *Still Water.* There was a memorial to Princess Diana. A granite oval fountain. At places the water ran smoothly; other places it was turbulent, like Diana's life. Ava would have liked to see that, but it would be guaranteed to always be crowded.

This was a waste. Ava clicked off the videos. She could close her eyes and see boats on the beautiful lake, imagine herself eating in one of the restaurants in the park, or strolling hand in hand with Jasper, stopping to kiss on one of the lawns or near Kensington Gardens. But it was only a fantasy. And not even a very good one, because it wasn't long before the little colored dots appeared.

One step at a time. A picture of a spider, then a video of a spider, then—

Get that fucking spider away from me before I kill myself.

Ava might just have to settle for London from her windows. The doorbell shrieked through the flat. It was only slightly less deafening than the buzzer to the building. Whoever it was, they were already in, waiting in the hall. Jasper. She had to slow herself down, stop herself from racing to the door as if her life depended on opening it. Play it cool. Casual. She opened the door, and was grinning before she even set eyes on him. When she did, she smiled even wider, for he was grinning ear to ear. God, his blue eyes were so beautiful. Priceless. "Hello," he said.

"Hi." She took one step, and he pulled her into him and kissed her. He moved her against the wall in the little hallway and pressed his body against hers, then took her hands and pinned them above her head, keeping them there with one hand, while kissing her neck. Ava sent up prayers of gratitude to the powers that be. *Thank you, thank you, thank you.*

Jasper pulled back. They were both out of breath. "I've been thinking about you round the clock."

"Me too."

"I can't get you off my mind. You're like an incurable disease."

"You really do have to work on the pillow talk."

Jasper laughed. "Well, how about this? I want you. I've never wanted anybody as much as I've wanted you."

"I want you too."

He stepped back slightly and cocked his head. "Your hair."

Ava laughed. She touched it. "Do you like it?"

"You are so incredibly sexy." Nobody had ever said that to her before. She grabbed his shirt and pulled him inside. He kissed her again. Then kissed her neck. Then her lips again. They were all alone. She could pull him into the bedroom. He seemed to be thinking the same thing until he looked up at the living room. He took in the rearrangement of furniture.

"What were you doing?"

"Forget it. Queenie's gone. Let's go to the bedroom."

"It looks like you've got a little jungle set up there." Jasper pointed to the plants.

"I could slip into something a little more comfortable."

"And you've moved the furniture."

Ah, barristers. Couldn't walk away from compelling evidence. "Intermittent Exposure Therapy," she said. He looked quizzical. "I start by looking at pictures of outside destinations, imagining myself there. This morning my living room has become Hyde Park. For the next step, I'll have someone actually go to Hyde Park, sit on a bench, and film it while I watch on my laptop. And then, hopefully, eventually, I can actually go to the park myself."

"That's brilliant." Jasper walked around the plants, then turned back to Ava. "I'll do it. I'll do it right now."

"Whoa, cowboy. Right now?"

"It's sunny. A quiet Monday. A perfect day to be in the park." He looked eager. Hillary was right. He loved the outdoors.

"You'd rather run off to Hyde Park than have your way with me?"

Jasper locked eyes with her, and this time the smile that came across his face was confident and sexy as hell. "Oh, don't you worry about that. I'm going to have my way with you. Not even you could stop me."

"Seriously. You start off good, but you need a bit of coaching."

Jasper laughed. "Sorry. All this fifty shades shite." He moved toward her, wrapped his hands around her waist, and pulled her into him. When he spoke, his voice was low, and intimate. "I do want to have my way with you. So very, very badly."

Ava groaned. "Why not now?"

"Because now, I'm going to the park." He planted a kiss on her lips, then her nose. "All right?"

"Okay. Let's do it," Ava said.

Jasper hugged her. "So what do we do? Video chat? I get to the park and video you from my mobile?"

"Are you sure you want to go right now?" Ava hadn't intended on taking it this far today. He was already moving on to the spider-in-a-glass-jar portion of the experiment and she had barely looked at the videos.

"What's wrong? You look pale."

"If it gets too much, I may have to disconnect rapidly," Ava said.

"That's okay. You do whatever you have to do."

"You won't be mad?"

"I am mad. Mad about you."

"Okay. Shit. Let's do it. You're going to the park."

"*We're* going to the park." Jasper kissed her, and was gone.

It was over an hour later when Jasper texted that he was ready. Ava sat on her makeshift bench and stared at her computer screen. She brought up the video chat screen. Within seconds, Jasper's face filled the screen. He was grinning like an idiot, and his face was so close to the camera that he could have been anywhere. Total goofball.

"I see you," Ava said. Abruptly Jasper pulled back, and began to pan over the scenery. Ava caught sight of the the Marble Arch. She cried out.

"Are you okay?" Jasper turned the camera back on himself.

"The Marble Arch!" Ava exclaimed.

"Someone's done her homework. How do you feel?"

"Fine." Ava took a sip of Scotch from a teacup.

"Ah, good, a cuppa. That will sort you out." Jasper smiled. Ava smiled.

Ava closed her eyes. It wouldn't be very romantic if she hurled in front of him, but that was a very real possibility. "Can you pan over to the horse head sculpture?"

"Certainly, madame." She kept her eyes closed. Her stomach felt as if she had just panned over the London Eye. She was starting to feel prickly. "Here it is," Jasper said.

"Never mind," Ava said, keeping her eyes glued shut. "Can you just sit on the bench?"

There was a pause. "Certainly."

Breathe, Ava, breathe. Why was this so damn hard? Why, why, why? "Faulty wiring!" she shouted.

"Pardon?" Jasper sounded alarmed.

"I have faulty wiring. Right now my skin is prickly, and it's harder to breathe, and little colored dots are dancing in front of me. I don't want to be this girl. This girl who can't even sit on a freaking park bench or kiss you in Kensington Gardens. I don't want to be this girl."

"Just keep breathing. No need to even open your eyes." She let his voice wash over her. "I'm here on the bench. We have a spot of sunshine. You're right next me. I have my arm around you, is that all right?"

"Yes." *Oh, yes.* Ava could feel his strong arm across her shoulder. "You smell good."

"I do?" Jasper said. "I mean, I do. A very manly cologne I bought just for your smelling pleasure." Ava laughed. And even though she didn't have her eyes open, she could feel Jasper grinning. "We're having a lovely day, a lovely chat." He stopped talking.

"Yes?" Ava said. Silence. Was he trying to trick her into opening her eyes? "Are you still there?"

"Sorry, mate, I told you earlier. I don't have any change." What was he talking about? Was this part of the script?

"You don't have any change?" A man's voice rang out. His accent sounded twangy. He was loud and rude. "In your fancy suit with your fancy briefcase? Why don't you just hand over your wallet and let me see for myself what you've got?"

"Jasper?" Ava opened one eye. Jasper had set the phone in his lap, and Ava saw nothing but the face of a stranger standing over Jasper. He was one big bloke. Scruffy, and red eyed.

"Go away!" Ava yelled.

"It's okay, Ava," Jasper said. His voice shook. "Why don't you disconnect? We'll do this another time."

"I'm calling the police!" Ava yelled at the man.

The stranger snatched the phone and brought it even closer to his face.

"Ava," Jasper called again. "Hang up." He sounded frightened.

"Who the 'ell are you?" The scruffy bloke's face filled the screen.

"I'm your worst nightmare," Ava said.

"Is that right?" the bloke said. "How's that? Are you going to jump through the mobile and kick my arse?"

"Jasper is going to kick your arse."

"Ava," Jasper pleaded.

"Jasper, is it?" The bloke started laughing and turned his head, apparently to look at Jasper. "That's a very manly name, Jasper. I'm shaking in me boots. Give me your fucking wallet, Jasper."

"Off with you, mate," Jasper said. If only he sounded more confident.

The bloke turned the phone to show his own pocket. He reached in and pulled out a knife.

Ava screamed, "No!" Could others in the park hear her? Could they see what was going on in broad daylight? Ava grabbed the laptop and ran to the rotary phone. She picked it up and dialed 999. As she was doing so, the camera panned to Jasper's face. He had gone completely white. "Jasper," Ava said. Jasper reached into his jacket pocket and removed his wallet. He handed it to the man.

"Emergency. Which service?"

"My friend is being mugged in Hyde Park. On a bench near

the Marble Arch. The man is ugly, and scruffy, and red eyed, and he has a knife."

"You need the police service," the operator said.

"I don't. My friend does. He's in the park—"

"Is the man with the knife still threatening your friend?"

"Hang up or I fucking cut him," the bloke said. He rested the knife just below Jasper's chin.

"Ava, please," Jasper said. "Hang up."

Ava hung up. "Done. You have the wallet. The police have been called. Now get the fuck away from him." The bloke pulled the knife away, and began to run. He kept the phone with him.

"Your bloke is a fucking joke," he said. He kept running, but was talking to Ava while doing so. "If he doesn't have some good cards and cash in this wallet, then I'm going to go back and cut him. Would you like that?"

"You're a sick person," Ava said. "You're going to get everything you deserve." The ground bounced up and down as the man ran. London was bouncing pavement, and strangers' shoes, and bicycle tires. Ava couldn't look away although she felt as if she was going to lose her lunch. "Take the cash. Leave the cards, and his ID, and everything but the cash, and leave the wallet and phone. You don't need them."

"Who are you? The Queen? You sound like a bloody Yank. Are you a bloody Yank?"

"I'm the fucking Yank who's going to cut your balls off—"

Loud laughter pealed through the phone. "I like you. You've got more balls than your bloke back there."

"You held a knife to his throat." Ava didn't know why she was still talking to him. She heard police sirens. They could be coming to help Jasper, or they could be racing to another million things going on in London. The man was moving the phone again. He put the camera on his crotch. She watched him pull his zipper down. She wanted to slam the lid down. She didn't want to see a small dick on a giant arsehole of a man. Then again, she could use it against him. Soon the tip of his penis appeared. "Suck it, bitch."

Ava tried to keep her voice calm. "No wonder you need to

mug people and threaten them with knives. Anyone with that small of a dick would have to compensate in all sorts of crazy ways." Then she did slam the lid of the laptop down. She wobbled her way back to the teacup and drank the rest of the Scotch. So much for sitting on a bench in the park on a lovely London day. She picked up her sketch pad and began to draw. If they ever came up with a penis lineup she was going to make sure she had something to show the police.

CHAPTER 28

Ava was starting to wear a groove in the wood floors from pacing when her phone finally rang. She pounced on it, expecting it was Jasper. "Are you okay? Are you hurt?"

"Just a couple of sore dogs from dancing." Her mother's voice washed over her. Ava didn't realize how much she wanted to hear from her until now.

"Mom. Sorry. I thought you were Jasper."

"Why would Jasper be hurt?"

"He had a challenging court case this morning. Said he might have a bit of a sore head after." God, she was an awful liar. What bad timing. Jasper was okay, wasn't he? Surely he ran away when the psycho with the knife left with his mobile and wallet. Then again, how was he going to get home without his mobile and wallet? Any other girlfriend would be rushing out in a taxi heading for Hyde Park. But how was she to know if he was still there? He wouldn't expect her to come, so it was not like he was waiting for her. Was he? She hoped he was on his way over here. This was why she was no good for him. She couldn't come to anyone's rescue. She'd better not let her mother know what happened or she'd be insisting Ava get on the next plane. "Are *you* okay, Mom? Why haven't you called?"

"The time difference. I don't want to wake you up."

"I've been worried sick."

"I'm sorry. Are *you* okay?"

"I am. I'm doing better than I ever have." It was true, wasn't it? Just because she hadn't been able to tackle the list didn't mean there wasn't improvement. "I threw a party."

"I want you to come home."

"Did you hear what I said?" *I threw a party, Mom! A party!* How did her mother become this person? This person who didn't pay any attention to her daughter? Ava supposed she'd used up all her chips in her younger years. Her agoraphobia had turned her mother into a part-time prisoner too. And now she was free of Ava and never wanted to go back. Ava couldn't blame her. Was that what would happen to Jasper if she stayed with him? Would he end up hating her? Feeling like a prisoner? "Why don't you come and visit?"

"Oh, now you want me?"

"Yes. Now I want you." Now was not the time to get in a fight. All she cared about was making sure Jasper was okay.

"I don't want to go to London anymore. This whole thing with your aunt Beverly makes me furious all over again."

Makes you furious? Ava had better watch what she said or she was going to get sucked into this. She glanced at the cabinet where all the letters were residing. Every time she even looked in that direction she could feel herself heating up. *Pick your battles, pick your battles, pick your battles.* "I think there were hard feelings on both sides."

"On both sides? Is Beverly talking from the grave now? It wouldn't surprise me a bit."

"I know she came to the funeral." Ava blurted it out. Her accusation was met with silence. "I know she tried to see me. And you wouldn't let her." Her mother wasn't going to respond? Of course; the most infuriating thing she could do. "How could you?"

"You don't know the whole story."

"Then tell me."

"I don't like your tone."

"I don't like being lied to." Kept in the dark. Just like she'd kept herself in the dark all these years.

"I'll explain everything when you're back home."

"I am home. I live here now."

"Have you been out of the house? It's been, what? Almost a month?"

"I'm surprised you know that. Given that you haven't tried to contact me."

"I've tried. You don't always answer."

"Did you leave a message?"

"You know I don't like leaving messages."

"Beverly has a rotary phone, and no caller ID. I thought you hadn't bothered calling me at all."

"Well, I have. And I've been waiting. Waiting for you to come home."

"This is my home now."

"For how long? Have you done a single thing on that ridiculous list?"

"As a matter of fact." Ava wanted to lie. Tell her mother she'd sat on a bench in Hyde Park with Jasper. She'd almost made it to the food market, and she'd lost her flatmate's lucky charm but was able to get him off to his audition with a pep talk, and just now she was sketching a perp's penis. None of it sounded very impressive. "I've been drawing. Everyone likes my cartoons." That part was true.

"I'll talk to you when you get home."

Her mother was about to hang up; she could hear it in her voice. "I'm in love," Ava said. She hung up. *There.* Let her mother take that little tidbit to her next line dance and stomp on it.

Someone pounded on the door. Ava opened it. Jasper stumbled in. His hair was messed up. His eyes were red. "Are you all right?" he asked her.

"You're asking me? I'm just worried about you." Jasper

grabbed her in a hug, then held her at arm's length. "Listen to me. That never happens. I've sat in that park a million times. A million. That is the first time I have ever, ever been mugged."

"Come in. Calm down."

"Scotch." He went straight to the bar. "You're almost out. I'll buy you more. I'll empty the off-license of Scotch." He poured a drink and downed it. "Never been mugged in my life."

"I'm so sorry. It's my fault. I told him to take your cash and leave your wallet. Did he?"

"No. Imagine that. A mugger without manners." He started to laugh.

"I'm sorry. I'm so sorry." This was all her fault.

"I don't care about my wallet or my mobile." He set his drink down and approached Ava. "I just wanted you to have a lovely day, sitting on a bench in the bloody park." Ava started laughing. Jasper looked at her, startled. Then he started to laugh too. "So was it good for you?"

"The best. He even showed me his shlong."

"He . . . what? His what?"

"Yep. Flashed me." Ava picked up her sketch and showed it to Jasper.

"Oh, good Christ."

"Just in case there's ever a penis lineup."

Jasper shook his head, and laughter rolled out of him. "What a tiny, tiny prick. Wouldn't you say?"

"The worst."

"Do you mind?" Jasper ripped it up.

Ava shook her head. "That was our only lead."

"Scotland Yard will have to survive." He threw his arms open, then wrapped them around her and hugged her. "So you're not scarred for life?"

"Honestly, that doesn't scare me any more or less than just sitting on the bench would. I know that sounds weird. It's just how I'm wired."

"Sometimes I hate the world," Jasper said. "I want to wrap it up, give it a nice little bow, and hand it to you like a present.

And what happens? Some wanker pulls out his pathetic little penis."

"He also had a knife. I was so worried. "

"I'm all right. Not a cut on me."

"I should have jumped in a taxi, come to your rescue."

"I'm here, aren't I?"

"I'm sorry. I'm so sorry."

"Please, stop apologizing. Let me apologize. I apologize on behalf of London."

"I have to change. I have to do something on the list."

"No," Jasper said. Gently he backed out of the embrace. "Look at what happened when I tried one thing on the list. I've never been held up at knifepoint. That doesn't happen. The bloody thing is cursed."

"Then I lose the flat. I go home."

Jasper snapped his fingers. "Queenie is the answer. You've been getting along with Queenie, haven't you?"

Ava nodded. Thank God she didn't admit to Queenie that she was the one who lost his lucky charm. He'd barely spoken to Jasper since. "But I'm still going to try to do everything on that list. Every single thing." Ava didn't know why she was saying that, but every time she did, Jasper looked so proud one minute and concerned the next.

"I don't want to put you in any danger," he said.

"It's perceived danger, not real danger."

"What if you pass out, have a heart attack?"

"You'll be there."

"I'm so sorry I let Beverly go ahead with this scheme. I didn't know. None of us realized."

"I know."

"I'm so sorry."

"I'm not. I feel alive. For the first time in a long time."

Jasper touched Ava's chin, tilted her face toward him. "Do you want to know a secret?"

"Please."

"I'm terrified too. Every single day, I'm terrified. But even more so since I've met you."

Ava shook her head. "Seriously. I'll have to start writing these down. You're horrific at this love talk business."

Jasper laughed again. She loved his laugh. Everything about him was like a gift. "I just meant I'm terrified at that thought of losing you. I know that sounds insecure, and I don't mean it that way. But I don't want this to end. Ever. I want you in my life. And I'm terrified of discovering this is just a dream. That I just dreamt you. Because if you are a dream, then I don't want to wake up. I don't ever want to wake up."

"Kiss me." He took her in his arms. They kissed in front of the open windows. When he pulled away, Ava had tears in her eyes. She went to the stereo, turned it on, and found a slow song. "Dance with me?"

"It would be my pleasure." They danced in front of the windows. They danced in the galley kitchen. They danced in the hall. Ava danced Jasper right into the bedroom. And then, she stripped while he watched. With Cliff it was always hurried. With Jasper it was slow. They delayed the moment, second by second, savoring each step. Jasper spent an eternity just looking at her.

"You are so incredibly beautiful," he said. Ava dived underneath the covers, and invited him in.

Later, they lay in bed, under the covers. Jasper was so nice to be around, so easy. He made her feel safe and warm. "I got you something," he whispered just as she was falling asleep.

"What?" Ava sat up.

"Maybe I should save it for later."

Ava punched him lightly on the arm. "Now, please." Jasper leaned over the bed and picked up his pants. "Thank you," Ava said. "But they're really not my style."

"Ha-ha." Jasper removed a little blue card from the pocket, and handed it to Ava. She read the word on it. "Oyster." It was the card you needed to ride the Tube or a bus. "Don't panic. It doesn't mean you have to use it. But you'll feel like a real Londoner with it in your pocket. You can ride the Tube, buses, trains, even the cable line that runs over the Thames. That would knock two things off your list in one go."

Ava stared at the card. She felt the hot tears in the back of her eyes, the lump in her throat. "Thank you."

"You're all right then?"

"Of course."

"It's not to pressure you."

"I know that."

"Okay, good. Because if you feel pressured we can cut it up, right now."

"I love it," Ava said. She didn't. She was downright sick. The Tube. Open spaces underground. The map alone sent her spinning. Lines going every which way. Going somewhere. Going nowhere. To Ava, it was all the same. It was just like her and Jasper. Barreling on, hurling through space, going somewhere and nowhere at the exact same time.

CHAPTER 29

Ava's habits were deeply entrenched. She had probably already made grooves in her brain, little trenches of action-fear responses. Could she visualize herself out of this mess? Was there any hope? There had to be. Ava had to get through this. She had to conquer the list. Not just to stick it to Hillary—oh, that was icing on the cake—but the real reason was . . . she wanted to live. Really live. Maybe if Ava continued to force herself to experience the fear, it would gradually decrease. Or maybe she would die. But she would die trying. Jasper wanted to be with her either way. Did she really want to drag him into such a small life? No, he deserved the whole world. And so did she.

She went to Beverly's closet, pulled out another dress. A tight purple one. The color of royalty, perfect for this new Londoner. Ava was going to make a bold move. It was Friday. Jasper had a rehearsal for his show, so she wouldn't be seeing him tonight. She planned on making it to one of his performances, but she had to practice going out first. She didn't want to ruin his show by passing out at it. Franco and Georgie said they were performing just down the street. She had the flyer in her clutch. A couple of blocks. Surely she could make it a couple of blocks. She'd already mapped out the directions. They were right. Pretty much a straight shot. She was, after all, in the heart of London. What a waste, staying inside. This was the day. No matter what the consequences, she would go. She would stand for at least thirty seconds on a dance floor. She wouldn't involve Jasper. Not yet. It would be delicious to surprise him. If she did it once, she could do it again. It would be easy enough to get proof that she'd been there. She'd pick up a book of matches at the bar or have someone take her photo.

For a second she wanted to call Vic. Ava had liked a few things about her. She wished Vic had been nicer. Ava liked Deven too. The three of them could be going to the club together. But Vic had a mean streak, and she might even have Queenie's lucky charm. Ava had seen the look in her eye when she heard that Ava might inherit this flat. The girl was trouble and Ava was going to listen to her instincts. One thing was clear. Ava wasn't alone; everyone in the world had his or her own set of problems. Right now, tonight, she was just going to be a girl out on the town in London on a Friday night. That wasn't fear in her stomach; it was excitement. Fake it until you make it. Even Ben Franklin knew he couldn't guarantee happiness, he could only grant rights to the pursuit.

Ava was dressed. She had her little black clutch, a hundred pounds, her oyster card, and Aunt Beverly's dark red lipstick, which Ava had applied liberally. It matched the streaks in her hair. Did she look Goth? Was that still even a thing? She'd missed out on so many fads, only watching them on television or reading about them in the gossip rags. Now she was going to be a doer. Maybe someone would make fun of her in an article for a change. How lucky would that be? She looked in the mirror. With the hair and the outfit, she looked like someone else. She grabbed the keys—*keys, keys, keys, keys, keys*—and was out the door. She locked the door. She didn't hesitate on the landing, and every time a thought came into her head she countered it. *I am just a girl out on the town, in London.*

She flew down the steps. She opened the front door. She stood on the stoop. When her heart began pounding she told it to hush. She was not Ava. She was not trapped. She headed down the steps. The light was on her side; it was signaling her to cross. She crossed. She was on the other side. She'd made it this far before; this was where she had slammed into Deven. She wanted to look back, feast her eyes on the apartment building, but she knew she must not. She kept her eyes on the sidewalk, terrified that vertigo would hit, make her feel as if the streets of London were flipping upside down. But she didn't like just looking at the sidewalk, so she cast her eyes about a foot up, so that she could see the knees of most passersby. It was a warm summer evening, and she was walking the streets of London. If only someone she knew could see her now. She kept going, forward, forward, forward. She wasn't Ava; she was someone else, an actress playing a role. What would her stage name be? *Sydney? Sydney Wilder? Savage. Savage Wilder.* That sounded ridiculous. And kind of cool. *Vanessa. Vanessa Wilder. Ava Keyes. Stop it! Married to Jasper, what a thought.* Nothing that wonderful could ever happen to her.

Stop thinking about the things Ava would be thinking about. Tonight, she was Beatrice. That's right. Something between Bertrand and Beverly. Why not Beatrice? Did they call her Bea? She was off with her little black clutch and all she wanted to do was stand in the middle of a dance floor. The little colored dots appeared. "No," she said out loud. "No, no, no." She began to jog. People moved out of her way; knees darted left and right as she approached. "No, no, no," she continued to say. Sweat was running down her face, but all joggers sweated, didn't they? *Oh, you don't normally see a girl jogging in a dress and kitten heels; well, screw you, it's a new trend. A new Goth, athletic, Septic-abroad trend.*

She had to find the club. Straight shot, they said it was a straight shot. The crowd was thickening, along with the noise, and the lights. Headlights, theater signs, business lights. *Go back, Ava. Go back.*

No. No, no, no, no, no, no. Bea would not turn back. Even though she felt the sweat dripping down the back of her neck. She stumbled, then was forced to look up when a pair of knees dressed in a gray suit stopped directly in front of her.

"Watch where you're going," he said.

"Sod off," Ava said. He swore, but moved out of the way and kept going. She laughed. She had just told a Brit to sod off. She'd even used a bit of a British accent. That was fun. She saw it, on the corner. The club. A bouncer sat on a stool just outside the door, checking IDs. She hoped that was all he was checking. If you needed a ticket, or a wristband, or a secret passcode, she would be out of luck. Ava joined the line. She had made this entire trip without raising her eyes past knee level. But it was working. Between convincing herself she was someone else and blocking out most of her view, she was doing it. And even though she hadn't left bread crumbs, she had pretty much stayed on a straight path since crossing the street from her flat. She should be able to get home. Soon she was standing directly next to the massive bouncer.

"ID," he said. Ava dug in her purse. She didn't bring ID. How could she when she wasn't herself? She never went anywhere, so she never even thought about ID. Keys. She brought her keys. She showed him her keys. He didn't seem to care.

"I'm a lot older than twenty-one," she said. She tried to get past him. She had to get inside. His arm shot out and she ran straight into it. It was like slamming into a lead pipe. He was all muscle. Apparently he was in the right job.

"ID."

"I'm twenty-nine."

"ID."

"My name is Ava—no, Beatrice. No. Bea."

"You don't even know your own name? Maybe you should carry some ID."

Wiseass. "I left it at the hotel." Might as well pretend to be a tourist all the way.

"Sorry, luv. I can't let you enter without ID."

"What if I don't drink?"

"You must have ID to enter whether you drink or don't drink."

"I've come so far."

"America?"

So much for her convincing accent. "No. Agoraphobia."

"I'm sorry, luv. Next."

"I'm on Canadian television."

"Off with you."

Poor Canada. It appeared that nobody cared about their telly. "I'm doing a social experiment."

"Bugger off. Or I'll call the coppers."

The colored dots were impossible to ignore. She was going to pass out. "Help me," Ava said. He sighed. She was annoying him now. But she couldn't turn back. Not after all this. "I'm going to have a panic attack," she told him. "Right here. Right now." She looked at the ground. Should she just get down now? It wasn't fainting itself that was the problem; it was smashing her head into the concrete.

"Step aside."

"Let me in. Let me in. Let me in." Her voice rose with each plea. She was making a scene in London. She gasped for breath as dizziness washed over her.

"Christ," the bouncer said. "Go on with you." Did he mean in or out? She stumbled forward. He grabbed her arm and shoved her off to the side.

She slid down the side of the building and sat on the ground. Her breath was constricting; it felt like someone's fist was in her lungs, squeezing the life out of them. She needed a paper bag. What an idiot, she didn't think to bring one. She was never going to beat this, never.

A beautiful blonde was flirting with the bouncer. After a few seconds, he allowed her to go in. Without showing her ID. "Next."

Ava pulled herself up, and lurched in front of the bouncer again. "Hey!" the girl who was next in line yelled. "No shoving your way in, you wanker!" Ava ignored her, and turned on the bouncer. "You just let that blond bitch go in without ID," she said. She hadn't meant to say *bitch;* it just poured out of her hot mouth.

"I know her," the bouncer mumbled. He was lying. Ava could tell. She'd sketched enough criminals to know a liar when she saw one. His jaw tightened and he looked away.

"You did not."

"Come back with ID or go someplace else."

"Why? I'm not enough for you? Not tall enough, not pretty enough—I didn't put my hand on your shoulder?"

"Listen—"

"No, you listen." The sweat was pouring off Ava now. She was sure she probably looked like she had just walked out of a sauna. For all she knew, mahogany streaks were running down her face. The bouncer pulled his head back as far as he could, as if he didn't want to be too close to her. It hurt her feelings, but not enough to stop her. "My father is dead. My aunt is dead. They're British. I'm an agoraphobic and I came to stand on the dance floor for thirty fucking seconds and you're going to let me pass."

"Oy, you have a mouth on you, you do, do you?" Ava didn't know how to respond. There were too many rhetorical questions stuffed into one sentence.

"Ava!" The voice rang out. Ava turned to find Franco and Georgie dressed in drag, barreling toward her. Everyone looked up when Franco passed; he was just too gorgeous not to stare. The bouncer actually turned red when Franco put his arm around him.

"She's with you, then, is she?"

"Team Ava!" Ava cried. She glared at the bouncer. *I have a team, you wanker.*

"She's our Ava," Franco said. Before she quite knew what was happening Franco had practically lifted her around the middle and was carrying her into the club. They went down a flight of stairs into a cellar-like entrance. Inside it was the kind of dark Ava liked. Bat dark. The kind of dark where you could just make out shapes, enough to know that there were other people and things in there with you, but blurry enough that you couldn't see every dirty detail.

"Darling, show is on at ten, but you can sit at the bar," Franco said. Sit at the bar. By herself. At a club in London on a Friday night. The only thing worse was the thought of having to make it back home.

"I can't think," Ava said. "I need a drink."

"Won't people think you're violating your social experiment?" Georgie said.

"Did anybody even believe the social experiment?" Ava asked.

Franco and Georgie shook their heads no. "I believed it for about five seconds," Franco said. "I thought, 'Girl, I can't sit still for five seconds.' You're in London! If you were in Manchester, I'd highly recommend locking yourself in, round the clock, but London? Nnnn-mmm. You'll just have to find another social experiment."

"We know plenty of specimens if you're ever in short supply," Georgie said. They laughed.

"Off we go, then," Franco said. He kissed Ava on one cheek and then the other. "Dancing and nibbles later?"

Tears came to Ava's eyes. "Dancing? Nibbles? Later? I never thought anyone would say those three little words to me ever." Franco and Georgie engulfed her in a hug.

"Get used to it," Franco said. "Team Ava."

"This is the new you now." They blew her kisses and were off. Ava took a deep breath and concentrated on the bartender. He was a young, good-looking boy. Ava was happy it was a gay club. Nobody was going to hit on her, or ask her for a date. She didn't have to worry about what she looked like. Given the looks of the crowd, she probably didn't even have to worry if she had a full-blown panic attack. They looked as if they could not only handle the drama but barely even notice it.

"What will it be, luv?" The bartender was talking to her. What was she supposed to order? Wine? Beer? She really wanted a cocktail.

"Xanax?" she said.

"I only serve drinks, luv."

"Do you have a drink list?"

"What do you like?"

"Something strong, that doesn't taste strong."

"That's how I like my men." The bartender winked. Ava laughed. More people were filing in. *Don't look,* Ava told herself. *Just drink.* She must have given him enough to go on, for he simply whirled around, grabbed a couple of shakers, and went to town. His biceps bulged as he shook the drink. Was it normal to be attracted to a gay man? She loved him. Music thumped in through speakers. Disco lights came up and pulsed. The noise level rose. He'd better finish that drink quick. Next to her sat a fat tub of napkins. Ava grabbed the entire tub and pulled it toward her. She began laying napkins out in front of her.

"Darling, if you plan on making that much of a mess, you should be onstage with the drag queens."

"Pen," Ava said. The colored dots were playing at her periphery. Sweat on the back of her neck. *No, damn it, no.* She needed Xanax. Did anyone do drugs in this club?

What an idiot. She was at a drag show in London. Of course someone did drugs. But who, and what? She highly doubted she could just turn to anyone and ask for Valium or Xanax.

The bartender slid her a pen and her drink. It was pink and frothy. She picked up the glass and drank it in one go. She slammed it down. The bartender stared at her, his beautiful mouth open. Then he planted his elbows on the bar and rested his face on top of his fists. "Darling, who broke your heart? You can tell me."

"Another please. And can you drop in some Xanax?"

"Are you all right, luv? You don't look all right."

Ava wrote on her napkin: *PANIC ATTACK.* She showed it to him.

"So you weren't having a laugh about the Xanax?"

Ava shook her head. She would never laugh about Xanax.

"Give me a minute, luv." She nodded, then picked up the pen and started to sketch the bouncer. His big squirrel cheeks, his red face, his bald, angry head. His rhetoricals. Payback was a bitch. Soon the bartender slid her a little blue pill. "It's E," he said.

"I'll take any letter of the alphabet," Ava said. And she swallowed the pill.

CHAPTER 30

Ava was about to start in on her third cocktail. She wouldn't ever do E again. It felt too good. Nothing that felt this good could be good for you. *Just shut up and enjoy it.* The cool, smooth glass in the palm of her hand. The thumping music. The smiling bartender. London rocked. *Gawd.* She wanted to touch it, all of London, just touch it all. Everything felt so good to touch.

Jasper, she wanted to touch Jasper. She wanted him, body and soul. They'd made love the other night; they'd made love. Three times in one night. It was so good, even better than she thought it would be, even better remembering it now. Was he thinking about her every single second? He got mugged for her. Who could ask for more?

Look at me, London. I'm out. I'm in a club in the West End. And it was on the list. Ava was doing something on the list. And she was loving it. Loving it.

She felt a hand on her shoulder. "Baby, it's showtime." Ava whirled around on her stool.

"Franco!" She threw open her arms. He raised his beautifully stenciled eyebrow and came in for the hug. He patted her back. She could feel the tips of his fake fingernails and was dying to ask him to scratch her back.

"Somebody is coming out of her shell," Franco said, extricating himself from the hug. Georgie stood next to him, grinning. Ava reached out to touch his lime green bow tie.

"I love that you wear these," she said.

"Thank you," Georgie said.

"I mean, they're ridiculous, you know? And you just don't care. That's so cool."

"Okay, luv," Franco said. "Stop while you're ahead." Ava just noticed Franco was no longer a blonde. He had a long black wig to his ass, massive eyelashes, and he was wearing sequins.

"Cher!" she cried out.

"Black Cher," Franco said. "You know she always wanted to go black."

"Sonny," she said pointing at Georgie. "With a bow tie."

"I like her better sober," Georgie said.

"Ironic, because she likes you better when she's blotto." He turned to Ava and smiled. "Showtime," he said.

"I took drugs," Ava whispered. "I never take drugs. Except as prescribed by my doctor."

"What did you take, luv?" Franco and Georgie stared at her in stereo concern.

"A," Ava said.

"A?" Franco and Georgie said at the same time.

"Old Macdonald had a farm," Ava said. "E!"

"Ah," they said. Franco put his hand on her shoulder. "Luv, you just enjoy yourself. I get the feeling it doesn't happen very often."

"It doesn't," Ava said. "London is magical."

"Uh-huh," Franco said. "Come on, now." Franco looped his arm through hers and hauled her through the crowd. Ava barely had time to panic. The colored dots were back. And this time, she liked them. Yes, it was hard to see, and it was hard to walk because they made her dizzy, but they were so pretty. Ava reached up and tried to grab a colored dot. They were slippery little things, and she ended up just grasping air. Ava stumbled. Franco stopped abruptly and she ran into him.

"I'll wait here," she said. "I can't see."

"You can't see?"

"I can't see a thing but colored dots. But this time, they're so pretty."

"Oh, luv," Franco said. He picked her up, threw her over his shoulder like the clichéd sack of potatoes. The next thing she knew, Franco was depositing her onstage. The lights went black, the crowd hushed, and then a spotlight illuminated the threesome. Disco lights began to pulse.

"Gentlemen, and boys, and sailors!" Franco yelled. Ava wasn't looking, but she highly doubted there were any sailors in the crowd. "I'm Cher, this is my Sonny, and this cute breeder is the late, great Beverly Wilder's niece."

A few whistles and whoops erupted from the crowd. Ava's eyes were on the crowd. Sweaty, tightly packed people with flying boas and leather pants in so many different colors. They were shirtless and sweaty. Loud. Exuberant. Happy. "Whoooo!" Ava screamed. "Whooooo!"

They screamed back. Should she jump out on them now? Would they catch her?

The music started. Franco opened with "It's in His Kiss." Georgie sang the "shoop, shoop" part. Ava tried to do the "shoop, shoop" part, too, but the music was too loud. Nobody could hear her. But she didn't care. She danced. She danced with her arms up, and her body moving without a single thought to all the other people in the room. She imagined her view from her window. She wasn't just dancing in a club; she was dancing in front of the city of London. *Whoo-hooooooooooooooo!*

She imagined kissing Jasper here onstage in front of the world. The audience grew in volume along with the music. They were loving it. Ava was too. She closed her eyes and moved to the music. She was dancing. She was dancing. She hadn't danced since—

"This one goes out to Ava's aunt Beverly. Our dear friend. It was her favorite song," Franco said.

"Tall and tan and lean and lovely," Georgie sang as Franco strutted the stage. "The girl from Ipanema goes walking."

Ava could feel the room spinning; she could see her father; she could see their shag carpet. Sunlight streaming into his Scotch. They were dancing to the door. Who cared what the neighbors thought? They were on the porch. The smell of roses mingled with that of marinara sauce. The spaghetti with the stretchy white cheese. One two, one two, one two, down the steps. *No.* She slapped her hands over her ears. *No.* She fell to her knees. *No, no, no, no, no.*

Dance with me!.

What will the neighbors think?

Dance with me!

What did you do, Ava? WHAT DID YOU DO?

Ava was aware that she was rocking, and crying, and talking. She couldn't stop. She was outside her body watching. She didn't know if anyone else could see or hear her. They didn't exist. She wasn't human anymore. She wasn't part of this planet. Why hadn't the Mother Ship called her home already? Hadn't she suffered enough? Someone touched her, tried to pull her up. She jerked away. She had to find an exit. She stumbled offstage. The colored dots competed with the strobe lights for attention. So this was where she died. In a gay club in London. Not bad, actually. Much better than she ever expected. She was in a back hallway. It led to a unisex bathroom. There was a line. *Trapped.* She needed to find a hiding spot and call Jasper. He was her safe person. And she wasn't safe. But she still didn't know his number. And she didn't have a mobile. *Stupid, Ava. Stupid, stupid, Ava. It doesn't matter how many drinks, how many drugs, how many friends, or how many songs. You can't do it. You'll never be able to do it. You're handicapped. A loser. You deserve to lose the flat; you deserve to lose Jasper. What did you do, Ava? What did you do?*

At the end of the hall was a door. She threw it open and stepped into a dingy stairwell. It smelled like stale beer and rain. The heavy door slammed behind her. She tried to open it again. Locked. She was alone in the stairwell. At the bottom of about ten steps was another door. It probably led out into an alley. She collapsed onto the top step.

Tall and tan and young and lovely . . .

The song wouldn't go away. She couldn't get it out of her head. She couldn't just sit and let it invade her. Ava walked down to the second door. To her surprise it opened with a squeak and soon she was indeed standing in a back alley. She wouldn't have to take the Jack the Ripper tour after all. She could just live it. Facing things by force. *This is it,* Ava thought. *I'm going to walk. I'm going to walk around outside. He's with me. My father is on one side. Aunt Beverly is on the other. I didn't do anything. I was a child. My tiny hands couldn't have saved him, couldn't have pumped on his heart hard enough even if I had taken CPR.* Ava imagined him standing directly in front of her. He seemed so real. He had tears in his eyes.

Please, Ava, he said. *You're my world.*

Dad.

Live, Ava. Dance. Love. Please, Ava. Please.

I can't. I can't. I can't.

You can. It was Aunt Beverly. Ava turned to Aunt Beverly. She wasn't old; she was young and beautiful, just like in her pictures. *It's your flat now. It's yours. Don't waste it. Live. Live for us. We're right here. We'll always be right here.*

Ava walked faster. There were still colored dots, but she could see between them, enough to keep walking. *It's my world now; it's mine.*

Ava had no idea how long she walked. She just knew that there was a moment when she felt compelled to stop and look up. And when she did, she saw Cupid. She was standing at a huge intersection with an open, circular space that housed a fountain. Piccadilly Circus. She stopped to take it all in. Her breath caught. She was actually standing in a place she had read about so many times. She was actually standing in one of London's busiest squares. "I've run away with the circus." She looked up at the statue of Eros atop the fountain. Cupid. She adored his wings, his spears. Aunt Bev and her father had brought her here. To Cupid. "I love you too," she said.

So many lights. They were beautiful. The world was like an orchestra. It made music. The cars, the people, the lights. There was a rhythm to it, a pulse she could feel through her skin. She just stopped and stared. She tilted her head back. Even the tears dripping down her cheeks felt so good. She waited for the crippling fear. She waited for her heartbeat to speed up. Was this the E? Would she always have to take it to feel okay outside? She couldn't trade in agoraphobia for a drug addiction.

It's a slippery slope.

Just walk, just walk. She never knew there were so many smells. Cigarette smoke, and rain, and French fries. She was suddenly starving. She still had money.

She could walk in a restaurant and eat. They wouldn't know it wasn't normal. They would seat her at a table and give her a menu. She could order French fries. Chips, they called them here. Or one could get them with curry, or gravy, or mayonnaise. She could order five plates of French fries and sure, they might look at her funny, but she wouldn't care. She'd offer them one. They wouldn't take it of course, because that wasn't polite or even sanitary to eat a stranger's chips, but she could do it.

Ava took a left, humming to herself all the while. She reached the corner. Too fast. Such a long street, so many cars, so much noise and light. People everywhere, scurrying like cockroaches. Ava ran. She ran until her lungs were bursting and her feet burning. She ran until she saw an English pub on the corner. It had a large crest, and welcoming sign. She pushed open the doors and before anyone could protest she sat at a large booth by the window. The waitress tossed a menu on her table with barely a glance. Just like she belonged!

She ordered curried chips and a pint of ale. When they arrived, she just stared at them. She wanted to cry. She called the waitress over and asked her to take her photo. She did. With her mobile. Ava didn't have a mobile for her to send it to. Did it count? If somebody took a picture of you with his or her mobile, but there was no second mobile to send it to, did it count?

Had they ever figured out the tree falling in the forest conundrum? God, this tabletop felt so good. Nice, thick wood. Oh, she was out. In London. On a Friday night. And she even got a seat. If Diana could see her now. If her mother could see her now. If Jasper. The entire pub smelled like curry and beer and Ava loved it. She loved it.

She wouldn't tell Jasper she was out. Not until she could repeat it without alcohol and drugs. She'd been foolish to take the E. Especially mixing it with alcohol. Now that was a real danger and she hadn't thought twice about it. How ironic. Danger was natural. Perceptions were the danger. From now on, Ava would pay attention to true danger, and to hell with the rest.

She took a bite of the curried chips. They were delicious. A little plate of friends. She took a sip of the ale. Smooth, and cold. She didn't need it on top of everything, but she'd just had to taste it. She pushed it away. She called the waitress over, left a generous amount of money on the tabletop. "Can you call me a taxi?" she said.

"You can just stand outside and flag one down," the waitress said.

"I can't," Ava said. "You're going to have to help." She'd had enough for one night. And she'd had enough for one life. From now on, people were going to have to help whether they liked it or not.

CHAPTER 31

Ava gripped a thick black marker and carefully crossed each item off the list, savoring the moment.

~~Go to an English pub . . .~~
~~Go to a show in the West End~~
~~Go to a club in the West End~~

Three things. Three things off the list. Monumental. She also had a mobile now, a gift from Jasper when he replaced his own. He'd programmed his phone number on speed dial. Ava felt like a real Londoner now with a mobile and a phone number and everything. She stared at the remaining items on the list and felt a shudder run through her. She didn't want to do any of them. Why wasn't the Tate Modern on the list? Or the Globe Theatre? As an actress and cultured woman, Beverly should have composed a better list. Ava didn't want to go to the Tower of London. Now that she tasted the outside, she wanted culture, and music, and flowers. She wanted life and the affirmation of life, and she wanted hope. On YouTube Ava listened to street musicians who were playing along the Thames. Lively, upbeat tunes. They didn't just sit on a bench; they played music on it. They owned that bench. One guy set up a beach chair near the water and sang his heart out in his yellow swimming shorts. He wasn't even very good. But he was thoroughly enjoying himself and anyone whose office was a speaker, a microphone, and a reclining beach chair probably had a pretty good life. The freedom to be who you were. London offered that. Ava wondered what it would take to get musicians to come and play on her street, just underneath her window. She could tell them about her social experiment. *I can't leave the flat, so just wondering if you will stand underneath my window and serenade me?*

From her windows, Ava watched as passersby helped a man on crutches. She watched an elderly lady pulling an oxygen tank behind her, saw how the crowd parted and offered her comforting glances. It wasn't fair, having an invisible disability. Maybe Ava could get her hands on crutches or an oxygen tank. Or she could procure a blind man's cane, or dog, for the afternoon. She wasn't at all trying to be disrespectful of anyone else's disability, but she was tired of having to prove hers. As long as she looked okay to others, then her challenges were her own bloody problem. That was what was wrong with the world today; no matter how much one shared the message, books were still judged by their covers. No, Ava didn't want to go to the Tower of London, or ride the stupid Underground, or the London Eye.

Why wasn't Borough Market on the list? That would be quite challenging for an agoraphobic, a literal outdoor marketplace. But at least Ava could buy herself a trinket if she survived it. Hell, if Beverly wanted Ava to be more like her, why not make Ava go skydiving too? Become the next Prime Minister of England? Seduce Prince Harry? *Oh, how small you were thinking, Aunt Bev.*

Ava needed to follow up her accomplishment with another one. She had to tackle something else on the list. Without taking Ecstasy. She could simply call a car service and have them drive her around, but that wasn't the experience Ava wanted. A change had taken place. There was now a small part of her who liked the fear. Now that she'd proven it wasn't going to kill her (as long as she got on the ground before she could faint), she realized the fear itself was a little bit like a drug. A jolt of adrenaline. In high enough volume, the fear could make her feel no pain. Was Jasper right? Would Queenie let her have the flat even if she didn't complete the list? It would help if she would get his lucky charm back.

She'd decided she would ask Deven about it first, but there'd been no sign of him. No smoking, no sweeping, no one going in or out. Ava was dying to know what was going on. Maybe Vic had dumped him and he was heartbroken. Maybe he had taken to staying inside. Would Ava like that? To have a friend who was also an agoraphobic? They'd never be able to get together.

Jasper had tried to call her, and left a sweet message alluding to their night together, but Ava hadn't called him back. She knew she'd end up spilling the beans about her night out— heck, she'd be surprised if Franco and Georgie hadn't already beat her to it, but just in case, she wanted to keep it a surprise. She wanted to do this for Jasper. She wanted to change. She wanted to prove she was the kind of woman who could have a good life. But first and foremost, she had to prove it to herself. Ava went to Aunt Beverly's wall of theater photos and studied them for inspiration. A thick binder was lying on the floor next to the sofa, by the far end of the wall. Ava picked it up. Bits of fabric and color swatches were sticking out of it. A note was on top.

QUEENIE,
THIRTY DAYS UNTIL THE SEPTIC IS GONE
AND THE FLAT IS YOURS!

CAN'T WAIT TO HELP YOU REDECORATE!

LOVE, HILLARY

Redecorate. That rat! Queenie was going to redecorate the flat. The red swatch. That's what that was. The reason he acted so secretive about it. Hillary was never going to let her uncle give up the flat. Especially if it meant Ava would be gone. She was the bigger enemy. Ava had to show her she wasn't going to win. Actors always looked at a script and asked, "What's my motivation?" Ava stared at the note from Hillary, and she had it. She had her motivation to get out of the flat. She had already been an immovable object; now she needed to become an unstoppable force.

Hillary stared at the twenty-five schoolchildren in front of her, lined up and glaring at her like a miniature firing squad. Eight years of age, all girls, expecting her to wow them with how and why she became a barrister when all they really wanted to be was Kate Middleton or Lady Gaga. How was Hillary to know whom little girls looked up to these days? Why had she agreed to do this? They were crowded into her meeting room, and smearing her conference table with saliva, gum, and heaven knows what else. She was supposed to talk for twenty minutes, but it was five minutes in and they were already getting fidgety. Since when did schools start bringing children to respectable workplaces? These little heathens didn't look as if they were open to learning anything. Time to wrap it up.

"Are there any questions?" she said. The teacher, who had been immersed in her mobile, looked up, startled. She glanced at her watch. *Yes, pay attention, you little wench. You're the one who wanted to become a schoolteacher, not me.* Hillary maintained a neutral expression.

"Do you meet a lot of bad men?" one girl piped up.

"No," Hillary said. The girl looked disappointed. "I meet a lot of people in bad situations. And I help them." The teacher smiled. The kids did not.

"What kind of bad situations?" the little girl insisted.

Shite. She wasn't going to get into that, was she? Surely they didn't want to hear about civil lawsuits, and insider trading, and corporate espionage. "Someone has to make sure the companies follow the law," she said. "And if someone is accused of breaking the law at his or her place of work, someone has to defend them." Several kids yawned. "I meet a lot of important people. Judges, barristers, police officers. And the money isn't bad either." Hillary laughed, and winked at them. They just stared back.

"Have you ever met the Queen?"

"No."

"What about Princess Kate?"

"The Duchess of Cambridge?" Hopefully chins tilted up, waiting for her answer. "No."

"Prince Harry?"

"No. And before you ask, I've never met Lady Gaga either."

"Who?" echoed around the room.

"Never mind."

"Well, who you have you met?" asked one cheeky little girl.

"I work hard for the people. The everyday British citizen. I make a difference in people's lives—" The door burst open. Hillary expected to see another child, or teacher. Instead, there stood Ava Wilder. Good Christ, she was actually out of the flat. And she looked unhinged. Her eyes were wild, her hair hadn't been combed, and she was visibly sweating. In her right hand she appeared to be clutching a rubbish bag, and some kind of binder in the other. She glared at Hillary and marched toward her as if she was completely oblivious to the room of eight-year-old girls.

"You're wrong about me," Ava said. She raised the binder. "You can take this back, because this Septic ain't going nowhere."

The children looked on, mesmerized. "What's a Septic?" a little girl asked. Ava turned and seemed to notice them for the first time.

"What's in the bag?" another one asked.

"She wears it over her head," Hillary said.

The girls giggled. Now that was a nice sound. "Why do you wear it over your head?" the same girl asked.

Hillary glanced at Ava. She was about three shades of red in the face, and little dots of sweat peppered her cheeks. Her hair looked a lot better than Georgie promised her it would. *Cheeky bugger.* She'd see how he liked it when she revoked their cushy gig at the club.

The teacher stood. "Off we go. We don't want to be late for Buckingham Palace, now do we?"

Ava straightened up. "You're going to Buckingham Palace?" she asked. The girls nodded their reply, their eyes glued to Ava. Ava stood for a moment as if lost, and then curtsied. The children laughed. Ava laughed, and then did it again. Several of the girls curtsied back.

"Are you one of the bad guys?" the girl who spoke up earlier asked.

"Me?" Ava said. "No. Why?" Ava stepped forward and lowered her voice. "What have you heard?"

"We heard you wear a rubbish bag over your head," the little girl answered.

"Rubbish head," another girl added.

"Where I come from," Ava said, "that's 'garbage head.' "

"Garbage head," they repeated. They all laughed.

"Ladies, your manners," the teacher said. "I'm sure she doesn't wear a rubbish bag over her head."

"Sometimes I do," Ava said. The class laughed again.

"Why?" several called out.

"Because I have a condition. A disability. Do you know what a disability is?"

"A disability?" Hillary said. She was calling herself disabled? She was a freak, that's what she was.

"Disabled people are in wheelchairs," a girl said.

"And they get to park in the front of the lots," another said. "But they don't get a ticket like my mummy does."

Ava laughed. "There are many kinds of disabilities, ladies," she said. "Some you can see, and some are invisible."

"Like a superhero?"

"Exactly," Ava said. "Like a superhero without any powers."

"Come on now," Hillary said. "Enough nonsense."

"Are you saying people with disabilities shouldn't be treated with respect?" Ava asked.

Everyone was looking at Hillary. *How could this be happening?* "You are not disabled," Hillary said.

"I have a biological and mental condition which severely inhibits my everyday functioning," Ava said. "What would you call it?"

It's all in your head. You just want the attention! "You seem to have mastered it, if you're standing here now," Hillary said.

"You have no clue what it took for me to get here today. It's not wrong to be unaware of someone's disability, unless and until you are educated. If you remain ignorant and dismissive after that, Ms. Swanson, then you are a bigot."

"What's your disability?" a girl asked.

"I have agoraphobia," Ava said. "It means that I can't just walk outside and enjoy it like you can. My body reacts as if the outside is dangerous. I'm terrified. Have you ever been terrified of anything?" The girls started calling out their fears. Snakes, spankings, tests, ghosts, grasshoppers, and at least one girl pointed to her teacher. "Most fears are pretty mild. You're afraid if you come into contact with that thing, but you can still lead a pretty normal life. But my body reacts to my fear immediately and so when I go outside my heart beats really fast, I get hot, and I can't see because little colored dots appear in front of my eyes."

"Off you go, then, ladies," Hillary said. "Don't want to keep Buckingham Palace waiting, now do you?"

The teacher nodded, and against their protests she started rounding the children up and herding them to the door. "Wait," Ava called. "How many of you know CPR?"

"Ava?" Hillary said. She stepped up and pinched the back of Ava's arm. Hard. Ava jerked away and scanned the room. None of them had their hands up.

"I think we've had enough for today," Hillary said.

"CPR is a lifesaving skill," Ava said.

"I know it." One little girl shot up. She grabbed the girl next to her and yanked her up. "Do this," the little girl said. She wrapped her hands around her own neck to demonstrate the universal sign for choking. The little girl next to her followed suit. The first girl grabbed her around the waist from behind and squeezed. "Spit it out!" she screamed. "Spit it out!"

"Enough, enough," the teacher said. The little girl let go, and then bowed. The other girls clapped.

"That's not CPR," Ava said. "But it's a good one too. If you'd like I could show you—"

"I think we've had enough demonstrations for one day," Hillary said. She grabbed Ava by the arm and began to pull her out of the room. The children protested once again, begging Hillary to let Ava come back and show them CPR. Hillary got them out of the room before they could witness her physically assaulting a Septic.

They stood in the lobby, facing each other, arms crossed. "How dare you barge into my workplace," Hillary said.

"I was motivated," Ava said, thrusting the binder at her. "And I don't think it's nice of you to get Queenie's hopes up."

"You care about my uncle then, do you?"

"I do. Very much." She loved him. She loved Queenie. But she wasn't going to tell Hillary that.

"Then let him have the flat."

"That's not how this works. I'm going to do everything on the list. I've completed several already."

"I don't believe you. You probably took a taxi here, wearing that bag over your head, and your pathetic driver is probably waiting at the curb for you to return. How much did that cost you? All to come up here. You look as if you're about to die, my darling. So excuse me if I don't quite see you touring the Tower of London or, God forbid, riding the London Eye or, better yet, the Tube."

"I'm sorry that Jasper broke your heart. But that doesn't give you the right to—"

"Broke my heart? He hasn't broken my heart. He's opened my eyes. He's got no ambition. I don't need to look any further than you to realize that."

"Then why? Why do you hate me so?"

"My uncle loved and took care of that woman for forty years. And you get the flat? It's a load of bollocks." There was an immediate gasp from the group of girls who were standing in the hall, waiting.

"She said 'bollocks.' "

"Children, let's go wait for the lift," the teacher said. She glared at Hillary. Only a few girls moved along with the teacher. The rest remained rooted to the spot.

"It's not my fault Aunt Beverly left the flat to me," Ava said.

"Then do the right thing and let Queenie have it."

"Maybe he'll get a starring role on the telly and can buy his own flat," Ava said. "Or don't you believe in him?"

"I want you gone. That's all I believe in right now."

"How sad for you. Because I'm not going anywhere."

"Oh, I know you aren't going anywhere. That's what I'm counting on. Stay in your flat and draw your stupid drawings. Tick, tock, tick, tock." Hillary smiled, then turned on her heel and strode away. The schoolchildren reluctantly headed for the elevators. Ava followed behind them. Somehow, it was easier focusing on the children than the panic waiting to seize her.

"You're going to Buckingham Palace?" Ava asked once again.

The girls chanted, "Yes!"

"We're going to see Princess Kate," a little girl said.

"We're not going to see Princess Kate," the teacher said.

"The Queen then."

"No. We'll see the guards. And the outside of the palace. And then we'll go back to class and you can write about how you didn't get to see the Queen or meet the Princess." The teacher looked at Ava. "Doesn't that sound like fun?" she said sarcastically.

"Yes," Ava said. "Can I come?"

The teacher looked at her phone, buzzing in her hand. "I couldn't possibly allow a total stranger on the bus."

"My aunt was Beverly Wilder." Ava dug in her purse. "I remembered my ID this time." She showed it to the teacher. "See? Ava Wilder."

"I'm afraid I've never heard of Beverly Wilder."

"That's too bad. She was brilliant."

"Was she a garbage head too?"

"No," Ava said. "She was brave."

"You do have a way with them," the teacher said. "If I let you ride on the bus will you talk more about people with disabilities?"

"I only know about mine," Ava said.

"They seem to be fascinated," the teacher said. She leaned in. "But you'll have to watch your language."

"I will. I swear." The teacher raised an eyebrow. "I mean I won't swear," Ava assured her.

"If anyone asks, you're a surprise guest."

Ava lifted her arms. "Surprise," she said.

"It's employment day. What is it you do?"

"I'm an aspiring cartoonist." The teacher didn't look impressed. "And a sketch artist," Ava said. "For the police department."

"You'll have to present to them on the bus ride there. But no swearing, and no gory details about criminal activity."

"I swear. I mean I promise."

"And you can only ride with us to Buckingham Palace. No farther."

"Great." It wasn't great. What if she couldn't catch a taxi right away? She shut the thought out. She'd force herself to cross that bridge when she got to it. London Bridge, perhaps. *London Bridge is falling down.* Ava slapped her hand over her mouth even though she didn't say it out loud. If she swore in front of the children again she might be arrested.

"Are you going to wear that bag over your head when we go outside?" a girl asked.

"Probably," Ava said. The children cheered. Ava looked at them, and when she spoke she was kind. "It's not nice to make fun of someone's disability. Do you like it when people make fun of you?" The girls shook their heads. "Good," Ava said. "It doesn't matter if it's a wheelchair, or a hearing aid, or a rubbish bag. You should be kind to people. You never know what they're dealing with inside." Big eyes stared at her, nodding. The teacher gave her a sideways glance. She looked impressed. Ava moved her hand down to her chin, solemnly, as if constructing class lessons in her mind. This was incredible. A spontaneous adventure. Buckingham Palace. Maybe they would see William or Kate, or the wee ones, or the Queen. How amazing if she could hold the royal baby. How exciting. Ava hoped she was feeling all right. Having babies. Ava should be thinking about having babies. That was another clock that was ticking. But God, Hillary was right about one thing. What kind of mother would she be? Would it force her out of the house or would her kids never get to play on the playground?

"Don't make me regret this," the teacher said. Ava shook her head. "If anyone asks, you're an expert, a guide." *An expert. A guide.* Two words that had never been used to describe her. Music to Ava's ears. The teacher nodded. "Right so." She reached in her purse and handed Ava a hairbrush. "My name is Miss Maggie," she said. "And there's a lady I work with whom I think you should meet."

"Thank you," Ava said. She had no idea what that meant, nor did she want to see any more people today than she already had. But Miss Maggie liked her, and so did the children, and she was pretty sure they wouldn't just step over her when Ava finally passed out.

CHAPTER 32

The school bus rumbled through London. The girls with window seats plastered their faces to the glass, wide-eyed and unafraid. Ava had wangled a spot in the aisle, although what she really wanted to do was crawl under the seats. She dug in her purse for her rubbish bag. It was gone. Had one of the schoolchildren taken it? That wasn't nice, but she couldn't accuse anyone without proof and she'd already made enough of a scene walking down the street in the middle of a gaggle of schoolchildren with a rubbish bag over her head. She scooted as far to the edge of her outside seat as she could get. Too bad it wasn't raining. London was bright and clear. London was America's big sister. Older, statelier, a land of tea, and Queens, and schoolchildren clamoring to be the next Duchess of Cambridge.

Bright red double-decker buses, trolleys, bicycles, scooters, motorcycles, and motorcars jammed together on the narrow city streets yet flowed, for somehow the traffic kept heaving and progressing. Spirals, crowns, and statues adorned the buildings. As commonplace as a hat on a Londoner's head. Once in a while, despite her best efforts to look away, Ava caught a patch of the outside world. A fountain, a bright square of green grass amidst concrete, a statue commemorating someone who had done something, sometime, that was more than she would ever do. If anyone ever erected a statue of her, they would have to place it inside. What would it say? Here She Sat. And That Was That.

If Ava focused on the periphery, she could make all the people outside blur into fuzzy colors, a walking bouquet of flowers, and weeds. People, people, people. There were too many. *Stop the bus; I want to stay on.*

"Ladies, quiet down," Miss Maggie said. Were they noisy? Ava couldn't hear over the roar in her head. "Let's go over our itinerary. First, we'll witness the Mounting of the Guards—"

Did she just say "Mounting"?

"—the State Room, the Queen's Mews—"

What was the Queen's Mews? Cats? Did the Queen have royal cats? Did they feed them Fancy Feast?

"The Throne Room—"

Royal toilets. Wouldn't that be funny? The Queen's Commode.

"Is someone laughing? Who is it? Who is it?"

One by one, hands extended and little index fingers pointed directly at Ava. Miss Maggie turned on her with a withering look. Even the bus driver glared through the rearview mirror. Should she share the joke about the Queen's cats and commode? Probably not. The bus was pulling around a huge stone wall, aiming behind a long row of them, all packed with schoolchildren waiting to take the tour.

"Ladies, we have to remain on the bus for a little while and wait our turn. Remember our manners."

"Can I just wait on the bus?" Ava said.

"Me too!" one of the girls sang out.

"No," Miss Maggie said. "Everyone will get out. Ava, this is where we part ways, remember?"

"Maybe the bus driver could take me home?"

"No, madame," the bus driver said.

Jolly jerk.

"I'll hail a taxi," Ava said. *Hail to the Chief.* "Could you help me, kind sir?" The girls giggled. The bus driver frowned some more.

"Help you how, miss?" She was no longer Madame. Probably because she was reverting to a child right before his very eyes.

"Help me hail a taxi?" *Put a rubbish bag over me head and throw me into the back of a cab, lad!* Why was it so difficult for people to grasp the obvious?

"Why aren't you going on the tour?" a little girl piped up. "Do you not like the Queen?"

Once again all heads turned to her. "I like the Queen," Ava said. "Well, you know. Not as much as you guys do, probably. But she seems all right. I liked when she pretended to jump out of a plane at the opening ceremony of the Olympics. No? My aunt Beverly jumped out of a plane once. She was an actress. And very brave."

"You don't have a Queen," another girl taunted.

"I have a Queenie. He's my flatmate."

"Men can't be Queens," a girl said.

"Is he a King?"

"No," Ava said. "He's a drag queen."

"Miss Ava!" Miss Maggie said.

"Oh. Sorry. I didn't know I wasn't allowed to say that. I was homeschooled, you see." Mighty prejudiced of them to react that way to the subject of drag queens, but Ava was on too much thin ice to start a row over it.

"What's homeschooled?"

"I didn't go to school. I stayed home and studied." Ava wanted to tell them it wasn't a religious thing, she just refused to go to school and her mother had no other choice.

"I want to stay home."

"Me too's" rang out all over the bus.

"How about that Princess Kate?" Ava said. "Isn't she pretty?"

"The Duchess of Cambridge," Miss Maggie corrected.

They were so into titles here. What would Ava's be? The Shut-in of Dubuque. The Insider of Iowa. The school bus in front of them was off-loading. Ava couldn't see much beyond the wall, but just within reach was Buckingham Palace, where the Queen's Guards marched, and the monarchy reigned, and schoolchildren learned more about life in an afternoon than Ava had in a lifetime. Could she do it? Could she take the tour? She wanted to ask Miss Maggie if there royal paramedics on standby and if so, would they be able to attend to an American if she passed out in the royal halls? They were probably paved with expensive marble. What if Ava's head cracked open and she bled all over the Queen's floors? She'd make the news. She'd draw more attention to herself than she would ever be able to handle.

She snuck her phone into her lap and texted Jasper. **Can you come get me?**

A few seconds later she heard a little chirp. She loved the little chirp. **Where are you?**

Just outside Buckingham Palace.

Are you having a laugh?

I'm having a panic attack.

I'm so sorry. In court. Call Queenie. *Wow.* He was texting her from court? Ava felt bad. And important. *Wait.* Did he wear one of those wigs in court? Ava would love to see that.

"No mobiles on the bus!" a girl yelled. "Miss Maggie, Miss Ava is using her mobile."

"Ava. Put that straight away and sit properly in your seat," Miss Maggie said.

"But I was just about to text Queenie."

"Straight away!" Ava complied. She was afraid not to. Miss Maggie had transformed into a wicked witch right before her very eyes. Ava's fear of whatever was out the window dropped a degree as she concentrated on Miss Maggie's dangerous expression. Ava wondered if she presented that during the interview. It could wither a cactus. Maybe Ava could hire this woman to follow her around all day and scare the bejesus out of her. Ava didn't like Miss Maggie glaring at her, so she did something that astounded her. She looked out the window. A woman entered the bus, dressed in a navy suit. She was holding a clipboard. She looked regal and professional. Ava made a mental note to buy herself a navy suit and a clipboard. The woman conferred with Miss Maggie.

"Children, there is a slight delay. We'll be eating our lunch on the bus while we wait." The ruckus was immediate. "We want to go home!" they shouted. "No fair!" they shouted. "I hate buses," they said. "Let's go to the park." There were wails, and fist-pumps, and even tears. The pint-sized people were revolting. The woman in the navy suit turned red and glared at Miss Maggie. Miss Maggie's stern composure buckled. She looked to the bus driver, who shoved his face in a newspaper. Ava glanced down by the driver's seat. There sat a rubbish bag, empty and waiting to swallow the remains of the girls' lunches. Miss Maggie turned to Ava with a pleading look. She needed her help. Ava stood up, and faced the rioting girls. She grabbed the rubbish bag and placed it over her head. There was immediate silence, followed by a few giggles. Ava ripped off the bag and, one by one, looked each girl in the eye.

"Miss Maggie wants peace and quiet right now. And you don't know how lucky you are. You can go outside, and touch the world. You're not afraid. You want to explore. You want to run, and jump, and see, and listen, and feel. You don't want to put a rubbish bag over your heads and hide under the seats, do you?"

An emphatic group "NO!" resounded through the bus. The woman with the clipboard looked impressed. She even made a note on her pad. What was it? *Who is this influential Yank?*

"Good on you, then," Ava said putting on her British accent. "Chin up, Mind the Gap, keep calm, and carry on!" Ava slipped the bag over her head and saluted. The girls applauded and cheered.

"Thank you," Miss Maggie whispered in her ear.

"Your turn, girls," the woman in the navy suit said. "Let's file out one at a time starting with Miss Ava."

"Can I bring up the rear?" Ava said. But the woman with the clipboard was physically dragging Ava off the bus. Perhaps she'd gone too far. They thought she was a nutter.

Oh, God. There was no place to go. An expanse of landscaped grounds, the palaces, and the entryway, all dotted by men in red suits. Like marching nutcrackers. They weren't allowed inside right away because they were to stay and watch the guards change. Why did the guards have to change? Ava was sure they were perfectly fine as they were. *You reaaly want to change?* Ava wanted to shout at them. *Rebel! Go inside.* Ava turned to Miss Maggie.

"I'd like to go back to the bus now."

"That's not an option," Miss Maggie said. "Are you ill?" Ava knew Miss Maggie had just zeroed in on the fact that Ava was sweating and shaking. The panic attack was coming. The little dots would be next. Ava didn't know how to control them once they started. Like a wave, she simply had to let them carry her away. She had no idea if it would be a little wave or a tsunami.

"Miss Maggie, if we don't get inside I'm going to have a panic attack. I think I should sit so that I don't pass out. You might have to call the paramedics." Ava sat on the ground before Miss Maggie could reply. So many people, all around her, this wasn't the perfect place to draw attention to herself, and all those eyes on her would make it worse. Much, much, worse. Queenie. She texted Queenie. **Help me. Buckingham Palace.**

Are you having a laugh?

By George, they were all talking alike.

NO! On the ground while the guards are mounting, Ava typed back furiously.

Lucky you.

Please.

Darling. I have callbacks.

TELEVISION?

TELLY!!!

Break a leg! You can do it!

He sent her an emoticon of a happy face in a wig with makeup and its tongue sticking out. Who knew they had smiley faces in drag? *Oh, please let him get the part.* She tried to send him mental waves of joy. Her joy was only temporary. She was stuck here. Alone. A low wail escaped Ava. *No, don't make a scene. Look at you, you stupid girl. You're in London at Buckingham Palace for God's sake, surrounded by guards, and children, and stern headmasters, and the royal staff. What kind of idiot doesn't feel safe here?*

The woman with the clipboard was kneeling down. "How can I help?"

"Can you take me inside?" Ava said. The woman helped her up, and the crowds parted. Waves of dizziness overtook Ava as step by step they headed toward the grand entrance. The woman flashed some kind of badge, allowing them to skip the line. Ava would have to bring her to the drag club next time. They crossed over the threshold, into the queue for the schools. This was it. She was inside Buckingham Palace. She could technically cross it off her list. Jasper wasn't with her, but there were plenty of witnesses to prove she was here. And Beverly never actually said Ava had to tour the entire inside of Buckingham Palace, and she certainly didn't require that Ava enjoy it. As far as she was concerned, been there, done that. The royal commodes and cats could wait for another day.

"May I ask what is happening?" the woman asked. She sounded kind. Ava wanted to answer, but she was having trouble breathing.

"Agoraphobic," Ava managed to spit out.

"Oh my," the woman said. "What can I do for you?"

"Do you have any pull around here?"

The woman glanced at her clipboard, then looked around as if to make sure no one was listening, then gave a quick nod. "What do you need?"

"I'd like to hide in the coat closet until a taxi can come get me. And then I'm going to need to wear this rubbish bag and someone is going to have to walk me to the taxi. And if they could also ride with me to the flat and walk with me into the flat, that would be brilliant."

The woman stared at her. "Miss Maggie called and told me all about you," she said. "She thought we should meet."

"She mentioned there was someone," Ava said.

"I have a son who is dyslexic."

"Sorry."

"Oh, don't be. I'm very proud of him." Using her clipboard

for support, she scribbled something on a piece of paper and handed it to Ava.

HIDDEN NO MORE

Join the Fight. Support Individuals with Hidden Disabilities.

"I don't like support groups," Ava said. *They should change that to "Invisible" so that it sounded more like superpowers.* She'd have to mention it if she ever met with them. Which she was never going to do.

"It's not a support group; it's a group that educates others, and refuses to be hidden." The woman pulled an iPhone out of her purse and scrolled through it. She turned it to Ava. There was a picture of a young man. He was out in the streets of London, with a girl posing next to him. He held a sign: Get Your Picture Taken with a Proud Dyslexic.

Ava handed it back. She didn't know what to think. But the woman was looking at Ava expectantly. She wanted her to react to this grand news. She wanted her to embrace the support group for those with hidden disabilities. She still liked "invisible" better. Their spokesperson could be the Invisible Man. That was kind of funny. Ava laughed. The woman frowned. Ava cleared her throat and posed the question as seriously as she could. "Do they ever meet inside?"

Once Ava was inside the taxicab she folded the flyer for Hidden Disabilities into little pieces and let it drop on the floor. Not normally one to litter, she just didn't want it in her possession. She didn't want to be associated with them. After all, a girl who routinely wore a rubbish bag over her head had no problems staying hidden.

CHAPTER 33

See Big Ben
Walk along the Thames
~~Visit Buckingham Palace~~
Tour the Tower of London
~~Go to an English Pub~~
Sit in a bench in Hyde Park
~~Go to a show in the West End~~
~~Go to a club in the West End~~
Navigate the London Underground (Tube/subway)
Ride the London Eye

For a solid week following the Buckingham Palace adventure, Ava didn't go anywhere. She'd missed her little perch at the windows, sketching, not worrying about the list, or the flat, or Vic, or Deven, or Hillary, or Queenie, or even Jasper. She just wanted to sketch anonymous Londoners from her emerald velvet stool.

She often lost track of what day it was, but in London she always knew when it was a Friday night. People literally had a bounce in their step. There were more girls in skirts, and dresses, and heels. Around four o'clock traffic was already jammed, as everyone had the brilliant idea to get out early. She wondered what most of them had in store. Who was going to their country house? Who was headed to the Tube to take the train to Paris? The station was only five blocks from her flat. It even had a champagne bar. People were sitting there, this very moment, drinking a glass of champagne, and waiting to zip off to a Parisian café, or nightclub. Ava was okay with the fact that she wasn't one of them. She wondered what people would think of their lives if they could see them in a series of sketches. Would they be forced to pay more attention to the little moments?

Although it would be fun to have a flat like this everywhere in the world. A little tree house of a place where you could gaze out at the people going by, sketch their lives for the few minutes you saw them. Ava had just finished sketching a woman with a dog in a handbag when the door opened and then slammed. Queenie was home, and it didn't sound good. Slowly, Ava put down her sketch pad and pencil and turned around. Queenie stood, red eyed, in front of her.

"I didn't get it," he said.

Ava stood. "I'm so sorry."

"I told you. I needed my lucky charm."

"What did they say?"

Queenie looked away. "That I was too old," he whispered. He turned back and raised his voice. "Too old!"

"You're right," Ava said. "It had to be the lucky charm."

"Why?" Queenie frowned. He was suspicious of her.

"Because that's a totally ridiculous thing to say about a man who looks like you."

"Are you taking the piss?"

"Why, it's like saying you're too purple." Queenie considered her for a moment, then flopped on the sofa.

"I'll pour you a Scotch," Ava said.

"You mean there's actually some left?"

"I bought two new bottles."

"You had Scotch delivered?" Queenie rose from the sofa.

"No," Ava said. "I stopped into a liquor store on my way home from Buckingham Palace." Actually, she had the driver of the town car run into the liquor store for her, but Queenie didn't need to get bogged down in the minutiae.

"You're cured?"

"I wouldn't go that far."

"Amazing." He was at the bar in seconds flat, and he downed the Scotch. He let it slam down on the bar. "So the flat will be yours, will it?"

Ava poured herself a Scotch, and took it to the window. "What do you mean?"

"You'll be able to complete the list."

"I don't know. I hope so." Now probably wasn't the time to ask him if she could count the porno for Big Ben and Jasper sitting on the bench for Hyde Park.

"Beverly would be very happy. And very proud."

"So you're fine with the fact that she left the flat to me, and not to you?"

"I'll admit I wanted this flat. I still do. And I never thought you'd be able to do anything on that list. Yet look at you. If you win it fair and square I'll be happy for you. I'll feel sorry for me, but I'll be happy for you."

"Hillary vehemently disagrees. She thinks I should let you have the flat no matter what."

Queenie shook his head and went back to the sofa. "Hillary has always been a pistol. My sister drank and smoked a lot during her pregnancy." Ava laughed.

"I found the decorating book she gave you." Queenie gasped. "And I took it to her office and shoved it in her face." He gasped again. It was rather dramatic sounding, and Ava had to laugh.

"You did not."

"I did. I'm surprised she didn't tell you."

"I've been busy with the auditions. You should have kept the decorating book. It had some lovely ideas."

"I'd hate to change a thing," Ava said. "It would be like changing Beverly."

"Eventually you'll make it your own," Queenie said. Her own. Ava had never even thought about that. "I'm starting to think you have the right idea. After that audition I never want to leave this flat again." He laid his head on Ava's shoulder. She liked it.

"So don't," she said. "We'll both stay here until we have moss growing on us."

"Gross," Queenie said. "And kind of nice too."

The buzzer shrieked. Queenie slapped his hands over his ears, and sloshed his Scotch. "We have to do something about that." Ava grinned. She was thrilled it wasn't just her. Queenie swore and padded to the door. He tried peeping out the peephole. "It's Jasper," Queenie announced. Ava's heart lifted. Queenie opened the door and Jasper practically fell in.

"Are you okay?" Ava said.

"Did you find my lucky charm?" Queenie said.

Jasper glanced at Ava, then Queenie. "No. Sorry, mate."

"You should be," Queenie said. "I just lost the television show of my career because of you."

"That's not true," Ava said.

"It is so," Queenie said.

Ava turned to Jasper. "Are you okay?"

"I haven't been to bed since my set last night." Jasper collapsed on the sofa.

Queenie gasped. "Your set. Your comedy set. Thursday night. Oh, Jasper, I forgot all about it. I'm so, so sorry."

"Not as sorry as I am."

"I'm a horrible person. Not showing up for a friend's show? That's only second to, say, losing someone's lucky charm right before the audition of his life!"

Jasper put his hand up. "Queenie, I will be eternally sorry. I don't know what else to say or do."

"I'm sorry I wasn't there," Ava said.

"I'm glad you weren't there," Jasper said. "I sucked. I failed. I bombed." He collapsed on the sofa. "I'm beginning to think you have the right idea. I never want to go out again."

Queenie gave Ava a long look. "Apparently you're contagious."

Ava brought the bottle of Scotch over to the sofa along with another glass. "What were some of your jokes?" she asked.

"British politics, the law, women," Jasper said.

"There's your problem," Queenie said. "You should only joke about what you know." Queenie and Ava laughed; Jasper did not.

"I'm sorry," Ava said. "But all great comedians have failed at one point or another."

"Some of them more and longer than others," Queenie said.

"Would you like some Scotch?" Ava said, readying the pour.

"There's some left?" Jasper said. The door shrieked again. This time both Jasper and Queenie jumped while Ava answered it. There in the hall stood Vic and Deven.

"Oh," Ava said. "Hello."

"You're a bollocks," Vic said to Ava. She pushed her way in, dragging Deven with her.

"What did I do?" Ava said.

"You made me fall in love with this terrorist." She swung and smacked Deven in the gut.

"I'm not a terrorist."

"Suspected terrorist," Vic said. "And then you had the nerve to promise me half the flat if I'd help you with the list, only to snatch it away again."

"You promised her half the flat?" Queenie said. Vic looked at Queenie and then Jasper as if just now noticing there were other people in the room.

"She did," Vic said. "She'd rather have me than you as flatmate."

"That's not true," Ava said quickly. "Queenie, that's not true."

"Queenie," Vic said. "So you're the bloke with the lucky charm."

Queenie gasped. "How do you know about my lucky charm?"

"Because Ava completely freaked out when she lost it."

Oh no. She did not just say that.

Queenie shot off the sofa and pointed at Ava. "You lost my lucky charm? You? Where is it? Where is it?"

"Do you have it, Vic?" Ava said.

"What would it be worth to you?" Vic said.

Just when Ava thought Queenie's gasps couldn't get any louder, he inhaled and then bellowed out a sound like a tuba.

"Queenie, please calm down," Ava said.

"Calm down?" Queenie said. "Calm down?"

"I'll get it back. I swear," Ava said. She glared at Vic, who was sporting a triumphant smirk. Meanwhile Queenie looked as if he was about to explode. He whirled on Ava and shook his fist.

"Can you also turn back time?" he yelled. "Can you turn back time and give me back the audition of my life? Telly! I was going to be on telly."

"Look on the bright side," Jasper said. "Telly adds ten pounds. So it's like you've lost ten pounds."

"No wonder you bombed," Queenie said. "There isn't a funny bone in your body!"

"All right," Ava said. "Everybody calm down."

"Where exactly did you lose my lucky charm?" Queenie said.

"I went to Sainsbury's, and then home. Between here and there."

"And you." Queenie whirled on Jasper. "Why did you lie?"

"Because he didn't want you to hate me," Ava said. "We were getting along so well."

"All good things must come to an end," Queenie said. "And the bad things too. I cannot believe the two of you and your little secrets. How long do you have to complete the list, Ava? A fortnight? Is that Big Ben I hear ticking in the distance? Tick, tock, tick, tock, tick, tock."

"Do you have the charm or not?" Ava asked Vic again. Vic pulled out a cigarette and lit it. Queenie started to cough. "Put that out. I told you he's allergic."

"The audition of my life," Queenie repeated. "The money. The fame. It's all your fault." Once again he pointed at Ava.

"That lucky charm wouldn't have made you look any younger," Ava said.

Queenie gasped. "Wanker!" he shouted.

"Ava thinks I'm funny," Jasper said. "Don't you, Ava?"

"Let's all calm down," Ava said.

"Why didn't you tell me? You let me go on that audition without it," Queenie said. "Did you even look for it?" He glared at Ava. "You didn't, did you? Because that would have meant going outside."

"Queenie, listen to me. You didn't need it. Whether or not you got the part has nothing to do with the lucky charm."

"Oh, it wasn't ridiculous that I didn't get it then? It wasn't like saying I was purple?"

"Purple?" Jasper said.

"And you don't need to be afraid of the outside either, do you?" Queenie said.

"That's not the same," Ava said.

"How is it not?" Queenie said. "Does this not look like a panic attack to you?"

"Actually, it just looks like an attack. On me. Why would you be panicking when the audition is over?"

"Thanks to you!" Queenie said.

"How much is the thing worth?" Vic said.

"What are you doing here?" Ava asked Vic.

"Visiting my mate," Vic said. "Aren't you my mate?"

"No," Ava said.

"British luck to you getting rid of me," Vic said. "I'm on a long smoke break."

"Me too," Deven said.

Ava was pondering what on earth she could say to that when the door opened without warning. Ava whirled around. "Don't you know how to knock?" There stood Hillary. And next to her—Ava's mother. Followed by Diana. This wasn't happening. She was dreaming. That's it. She was dreaming. Vic was sitting on the sill swinging her leg. Ava kicked her in the shin.

"Crikey! What did you do that for?"

"Pinching is too cliché," Ava said. "I have to be dreaming."

"No hug? No kiss? No hello?" her mother said.

"Mom. Diana. What are you doing here?" Ava hugged her mother, although she didn't want to. The feeling must have been mutual, for Gretchen didn't even hug back; she just patted Ava. People weren't just supposed to turn up from America. There were supposed to be multiple conversations and excuses, and postponements first.

"Knock, knock," Hillary said.

"Who's there?" Jasper answered glumly.

Ava went to hug Diana until she saw her recoil. These were her people? She'd never realized how cold they could be. Not until she had warmer people to compare them to.

"It's smaller than I imagined," her mother said.

"What are you doing here?" Ava asked Hillary. She seemed to be asking that question a lot and getting very few answers.

"I'm glad you asked. I'm here because I would like to make you an offer. I want to buy this flat." Hillary flashed her teeth. Ava wanted to pull down her pants right here and moon her, and she'd never mooned anyone ever.

"It's not for sale," Ava said.

Hillary smiled. Why was she smiling? "Perhaps you should discuss that with your mother."

"Mom?" Gretchen didn't answer. She was too busy checking out all the photographs on the wall.

"I knew it," Gretchen said. "We're not in a single one."

Hillary approached Ava. "All she has to do is have you declared a nut job and then the flat will legally be hers, and she's already agreed to sell it to me."

"Mother," Ava said. "Are you here to have me declared a nut job?"

"And go line dancing," Gretchen said.

"Mother!"

"Calm down, Ava. We can discuss this calmly later."

Ava turned to Queenie. "Queenie, tell your niece from hell that you're not going to let her get away with any of her diabolical plans regarding this flat."

"Better her than me," Vic said. She lit a cigarette.

"No smoking in the flat," Ava said.

Vic crawled out to the tiny balcony. "Happy now?"

"Not at all," Ava said.

Deven picked up the binoculars and aimed them at his place.

"Ava, you think I'm funny, don't you?" Jasper said. The buzzer shrieked. Everyone jumped. Ava opened the door. There was no one there.

"It's the intercom," Queenie said. "The buzzer is the same." He answered.

"Hey, bitches!" Franco yelled through the intercom. Queenie buzzed him up. A few minutes later, Franco and Georgie entered.

"Ava," Franco said. "Remember that cute bartender who gave you drugs?"

"Drugs?" Diana said.

"You're doing drugs?" her mother said.

"Sounds like she's unfit," Hillary said. "Very, very unfit."

"Do you have any left or did you use them all yourself?" Vic yelled.

"Unfit," Hillary said.

"You're having another party?" Georgie said. "Without us?"

"It's not a party," Ava said. "It's my public execution. What about the bartender?"

"Oh. He asked when you were coming back."

"He did? He asked when I was coming back?"

"Apparently he sold every one of your napkin sketches," Franco said.

"You're the one who should be selling them," Georgie said.

"There are a lot of people in this flat," Ava said. She was dying to go hide under the bed. But her mother was already contemplating having Ava declared unfit. She couldn't give her any more ammunition. Which meant she had to get out of there.

Ava looked at Queenie. Then Jasper. Then Hillary. Diana was making tea. As if she lived here. Ava's mother was picking up the photographs and looking behind them, as if one of her could be lurking there. Franco and Georgie were hanging around the piano, going through sheet music. "I could stay here all day," Franco said.

"Me too," Georgie said.

"Great," Ava said. She picked up her purse. And her keys. Then her sketch pad and pencil. Ava didn't have to wait for an opportunity to escape. Every single one of them was staring deep into his or her own navel. Nobody even looked up when she walked out the door.

CHAPTER 34

For once in her life, the fear of being inside the flat with all those people who were upset with her, or wanted something from her, was more overwhelming than being outside. Ava took a left on the street instead of crossing it, a direction she had never gone before. The shops soon disappeared and tree-lined homes replaced them. She clung tightly to her sketch pad, and looked at nothing, just kept moving. She plunked herself down on a top step shaded by an alcove. She got out her pad, and began sketching the footpath, the weeds poking through the cracks in the sidewalk, the generous front tree, and the back of a lorry as it trundled by.

Soon a boy and his mother strolled down the street and she began to sketch them. They didn't even notice her. It was almost like looking outside her windows. Maybe she didn't have an invisible disability; maybe she was just invisible. She thought of the woman from Buckingham Palace and her dyslexic son. She'd promised that woman she would look into the group, but she'd lied. What good would joining them do? In the past she might have said it would have made her feel less lonely, but she wasn't lonely anymore, was she? Then again, she'd just left everyone in her flat to be on her own. Her heart began to trip; the colored dots appeared. She wasn't cured. But they didn't happen right away. That was progress, wasn't it? She tucked her sketch pad under her arm, kept her eyes fastened on the sidewalk, and began to walk home.

She was almost to her own flat when a black limo pulled up in front of the building. Ava stopped. "There she is," her mother called out. Ava turned. Jasper, Queenie, Vic, Deven, Franco, Georgie, her mother, Diana, and Hillary were on the stoop.

"Ava," Jasper called out first. "We were so worried." He ran up and hugged her.

"We were going to look everywhere," Franco said.

"In style, apparently," Ava said. "Why didn't you pick me up in this at the airport?" Ava said. Jasper laughed.

"It's *my* limo, luv," Franco said. "I have friends in low places."

Her mother and Diana approached. They were pale. Diana's hand flew to her turtleneck.

"Are you guys okay?" Ava said.

"Ava," her mother said. "You're out."

"You make it sound as if I've been in prison," Ava said. Although she had been. Self-inflicted solitary confinement.

"You're not having a panic attack?" Diana said.

"The colored dots just started," Ava said. "I'm going back in now."

"Shouldn't we all go out to dinner?" Diana said. "Now that you're out?"

Shit. Ava was done. She wanted to go inside. Alone. Jasper came up behind her and wrapped his arms around her.

"You should all go to dinner. In the limo. Ava and I have already made private plans for dinner." Ava leaned into him, more grateful than she'd ever been in her whole life. He knew her better than her own therapist. Ava and Jasper waved from the stoop as the gang piled into the limo. *British luck to you,* Ava thought. *With my mother and Diana in tow, you're all going to need it.*

* * *

Jasper ordered curry. Ava poured wine. The sun was starting to set over London. It was only looking out at the lights twinkling, and having finished a delicious meal, clinking wineglasses with a man who was totally into her, that she realized something. Good and bad, today had been the best day of her life. Jasper grabbed her hands and kissed them. "You should have seen the look on everyone's face when they realized you were gone."

"Oh, God," Ava said. "Did you look under the bed?"

Jasper flushed, then nodded. "First place I checked," he said. Ava laughed. She wished she could have seen the looks on their faces.

After dinner Jasper pulled out the list. "You have two weeks left," he said quietly.

"I know," she said.

"Do you want to strategize?"

"That depends," Ava said, grabbing him by the tie and pulling him toward her. "Can we do it horizontal?"

"Right after we give vertical a fair shot," Jasper replied.

Late that evening, Diana and Gretchen returned from dinner and Jasper went home. Ava hated to see him go, but it was a little crowded in the flat with her visitors. Even Queenie packed a bag and headed out. Diana and Gretchen set about exploring the flat while Ava made tea. It was her "go to" now, the thing she did when she was tense. Although with those two in the house, she might have to resort to her old "go to"—the minibar.

"It's small," her mother said, once again coming into the kitchen.

"It's London," Ava said. "It's actually quite big, considering it's London." Was her mother always this negative? Ava couldn't remember.

"I think it's quite lovely," Diana said, stepping in.

"Thank you. Would either of you like a cup of tea?" Ava watched her mother's face. Gretchen was definitely thrown. Ava had never offered anyone anything to drink in her life.

How awful was that? The pair sat at the kitchen table, slowly, almost reluctantly, as if they didn't trust what Ava was going to do next.

"I'd love a cup of coffee, thank you," Diana said.

I didn't offer you a cup of coffee. Had Diana always been this passive-aggressive? She could get out Queenie's espresso maker, but that was a lot of work. Not to mention she was on shaky ground with him. "Sorry, all I have is tea. But there are coffee shops within walking distance if you fancy." Her mother finally accepted the tea, but Diana simply frowned and played with her turtleneck. At last she dived into the sugar cookies that Ava placed on the little table.

"We just had a big meal. I don't know if I can do tea," her mother said.

"Just pretend then. It's like breathing here. You have to at least go through tea-like motions."

"Interesting," Diana said.

"Isn't this some view?" Ava said. She would change the subject. Chitchat for once like a normal person. She would not let Diana or her mother get to her. Not anymore.

"It is a nice view," her mother said. "How much is this flat worth?"

"I think it's poor form to discuss things like that," Ava said.

"You've changed," Diana said, jabbing a sugar cookie in Ava's direction. She watched the crumbs fall to the floor.

"I'm glad you noticed," Ava said. "I *have* changed. There's no need for either of you to be here."

"I'm your mother," Gretchen said. "I have a right to visit my daughter, don't I?"

"Of course." The teakettle shrieked. Ava wished she could shriek along with it. She poured the tea, one for herself, and one for her mother. "Would you like sparkling water?" she said to Diana.

"God, no," Diana said.

"Tap water?"

"Coffee."

"I don't have coffee."

"You used to drink coffee."

"I used to hide under the bed too."

Diana squinted and bit into another cookie. "We both know you still do," she said. "There's not a speck of dust under that bed."

"Why are you checking underneath my bed?"

"To see what you've been up to," Diana said. "And I can see you're still doing it."

"Not as much," Ava said. "I have made significant improvement."

"Hillary wants to buy the flat from us," Gretchen said.

Ava stepped closer to her mother. "Us? There is no us. It's my flat. Or maybe Queenie's. But either way, it's not yours, and it's not Hillary's."

Gretchen set her teacup down and placed her hands on the table as if bracing herself. "I have taken care of you your entire life." She looked up at Ava and did not break eye contact.

This was it. Ava might not ever get the chance again. Especially with a therapist in the room to referee. "Taken care of me? Or enabled me?"

"What are you saying? I'm to blame for your condition?"

"My agoraphobia. You can't even say it."

"It's a ghastly word."

"It's a ghastly way to feel as well, Mother."

"I did everything I possibly could," Gretchen said. "I sent you to psychiatrist after psychiatrist."

"Some were better than others," Ava said with a glance at Diana.

"Baby steps," Diana said. "There's no cure."

"I thought you were afraid to fly," Ava said to Diana. Diana glanced at Gretchen. One look and Ava knew the story. Gretchen had promised Diana a chunk of the profits from the sale of her flat. "Look at me, Mom." Gretchen looked out the window. "Why aren't you happy for me? Can't you see how well I'm doing?"

Finally, Gretchen looked at her. "I do see. And I'm proud of you. But what's the game plan? Live here the rest of your life?"

"Why not?"

"You don't belong here. I'm too far away. You're doing very well at the moment, and I'm thrilled for you; I am. But what's going to happen when things aren't going well?"

"I'm not selling the flat."

Gretchen set her teacup down. "Our only other option is to go to court and explain to them that you have a disability."

"I see," Ava said. "And why is that?"

"So that man doesn't get the flat!" Gretchen said.

"That man is my friend. And I have decided to abide by Beverly's wishes. I only get the flat if I complete the list."

"That's absurd," Gretchen said.

"I've done several already."

"Show me the list. Show me which ones you've done."

"Drink your tea, ladies," Diana said. "It is rather soothing."

"I shouldn't have to show you the list. I told you what I'm going to do. I need you to be on my side this time."

"I'm trying to help you. Let's go to court and tell them to throw out this ridiculous list."

"I'm going to do the list."

"Walking a few blocks down the street is not the same thing as riding the Tube, and touring the Tower of London," Gretchen said.

Ava put her tea down. She wished it was scalding. She'd drink it. She'd welcome a burning sensation along her throat. "How long have you been talking to Hillary?"

Gretchen slammed down her teacup. "She called me. That's a lot more than I can say about my own daughter lately. Do you have any idea how worried I've been?"

"I've called you numerous times. You don't always answer."

"Are you referring to the call where you said, 'I know,' and hung up?"

"Oh, we talked after that. Selective memory, as usual. Shall I remind you what we were fighting about?" Before Gretchen could respond, Ava exited the kitchen and went to the bookshelf in the living room. She pulled out the picture of her father's headstone and handed it to her mother. Gretchen sipped her tea and barely glanced at it. "Queenie said she stayed on for days. Even missed a matinée performance trying to see me."

"What kind of a name is Queenie?" Diana said.

"It's a nickname," Ava said. "He's a drag queen."

"Fascinating," Diana said. "And he doesn't drink coffee?"

"You're in London," Ava said. "Drink tea."

"You've run out of your Xanax, haven't you?"

"That depends," Ava said. "Do you have any on you?"

Gretchen reached underneath her seat where her purse was stashed. She reached into it and removed a stack of papers. "I think you should at least look at Hillary's offer. It's more money than either of us have ever made in our lives." Ava grabbed the papers and took them straight to the stove. She turned on the gas, touched the edges of the papers to the flame, and held them over the sink as they burned.

"Ava," her mother said. "Stop that."

"Interesting," Diana said.

"I am never selling my flat to that woman," Ava said. "Did you know that Jasper used to date Hillary? She dumped him. Then I came along, and guess what? He fell for me. Me. Now she's jealous and it's the only reason why she wants me to lose this flat. What she really wants is for me to be out of Jasper's life for good."

Gretchen went to the living room window and looked out. "Is that where the terrorist lives?"

"I'm going to kill her," Ava said.

"Now *those* people drink coffee, I bet," Diana said, joining Gretchen at the window.

"Deven is not a terrorist." Vic never did answer Ava's question about the lucky charm. That wench had it. Ava just knew it.

"This is a terrible city," Gretchen said. "You don't belong here."

"This is an amazing city," Ava said. "I belong here more than I've ever belonged anywhere."

"Ava, don't make us do this," her mother said.

"Make you do what?"

"We can go to a judge. Tell him you're not well. Certainly not capable of completing that list or deciding whether or not to sell this flat."

"How dare you. You know there's nothing wrong with my intelligence."

"Then start using it, Ava. Sell this place, take the money, and run."

"I'm staying."

"You've always been impulsive. I knew you would do this." She turned to Diana. "Didn't I tell you she would do this?"

"Did you also know I would fall in love? Go down the block? Go to the market? A nightclub? An English pub?" *Hide in the closet of Buckingham Palace? Take E at the club? Put a rubbish bag over my head in front of a busful of schoolchildren? Watch a British porno?* They didn't need to know everything.

"I want to see your prescription bottle of Xanax," Diana said.

That wasn't good news. She'd see it was empty. "Why?"

"I want to make sure you're not overdosing."

"Because I'm finally making progress? You two are unbelievable."

"We're only trying to help."

"No, you're pushing your own agendas. And what is with the turtlenecks? Why don't you wear anything else?"

Diana's hand flew up to her neck as if to make sure it was still there. "I need to present a neutral palette to my clients."

"Most of your clients are wondering exactly how many turtlenecks you own, and whether or not you change your clothes at all."

"Interesting," Diana said.

"I think you're overusing that word," Ava said.

"Ava Wilder," Gretchen said. "Apologize at once."

"I have fifteen turtlenecks," Diana said. "I wash them on Wednesdays."

"Ava, I'm taking you home, and that's that. If you don't want to sell this flat to Hillary, then just leave it to the queen and we'll be on our way."

"That's not your decision to make," Ava said.

"You don't know Beverly Wilder. She was a manipulative woman. She ruined our lives."

"How, Mother? How did she ruin our lives?"

"We've been over this."

"Actually, we haven't. I want to know why you two hated each other so much. Because it makes me sad. And it made Daddy sad."

"It wasn't my fault. That woman hated my guts. I never asked him to choose, but she did. And he chose me. She never got over it."

"I'm sorry. But I was just a child. And I had a right to know my father's sister."

"She wanted to take over. Once Bertrand died I thought she'd show me some kindness. She was worse."

"Worse, how?"

"You don't need to know."

"Stop sheltering me!"

"She was going to kidnap you. All right? Is that what you wanted to hear?"

"What do you mean?"

"She wanted custody of you. Said a change of atmosphere would snap you out of it. That's why I didn't let her near you. And I would do it again. I don't care what her little London friends say. She was not a nice woman." Gretchen moved restlessly about the flat. She grabbed the nearest picture off the wall.

"Mom," Ava said.

"Her, her, her, her, HER." Gretchen threw the picture to the floor. It landed on the throw rug. A crack formed in the center. Ava dropped to her knees and grabbed the picture. "Stop it. This isn't yours." Ava lunged at the wall and began removing Beverly's posters. She would put them back later; she didn't want to see another one cracked. Her mother grabbed another one. *Cats.* Ava lunged for it and grabbed the other end. They tugged back and forth.

"Let it go," Ava said. "It's not yours."

"Where are all the pictures of you, and Bertrand? If she loved you so much?"

Gretchen let go of the poster, and Ava stumbled back. Gretchen collapsed onto the divan. Diana watched from the corner of the room, playing with her turtleneck.

Ava went to the side cabinet and withdrew the envelope. "They're here." She threw the envelope at her mother. She caught the edge of it, and the cards tipped over and onto the floor. Photos slid out of several of them. Photos! Aunt Beverly had sent her photos. "You sent every one of them back," Ava said, staring at the mess on the floor. "These were for me."

Gretchen too stared at the photos and cards. "She was poison."

"And you weren't?"

Her mother gasped. Ava didn't mean to say it. But she couldn't take it back. It had been too long, boiling inside her, everything she'd never said. "I loved you more than anyone else in the world," Gretchen said.

"You blamed me."

"For what? I blamed you for what?"

"For Daddy's death."

"Please don't start this again."

" 'What did you DO, Ava? What did you DO?' "

"I was in shock. My husband was lying dead in the street. I was in shock."

"But I believed you. Don't you get it? I thought I had caused it somehow."

"That's not logical."

"Gretchen," Diana said. "I think you need to listen."

"I spent years replaying that night. Years. Figuring out what I could have done differently. Said, 'No, Daddy, I don't want to dance.' So many years. Torturing myself with what I could have said or thought differently so that my father wouldn't end up dead and my mother wouldn't end up blaming me. I couldn't stop replaying the worst day of my entire life over and over and over again. And you watched me. And you never once truly looked me in the eyes and tried to convince me it wasn't my fault. You've never even said you were sorry for doing that to me."

"You were a child. You were in shock. You're not remembering it clearly."

Ava looked at Diana, who was suddenly inspecting a spot on the wall. "Now would be the time to step in with some therapeutic advice," Ava said.

"Is that a camera?" Diana said.

Gretchen and Ava turned to the wall where *Cats* used to be. A little red light stared back at them.

"Holy shit," Ava said. She approached. It was duct-taped to the wall. A little recording device.

"We're on film?" Gretchen said.

"Oh, God," Ava said. *Big Ben. Big Ben. Big Ben.* Who had done this? Hillary? Queenie? Definitely not Jasper, right? Was someone spying on her 24-7? Ava ripped it off the wall. She threw it to the floor and stomped on it. "We're going to have to check for more," she said. Gretchen walked up to Ava and put her hand on her cheek.

"I've missed the happy, daring little girl you used to be," she said.

"I miss her too," Ava said. "That's why I'm here, Mom. Not to hurt you. I'm proud of you too. You didn't crawl into a ball when Daddy died like I did. You took country line dancing. I should have told you how proud of you I was. I know I wasn't an easy daughter to raise. But you have to see me, now, Mom. Really see me. And you have to look at me and tell me that it was not my fault that Dad had a heart attack and died. That you know there was nothing I did or could have done."

"I know that, Ava. I do."

"I need you to say it, Mom."

"You're being ridiculous."

"I need you to say it."

"You may never get another chance," Diana told Gretchen. She took off her turtleneck and stood in the living room in her bra.

"Diana, what are you doing?" Ava said.

"I'm changing. You're changing; now I'm changing. It's your mother's turn."

"There might still be cameras," Ava said, trying not to look at Diana's breasts.

"They've still got some bounce to them," Diana said.

Gretchen ran her hands down her sides. She cleared her throat. She looked at Ava. "I'm sorry I blamed you for your father's death. He had a heart attack. The doctor said there was nothing we could have done to save him. Even if we did CPR. It was too massive. If it hadn't happened while dancing, it would have happened at the dinner table. Or on his way to bed." She stepped up to Ava. "You didn't do anything. And I'm sorry I said that to you. I truly don't remember, but I just as truly apologize." Tears welled in Ava's eyes. She grabbed her mother and held on to her. At first Gretchen was stiff. Then she wrapped her arms around Ava. "You're my little girl. Maybe I did enable you. I didn't want another bad thing to happen to my little girl."

Ava pulled away. She reached up and wiped a tear from her mother's cheek. "I'm sorry. I'm sorry I didn't handle it better. I'm sorry Aunt Beverly didn't treat you better. But please, Mom. This is good for me. I need to be here."

"I know," Gretchen said.

"You do?" Ava said.

"A mother knows," Gretchen said. She hugged Ava again. "I'm proud of you."

"Thank you."

"We're both proud of you. But what are we going to tell the judge? I think the only way out of this is to tell him you aren't capable of doing the things on that list."

Ava sighed. Her mother wasn't going to change. People never really did. "I'm only going to say this one last time. I'm either going to finish the list or Queenie is going to get the flat." Ava picked up her mobile and called Jasper. He answered on the first ring. "Do you have plans tomorrow?"

"It's Saturday. So I'm flexible. You want me to come over?"

"No," Ava said. "I want you to take me out."

"Really?" he said. "Where?"

She glanced out the kitchen window and looked into the distance. "How about the Thames?" Ava said.

"Brilliant," Jasper said. "A walk along the Thames sounds brilliant." Ava hung up the phone, and lost herself in the moment, thinking of Jasper, imagining holding his hand as they walked along the river. She came out of the daydream to find her mother and Diana staring at her.

"What?"

"Do you always smile like that after you talk to him?" Diana said.

"Yes," Ava said.

"Interesting," Diana said. Ava's mother looked worried.

"What is it?" Ava asked.

"Do you think he knows about the camera?" Gretchen asked.

CHAPTER 35

The next morning, at ten o'clock, Jasper picked her up in a town car driven by a professional driver. Jasper was sitting in the back and ushered her in. The colored dots appeared within seconds, but Ava told herself she was having a disco party for one and who didn't want that? The minute she slipped in next to him, Jasper took her hands. "I had a million things I wanted to say to you, but they've all slipped out of my head."

"Me too," Ava said. Jasper scooted over and kissed her. The driver started the car. Looking at Jasper, Ava realized she didn't care about the list. All Ava wanted to do was make out with Jasper as they drove through the streets of London. And Jasper must have had the same idea, for a few minutes later the car pulled up behind a food cart.

"They have the best enchiladas in town," Jasper said. "If you like—"

"Love them," Ava said. Jasper grinned, handed the driver money, and went back to kissing Ava. The driver had to interrupt them about ten minutes later. Soon they had a feast of enchi-

ladas, chips, and guacamole. Jasper pulled a bottle of champagne
out of a bucket at his feet. Ava hadn't even noticed it.

"What are we celebrating?" Ava said.

"You completing the list," Jasper said. He pulled it out of his
pocket. "Look how many you've accomplished already." Ava
took the list. Jasper had put a line through the ones she'd accomplished.

~~See Big Ben~~
Walk along the Thames
~~Visit Buckingham Palace~~
Tour the Tower of London
~~Go to an English pub~~
~~Sit on a bench in Hyde Park~~
~~Go to a show in the West End~~
~~Go to a club in the West End~~
Navigate the London Underground (Tube/subway)
Ride the London Eye

"You're counting the porno for Big Ben and you sitting on
the bench instead of me," Ava said.

"I talked to Queenie. He said you could count them."

"After he blew up about me losing his lucky charm?"

"Yes," Jasper said. "After." Tears came to Ava's eyes. That was
awful big of Queenie. Especially since he really wanted the flat.
Was he trying to support her or was he just that convinced she
couldn't do the rest? She was so cynical, but it was hard to believe that he would give up the flat for her. And what if he was
the one who planted the camera? Why would he do it and what
was he hoping to "catch"? Ava certainly didn't want to think
Jasper had anything to do with it. And she was too afraid to ask
him. She was out in London with a handsome man. Who knew
if a moment like this would ever come again? She was having an
experience. Not reading about it, dreaming about it, or sketching it. She was living it. She'd have to be even more insane than
she already was to ruin it.

"There are only four items left on the list, and my driver is headed to the Thames as we speak," Jasper said. Ava nodded, and Jasper held her hand as the car progressed through the streets. "We can simply find a spot to pull up to next to the Thames," Jasper said. "Or."

"Or?"

"There's a boat we could ride. It will go under Tower Bridge. I think we could technically count that as seeing the Tower of London."

"I seem to be getting by on a lot of technicalities."

"What's wrong?"

"Is it fair? Am I playing by the rules?"

"I think we've all come to realize the list wasn't fair to begin with. We knew Beverly. She was trying to welcome you to the city, not paralyze you."

That would leave only two more items on the list. A boat ride along the Thames with Jasper. So romantic. So crowded with people. So nowhere to go if she had an attack. What could she do, jump overboard? Just the thought of all those people staring at her and wondering what was wrong with her was enough to ruin all ideas of the romance of it.

"It's a good idea," Ava said. "If we were rich with a private boat."

"Ah, a high-society girl," Jasper said.

Ava laughed. "Wouldn't want you to make that mistake again," she said with a playful punch to his arm. "No. I just need to make sure that wherever I go, I'm somewhat in control. I don't want to lose it in front of a boatload of strangers."

"Sorry. I didn't think about that."

"Nor should you," Ava said. "And I really do love the idea. Someday. But I need to prepare for it."

"Are you still up for just walking along the Thames?"

"Absolutely."

"The South Bank walk starts at the Tower Bridge, so we can snap a quick picture in front and cross it off your list."

"You're sure I don't have to go inside?"

"Only if you want to." Ava nodded. "Do you want to?" Ava shook her head. "Okay. A photo op in front of the Tower will have to do."

"As long as I'm with you, and I can control when we go back to the car."

"Of course."

The driver looked back through the rearview mirror. "I can't just hang out at the curb waiting for you. I'd get a ticket."

"What?" He was just going to dump them out near the Tower and disappear. Was that what he was saying?

"No worries," Jasper said. "It's a touristy area. We'll find a taxi whenever we need one. I promise."

"We're jammed up at this time of day," the driver said. "You could wait for hours. Better if you take the Tube or bus home."

The driver was smiling, clueless that he'd just shot Ava in the chest twice. Tube or bus. Death by Tube? Or death by bus? Was cake even an option this time? "Oh, God," Ava said. "Maybe we should try this another time."

"You definitely should if you expect a taxi to be waiting for you like you're the Queen," the driver said, wagging his finger at her.

"Do you mind just doing the driving and letting me do the talking, all right, mate?" Jasper said. The driver shrugged. Jasper snuck his hand across the seat and took Ava's. "If we did take the Tube home, you'd only have one more thing left on your list." He was whispering, in case she couldn't handle the things he was saying at any higher of a volume. And he was right about that. "And maybe, we could even take the Tube to the London Eye and just get it all over with today."

Ava snatched her hand away. It was too much. He didn't understand. She hadn't planned on doing anything other than running out of the taxi and up to the Thames, then turning around and going straight back to a waiting taxi. She didn't know the path started at a touristy spot like Tower Bridge, she didn't realize the taxi couldn't wait for them at the curb, and she certainly didn't expect to ride the Tube or the London Eye today.

Just get it over with? If it were that easy she would have done it already. Jasper was never going to understand. Her mother didn't understand. Diana didn't understand.

Hidden Disabilities. Would that group understand? Was she wrong to judge them, not give them a chance? Did she need the strength of a group to educate others about herself?

"I need to go home now," Ava said. She whispered it too. But she didn't have to repeat it. Jasper heard it loud and clear.

Later, as their taxi idled at her curb, he tried to apologize. She held her hand out. "It's not your fault. It's mine. For acting like I could beat this. For arguing with the people who say I can't, but also for agreeing with the people who say I can. I wanted to do this. For you. For me. For Aunt Beverly. For my father. The world. I've missed so much. And I can't get it back. And I love it and I hate it and there's too much and there's not enough and I want to see and touch everything and I want to spend my life curled up in a bathtub with the curtain drawn. I'm two sides of a coin and I don't know how to be victorious on either side. Because it's one thing if I wanted to be this way. But I don't. I don't. And it's another thing if I could just presto change, but I can't, I can't."

Jasper was silent for a moment, but Ava knew he was listening, taking it in, and she also knew why so many women complained when they felt as if the man they loved wasn't listening. Because when they did listen, like Jasper was now, it was everything. He didn't have to have any answers or the right words, for the biggest gift of all was simply to feel heard. And when Jasper placed his hand on her knee and squeezed, Ava felt heard. When he did speak his voice was soft but sure. "I know you might not believe me, Ava, but that's how most people feel about the world. You inspire me, Ava. Just being near you." He removed something from his pocket. It was another brochure from the comedy club.

"I missed it," Ava said. "I missed your show." She missed everything. Why couldn't she just change already? Why couldn't she just talk herself into being somebody else?

"I'm going back. Not because I was great, or they laughed, or it was such a wonderful experience. It was terrifying. I'm totally out of my comfort zone. And you taught me that, Ava. You did."

Ava wanted to tell him he'd do great. She wanted to tell him she'd be there. She wanted to assure him that they would walk along the Thames another day. But she didn't want to lie. Not to him. Not to the man who really listened. So she smiled and nodded to him, and refused when he said he'd come with her into the flat. She faced the open door of the car, and the sidewalk, and the steps going up to her building, and the entrance. She endured her heart hammering all the way up four flights, not slowing down until the moment she finally burst into the door of her flat. It felt still, and silent. Her mother and Diana were out sightseeing. *Thank God.*

Ava went to the window and looked out. Jasper was still waiting, at the curb, looking at the flat. Ava went to wave. That's when she realized she was clutching the flyer for Jasper's comedy show in her hands. Jasper looked up, saw her, and waved back. The car pulled away from the curb. He was there for her. Even when she changed her mind, he was there. The least she could do was try to return the favor. She'd missed his first show. She would be damned if she missed the second. And she didn't care what any of the rest of those wankers did; Ava Wilder was going to laugh. Even if he wasn't funny, she was going to laugh.

CHAPTER 36

Ava kept her sunglasses on, even as she descended into The Laughing Den. Franco and Georgie were on either side of her, literally holding her up at times. Franco was dressed like Marilyn Monroe. Georgie was in a gray pinstripe suit with an orange-and-white polka-dotted bow tie. "We're here, Miss Ava," Georgie said.

"Thank God," Ava said.

"Can't wait to see straightlaced Jasper cutting a rug," Franco said.

"That's dancing," Georgie said.

"Which is exactly what we'll be doing after his little comedy routine," Franco said. They took the three-seater by the exit. Ava was on Xanax, with a little help from Diana, who had waited until now to admit that she had brought Ava a refill. It was only under the condition that Diana dole them out. Ava was ready for her and her mother to leave. Here they were in London and so far they'd spent more time lounging around her flat than doing anything else. At least Ava had a good excuse.

"This is so exciting," Georgie said.

"He's not meant to be very funny," Franco said. "But let's clap and cheer as loud as we can, bitches." Ava laughed. A few people turned and gave them a dirty look. "What?" Franco stared at them. "No laughing at the comedy club?" There was no one onstage. *Great. What a loser of a crowd. No laughing at the comedy club!*

Ava put her hand on Franco's arm. "I love your enthusiasm," she said. "But if you make a fuss, Jasper is going to see us. I'd rather surprise him after the show."

"Good idea," Georgie said. Franco gave a bit of a pout.

"I'll sketch you again," Ava said.

Franco mimed zipping his lips and tucking the key into his fake cleavage. Soon they were finishing their first of the two-drink minimum.

"Where is everyone?" Ava said. She'd invited them all. Queenie, her mom, Diana, even Hillary. Jasper deserved everyone's support. Just before the lights dipped they finally arrived, and the four of them took the table directly in front of Ava. She was relieved. For even if Jasper saw them, he wouldn't see her. She would have the element of surprise. Soon an MC trotted out onstage and faced the audience. "Straight from the courtrooms of London, get ready to hand down a verdict to our very own Jasper Keyes."

Polite applause clattered around the room. Jasper stumbled onstage. Was that on purpose? It wasn't funny, just awkward. But Ava wasn't going to judge. She was going to support him no matter what. Jasper stood in front of the mic. He looked slightly shocked. Poor fellow. She bet that's how she looked whenever she was outside. Absolutely terrified. "Hello, London," Jasper said. "How is everyone this fine, soggy evening?" Ava slipped down into her chair a little. So did Franco and Georgie. *Oh, no.* If he was already embarrassing the drag queens then Jasper was in real trouble.

"So, I've been dating an inside girl. Not because she's in the know, or connected somehow, but because she literally has to stay inside." Hillary's laugh rang through the room. Even Ava had to admit her laugh was so obnoxious it was funny, and funny was infectious, and soon several were laughing along with her. Now Jasper knew that Hillary was there. And thoroughly enjoying the jab at Ava. Would that slow him down? Ava could feel Franco and Georgie staring at her. She also saw the table in front of her, with the obvious exception of Hillary, completely tense. Queenie, her mother, and Diana sat like they had poles for spines. Oh, how they wanted to turn around and see Ava's reaction. It was amusing to watch. *I'm the one who told him to talk about what he knows!* Ava wanted to shout at them. *Lighten up. I'm not upset. He's following his dream because of me. He's getting laughs. That's all that matters.* But still, Ava couldn't produce a laugh. She felt like a block of ice.

"If you've never met an agoraphobic you should probably stay in more. Then again, I never seem to get lucky when I try and take her out. It's a bit hard on the ego, knowing that going out with me nearly kills her. Whenever we have a fight she gets real stern and says, 'Let's take this inside.' " Ava laughed. That one was funny. It caught her off guard. This time, the table did turn, en masse, and look at her. Ava smiled and waved at them. Hillary frowned. "It's really hard to go on vacation. I guess if we stay together I'm going to need a mobile home."

Ava laughed again. That was a good one too. She'd never thought of that. Maybe she would like a mobile home. She'd managed on the bus full of schoolchildren, hadn't she?

"I think an outdoor wedding is out, and I never have to worry about her stalking me. She says she has an invisible disability. I'd rather she had an invisible friend. A really hot one who wanted to join us in the bed. Or under the bed as the case may be, because that's where my girlfriend likes to go when she's scared. And I grew up worried there were monsters under the bed; imagine my relief to find out it was only girls."

Whoa. Did he just say that? A roar rose from the crowd. Diana was laughing so hard she had to tug on her turtleneck as if she couldn't breathe. Come on. It wasn't *that* funny. They were supposed to support Jasper because he was flopping, not roar with laughter over her faults. Why didn't he pick on someone else? Why not make fun of Hillary? There was enough material there for a lifetime of jabs. "But the best thing about dating an agoraphobic is that I never have to go to the ballet again. I hate the ballet. My last girlfriend said it was either her or the ballet. So I picked the ballet." Ava laughed, but nobody else did. Jasper's head suddenly jerked up. *Shit. Did he recognize my laugh? Go back to making fun of me!* Ava wanted to shout. "But all jokes aside, I'm in love."

He's in love? Did he just say that out loud to a roomful of strangers? The crowd applauded and cheered. Hillary whirled around in her seat and glared at Ava with a look so hateful that Ava actually stopped breathing for a few seconds. The colored dots danced onto the scene. *Great.* A man tells her he's in love with her—or rather tells a roomful of strangers—and she panics. *You love him too. You do. You love that quirky, nice British man.* He couldn't be talking about someone else, could he? What? Did she think he was seeing another agoraphobic behind her back? He loved her.

Franco and Georgie looked at her without turning their heads. But she could feel their eyeballs sliding in her direction. "She tells me that when she goes outside her body goes into fight-or-flight mode. It's as if she's being chased across the Serengeti by a wild boar. Londoners can relate, can't we? It's called Tuesdays at Tesco." When another wave of laughter hit, Ava hunched over, and dived underneath the table. It was too much. Too many people looking at her. But Jasper was good. He was funny. Most of the time. Franco uncrossed his legs to give her more room, and Georgie patted her on the head.

Jasper paused as the place filled with laughter. It felt so good. He was surprised to see Hillary, and Queenie, and even Ava's mother sitting next to that tiny woman in a turtleneck. He wished Ava were here. She would be a good sport; he knew she would. She encouraged him, practically gave him permission to joke about whatever he knew. "I joke around, but I want to get serious for a moment. You see, I never would have imagined that someone who stayed in so much could know so much about the world. Ava cares about people. She loves people.

She's done nothing but support me, and you too Queenie, and everyone else she's met since the day I picked her up at the aeroport with a rubbish bag over her head." There was laughter at this, but Jasper held his hand up. "She's opened my eyes to the fact that there are so many people out there struggling in ways we can't comprehend. We Londoners live such busy lives, filled with our to-do lists, and our social activities, and our clubs, and our bands, and our loves. We couldn't imagine spending a sunny day inside—we get so little of them. We don't think of the grocery store as a battlefield, that is, unless you shop at Tesco on Tuesdays. Sorry. I did that one already. Right. There are a few Londoners I think who could and should take a page from Ava's book. Prince Harry, for one. He'd get in a lot less trouble if he would just stay inside. I see my ex-girlfriend is here tonight. Hello, Hillary."

Hillary looked appalled, but she managed to nod back. "I want to thank her for breaking up with me, so that when Ava came into my life I was available. Because before Ava, I had a disability too. I always fell for the wrong girl. The hard-to-please girl. The disappearing girl. The nothing-is-ever-good-enough girl. I always tried to change myself so that they would like me better. You see, I'm the dreaded Nice Guy. And nobody has ever liked that side of me, until Ava. Including me. So I don't give a damn if I have to bring the entire world into her living room. I want to be with her, and if that means I'd better lose a few stone to fit under the bed then that's what I'm going to do. And since I've now completely faced my fear that you wankers would boo me off the stage, I'm going to use you to help me face another fear. I just want to practice what I'd say to the most amazing Yank I've ever met if she were here right now. Are you ready?"

Jasper got down on one knee. The audience erupted in cheers, and banter.

"Go for it."

"Ava," Jasper said. "I don't tan very easily anyway." The audience roared with laughter. "You think you're the one who's got a disability, but it's nothing compared to how dysfunctional I would be if you were to disappear from my life right now. I don't care if we ever walk along the Thames—"

"Why would you? It stinks!" a heckler yelled out.

"Or ride the Tube—"

"The Tube is bloody awful—"

"Or see Downton Abbey in person—"

"Free Maggie Smith!" A few cheers mixed with boos rang from the crowd.

"I love you. I want to be wherever you are. Ava Wilder. Will you marry me?" The crowd cheered, and clapped. A few stood and applauded. Jasper bowed. He bathed in the praise and stood until the room was quiet again, and just as he was about to exit stage right a familiar voice called out.

"Bloody hell." Jasper stopped in his tracks and turned to the audience. It sounded like Ava. Heads turned to the back. Franco and Georgie sat at the last table. Georgie's cheeks were puffed out as if he was holding his breath. Franco glanced down at the tabletop as if he could see through it.

"Oh shit," Jasper said. The voice. It definitely belonged to Ava. And it had come from underneath the table.

Hillary was standing by the table. Ava recognized the smell of expensive heels. Soon her face appeared underneath the tablecloth. Everybody else at Jasper's request had politely left. He was in the loo. He was probably terrified he'd hurt her feelings. But the opposite was true. He was funny. She was proud of him. But in order for her to tell him, he'd have to come out of the loo and she'd have to emerge from underneath the table. At this moment they were about as star-crossed as lovers could get. But Ava still couldn't stop smiling. He'd proposed. Sort of. At least practiced proposing. To the shut-in. The Inside Girl. What was considered bat-shit crazy in America was adorably quirky in London. She belonged.

Marriage. Yikes. The thought of it made Ava's little colored dots to go at warp speed. Her sense of smell was suddenly heightened, too, and in a dank club that wasn't a good thing. Stale cigarettes, and spilled beer, and dirty feet. She really needed to get out from under the table. On Diana's way out she had handed Ava another Xanax. She was just waiting for it to kick in. She dug in her purse. Wallet, lipstick, mirror, brush. She'd forgotten to carry a rubbish bag. That was progress, but boy, she wished she had it.

"Good luck proving you're of sound mind now," Hillary said.

"Screw you," Ava said.

"Do you love him back?"

Hillary's question startled her. For a moment Hillary looked human. Maybe it was because Ava was sitting on a dirty floor. "Yes," she said. "Very much."

"Then do the human thing. Let him go."

"How dare you."

"How dare me? Do you want to know why I broke up with him?" Ava simply stared at her. "Because I saw what a truly great person he is. I mean really great. And I didn't love him."

"But I do."

"Love isn't everything. You're condemning him to a virtual prison."

"I'm out now, aren't I?"

"You're underneath a table in a dank cellar on a filthy floor." She had her there. "He'll spend the rest of his life doomed to a little, little life. Don't do that to him. I'm sorry you have this condition. But at least be honest about it. You don't need a flat in London. You don't need a vibrant, adventurous guy like Jasper. Let me buy the flat for Queenie. Hell, we both know you aren't going to complete the list, so it's a very generous offer. At least you and your mother can buy a place back in the cornfields of Indiana or wherever it is you live."

"Iowa," Ava said.

"You owe me, what?" Hillary said.

"Leave her alone." It was Queenie. It was good to hear his voice.

"Uncle," Hillary said.

"Don't call me that in the same breath that you're tormenting this poor girl."

"I'm only telling her the truth."

"Ava? Can I come in?" Queenie's face appeared underneath the table. Ava hadn't meant to start crying, but one look at Queenie's concerned face and her eyes filled with tears. Ava nodded and Queenie sat on the floor with the tablecloth over his head, staying at the edge because he was too large to fit underneath the table.

"She's right," Ava said. "I'd ruin Jasper's life."

Queenie took her hands in his and held them. "Don't you listen to her. You've earned your place under this table," he said. Ava burst out laughing; then Queenie threw his head back and roared.

"I'm so sorry about your lucky charm," Ava said

"I know. And I'm sorry about your agoraphobia."

"But that's not your fault. The charm was my fault."

"Did you lose it on purpose?"

"Of course not."

"Enough said."

"I want you to have the flat," Ava said. "It's only fair."

"Finally," Hillary said. "She's finally making sense."

"I'm not taking the flat," Queenie said.

"You don't have a choice," Hillary said.

Queenie backed out from underneath the table. Ava peeked out. He faced Hillary. "What are you saying?"

"You know what I'm saying. You're in debt to me, Uncle. Twenty thousand pounds. And if you don't fight for that flat then I'm going to collect."

Queenie gasped. "It's okay," Ava said. "You can have it."

"Sell it to me," Hillary said. "Then everybody wins."

"I'll pay you the twenty thousand pounds," Jasper said. His voice came out of nowhere. Ava came out from underneath the table. Jasper ran up to her and pulled her into him. It felt so good to be crushed against his chest. "You came," he said. "You came."

"You were funny. You were truly funny."

"You didn't take offense then?"

"No. I told you to use me."

He looked into her eyes. His were sparkling. "I'd never use you. Unless of course you asked me nicely." He kissed her neck.

"Gross," Hillary said. "So you're going to pay me the twenty thousand pounds, Jasper?"

"No," Ava said. "I won't let you."

Queenie raised his hands in the air. "Ava Wilder, you only have four items left on that list. And we're not going to let you give up."

" 'We'?"

"Boys?" Franco and Georgie popped their heads out from underneath the neighboring table.

"What are you doing?" Ava said.

"We had to try it for ourselves," Georgie said.

"It kind of stinks," Franco said. He threw his head back and laughed.

"Your mother and her friend are behind you too," Queenie said. "Literally. They're standing directly behind you." Ava whirled around. Sure enough, her mother was back. Ava hadn't noticed her outfit before. She was back to being a cowgirl.

"You look beautiful, Mother." Ava meant it too. Her mother was brave, and funny.

"This old thing?" Her mother played with the red bandana around her neck. "What would your father think?"

"He'd be happy," Ava said. "He'd be so happy." She ran up and hugged her.

"What about me?" Diana said. Ava looked over. Diana wasn't in a turtleneck. She was wearing a low-cut sequined top.

"Holy shit," Ava said. "I'm going to need therapy to process this." Diana laughed, then reached up to play with her invisible turtleneck.

"What is this?" Hillary said. "Group therapy? She's playing every single one of you, can't you see that?"

"Shut up, Hillary," Jasper said.

Queenie, Franco, and Georgie held hands and stepped up. Queenie spoke up. "We're here to tell you that we're Team Ava.

We'll stroll along the Thames with you, take a photo under the Tower—no use going up—"

"TOURISTS," they said together.

". . . we'll ride the Tube with you, and then the London Eye. We'll carry you, we'll talk to you, we'll sing to you, and we'll put as many rubbish bags over your head as you'd like." They stepped forward. "First thing tomorrow, Ava. We all do it all. What do you say?"

"Tomorrow's the deadline," Ava said. "If I don't get it done . . ."

"The flat belongs to Queenie," Hillary said.

"You can do this, Ava," Jasper said. "*We* can do this."

Ava spanned their faces as she sucked in her breath. Her little London family. And her American one too. "On one condition," she said. They waited. "Fair and square. No more cheats. Once we head out tomorrow the clock starts. If I don't get it done within the day, I'm done. This whole thing is done. And Queenie, you have to agree. If I can't do it the flat is yours."

"Agreed," he said.

"Let's get out of here and go for a drink," Diana said.

"And dancing," Gretchen said.

Jasper slipped his hand into Ava's. "We're going to have some alone time at home," he said. Ava squeezed his hand and thought of all the ways she was going to thank him later.

CHAPTER 37

They arrived at the London Eye as a group, all holding hands. Ava was in the middle. Jasper was on one side of her and Queenie on the other. When they got close to the queue, Diana broke free. "I'm not riding that," she said. "I don't like heights."

"If I'm doing it, you're doing it," Ava said.

"So don't do it," Diana said.

"I'm seeing you in a whole new light," Ava said. Ava was exhausted. The comedy cellar was her one outing for the week. Here it was the next day and she was already out again. She would never ride this contraption. Ever.

"Queenie, if you get the flat will Hillary really try to take it from you?"

"In a New York minute," Queenie said. He looked at Ava. "Oh, honey. You're shaking."

"I can't. I appreciate all the support. I just can't. I want to go home." She turned to Queenie. "Appeal to Hillary. Work something out. Something that benefits you. I'm willing to sell it or let you have the flat. As long as it benefits you, and not her."

"Fight," Queenie said. "We're here. So just fight."

Jasper slipped his hand through hers. He leaned in and whispered, "Beverly would be so proud."

"If I have to watch that thing rotate once more, I'm going to hurl," Diana said.

They turned and started to walk away. Just then one of the staff members from the London Eye came running toward them.

"Franco, Franco," he said.

"Hello, Louie," Franco said.

The young man blushed. "I can take her," he said. "But we've got to do it now. And I can only take one more."

"What?" Ava said. "By myself? I can't."

Georgie took over. "If you go up, you're going to see Big Ben, Ava. The real one. You'll also spot the Tower."

"And we're on the Thames," Franco said.

"The Tube is out there somewhere too," Queenie said. "We've already discussed it and agreed. This will count as everything."

Everything. "That's cheating."

"We all agreed," Queenie said. "It's why we came here first." He turned to the group. They all gave thumbs-up. "See? Team Ava."

Ava nodded. She was afraid if she opened her mouth to say anything she would hurl too. She'd make sure to aim for Hillary.

They all walked with her to the car. Ava stepped in. Soon she was sandwiched in with tourists. *Look at the ground, look at the ground, look at the ground. Breathe, breathe, breathe.* She could do this. Well, she had no choice, now did she? Oh, why didn't she have a scarf? Something soft to land on in case she passed out. At least it was a small space. That was actually somewhat comforting. Were they all staring at her? Could they see her sweating? Suddenly Jasper's face appeared on the other side of the window.

I love you, he mouthed.

I love you too, she mouthed back.

The car lurched forward and up, rotating just a few feet as the next car took the place at the bottom. Her car swung slightly.

"Let me off, let me off," a little girl said. All eyes turned toward the little blond girl, eyes wide, lips quivering. "Mommy, off. Off, Mommy, off." She was American. Ava forced her eyes away from the ground and looked to the door. She looked around. Was there an emergency button? The car rotated again, and this time it kept going. The little girl started to scream. An ear-piercing scream. Everyone on the car slapped their hands over their ears. Ava made her way to the little girl.

"Can I try something?" she asked the father.

"You can try anything," the father said.

Ava knelt down next to the little girl. Ava spread her hands. "Look at the lines on my hands," she said. At first the little girl continued to cry and scream. Ava kept moving her hands just underneath the little girl's face. Finally, the girl looked.

"What?" she said. Ava began tracing the lines in her palms. "What are you doing?"

"I'm drawing a picture."

"Of what?"

"This is you," Ava said. "And your favorite animal in the whole world."

"A dog?"

"A dog. See? He's right here." The wheel kept turning, and others were eagerly looking out the window for the view. Ava kept her focus on her hands. Soon the little girl snuck a finger out, and touched Ava's palms. She copied Ava as she traced the lines.

"Do more," the little girl said, placing her hands out, palms up.

"Look at those beautiful lines on your palms." Ava didn't know a thing about palm reading but she was pretty sure the little girl didn't either. "This line means that you're very smart. This line means that you're very brave."

"Am I pretty too?"

"Very, very pretty," Ava said.

"I don't like this ride," the little girl said. "I want to go home."

"If you sit down here, with me, we can pretend we're under our bed at home," Ava said.

The little girl sank to the floor. The ride kept rising, higher and higher. A teeny, tiny part of Ava wanted to look. They were nearly at the highest point. The best view in town. Except, of course, nothing could compare to the one from her flat.

"Yes, see all the legs," Ava said. "It's like we're hiding under our beds, watching everyone."

"Good," the little girl said.

"But I kind of want to pop my head up, just for a second, and look around. Then I'll come back under the bed."

The little girl snuck her hand into Ava's. "Me too," she said. The father looked down and smiled at them.

"On three," Ava said. "One, two, three." Ava stood, and lifted the little girl in her arms. This time, she gasped. They were practically in the clouds. London unfurled below them. Big Ben standing proud; the Thames littered with boats; tiny cars and red trolleys making their way across London Bridge; Westminster Abbey, swaths of green, the Tower of London, Buckingham Palace, and the Queen's Guards. All of London was below her, around her, a part of her. She was doing it. She was riding the London Eye.

The little girl reached up and touched a tear rolling down Ava's face. "Why are you crying?"

"Because I've never had a to-do list before," Ava said. "And it feels good to check things off."

"You don't have to do this, you know," Jasper said.

"You're wrong," Ava said. "I do have to." She pulled her oyster card out of her pocket. "It's rude not to use a gift."

On the way to the Tube, the car passed a group of people marching with signs. Ava caught a few as they idled in traffic.

Proud Dyslexic
Can You See My Autism?
I'm Epileptic, but You Wouldn't Know It.

No way. Was it a sign? *Several signs, ha. Life's talking to you, Ava. You'd better listen.* Every person had their own troubles on their backs. Ava wasn't going to ruin Jasper's life any more than any other woman on the planet. As long as he didn't limit himself, and they were happy together, she would continue to take baby steps toward living a more normal life.

She would introduce herself to the group. Eventually. Right now she had more pressing things on her mind. The last item on the list. The telltale signs of anxiety were there—heart beating, colored dots, sweats gathering on her brow. But she felt another feeling well up inside her. Competitive. Especially with Hillary standing at the entrance to the Tube with a stopwatch. "Are you okay?" Jasper asked. The London Underground. Lines from the map Jasper gave her once rose in her mind and began strangling her.

"Yes," Ava said. "I'm okay." Do or die. This was it.

"Bloody hell," Jasper said.

"What?"

"Based on your progress, I'm going to have to come up with a whole new act." Ava laughed, then scooted closer, and kissed him. She glanced out again and saw Vic and Deven standing with her crowd—Franco and Georgie, her mother, Diana, Queenie, and of course Hillary and her stopwatch.

"How did they know about this?" Ava said.

"Vic probably saw the promenade from the flat. All your fans."

"That stalker." Ava looked away as she was hit with a dizzy stick. "Guess there's no turning back now."

"You don't have to do this," he said again.

"I do." Before she could talk herself out of it, Ava pressed on the door handle and stepped onto the sidewalk.

"Fifteen minutes to catch a ride," Hillary said.

"Screw you."

"Ava, Ava, Ava," the rest chanted as she approached the entrance to the Underground. *You can do this. Don't think. Your dad is here. So is Aunt Beverly. Hand in hand, feel them?* Queenie stood at the back of the crowd. Was he upset about losing the flat? He looked pale. He was gripping his left arm, as if literally trying to hold himself together.

Ava passed them, and took the first step down to the Underground. She gripped her oyster card so hard it cut into her fingers. *Let it bleed.* The pain felt good. Her posse followed her, right behind, ready to catch her if she passed out.

"Ava!" It was Vic, yelling at her from the top of the stairs. *Ignore her.* "Lookie here," she said. Ava stopped. Turned. And looked. Vic was holding something up, dangling it from her fingertips. Queenie's lucky charm.

"Give it back," Ava said. She tried to go up the steps. Queenie was in her way. "Move, please," she said.

"What are you doing? Hillary's counting down."

"Vic has your lucky charm," Ava said.

"Let it go," Queenie said.

"No," Ava said. "It's your lucky charm." She dodged Queenie and ran up the steps. Vic saw her, turned, and began to run. Ava chased after her.

"Ava, Ava." Queenie was right behind her.

Ava didn't stop. She kept running, trying to keep a glimpse of Vic in the crowd. She could hear Queenie behind her, his breath ragged, his heels pounding on the pavement. She never guessed he could run like that. She never guessed she could run like this either. She was gaining on Vic. She had to dodge people, and bikes, and children, and dogs, and skateboarders. She didn't have time to think; she was all machine pumping her arms and her legs. She closed the gap enough to grab Vic's shirt and she yanked.

Vic flew back, almost hitting her head on the pavement. Ava caught her, then ripped the charm out of her hand. Vic was laughing hysterically.

"That's not funny."

"Your flatmate looks like he's about to burst."

Ava turned. Queenie was red in the face. Gasping. He grabbed his left arm. His left arm. "Queenie!" Ava said. Queenie's eyes bulged and he clutched his heart.

"Queenie!" Ava screamed. Queenie fell to the ground. *Heart attack. He's having a heart attack. CPR. It's a lifesaving skill.* She dropped to her knees. She checked his head to make sure he hadn't cracked it on the sidewalk. She didn't see any blood. *Thank God. Thank God.* "Call nine-nine-nine!" she yelled.

"Calling," Vic said.

Ava didn't think; she acted. She tilted his head back and pinched his nose, and breathed into him. *One, two, three, four, five.* "Breathe, Queenie, breathe." She folded her hands together in a fist and placed them over his heart. *One, two, three, four, five. Back to breaths. One, two, three, four, five. Back to the chest. One, two, three, four, five. Back to breaths. One, two*—Queenie jerked. His eyes flew open. He took a breath.

"You're back," Ava said. She plastered his face with kisses. Queenie tried to get up. "Stay down. The ambulance is coming."

"Ambulance?" he said. "Are you hurt? Did you pass out?"

"Ava." Ava looked up. It was Jasper. The posse was here, all gathered around.

"She saved him," Vic said.

"He had a heart attack," Ava said. "Help is on the way."

"Help is already here," Jasper said, looking at Ava. "It's already here."

Three Months Later

CHAPTER 38

Ava stood in front of her windows, watching the lights come up. London was spread out before her, like a jeweled necklace. She couldn't wait to slip it on, dance until dawn. She would never get tired of this view. London was wonderful. And London was terrible. It was in constant flux, and turmoil, and motion. Just like the flat would be when Queenie and his cast returned. They'd already shot the first nine episodes. It had been so lonely around here without him. She couldn't wait to have him back. Ava smiled to herself when she realized she couldn't remember the last time she'd heard him gasp. He'd refused to accept that the flat was his. For now they were both content to be flatmates for the rest of the year. And this time Ava was going to pay half of the expenses. Nobody was pressing about the legalities of the flat except for Hillary. Jasper came up behind Ava, wrapped his arms around her, and kissed her neck.

"Do you have to work tonight?" he said. Ava had been sketching at the club a few nights a week after the drag shows. The money was fantastic.

She turned, and kissed him. "No," she said. "I'm all yours."

"All mine. I love the sound of that."

"May I have this dance?" Ava said.

"There's no music playing," Jasper said.

"I can fix that." Ava went to the record player, lifted the needle, and stepped into Jasper's arms as the needle touched down. They began to dance. Ava stopped.

"Are you okay?"

"I have to ask you something." They were in the spot where the camera had been positioned. She told him about discovering it and smashing it. Jasper hit his forehead with his hand.

"I can't believe I forgot."

"What?"

"Beverly installed the camera. So she could tape you a message. I was supposed to give it to you after you finished the list. But—"

"I never finished the list."

"The tape is here though."

"What's on it?"

"I've never seen it. But if I had to guess. Everything she ever wanted to say but never got the chance." He reached up on the top shelf and came back with a USB plug. Tears came to Ava's eyes. He held the USB plug out to Ava. She didn't take it. "Don't you want to see it?"

"Yes," Ava said. She sat on the emerald stool, and perched her laptop on her knees.

"Do you want me to leave?" Jasper said.

"Please stay," Ava said. She plugged in the USB and soon the video was up on the screen. Beverly's face came into view. Such kind blue eyes. Beverly smiled and Ava lit up inside. She was still so beautiful. She wore an ivory dress with a faux fur collar, and a little matching hat. Glamorous to the end. Beverly clasped her hands in front of her, still grinning. "Hello, luv. I'm so glad you're here."

"Me too," Ava said.

Beverly opened her arms. "I hope you feel at home here in my little flat."

"You have no idea."

"One of my favorite things in the world was to sit on my emerald stool and look out over London." Ava turned to Jasper at this and he winked. "I hope you feel the same." Ava laughed. She couldn't believe it. She looked out over London now, so beautiful in front of her. The same view that Beverly looked at for most of her life. Beverly looked away for a second as if speaking to someone off camera, then nodded, and turned back. She looked Ava right in the eyes. For a second Ava forgot Beverly wasn't actually there in real time. "I hope you can find it in your heart to forgive such an old fool."

"I do, I forgive you. I'm sorry too."

"I wish I could turn back time. I would do everything differently."

Me too.

"But you're here now, or else you wouldn't be watching this, and that makes me the happiest woman alive. You're here, and you're okay, and I want you to have the entire world. It's a wild ride, this life. Enjoy it. Every day. Don't be like me. Don't be too afraid to admit when you're acting the fool. I see it now, so clearly. I blamed others, but I was wrong. I had the power to change me. I was a bit stubborn, if you must know. And I have a feeling you do. It's a Wilder thing." She laughed. It sounded a lot like Ava's laugh. Ava reached out, as if she could touch her. And just then, Beverly reached out too. Ava gasped. She turned and looked at Jasper; he had tears in his eyes. "I know Queenie and Jasper are taking good care of you." Ava smiled at Jasper. He smiled back. *If only she knew.* Ava turned back to the screen.

Beverly put her hands over her heart. "I've never been very good without a script. So here's what I have to say. I love you. I'm so sorry. I know I'll be with Bertie again, and I'm so happy. I saw him when I was skydiving. He wanted me to reach out to you. He knew there was a hole in my heart over you. I saw him, darling. We still exist. We're just on the other side of the curtain, and we'll be watching over you, the two of us. We'll always be here for you, luv. Through the good and the bad. And I will see you again. We will have a proper introduction. But until then, remember that all the world's a stage, my darling. And it's your stage now. I'm ready for the curtain to go down, but one day, it will come up again, and you'll be on the other side. That will be the second-happiest day of my life. Until that day, my darling, I'm grateful you have your mother, and now you have Jasper, and Queenie, and your own little slice of London. But wherever you are, Bertie and I will be there, which means no matter where it is, you'll always have us; you'll always have a home."

Ava wiped tears from her eyes. Beverly kissed her fingers and touched the screen. Ava kissed hers and quickly put her fingers over Beverly's. And for just that second, she felt her. She knew she would carry that the rest of her life. The screen went dark. Ava sat for a moment, taking in London in the silence. Jasper came and put his hand on her shoulder.

"Are you all right?"

"Better than all right," Ava said. She stood, fetched her purse, and removed the oyster card Jasper had given her. She held it up. "First things first," she said. The tape was just what she needed. A hello and a good-bye from Beverly. *Motivation.*

Jasper smiled. "Would you like some company?"

"I thought you'd never ask." They held hands, opened the door, walked down four flights of steps, and exited the building. Ava only hesitated a moment; then they were off. The air still held its warmth. She could feel the buzz of London through her fingertips. It wasn't until they were across the street and Ava looked up at the twinkling lights that Ava stopped. "They're gone," she said.

"Who's gone?"

"The colored dots." Jasper squeezed her hand. "Let's take the Tube to St. Pancras," Ava said.

"Brilliant," Jasper said. "It's only a few stops, so we can turn right back—"

"Actually, there's a champagne bar at the station," Ava said. "I want to have a glass and pretend we're waiting for the next train to Paris."

"*Oui,*" Jasper said. "*Oui.*" Their steps joined the others on the sidewalk, so many people, going so many places, and somewhere maybe someone was watching, wondering where they were all going, wondering how they could do it, Yet here she was; she was doing it. This was her moment, and it was going to keep on going. Every moment was waiting, the next life sketch, just a step away. She squeezed Jasper's hand, sent a prayer up to her father and Aunt Beverly, and joined in with all the other Londoners, who, be it in high heels, cowboy boots, or sneakers, were simply in the moment, bravely putting one foot in front of the other. *Bloody hell.* She was going to have that Christmas song stuck in her head the rest of the night.

"Come on, what's so funny?" Jasper said. "Give us a laugh too."

"Forget the champagne bar," Ava said.

"That's all right." Jasper squeezed her hand. "We'll do it next time. It's absolutely all right."

"Good," Ava said. "Because I would just die if we missed the next train to Paris."

LONDON FROM MY WINDOWS

Mary Carter

ABOUT THIS GUIDE

The suggested questions are included to enhance
your group's reading of Mary Carter's
London from My Windows.

DISCUSSION QUESTIONS

1. Ava's agoraphobia surfaced after the death of her father and is exacerbated by the guilt she carries. Do you think Ava would have ever experienced agoraphobia had her father not died? Would *any* tragic event have yielded the same results? Discuss.

2. Do you think agoraphobia is a true disability? Why or why not?

3. Do you think Ava's mother Gretchen is at all responsible for Ava's condition? Do you think Gretchen feels she has any responsibility? Does Ava blame her mother?

4. Do you think people with invisible disabilities have it harder than people with visible ones? Does Ava ever come to accept herself as having a disability? Discuss.

5. When Ava first meets Jasper he's pretending to be a limo driver. How does this meeting affect the rest of their relationship, positive and negative? Would they have ended up with the same bond had they met under truthful circumstances?

6. Ava always had regrets about not visiting Aunt Beverly. Is she to blame, or is Aunt Beverly? Or both?

7. How does watching people and places outside her window start to affect Ava? If Aunt Beverly had a flat without a spectacular view of London, would Ava have had the same experience? Why or why not?

8. How does being in Aunt Beverly's flat and surrounded by her things start to change Ava?

9. Ava quickly impresses all of Queenie's friends, and several form a bond with her. Does Ava owe "Team Ava" for her recovery?

10. Jasper says he's fallen in love with Ava partly *because* she's imperfect. Is he finally making better choices, or is he repeating the pattern of falling for unavailable women?

11. What are some of the cultural differences Ava experiences between America and London? In which place does Ava feel more at home? How can living someplace new make a person feel freer to be who they truly are? Would Ava have grown no matter what city she had moved to, or was there something about London that helped heal her?

12. Was it unfair of Beverly to require Ava's participation in life if she wanted to inherit the flat? Why or why not?

13. Do you think Jasper and Ava will make it as a couple? Why or why not?

14. Will Ava continue to improve, or will she backslide? Is she cured?

15. By the end, how have Ava's relationships changed toward her father, Aunt Beverly, and her mother?